Chanting the Feminine Down

A Psychological, Religious and Historical Novel

D1714774

ISBN: 197905990X
EAN: 9781979059909
Printed by CreateSpace, An Amazon.com Company

This book is dedicated to Boccaccio's Famous Women and all their daughters across the centuries who have served as anthem, prayer and eternal chorus.

Prologue

Colette stirred in what felt like an amphitheater. Tied to what must have been a hospital gurney, she saw images on screens. In one scene a very young Michael Caine in his 1966 movie role of "Alfie" sounded off in his best Cockney accent about how badly the world was treating him. It was blimey this, and blimey that, and you bloody well get what you ask for. He was the master of ceremonies, an omniscient cagey gent who could coax any number of lovers into his Morris Minor to take them for a roll in the hay at Shepherd's Bush.

She heard Alfie chatting. He was excited, dropping "you know what I mean, love" in sentences that ran together in musical incoherence. He pointed to a black curtain. She heard noises coming from behind it. A doctor and several nurses appeared. They displayed tools and instruments, as if they were working at a construction site, showing off what was hanging from their carpenter belts. She heard screaming from behind the curtain and felt a sucking sound at the center of her being. She couldn't make out what she was hearing. Was it the sound of a baby crying? God knows, something had to give.

Colette Maria McGovern felt as if she were down some dark well in Western Ireland, filled with the smell of death and the sobbing of children. She saw a craggy face of a nun who covered the well opening with her scowl. This was the Sister Anne of her youth, with bad breath and throbbing jowls, who was meant to breathe the fear of God into her. Colette heard shushing sounds and couldn't tell if it was the nun, the wind, or the voice of God.

Then, written on an old classroom blackboard located in County Galway, Ireland, were the words *Bon Secours Sisters*. Colette saw nuns and read succor as help, but felt helpless because a line of ropes marked off places for the saved and the damned, directional arrows and all. The Shepherd's Bush crowd, plump with illegitimate children, walked toward distant huts and cottages, just beyond the tree line, beyond the human touch. Dead children would surely be tossed down the well without prayers or remorse in response to some ancient curse.

She was back in the dark well, listening to voices in Latin and Gaelic, speaking about the wishes of Holy Mother the Church, while women wept because their pelvic bones were severed with surgical saws, making a blessed, endless, theologically correct birth canal that delivered righteous souls. The wailing she heard was in a foreign tongue, though vaguely similar to Latin prayers from her childhood, as if other places also wept for this monstrosity.

Colette was still tied to a gurney inside a sanctuary. Now she had a fuller view of an altar, which looked like it had been prepared for Lent with a purple altar cloth. The surrounding statues were also covered in the color of the Passion. She wanted to roll that word around in her head, comparing it to the smaller case "p," but the weight she felt against her was historical. The capital remained out of reach.

Everything seemed quiet, holy and restrained, waiting for the Resurrection. Colette daydreamed about the poor souls who would not have that chance. She felt no mercy in her heart.

She saw herself rising from the gurney and moving through the air, as if she had wings, level with the statues. She removed the purple garments from the icons and watched the coverings drop to the floor as from a body. Colette was in familiar territory now with images of Jesus, Mary and Joseph.

She paused in her reverie, reflecting on the cost of this passage and whether venial or mortal terms would apply. She lingered for a while in a gated, ill-defined place called Limbo, reaching back for all the children who had been discarded in plumbing and in septic tanks. She vaguely recalled that some Vatican committee had announced that Limbo for the unbaptized who died in infancy had been closed down, just like that. She thought that this announcement was as casual as a memo announcing St. Peter's in Rome was closed for a cleaning. She had lost track of who was writing the rules.

Colette stared at the black screen, halfway expecting Alfie to show up, stage left. She was drained, body and soul. The doctor and nurses had left her room. She could feel the emptiness in her uterus. The nurse said she was feverish and talking a lot. The well with hundreds of dead babies was damp and deep.

Colette imagined she was with the damned and discarded babies in the deep throwaway well in County Galway that was still giving up the dead to this very day under the wrathful eye of the Church.

Chapter One

"You want what?" responded Professor Gleason, only half-listening.

"Trent, sir! I want Trent, sir."

Colette preferred calling him sir, rather than Father, even though he was a Jesuit. She wanted to leave church trappings outside the conversation. There were already too many Fathers in the room.

"Ms. McGovern," he said, "the Council of Trent is so boring. It's a bunch of old men who put a catechism together while ignoring Luther, Calvin and the rest of that tribe. So much for the Counter-Reformation!"

"Why don't you look at the First or Second Vatican Councils? They both bear a lot more directly on contemporary issues and doctrinal matters. These councils are still problematic for the Church."

"Thanks. I'm sure I'll get around to looking at the recent councils. I am interested in what Trent accomplished and why it was the last council for four hundred years."

"Very well. Please check in with me at any time. I'm here to help."

"Thanks, Professor."

Colette was glad that was over. She didn't really care whether her senior project was about Trent or the man in the moon. She wanted something simple, unexciting, and far enough in the past that no one would really give a damn. Mostly, she wanted an excuse to get away from the Bronx without arousing her mother's curiosity. Colette felt a vague need to take some religion back inside her soul in exchange for what she had given up behind that awful curtain. She felt she was inside a foreign body.

Deep down, she knew that this was compensation but had a hard time finishing the thought. She wanted to stay on the surface of things. Trent was outside her, vague and historical. Colette tried to conjure up a tidy, nondescript church-like building called Trent but all she could imagine was a narrow, vertical, coffin-like structure that reminded her of a confessional with dark curtains separating the priest from the penitent. Above the confessional were the words: Trent the Confessional. She shuddered and quickly returned to the other Trent.

Colette figured Gleason must have had a change of heart since giving the assignment weeks earlier. "Since the time of Constantine there have been dozens of councils up to the early 1960s which redefined the character and mission of the Church. Pick one and describe in your thesis how your council influenced the Church for good or ill. We would expect more good than ill, of course."

She put herself in the Gleason's shoes and figured it more likely that he was trying to save himself the bother of reading about Trent. Or was he hiding something, she thought, laughing at the idea. But she stayed with the idea. Colette sensed that the Jesuits were somehow involved in the almost five hundred years of church stuff since Trent because they were rumored to have secret societies everywhere, even in Sao Paulo, Brazil. Her grasp of geography was no more certain than her grasp of theology.

After a few days of research Colette wondered whether reaching back to the Council of Trent would be more problematic than she first thought because, having met for almost twenty years, starting in 1545 and ending in 1563, the council could have produced enough doctrine to keep a century of popes happy. She felt odd praying that the Trent proceedings would be mainly in Latin, so she could get by on excerpts and translations.

Her mother Patricia still attended the Latin Mass celebrated every Sunday in the Bronx. Her mother knew the Latin Mass by heart. Colette thought Mass in the vernacular was normal, but her mother clung to the Latin version as if she were a nun in a medieval village. She was sure her own birth was celebrated in Latin.

Colette would listen to her mother singing *"Pater Noster, qui es in caelis, sanctificetur nomen tuum,"* while she was cooking, lifting her voice when referring to daily bread and forgiving trespasses and debts. Patricia unfailingly looked at her husband's black-and-white photograph on the piano when she got to *"Sed libera nos a malo,"* and left her daughter wondering who was being delivered from evil.

Patricia was not above dropping Latin into conversations with her daughter as a way to gain the theological high ground. "Colette, that boy, the young man from Boston College, he is Catholic, yes, but I fear he is *malo*." She didn't seem to be concerned whether the preferred Latin word was syntactically correct or not. Colette wanted to bring that to her attention, but then her mother would come back with the big guns, such as *tentationem*, convinced that this boy was tempting her dear daughter and leading her up the garden path. Or was that down?

"Don't worry, Mother. I'm a big girl, and I am careful."

Colette wondered, what was the price of a lie when the conversation was in Latin?

Sometimes she wanted to strangle her mother for slipping into Latin to put her on the defensive. How often had Colette pleaded with her to speak English and stop bringing up a dead language belonging in some Roman tomb? "Mother, there are reasons we call it a dead language because it's dead, done and buried. Why don't we learn Italian together so we can go on vacation and have a good time? That's the new Latin, you know, but filled with life, wine and song."

Her mother didn't like the reference to a tomb because that reminded her of the death of Christ and her poor husband Jack, God bless his soul. "My daughter, this was the language of the Church from the earliest times. Latin holds the mystery of Christ and two thousand years of history. It stops me in my tracks, you know. It's like music to me that doesn't stop but picks away at my heart until I'm almost in tears. I can't tell you what it means to me. I feel closer to your father when I'm in my Latin state."

Game, set, match, Colette said to herself on more than one occasion. Her mother's Latin missal was next to the stove, and any dish from cockles, to mussels, to lobster bisque would include hymns, prayers and tears in a language that became increasingly unintelligible. Colette thought this was food for thought, not her stomach.

She had read Simone de Beauvoir's *The Second Sex* as an undergraduate and remembered that the author told her mother at age fourteen that she would no longer attend Catholic Mass. Colette wished she had the courage of the young French woman. She was still trying to get her head around de Beauvoir's feminism. She could almost hear the author saying with Parisian charm and finality: "This is not your Body."

Colette learned about the word association test in a psychology class on Carl Jung at St. Anselm's College in the Bronx. Certain words could trigger particular emotions and tics. Jung's work was instrumental in the development of the lie detector test. That's what Colette thought her mother was doing by dipping into her Latin cosmology. She thought it was a test, and it made her feel like a criminal tied to a chair with her pulse points charted.

When Colette relaxed and let her guard down, her mother would pounce with her trump card, *tentationem*, fishing for her temptations. What annoyed Colette most of all was that it worked, and she wasn't sure whether this was the Jung thing or some divine intervention. She went with the psychologist's view because it was the logical choice but, with a mother who had filled the house with Latin since the time of her birth, she couldn't be one hundred percent sure.

Lately she had been taking comfort in binge-watching Michael Caine's "Alfie" for a film class. Every time she was taken in by his charm, his accent and his asides to the camera. She was still trying to figure out why

9

he announced early on that the film would have no upfront credits. It didn't seem like the actor was taking over the director's role. She thought it's more like he couldn't be bothered. He was beyond convention. He sucked you in with that glib Cockney chatter and you even felt sorry for him when his son's mother married a bus conductor and he's left out in the cold. What's it all about, Alfie?

"Alfie is a charming character who seduced women in a sexually-liberated London in the 1960s until he is seduced by time and replaced by a younger man. Actress Shelly Winters is in fine form." That was what a film critic wrote fifty years ago. It was probably still true, but didn't get to the heart of the matter for Colette. What did was the scene in which Alfie took the married woman Lily for a boat ride on a London lake before getting her pregnant. The chattering charm of the young man who told his audience stage right that his married passenger wasn't half bad ran aground during the abortion scene. This seemed to be the turning point for Alfie, who might as well have turned into a stone wall. Colette trembled, imagining a black curtain, resembling a Lenten shroud, rising over her own abortion.

She also vaguely remembered the song by the Divine Comedy Band called "Becoming More than Alfie" on an album titled "Casanova." She didn't remember how that song ended but was certain her own story was closer to Lily's boat ride on the lake. He said, "My darling Colette," in the soft Irish tongue that he must have borrowed from his Irish father. Already on the flat Charles River under Longfellow Bridge in Boston, he was becoming more than Alfie, upwardly mobile and law-school bound, with a lilt in his voice and bespoke summer clothing to boot. He was taking her upstream to the tune of the paddle song.

"Yes, my love, I must show you the heather on the side of cliffs in the west of Ireland where our family has a cottage. Now, love, you mustn't accuse me of acting the maggot, though I might sound like a foolish person. Sorry, I fall back on Irish slang when I'm in the presence of a gorgeous girl, who we would call a *feek* but now in your presence that sounds like bar talk.

"Still, I have this powerful urge to score. And, no, it's not that randy American notion common to baseball but it's to kiss a beloved and, not to be crude, to offer a *shift* or a French kiss as slow as this river flows."

Colette wanted to laugh at the torrent of cant, delightful slang, and marginal love-making, but she couldn't. She secretly wished that Alfie would show up with his self-centered monologues as he was maneuvering to get laid. She wondered whether Jerry O'Connor, a senior at Boston College on his way to great things with the Catholic fraternity, would be chatting with an invisible audience on the port side of their canoe about the vicissitudes of life, including his long-suffering Irish passion. If he had such a conversation, it must have been quick because, before she could bless herself, O'Connor, steadying himself with an oar, was leaning over her, gaining traction and confidence before he delivered to Colette her very first shift, a current-changing French kiss.

She thought he was now talking French to her with a repeated reference to an Esplanade. She had a vague notion that this was foreplay, as he helped her out of the canoe and up the bank of the Charles River to the fabled Esplanade, mumbling bits and pieces of poetry which could have been from John Keats or Matthew Arnold. Did he really say, "Ah, love, let us to be true to one another," or was someone just acting the maggot, as her Jerry had said? Would a real Irishman dare to recite to a beloved that "Oh our love is like a red, red rose that is newly sprung in spring" straight from the lips of Robert Burns, the proper Scotsman?

She waited for something thoroughly Irish, sure as dew from the west, the home of all moisture. She looked for a sign of Yeats on his lips and face. She might have seen the outline of Yeats's melancholy "Adam's Curse," where women were told they must labor to be beautiful, though the poet said he had practiced the old ways of love. Colette turned away from those words and that face because she thought a priest might be talking. She had been hearing about Adam's curses for at least twenty years.

The Esplanade was a promenade lined with fruit trees and low-hanging forsythia. She was walking upright and felt more at home. Jerry O'Connor seemed to have lost all his Irish slang and was focused on ripping her clothes off. She remembered that Alfie was a bit of a bastard in life, but his love-making was slow and easy. Her boat ride up the lazy river was gentle, but now, as he entered her, mumbling in his discovered Gaelic tongue about how "bullin" or randy she was, Colette wanted to cry out in the vernacular, "Yes, yes, yes" but couldn't recall the Latin. The glow quickly passed, and she was left staring at her lover's wide back as he preened before the sunset, cigarette in hand.

Faintly, faintly, she heard the poet Rainer Maria Rilke whisper, probably in some nondescript cirrus cloud, "Someone is watching you; you must change your life."

Chapter Two

"They have cut out my tongue."

"Oh, Mother. Don't be silly. Your tongue is in plain view, and it is moving quite well."

"You know what I mean, Colette, the mother tongue."

The daughter was uncomfortable about where the conversation was going.

"Don't worry, Mother. I'll get it back. Maybe I'll go to Trent."

"Never heard of it. Sounds like a horrible place like Brackdish or Drinkbeastly in Northern England. Why don't they learn beautiful names from the Irish like the River Liffey?"

"How about Trento, the Italian version?"

"Your father told me about the Italian trick. You know, they add letters like an "a" or an "o" to a bottle of wine or a lump of salami and charge a couple dollars more. What do you call them?"

"Vowels, Mother."

"You father wasn't educated, but he had a good nose."

Five years after his death she could hardly remember his nose.

"Anyway, Mother, Trento is in the northwest of Italy above Milan and Venice. The Catholic Church had meetings there in the sixteenth century which gave us the Latin Mass and the missal and bible you still use. Fancy that."

"That's a long way to go. Can we afford it?"

"Perhaps I'll take up a collection: Colette's Pence. Think the Vatican would contribute?"

"Funny girl! Poking fun at Peter's Pence is probably a sin."

Her mother changed the subject.

"I see you have lost weight."

Colette had a hard time looking in the mirror.

"Just a little baby fat."

Her mother always went there when the conversation got awkward. Colette felt she had stumbled backwards into the truth. It was two months since her abortion.

Colette was telling the truth. Didn't the flesh she lost come from all parts of her body and every inch of her skin? The flesh also came from her lover Jerry O'Connor. It came from the promises that found and entered her under the Promenade tree; the vulgar lines of his chest, his deep-throated musical shift that parted her tongue. She had read the book of gutter slang and knew that *slag* and *skank* found prominence in a later chapter yet to be lived. She wondered who was acting the maggot now.

"Mother, if the bishops take Latin away, you can go down to the Village or St. Patrick's. This is New York City, you know," said Colette.

"It's not the same. Take the tongue and they will also take Father Stravinsky and bring in someone who wouldn't know Latin if it hit him in the face."

Colette knew she was referring to Spanish-speaking priests from the Philippines who were taking over churches in the Bronx. She wanted to say that the Spanish had their tongue too, and it was more widely spoken than Latin and important to the Church's future. But she kept quiet.

She drifted off into safer territory, and today that was Father Stravinsky from Croatia, who wore vestments with the cross of St. Andrew which seemed to bewitch her. She had no idea why. She recalled from her religious training that St. Andrew was said to have established the Church in Constantinople and was the patron saint of Romania, so why not Croatia? That would explain the cross. As the story goes, St. Andrew was crucified on an X-shaped cross because he considered himself unworthy to die like Christ. After his death, his knees, upper arm, tooth and fingers found their way to Greece, Scotland, Ireland and England. Part of this story was based on a monk's dream, so she had to be careful.

Colette thought Father Stravinsky might be worth talking to for her Trent project. She could imagine the priest with St. Andrew emblazoned on his vestments standing in the Trent town square holding back the hordes of Lutherans, Anglicans and Anabaptists. This view seemed as reasonable as the CliffsNotes version of the Council of Trent she consulted, one that was probably written by a Jesuit who drew a straight line from the sixteenth century council to the Second Vatican Council in the 1960s, which told her all sexual congress must contain the potential of birth. Colette felt a shiver down her spine.

"What if I would give you Trent, Mother?"

"Wouldn't the Italians mind?"

"I don't mean the city. I mean my graduate thesis. I'll dedicate it to you. I'll even put the dedication in Latin."

13

"Thanks, dear. That's very kind of you. Could you include your dad, too? He loved that you were going to college."

"Of course, Mom."

"If you do go, will you see the pope?"

"I don't think I'll go to Rome. It's hundreds of miles to the south."

"Well, if you do, please have him bless my St. Christopher medal. It's the last thing your father gave me. It's a new version with the saint much larger."

"Of course. And if not, I'll get a Latin-speaking priest in Trent to do the honors."

Her mother sighed as if she were finding the very last sale item on the discount rack, thoroughly picked over by the throng and ultimately discarded.

That night Colette heard in a dream the sounds of a large throng of worshippers outside the Vatican chanting "*Santo Subito, Santo Subito,* Sainthood in our time," urging quick sainthood for Pope John Paul II. The Latin felt unrehearsed and might well have come from the catacombs.

On waking, Colette recalled the essence of the dream. The pope wore a four-cornered hat, a white cassock and a blue stole. He slipped into the earth. In the background a Mass was in progress. She was kept from the ceremony by a rope. A priest had dressed her in a black robe and painted her face white. She spoke in Latin" "*Introibo ad altare Dei*—I will go to the altar of God."

She said the Gloria, confessed her sins, and a voice asked her to turn her back to the altar before the Communion feast. She was turned again, watching the celebrant in purple vestments fisting a bloodless chalice with an altar cloth. "*Dominus vobiscum,*" he said, "the Lord be with you."

Colette scribbled down a few more details she remembered from the dream, eager to get out of the house and out of the dream. At first she saw the dream as a gift and then it seemed like a punishment and a weight. She was astonished that Latin phrases came back with such ease. She had the uncanny feeling that her mother was getting inside her head, though she knew the idea was nonsense. The dream seemed so stark, dramatic and threatening. She had never experienced anything like that in her life.

Colette knew she needed help and decided to schedule an appointment with the campus counselor.

Chapter Three

"Since this is our first session, Ms. McGovern, here is a little background. I have a MS in Behavioral Psychology, which I hope is enough for students who need a willing ear. I have also studied Carl Jung extensively. Now what can I do for you?"

Colette had read O'Connell's resume on the college web site. His study of Jung caught her eye. And two of her friends had had sessions with him. Nonetheless, she was not eager.

"Well, Mr. O'Connell, I am having trouble sleeping and generally seem tense."

"Any reason for your insomnia and feeling tense?"

Colette was having trouble talking about a very feminine pope and any link that dream might have to her abortion. And she didn't know how to talk about a priest fisting a chalice.

O'Connell said nothing. Colette thought minutes must have passed. She thought about her mother and the Latin Mass. She thought about the last time she went to confession. She thought about cold churches. She thought about her father's silence on most matters of the heart. Colette worried about what she had set in motion.

"It's okay, Ms. McGovern. Please take your time. We can reschedule if you like."

"I had a very troubling dream about the late Pope John Paul II."

Colette felt as if she had blurted out this thought during an imaginary confession, except this time there was no screen to filter her words and give her cover. For some reason she remembered that a Milanese bishop had invented a screen for the confessional so that those involved could not see each other. Colette knew there was no darkness to hide in.

"Any particular reason you are dreaming about him now?"

It was as if someone or something had control of her tongue.

"I'm not sure. I recall seeing some news accounts a few years ago about the Italians pressing for him to become a saint immediately: *Santo*

Subito or sainthood in our time. At first I didn't really know what it meant, but the phrase stayed with me."

"You know Pope John Paul II became a saint in 2014?"

"I remember my mother going to Mass to celebrate his canonization. I don't think it was a big deal for her. She was more worried about the church closings and losing her Latin Mass."

"Did you have any particular impression of him when he was alive?"

"Not really. I guess it was filtered through my mother and father. I was in grade school when I first heard his name. I had read that Pope John Paul wasn't very progressive on women's issues, but he seemed to become softer after he got Parkinson's. I saw him on television a few times."

"Okay, that brings us back to the dream about Pope John Paul. Was the 'softer' pope in your dream?"

"I guess so. After the cries of the crowd demanding that he be made a saint now, he seemed to wrap himself in soft robes and literally sink into the ground."

"Does that suggest anything to you?"

"I'm not sure. He's sinking into the earth, but he's getting softer. Maybe it's not odd for the pope to wear lace. I mean, some of the outfits the priests wear make you wonder. It felt gentle and feminine. I don't know how else to say it."

"You say it very well. I was wondering whether this feminine feel is awkward for you, him being the pope."

"I don't really know. I mean, the vestments and all, the celibacy of priests, and the absence of women in the Church is confusing to me."

"Confusing?"

"That might not be the right word. I don't really know. The pope in the dream was sinking into the earth, and the feel was feminine. It's not the image that usually comes up when I think of the Church."

"And why do you suppose he was doing that?"

Colette laughed and wanted to say, how the hell do I know? Deep down she thought this dream might be a price she was paying for the abortion and thumbing her nose at the Church.

"I don't know about dreams. I read something in Jung that dreams are what we ignore during the daylight hours."

"You have been ignoring the pope?"

She laughed again.

"I really haven't given him much thought. This dream just came."

"And was that the end of the story?"

"I wish it was. What I remember next was standing in front of the altar at the beginning of Mass. A priest dressed me in black and painted my face white. Before Communion, he turned me away from the altar."

16

"My goodness! No wonder you are upset. Do you need a break?"

Colette wanted to get the hell out of his office but had a gut feeling that the dream was much bigger than her.

"No, I'm all right. I just want to understand why this is happening to me."

"Why do you think?"

"I just don't know."

Colette recalled the unwanted children who were tossed down abandoned wells in County Galway. Sometimes it seemed like the place was calling her.

"Okay. You mentioned the priest dressing you in black, painting your face white and turning you from the altar. What do you think that means?"

"I recall writing in my journal that it felt like a shunning. I heard that some religious groups in Ohio turn people away from the community. I remember being behind a rope. I was roped off."

"Please, go on."

"I have joked with my mother about excommunication. She warned me: don't joke about religious stuff. Now the joke seems to be on me."

"Does that explanation feel right to you?"

She wanted to say yes in order to end the session but knew something else was in the air.

"I really don't know. Now that I think about it the dream seemed really old and medieval. At least they didn't burn me at the stake."

Colette didn't like her attempt at humor but felt she was recovering her balance.

"Yes, Ms. McGovern, it seems to have that sense. You mentioned earlier a shunning. In the dream you seem to be held hostage behind the rope with your face painted, as if on display in the public square. Does this suggest a punishment to you?"

She was not ready to go there under any circumstances.

"I'm not sure. I rarely go to church. My mother still attends the Latin Mass and sometimes fills the house with her Latin phrases. But that seems to be more play than doctrine. We joke about it a lot in a harmless sort of way."

"Understood. What you describe does seem like banter and play. Then why do you think such complex and very organized religious themes pop up in your dreams? The dream you described seemed to be structured like a story or perhaps a play."

"I hadn't thought about it that way but there is certainly a structure and a storyline to the dream. I wrote in my journal that when the dream opened it seemed peaceful and quiet, then the other scenes seemed dark and threatening. But I wasn't just watching the dream. I was inside it, standing in front of the altar as if I was a statue. The more I describe the dream, the more it did seem like a punishment."

"Please go on."

"Well, I'm clearly outside the worship circle, not deserving of participation. As I said before, this punishment seemed of another time, outside my experience. I'm not close enough to the church to be having dreams like this. I don't want and don't deserve them. It's not like I'm living in a convent in the 12th century like St. Hildegard of Bingen eagerly awaiting visions from God. And to recall all that Latin from a service I don't even remember seems absolutely crazy. Hell, I can hardly remember what happened yesterday."

"But you don't just stand there, right?"

"Right. I'm listening to the Latin Mass. I guess it's all in Latin. When the priest said, *Dominus Vobiscum* or 'The Lord Be with You,' I responded, 'And with you Father' and then 'And you Mother.' It was if something was missing and I had to fill in the missing part."

"What was missing?"

"I'm not sure. In the dream Pope John Paul slipping into the earth was not an ending but a beginning. In the dream what seemed to be missing in the Mass was the feminine. I don't know what that means. It was just a feeling. I recall the words 'And you Mother,' as an emphatic statement that I wanted the Mother to be part of the ritual."

"Very good! You invoke the mother. Which one?"

Colette laughed.

"Well, my mother must be in the mix. I guess Mother Church, although it didn't really feel that way. It was as if something was missing from the service. I acknowledge the Son and the Father but I seem insistent that the Mother be part of this. Isn't that crazy? What on earth was I thinking?"

"I don't think your remarks sound crazy. You keep coming back to some missing element."

"Yes, the service seemed incomplete. The pope was leaving the earth gracefully, with a hint of the feminine. Then I am put on display and turned away from the service. I'm not sure but in the dream I seemed to be a little pissed off, if you don't mind me saying."

"Pissed off?"

"Yes and I'm angry. My back is turned away from the altar during the lead up to the Communion, but I can still hear the prayers. I invoke the Mother and ask for our daily bread. Actually, it's more like a plea or a prayer. Perhaps it's a demand?"

"What do you think that means?"

"It might mean me and perhaps all female worshippers want to be fed our daily bread by some goddess."

"Is that a joke?"

"Probably. I realize it's a little presumptuous of me, trying to rewrite traditions and theology, but the dream was emphatic about the need for the feminine presence in the Mass."

"Please, go on."

"I'm struggling. The dream seemed so personal and so close. I swear to God it felt like I was standing before the altar."

"Why do you think the dream put you in that position?"

"That's an interesting way to put it. I seemed to have a vested interest in the dream. I mean, the dream was not hanging out there in the distance. Yes, it felt very personal but there's more to it. In asking for our daily bread from a mother figure, I was challenging the church in some way. Perhaps the dream was trying to balance the patriarchy of the church with the feminine element. That's what it felt like but I just don't know why."

"There's nothing in your life or psyche that might have brought this on?"

Colette was thinking about her baby and why she felt hungry all the time; then she retreated to Trent.

"Well, I have started to research the Council of Trent for a senior thesis. The objective is to analyze the importance of the council to the modern Church."

"Making any progress?"

"I've just started. The Council of Trent seems heavy, distant and a little foreign. Actually, I have been thinking about examining how the feminine was handled at Trent and at other times in Church history? It's a little vague at the moment."

"Perhaps that was the spark for the dream?"

"The spark?"

"Well, sometimes these things just bubble up. I think Jung said that these represent archetypal forces that bubble up from the collective unconscious. We greet them when we are ready."

Colette wondered what energies had produced a dream that suggested she was waging a war on theology. Then she had to suppress a laugh.

"Then I'm not responsible for these energies?"

O'Connell laughed. "I guess it depends on what action you take."

"I promise not to do anything stupid. It looks like the Council of Trent is about to take over my life. From what I have read so far, it might have a very long shadow."

Colette sensed the session with O'Connell was coming to an end.

19

"We hope not, Ms. McGovern. As long as these things come to the surface, we can deal with them. May I ask what you will do with the dream we discussed?"

"Sure, I think I'll work it into a poem and post it on the front door of Holy Angels Church in the Bronx. I'll call it 'Chanting the Feminine Down.'"

"You mean like Luther?"

"I hope not. Didn't the pope banish and try to kill him?"

"I'm not sure about the pope. Now that sounds like a protest."

"Then perhaps I won't sign the poem."

"And miss the notoriety?"

"We do our best work in the dark."

Chapter Four

The word Colette used to begin most dream journal entries was Tumbleweed. She intended no Western association or sleight of hand. She had no interest in going to Texas. She was being absolutely literal. What she was about to record was as predictable as tumbleweed tumbling aimlessly across tundra and sand without meaning or purpose. This double-barreled word said it all in a breezy incantation: What follows should be considered suspect, exaggerated, unreliable, and very likely fiction.

Colette remained of two minds about her journal entries. The entries might be bad fiction or an ominous prediction. She had gone to the psychologist because she was troubled and offended by the lucidity of "Chanting the Feminine Down." Why would Pope John Paul II, the blessed, patient, suffering man, appear out of nowhere in her dream?

Colette only vaguely remembered the pope, except for his final days when he showed enormous dignity while battling Parkinson's. He seemed to kiss the ground everywhere he went, especially in his native Poland, as if he really loved the place. Why had he shown up on her doorstep unannounced and uninvited? Was he reaching out to her? Was his feminine dress and descent a final response to the Church's theology of sex? Colette shuddered.

Something was eating at her. Colette felt there were forces inside of her she couldn't control, as if she was giving birth to something. Since her meeting with O'Connell, her dreams increased, as if they were opening up strange, new and dangerous worlds.

Days later, Colette dreamed she was in a swank psychologist's office on Park Avenue with a therapy group that seemed to fade away upon her arrival. The psychologist could have been either a man or a woman. He or she said that we begin to get better after five or fifty minutes. Colette disagreed, saying that she just buried her father and the healing began when you started the process.

The psychologist was losing some authority and talked about failures and insecurities. Colette looked closely at the psychologist's face. It was now very feminine and became more so as she stared. She sensed that this transition from man to woman happened before her eyes, and therefore she bore a certain responsibility. The more she stared, the better she felt. The more fragile the psychologist became, the more healing occurred in Colette.

On waking, Colette recorded this dream in her journal, making a note that the dream seemed to be about transformation and healing from within. Colette wondered why the psychologist became more fragile as the patient experienced healing. What was going on here? She recalled learning about transference in a psychology class which referred to the redirection of repressed feelings on another party. Can you really do something like that in a dream, she wondered. She also wondered whether dreams could kill. Colette looked in the mirror, half expecting to see her dream figure. Her own red hair and blue eyes looked familiar but her face looked thin and worn.

She longed for something sturdy and opened her journal to an entry for December 8, 2016. She remembered that there was something magical about December 8th. Not Pearl Harbor, but the Feast of the Immaculate Conception courtesy of Pope Pius IX, December 8, 1854, finally delivering the feminine in her most virginal form into the symbolic pantheon.

Colette reviewed an earlier dream she had recorded in her journal on that special day. In the dream she had seen Pope Francis emerge from the heavens or a star cluster. Now only his eyes seemed visible, and she felt she was in the presence of God. The pope spoke and said something to the effect: "I know where the text comes from" or "Don't you know where the text comes from?" or "This is where the text comes from." The scene shifted to a line of young girls in Catholic school uniforms waiting to receive Communion.

This journal text was followed by some scribbling in a handwriting she didn't fully recognize. She read a number of questions. Did the traditional text still live? Why did Pope Francis sound like an angry Jehovah? Why the shift to the peaceful Communion scene? This dream was impressive and scary. What the hell was she supposed to do with it?

The next morning at breakfast Colette spoke to her mother.

"I dreamed of Pope Francis last night."

"Why, that is wonderful, Colette! What did he look like?"

"Well, it was like he came out of the heavens and said he knew where the text came from. Then I saw a group of Catholic school girls waiting for Communion."

"That's so beautiful, my dear. Was he referring to the bible text?"

"I'm not sure, Mom. It could mean he had or knew the true text, you know, the Word."

"But don't we already know that?"

"Yes, but perhaps the dream was a reminder to a certain college girl to watch her Ps and Qs."

"Now, how many times have I told you that? Mark my words."

"Your words and the pope's words are all duly marked, Mother."

"Well, it's about time, my dear. And thank you for the confession."

Colette winced. Her mother never joked about religion. She wished dreams would sooth her like they did her mother.

She thought of Pope Francis showing up on the Feast of the Immaculate Conception. Searching for serendipity, Colette looked for entries for August 15th, the date of the Feast of the Assumption. No luck this time, as the entry would be likely found in a religious book under the heading "profane." She promised to return to this mystery.

Colette scrolled through her journal, still looking for answers. The dream she came across was about a beautiful woman, a beautiful tease who emerged from a cloud of Arabian sand in a flowing white, bouncy dress, crossing time zones, oceans, and parking lots looking for a man who came out of a cloud. She kissed him slowly on the lips, long enough for the mystery to settle in, leaving Colette time to wonder whether this vision was a sign from God or just the luck of the draw.

Colette saw a note in the journal margin: "When love finds soul it loses compunction." She had no idea where the quote came from and didn't really understand it. Whatever it meant, she didn't seem to have it. She liked the feel of the dream and the mystery woman she would like to be, crossing oceans and time. She prayed that her psyche would send to her more voluptuous sex dreams and keep the pope and all that theological stuff out of her bedroom, at least for the time being. It was driving her crazy. She would settle for the occasional dream of Catholic schoolgirls waiting for communion in a patient, pious line. She wouldn't mind a little orthodoxy for a change. She would not hum Billy Joel's "Only the Good Die Young" because she had found herself in his lyrics too many times, even when she wasn't wearing that provocative Catholic high school skirt.

Her father was a fan of Johnny Cash and listened to his music until the day before he died. He must have played "A Burning Ring of Fire" a thousand times, often while he danced with her and his wife in their small Bronx apartment, bumping into furniture. Colette had never really thought about the words and how love was a burning thing. She now felt she was in that burning ring of fire, but the burning issue was not love but theology and conscience.

The weight of theology sent her back to her childhood and the sound of simple prayers. She could dig out that rosary given for her First Communion and now at the bottom of her underwear drawer. She loved reciting the Glorious Mysteries in Catholic school but had trouble concentrating when she got to the Agony in the Garden and the Scourging at the Pillar. These scenes, carved in church walls right under her nose, begged for year-round Lenten cover. To make matters worse, in seventh grade her teacher Sister Teresa often acted out these mysteries, going so far as to whip herself with her own tassel or whatever she called it, perhaps trying to mimic the early Christian crazies. As a kid Colette thought the nun was a little crazy but now she was beginning to feel she was on her own knife edge of theology.

For some reason the August 15th date stuck in Colette's head, and she went to her college library for peace, comfort and reflection. She found a replica of Titian's "The Assumption of the Virgin" in one of the rear library study rooms. It was enough to take her breath away. An accompanying note said that the work was painted between 1516 and 1518. She had read about the wars, the burnings and the smashing of religious items during this period. She wanted to weep.

The arguments that surrounded the doctrinal basis for the Assumption, the weird orthodoxies, and attendant heresies, seemed to disappear in the beautiful painting. She felt like the schoolgirl in line for Communion reflecting on a scene where dogma was replaced by a mystical scene set in an ancient hierarchy that joined heaven and earth.

Colette imagined for a moment how it would be if the Church let its art tell her story rather than the old hoary books that seemed designed to send every reader to hell, usually for some sexual sin. She suddenly felt a chill. She thought that this painting held a lifetime of meaning. At the bottom of the hierarchy were the anxious apostles looking up as the Blessed Mother was lifted towards heaven by the cherubim. The apostles were at ground level and anchored where mortals stand. She was pure radiance and golden as she was lifted to God, who seemed to glow with fatherly affection but not without a hint of Jove. Colette wondered how Mary added a touch of the feminine to the Godhead.

Was it her father who said God was in his heaven and all was right with the world? Perhaps it was Milton, who saw celestial orderings through his blindness better than most. The Elizabethan Great Chain of Being celebrated those layers and strata of humanity and divinity all in the proper sequence. Aristotle got the chain started with mere mortals, and Aquinas added the angels, God and more than a hint of misogyny. Colette felt her body was trapped in this ancient text.

24

She would buy a copy of the Titian print and put it over her desk as a counter to what she knew to be the Reformation and the Counter Reformation and all the other little counters that had popped up like boils in the recent past and remained the sword over the entrance. And her mother would be pleased, even if Colette could not tell her she was circling Trent, resting, living and learning in the rich reds, and blues and greens of Titian, finding soul and majesty in this hierarchy of wonder.

At times poetry fought with religion for Colette's attention. Just when she began to feel comfortable, if only for a spell, with those blossoming hierarchies and proper angels on high, the poet Rilke, who she was studying, came with his visions, and spells and wonderment of language that would make her weep, creeping in from Germany, the now-Czech Republic, and the old Austro-Hungarian Empire.

She cautiously welcomed Rilke and his *Duino Elegies* and joined him in reciting: "If I cried out, who would hear me up there among the angelic orders?" The poet was no Titian imagining order and hierarchy and angels lifting Mary into heaven, a move full of Assumption and belief. For him, every single angel was terrible, giving off beauty, which was the first touch of terror. Where do we turn in our hour of need when faced with such horrors? Not to angels, people or even the cunning animals. Perhaps to the tree on the hillside we have always taken for granted?

Rilke spoke to her heart and Colette spoke with him.

"You request no more wooing from the demon voices, no more hints about that spotty path of transcendence. Your words: Just to be here is a delight. There is nowhere the world can exist except within. Our lives are used up in transformations and what's outside us, always diminishing, vanishes. The town criers who announce the Zeitgeist have forgotten the temples inside of us. The answer is not to kneel, pray, and wish but to build temples inside ourselves. Gaze at it, angel, it is us."

She imagined the poet picking his way through Europe before World War I, looking for silence, turning his back on many friends, supporters and family, rejecting the old dead gods out of hand. His search was for quintessential silence in which he could hear the whisper of trees he found when dying in an asylum. He was no Dante looking for inspiration and support from the gods. He turned away, looking for salvation inside himself. She recalled his words from another place and time about people growing by being defeated by increasingly powerful angels every day. And she prayed for Rilke's clarity of mind and his muscular response to the heavens.

She tried to remember the ditty that helped her recall in grade school the difference between the seraphim and the cherubim but couldn't find the words. Colette thought of hierarchy and one foot in front of the other.

She thought about her father's simplicity and Titian's grandeur. The artist imagined the Virgin Mary in rich red and green colored clothing and with full figure being assumed into heaven. The phrase, "assumed bodily into heaven," became strangely human under the riveting gaze of Titian where he showed Mary in voluptuous, provocative, Renaissance flesh.

Rilke might have shaken an occasional fist at the terrifying indifference and perfection of angels, but his journey was mainly about Laments and Lamentations. But even in his poetic despair and understanding that everything eventually falls away from us, he knew "our hearts survive like a tongue that is between our teeth and in spite of everything goes on praising." She thought of the soft and feminine Pope John Paul slipping into the earth, heart filled with love and silent praise. Was the blessed man slipping away from dogma and into a feminine repose?

She would revisit "Chanting the Feminine Down" as poetry and art, eager to find these virtues in what seemed like a medieval morality play in which she was turned away from her God and the altar of her youth.

Chapter Five

Colette's mother was surprised to learn that her daughter had purchased a large print of Titian's "Assumption of the Virgin."

"This must have cost you a fortune, dear."

"Actually, thirty-five dollars, plus shipping and handling."

"Why so cheap?"

"This is a digital copy of a good photograph of the painting. Only costs a few dollars to produce."

"I didn't know you were interested in the Assumption."

"Well, I just came across this. It's simply beautiful in every way. Titian pictured Mary as a full-bodied woman and not some anemic female carrier of the Christ child."

"Now, Colette, is that any way to talk?"

"Mother, I'm just warming up."

Her mother looked down at her feet, a tactic her daughter was familiar with.

"This doesn't mean I'm going to hell, Mother. You are so dramatic."

"What are you warming up for?"

"You know; the Trent project."

"Oh, right. You're going to bring back the Latin tongue to the Bronx."

"I just promised to dedicate my thesis to you and Dad in Latin."

"That and $3.50 will get you a cup of …"

"Mother, you know you can get coffee for $1.50 from one of those carts on Kingsbridge Road."

"It's not about the coffee; it's about the Church. Did I tell you that the Holy Infancy School will be closing down? I think they will soon sell the nun's house. As far as I can tell there are only two nuns left in the place, and they are both over eighty and hobbling."

"I'm sorry to learn about the school. I had a few good years there. Is this for sure?"

"You know how this works. The diocese comes up with a list of schools, churches, and other buildings, and the bishop takes out the meat cleaver."

"You could get a bus to St. Catherine's. It always seems to have a full house."

"It's not the same."

"Want me to talk to the priest?"

Her mother laughed.

"Better take a check with you."

"I was thinking about a poem."

"Right, those things really move mountains."

"The Bible is filled with poetry, like in the Book of Wisdom."

"I don't think Father Stravinsky cares about that kind of thing. He's trying to figure out how to fix the hole in the roof and replace the gutters and downspouts."

"You remember the flash mob that took over the Wakefield section of the Bronx a few months ago?"

"You want to send a poetry flash mob to harass our Church?"

They both laughed at that prospect.

"No, of course not, Mother. I just want to create some attention. Post something on the church door like Luther did, you know, the Protestant stuff. Then send out notices on social media, invite the press and all that."

"You're becoming Protestant? I don't know much about Luther, but he sounds like he's related to Lucifer."

"Heaven forbid on all counts."

"Still sounds like funny business to me. I'm sure you're not thinking about Mary having a little lamb."

"Not exactly, though I've always thought that nursery rhyme had a dark, nasty side, like Little Boy Blue. I also think it's time for Mary to grow up. I'm working on it."

"Like you, Colette?"

"Mother, you sound like you have a priest whispering in your ear."

Her mother rolled her eyes.

"Anyway, it'll be nothing the Church would consider vulgar, Mom. It's a poem based on a dream about Pope John Paul II becoming feminine and slipping into the earth."

"My goodness! You're dreaming of our dear pope becoming a transvestite? Aren't we getting enough of that in the New York Post? I don't think the Church approves of transvestites."

"I don't know about that, but he did show a delicate piece of lace on the bottom of his silk garment."

"This sounds like—what do you call it—blasphemy! I hope you don't hear from the Vatican."

"Well, Mother, I hope I do."

Her mother remained quiet.

"Don't worry, Mother. Everything will be in good taste. This is just a little experiment to launch me into my Trent project. I'll print a copy of 'Chanting the Feminine Down' for you. Share it with your friends."

"That sounds a little—I don't know how to say it—sexual?"

"Sorry, Mom, clean as a whistle. It's about a sense of the feminine, Mother Earth and the ways the Church has turned its back on this and on us."

"Could they kick you out of the Church? What's that called?"

"It's called excommunication? Don't worry; no one in the Bronx can either spell or pronounce that word."

"Mark my words, dear. This is not going to end well."

"Hope springs eternal, Mother."

Colette was aware of her own bluster. She put greater weight on her mother's predictions than on her own. But she pushed ahead with her poetry project. She wanted the poem to rise and sing like Titian's painting. Colette spent a weekend with her dream journal trying to find soul in her entry about the pope. She found herself once again caught between Catholic doctrine and a very feminine Pope John Paul. That was where the battle lines were drawn, she said to herself in language that seemed out of character and pretentious. Colette told herself that she wanted something in writing so the dream, once in public view, would be less of a burden to her. "That's not the half of it," she heard her mother say.

Colette worked her journal entry and other notes into a poetic form for "Chanting the Feminine Down." She wanted to bring her dream to life in its raw form. She wanted to get out from underneath the weight of the dream. She wanted to make it public so others could feel her pain. Colette wished Rilke had been at her side during the composition if only to offset the fear she had confronting the powers that seemed to threaten her.

She scheduled a meeting with O'Connell, to whom she had emailed a copy of the poem.

"Ms. McGovern, you were true to your word."

"Thank you."

"I'm no judge of poetry, but this seems balanced and understated."

"Thank you again. I've been a closet poet for some time, recognizing it was no way to earn a living. This dream really hit home, and I've been reluctant to let it go. Perhaps it's a way to take some of the sting out of the dream."

29

"Will you publish it in a magazine or online?"

"Not right now. Frankly, I think it is a little uneven and perhaps follows the dream too closely. The dream was so lucid and my writing fell short. The feeling of the poem seemed to overtake the poetic form, if you know what I mean. I need some distance from it. I intend to nail it to our church door, as I mentioned to you a few weeks ago."

"Yes, I recall, but I still don't fully understand why."

"In a way it's a lark, but there's more to it. It's a declaration of sorts. Maybe it will give me courage to push into the Trent project. I've been reading about Venice in the late sixteenth century when the printing press had taken over society. Everyone seemed to be printing their own newspapers and books, often under pseudonyms, because people were being killed for the written word. It seemed so romantic, and dangerous and gutsy. Compared to Venice of the time, social media seems fairly tame, even with all the personas."

Colette thought her remarks sounded like bullshit.

"I see. You mentioned a declaration. Of what?"

"My project, my intentions, my hopes? I know this doesn't sound very convincing."

"Only you would know that. You don't have to have everything nailed down. It's a process and an adventure. Didn't you say you'd be going to Trent or Venice?"

"I was thinking about it but lately, Trent and Venice seem to be coming to me."

"One question: I don't have the impression that you are—forgive the expression—a feminist in the traditional sense?"

"Well, these days that phrase seems so charged. But I am a fan of Simeon de Beauvoir's work and embrace her rejection of the patriarchy. She was a very brave woman."

"And you're not?"

"Not so much."

"All right, I understand. So where do you think this push to go public with the dream is coming from?"

"I'm not sure. The push probably comes from where the dream came from, my psyche, right? It's like a creative urge; a desire to give birth to something. Like a little incarnation. There have been other dreams, not as momentous as the one about Pope John Paul. Something is going on. I'm paying more attention to art work with these themes, like Titian's 'Assumption of the Virgin' which seemed so colorful and full-bodied. I'm feeling these things in the pit of my stomach."

Colette could have kicked herself. She hoped he would not be thinking pregnancy.

"Welcome to Venice," he said.

"Fingers crossed."

"And we need to respect this kind of indicator. Any reason you haven't mentioned these other dreams?"

"They didn't seem to resonate so deeply, if you know what I mean. Perhaps I need to think about them some more."

"Understood. Please let me know how your excellent adventure turns out."

"Thanks again."

Her excellent Italian adventure began when she held a final copy of "Chanting the Feminine Down." It was if she were reading it for the first time.

Chanting the Feminine Down

"Santo Subito, Santo Subito"
Sainthood in our lifetime
Chanted the Vatican throng
Clapping the dead pope
Into his sepulcher.
Soon the lame will walk
And hands will remember
What the brethren already know
About Lenten wounds.

I began my reverie
In geometry with his red
Four-cornered hat
That touched the cardinal points
Of his compass and vision
Then the slow drag
Of gravity; broad lumber
Jack shoulders round into
A feminine curl, inward
As if they were reaching
For the heart while his white
Cassock slipped to the floor
Showing a hint of bottom lace.
The blue stole wound around
His body which was falling into itself
Like a circle of peace.

Mass was about to begin.
I am kept from the ceremony
By a thick rope.
A priest dressed me in a black robe,
Painted my face white
And covered me in a shroud of incense.
I am standing on a round stone
And heard the strains of my youth:
"*Introibo ad altare Deï*"—
I will go to the altar of God;
"*Kyrie eleison*"---
Christ have mercy on us;
I say the Gloria
Confess my sins
And then my back was turned to the altar
Until after the Communion Feast
As if it was a shunning.
I heard the shuffle of a thousand feet.

And when I am turned again
I am a statue
Watching the celebrant
In purple vestments
Fisting a bloodless chalice
With an altar cloth:
"*Dominus vobiscum*," he said—
"The Lord be with you
And with you, Father,"
I scream, fighting
My way out of ritual
As if coming up for air,
"And with you, Mother."
"*Dona nobis pacem*"
Grant us your peace
At your table
In your grace
As you slip into the earth
Becoming for us
Our "*panem nostrum*"—
Our daily bread

Harking back to the first meal
The first mystery
And the Feminine Incarnation
We take slow.

She showed the finished copy to her mother, who glanced through the stanzas as if reading an electric bill.

"I like the Latin parts," she said before returning it.

"I told you I would bring you Trent. This is the first installment."

Colette decided to give the poem an embroidered edge, photo-shopping 10th century images of a Byzantine-looking Mary from *The Book of Kells*. Her parents loved this beautifully illustrated rendition of the gospels of Matthew, Mark, Luke and John by monks on the island of Iona off the coast of Scotland one thousand years earlier. Her father had promised to take his wife to Trinity College, Dublin, where it was displayed, on his retirement.

Colette knew the images from *The Book of Kells* did not resonate with her poem, but this was a gift to her mother and dead father. Anyway, the book suggested a deep reverence which transcended theology. Moreover, this ancient book was just so beautiful and brought such hope and artistry from the Dark Ages. She didn't bother to explore a parody book titled *The Book of Kells: Copulating Cats and Holy Men*. She knew there would be a price to pay for dragging a lot of stuff back into the daylight, but she would do her best not to be distracted by cats or listicles. She could hear her mother say with exasperation that nothing was sacred anymore.

She left a copy of the poem on her mother's pillow. She went to her church in the late afternoon and posted copies of the poem and artwork on the front door, the bulletin board, and in the help wanted area. She left a stack of about thirty poems between the rows of prayer books and the poor box. Colette thought about placing copies of the poem in the various pews and on the altar steps and rails. She imagined the devout showing up for Mass and using her dream words instead of the regular missal. Soon attendees divided into two unequal camps with most of the congregation joining the priest in railing against and shunning Colette and one or two other women who joined her in celebrating a feminine Mass in the shadow of the feminine pope sinking into eternity. In Colette's imaginings the small female voices were drowned out by the angry religious mob.

She wondered if this was what the Council of Trent would be like.

Colette had personally signed every copy, though the signature was hardly legible to the uninformed. She guessed her courage failed her at the last minute.

She decided to make no announcement on social media.

She waited for five days but heard nothing. On her next visit to church, she saw her weathered page hanging by a thread on the front door. "Fuck you" was scribbled over the word "Feminine" and a crude drawing of a penis appeared over "Chanting," as if the organ had a mouth and was taking everything in. The graphic was on its way to becoming a cartoon, with room enough for additional contributors. She was not laughing.

She noticed more scribble on the church door: "Your poetry sucks the Big One. Fuck off with your faggot Pope. See you ladies in hell!"

There was more vulgarity.

"Fist this you fucking whore." The words were followed by a rough drawing of a fist penetrating a vagina. "And up your ass too."

Colette was close to tears when she returned to her home. She was glad her mother was nowhere in sight. She went to her bedroom and opened her journal to the Pope John Paul dream. She was beginning to understand that dreams, whether left as poetry in a church vestibule or contained with the center of her being, could be very dangerous territory.

She tried to laugh at the thought, recalling graffiti on the Bronx No. 6 train stating with some finality: "The Bronx is full of dicks."

It didn't help.

Chapter Six

If Colette had believed in astrology, the signs would have surely recommended that she get out of town, chasing after some planet which happened to be rising. She was already on her way, mentally, thanks to a course by a take-no-prisoners Jesuit, as he called himself, who explored his order's efforts to "convert" native Brazilian Indians to Catholicism, a task recounted in numerous letters from priests written in Portuguese, with some translated into Latin, Spanish and Italian. These two hundred or so letters were written in the middle of the sixteenth century.

Colette imagined that she was circling again like a wily beast, toward and away from Trent, picking up hints, animal spores, and markings on trees. She would embrace the signs, make notes and parse them in her journal, praying that they wouldn't come to life in the middle of the night. She still saw Trent as cold and forbidding, like the snows blowing in from the Alps, stopping both traffic and the heart. She wanted her blood warmed and her body prepared for a later, slow-boat journey to Trent which would be accomplished by going south, going under, going down through latitude and longitude to another place and time.

Her mother and probably a few nuns had taught her to believe in serendipity; that was easy enough. She had also learned about Carl Jung's synchronicity in psychology class, and that took a little getting used to. She understood this concept as the connection between two unrelated events, either physical or psychological. On the face of it, this seemed like pure coincidence, but Jung reminded her that the connection was not meaningless.

She laid down a few markers. Everyone agreed that the Council of Trent occurred between 1545 and 1563. The two hundred letters from Jesuits in Brazil were written between 1549 and 1563. Was this a coincidence, serendipity or full-fledged synchronicity? She could imagine prelates, nuncios, friars and other dignitaries, most under the authority of the pope, pushing back against the Protestant Reformation under the watchful eyes of Germany, France and Spain, while boatloads of Jesuits were well into their 6,000-mile journey to Brazil. It could take months or years. Were these voyages under the radar? Were they under God?

"If you can get your noses out of your mobile devices for a paltry hour," said Professor Merkel, playing the role of the scolding teacher, "we can reflect on a most remarkable century for the Church and the world. Now what am I talking about?"

"The Council of Trent," replied someone in the back of the room.

"That's a decent answer and not surprising since that's one reason we are here. After all, Trent defined the Church for the next four hundred and fifty years. Anything else?"

"This was the century of exploration," responded Colette. "It now seems staggering that Spain and Portugal could explore so much of the world and at the same time take the Church with them."

"Yes, this is the story of the century; how Portugal and Spain divided up the uncivilized world and set out to explore and conquer it, looking for gold and spices while bringing in Christ through the back door. One issue we will deal with is the relationship between the events at Trent and what was going on in the outside world, so to speak. Was there a relationship? For those of you who have read accounts of Trent will know that there is little, if any, discussion about the Church's global evangelizing taking root at the time of Trent.

"We will want to consider whether this was because such activity was a given, that the popes controlled the agenda, or that the attendees at Trent really didn't know about what their comrades were doing in Brazil and elsewhere. Keep in mind that a letter could take months or years to arrive, if at all. Everyone was in the dark to some degree. Was the Council of Trent a closely held script and the forced conversion of natives an unimportant event happening on the other side of the world? Was Trent a mid-sixteenth century soap opera, Italian style? Was the pope just buying time while the Portuguese and Spanish were carving up the world, one chunk of latitude after the other?

"Anyone?"

There was silence.

"All right, it's apparently time for the big guns, Vatican style. Pope Nicholas V signed a papal bull in 1456, authorizing the Portuguese king to crush, subdue, crucify, rob and castrate all pagans and other enemies of Christ in West Africa. Pope Alexander VI in 1493 stayed with essentially the same murderous script when he divided up the 'uncivilized' Americas between Spain and Portugal. The stage was set for a thousand years. Do I hear an 'Amen' from anyone?"

There was silence.

"Moreover, our intrepid Jesuit explorers were given permission to reduce pagans and other non-believers to perpetual slavery and take charge of their possessions, which I assume also meant their bodies. Free sex anyone?"

Still nothing.

"There is a doctrine imbedded here somewhere that is showing its ugly face today in the Middle East," Merkel continued. "It's all right for men to rape women who believe in polytheism, the most god-awful heresy. This is an ancient wound, my dear friends of theology, and don't you just know: this barbaric and un-Christian doctrine has never been repealed. No wonder Native Americans take turns protesting in front of the Vatican. No wonder American nuns are up in arms. My goodness, even the Episcopalians and Unitarians have rejected this bull. Is it any wonder that the Vatican hides its shame behind purple vestments? Pope John Paul II apologized for these actions in 2000, but the doctrine and shame still stand.

"Stay with me, dear students. You have a GPS for your petty, indulgent tasks, but the Portuguese and Spanish sailors had crude maps, the North Star, wobbly chronometers, and a sextant that wasn't exactly bringing down the heavens.

"So what do we have?"

"A mess?" responded a muffled voice.

"A mess is correct, Mr. Jones! It was a bloody mess and the sailors were up the creek—shit-creek, that is—without a paddle. I am sure you have all been in similar circumstances. Anyway, the real problem was that they never really knew from one day to next where they were. Talk about divine guidance. As you probably know, they were looking for India, spices, the Silk Road, and guns from the Japanese. These brave men and a small battalion or so of Jesuits stumbled onto Brazil, and the heavens opened up and they were all anointed on the spot, exclaiming, as if they came from the same choir: 'Jesus my Lord, my God, my All, how can I love Thee as I ought.'

"Now don't go overboard with this or take it with a mustard seed of truth. I'm re-visioning history a bit, taking a clue from psychologist Carl Jung, who told us to dream the dream forward, tacking along latitude lines for safety. Now there's a tip for the weekend sailors, especially for those in this class who have parents who can park yachts at Newport or have to settle for Tarrytown, under that bridge named for some Indian tribe or dead governor, long praised as a one-way ticket to the Rockland Psychiatric Center where electroshock was once a religion and an art. I feel your pain.

"Now, speaking of latitude lines that can be as tricky as understanding the pagan underpinnings of the Holy Spirit; they hold the key to the religious conversion of the Americas. Some popes, taking advice from a cardinal who must have summered on the Tigris or the Po, decided to give what is now Mexico and the rest of Central America to their Spanish friends and everything south of these lands to the Portuguese, more or less, thus preventing war, exporting a God, condemning the damned, and pumping up the Vatican's coffers. I am not sure if this brilliant decree of pontifical cartography became infallible doctrine, but it had the same effect.

"Now I don't want to hear snickers from the Matthew, Mark, Luke and John crowd that what this really tells us about the Vatican was that the College of Cardinals was—and perhaps still is—going around in circles, that the pope wouldn't know the North Star from a frittata, and what right did he have anyway to carve up the New World like a submarine sandwich?"

With that, Merkel leaned into a medieval map of the world, full of dragons and other fire eaters and briefly became part of the cartography.

Colette had learned not to laugh at Jesuit jokes because you could rarely tell where they were coming from. But Merkel seemed to be coming from the right place, a little fuzzy, somewhat mysterious, and not necessarily a safe place for the ruling Jesuits. He was circling Trent in his own way, filling in the script, while reflecting on some large screen outside the conference room which held the new science, adventure, and audacity. Copernicus's sun-centered model of the universe was outside looking in by 1543, greeted by the Vatican as anathema, a black veil over another birth.

Colette imagined the blistering hot sand at Porto Segro where the Portuguese landed in 1534 and their desperate need to plant a stone marker bearing a cross and the country's coat-of-arms. They called the inhabitants Indians and the country Terra da Santa Cruz, but the popular name Brazil, named after brazil wood, held. The luscious coves, islands and inlets along the coast became popular baptismal fonts and were given Christian names which held to this day.

Colette imagined Professor Merkel rising out of the South Atlantic foam, his long black tunic dripping with ocean creatures, his right hand holding aloft a large crucifix, blessing everything and everyone in his path. "Let us meditate and pray, on the blessings we received from Ignatius Loyola and the founding of the Society of Jesus to seek unrelentingly the salvation of souls and the conversion of infidels. So help me God.

"Remember that our dear Ignatius, with his demanding 'Spiritual Exercises' which included the cleaning of toilets and working with prostitutes, devoted himself to Christ, but there were those who were suspicious and who spread rumors that our great founder was a lunatic, a

Lutheran and even an Anabaptist. It was by the grace of God that favorable winds blew for the Jesuits, and they were granted by His Holiness the opportunity to tame this wild and desperate land, convert the savages, and baptize the unredeemed into the Holy Spirit.

"Pope Julius III, famous for looting Vatican coffers, buggering his adopted nephew, and God knows what else was of little help to our intrepid explorers. But thank goodness they could read the holy man's mind. These good souls went all in for the Brazilian Indians who would enjoy the same blessings as their brothers and sisters in Rome. Visit four churches in thirty days and all sins would be forgiven in this untamed, unredeemed land.

"Any comments, my inveterate students?"

"Sure," responded a young man who seemed to be dressed like a Jesuit. "After the initial positive remarks about the Jesuits and their early role in Brazil, your remarks seem to become a little fantastic if not critical."

"Thank you, Mr. Braun. Very astute. But tell me, why would I bother with the charade? I'm the professor, right? Am I not the truth and the light?"

"Maybe you wanted to lull us into the usual view of the good work done by missionaries; the good versus evil dance that the Jesuits loved. I mean, waltzing into Brazil or whatever it was called, and trying to convert everyone, with a corrupt, buggering pope in the rear view mirror. That seemed a bit much!"

"Lull is a good word. Most of America is lulled to sleep on a regular basis! I was bound to have some success here. We will get to the buggering, corrupt and infamous Julius whose name was forever engraved on the underside of an abandoned altar rail. Now what about the raw theology behind our Jesuit tale?"

No response.

"All right, we've read about the 'Spiritual Exercises' of the Jesuit Founder Ignatius Loyola. So, were our beachgoers doing pushups, mumbling some code to an unknown god, or beating themselves silly with a switch until the blood flowed?"

"None of these," responded a girl Colette didn't know. "'The 'Spiritual Exercises' were meant as a way to focus prayer and contemplation. And they gave guidance regarding what the individual should seek."

"Very good, Ms. Aimes. Now what were our creatures from the deep seeking?"

"Well, we know from our readings that individuals ought not to seek health, wealth and honor and the like. This obviously applied to men. The updated view of Loyola in drag is that for women the banned list might include beauty, body shape, youthful appearance, dependence on eternal validation, stylish dress and so on. It doesn't leave much to the imagination. This put an end to at least one industry."

"Bummer. Thanks for the post-modern take with a feminist twist. It all sounds very familiar. I think our Jesuits who came out of the sea probably needed all the prayers they could muster to handle this untamed, unknown, fantastical land named Brazil. Don't get me started on women."

"What do you think they called this place, Ms. Aimes?"

"The end of the world?"

"According to their cartographer, that's exactly where the land was. You're warm, so to speak. Can you get a little more Biblical?"

"The Garden of Eden?"

"Exactamente! What they saw or imagined they saw was Eden. Think about it. They stumble out of the water dragging their heavy, wet tunics behind them. The sand is finer, brighter, and more golden than anything they could experience on the Portuguese coast. If that wasn't enough to get their imaginations going, out from behind the trees and sea grasses came naked male and female Indians, some carrying weapons, others just curious. These people were buck naked, if you can excuse the expression; I am not trying to denigrate the feminine. You might read Roberto Gambini's book, *Indian Mirror: The Making of the Brazilian Soul* on this. The Indians displayed absolutely no shame.

"Now from a psychological point of view: just what the hell is going on? The hell is for effect, you understand, because current theology raises doubts about a literal hellhole, as residents of the Outer Boroughs in New York City might attest. Let me take you back to the Jesuits' dark, wool tunics, wooden crosses banging against their hollow but repentant chests, and their heads still in some medieval dungeon or whorehouse in Cairo, where they were helping the abused and the damned, God bless their souls."

"These guys must have been very confused," suggested Colette. "Someone mentioned that Brazil represented the Garden of Eden. But wasn't that where all the trouble started? I mean the temptation of Eve, the Fall, the shunning by God and the exit from the Garden? What about all the stuff from Aristotle up through Aquinas claiming women were inferior and empty vessels and sperm was the beginning and end of life? Catholic morality seemed to be sexual morality. I guess the Indians didn't get the message."

"Good point. But was that really true about the Indians not getting the message? Perhaps Aristotle, Augustine and Aquinas arrived on an earlier ship, speaking in tongues. There were already Europeans in Brazil before the Jesuits arrived and perhaps a bible or a missal was available, but the

40

Indians would have been unable to read the script. Maybe someone whispered in their ears."

Colette continued, "I said before that these guys were confused. Maybe it was worse than that. They looked at these naked bodies and saw what? Wouldn't they see what they wanted to see?"

"Luscious naked bodies!" said a voice from the back of the room.

"You are half-right, Mr. Martin. Please listen to Ms. McGovern. The Jesuits saw what they wanted to see. They were only human, after all. And they had that irrefutable Doctrine of Discovery in their back pocket for good luck. Based on their training and 'Spiritual Exercises,' what did they see and what did they imagine?"

"They saw naked people who were banished from the Brazilian Garden of Eden because they were likely having sex with each other and probably monkeys and other friends in the animal kingdom."

"Ouch! Someone is feeling that pain, Ms. Aimes, but well done. Now can you or anyone else tell us where all this sexy monkey business was coming from? I don't recall that primates having sex was included in our reading list."

Colette was enjoying her professor's line of questioning and Ms. Aimes' spunk. As soon as sex entered the discussion, everyone wanted to talk.

"Let's put down some fence posts," said a voice that might have been her professor. She fought the suspicion that she might be in Texas and back with the tumbling tumbleweed, looking for her father.

"The Jesuits saw all these naked bodies. Remember, the Indians covered nothing, not even the penis and vagina. These horny priests who had been at sea for months or years, fighting rough weather with Loyola's 'Spiritual Exercises' until they were blue in the face, crawled out of the muck and saw dicks, breasts and the whole nine yards. They probably dreamed about carrying out sexual acts of penance on these worshippers of many gods. Polytheism demanded a stiff sentence. What was their first reaction?"

"Everyone got blessed erections?"

"Young man, must you bring your dirty little mind into these deep theological discussions? Now, where's my sextant? And why the erections?"

"Wouldn't you?"

"I'll take the fifth," said a voice.

"I'd like a fifth," said another.

"Let's bring this baby home!" said Merkel. "We know that the Church had been trying to channel all that nasty, foreign libidinal stuff from the dark continents into doctrines, rituals and especially the confessional, that well-known porn studio. For centuries! Have you heard the one about having sex before Communion? The child born of this union would be a dwarf. Sex had obsessed the theological mind since the beginning. The Church had tried to cover nakedness for two thousand years and from the beginning—St. Paul, right, chastity and virginity are next to godliness, though not all priests and monks got that memo.

"Now reimagine our Jesuit friends looking at these well-tanned, well-shaped bodies that were playing the fool and perhaps engaged in an early-Brazilian version of cat's cradle or the Texas line dance without the boots.

"Keep in mind that our dear priests didn't know the country, language, or customs. For Christ's sake, they thought they had landed in India. You can't be wearing heavy wooden crosses from a Lisbon sweat shop around your neck, mumbling the exercises and then just dump baggage like original sin on the beach like a pile of old seaweed. Any fool could tell that those poor bastards emerging from the brush needed to be saved.

"Can you imagine the anguish our dear, burdened, blessed Jesuits felt? Can you imagine their urgency as they plotted on the fly to save these poor bastards before they escaped from this garden, running without soul but considerable alacrity into some concupiscent sexual fantasy? If anyone is not hot and bothered by this ecclesiastical text, this randy footnote to a divinely inspired Jesuit invasion, please leave the room until the feeling finds you.

"The center of meditation is God; everything else is secondary. Man can be saved only through total submission to God. Man can have his own visions, but they must be logged in some epistle and approved by the proper clerical authorities. Think allegory. Think morality play. Dreamers are not welcome in this universe. Nor are those poets who have vision after vision. Some of you know who I am talking about. Rilke for starters, forever accused of shaking his smallish, angry, Germanic fists at the heavens! Eventually we'll get to Trent and will really nail this sucker.

"Remember Loyola's vision of three keys to an organ that gave off the sound of beautiful harmony, like angels in heaven? And the correct answer is: the Trinity. Loyola's vision didn't mess around with multiple choices and monstrous, personal and private symbolism, such as dreams and the stuff found on a bathroom wall. He knew which side his bread was buttered on. The beautiful thing about this man is that even his hallucinations delivered clear messages from God. If that isn't the divine speaking, then all I have to say is, Bob's your uncle."

Colette knew no Bob, and didn't think she had an uncle, but remembered vaguely her mother stitching together Bob and Uncle until they both lived happily ever after in some exalted family tree.

Professor Merkel continued, "Now, please don't give too much thought to Bob, who shows up from time to time, especially when I have to take a toilet break. This is getting edgy and away from our pure Jesuits who were supposed to have no inclinations, so we won't look for any long-hidden love letters. Sentiment is out the South American window. Forget about lines of latitude. What interested these guys the most were the lines of the cross, which was the perfect intersection to record their sins. They came in abundance. I mean, the sins, the crosses, and the indulgences, all recorded in Latin and sometimes Portuguese, all sent in ledgers to clerics back home who devoured them without crossing their eyes or, God forbid, reading between the lines. These missives were rightly called letters of edification, and today might be written by some PR hack.

"I wander; you wonder; we all pray for ice cream. Let's get back to the beach. Understandably, the Jesuits weren't going to change their hymn book, so to speak, when they encountered hordes of naked, unsaved, unwashed Indians emerging from the heather, to bring in a feminine touch. What do humans do when faced with such circumstances? And please, no selfies."

"Punt?"

"That's the coward's way, Mr. Martin, and you are not one."

"Fall back on what you know?"

"Excelente! And what might that be, Ms. Aimes?"

"Their training as Jesuits, their 'Spiritual Exercises,' and prayers, I guess."

"You are correct! Their training focused on their meditation on certain sins, especially those associated with the fall of Adam and Eve, the big sin, the Original One, and sex on the down low which we poor, buggered bastards have engaged in for centuries. The confessional has been more useful than a sex manual. This was essentially a mental exercise, and it might take some time for an individual to thoroughly suppress the senses. And keep in mind that our Jesuits were not on holiday. They brought few comforts with them from home, including beds, straight razors or the midnight rations celebrated in their handbook because these guys burned a lot of midnight oil. The body was evil and the flesh was temptation, so they should be shut down, denied, and suppressed. And no sneaking out after dark into the bush and perfumed sea grasses!

"How are you folks holding up?"

"Bummer," someone said.

"Ah, I'm glad you still have a sense of humor, you voice out of nowhere! Stay with me on this. We have the narrative down pat; the invasion from the sea; the theological baggage our Jesuits lugged up over the burning sand; the joy with which the natives received them, at least

43

according the passionless letters written by our invaders; and the ready-made, fresh from home, divinely inspired training program the Jesuits used to breathe the fear of Christ into these people.

"Now, think back to your courses on Carl Jung. What do we call it when we identify characteristics in a stranger or, as Jung puts it, the Other?"

"It's called projection," said Rebecca Aimes.

"And what is that?"

"It's when we project our negative traits or what we have repressed and don't recognize on another."

"Good! So what were our Jesuits projecting on the Brazilians?"

"Fear of the body and the flesh."

"What else?"

"Original Sin."

"What else?"

"All that righteous spiritual stuff; you know, the spiritual exercises we have discussed."

"What else?"

"The Adam and Eve thing. The Fall and the wandering for a zillion years."

"What else?"

"Maybe they saw hell in the Indians? I mean, they were naked, sexual, eating all that forbidden fruit, like pomegranates. Maybe the Jesuits figured they were already in hell."

"Okay. The Jesuits were projecting all this stuff on the Indians. What does their projection tell us about them?"

"They felt superior."

"They felt morally superior."

"They felt they were the chosen ones. The Indians were savages, living in sin and going to hell. They were there to save them."

"And what do we call this feeling of superiority, psychologically speaking? Think of Jung."

"I think Jung called it inflation."

"Indeed it is, Ms. Aimes! Now what is actually inflated?"

"Well, everything about the Jesuits seems inflated: their sense of mission; their desire to save the souls of the inhabitants, and I guess their theological grounding."

"Whoops! Are we getting stuck here? What does that mean in the psychological sense?"

"Like walking in mud?"

"Yes, but a little more meat and potatoes and less mud, please."

"Psychologically stuck means an inability to advance; to stay in the same place or pattern of behavior."

"Nicely put. Anything else keeping our Jesuits down?"

"Professor Merkel," asked Luther Martin, "weren't the Jesuits carrying a lot of psychological baggage, courtesy of Rome? Surely they knew the stories about Pope Alexander VI, Pope Paul III and Pope Julius III, now considered three of the most corrupt popes in Church history. I read Pope Paul III took control of 45,000 prostitutes in Rome and a cut of their earnings. Maybe the Jesuits were projecting all that evil stuff on the Brazilians. You know; the sins of the Father and all that."

"I'm not sure that particular missive reached Brazil, Mr. Martin, but rumors do travel at the speed of the gods. Yes, the word was abroad about this papal corruption and, even if our explorers were cut from a finer moral cloth, they likely carried some of this weight, at least unconsciously. Perhaps they were expiating the sins of the Fathers and that became part of their psychological makeup. If so, what are we to make of this?"

"I had read that Spain and Portugal didn't care whether Pope Paul III was sleeping with his daughter or Pope Julian III got off on frescoes of boys having sex," replied Colette. "They just wanted new trade routes, land and slaves. They wanted wealth. It's always about the money."

"So the Jesuit banner was a fig leaf, Ms. McGovern. What happened to the go forth and conquer command?"

"Perhaps we slow down and rethink the narrative, Professor."

"Perhaps we do," Merkel replied, taking a deep breath. "In that spirit, should we still take literally the biblical call for us to go forth and convert all nations? Or have we taken that book too seriously for centuries and should now put it on the back burner? As soon as Constantine declared the Roman Empire Holy and Christian, the good Christians proceeded to destroy the icons and altars dedicated to Zeus, Athena, Hera, Aphrodite and others. They would get around to the Temple of Artemis, replacing that god with the newly enshrined Virgin Mary, hymen intact according to some neighborhood gossip.

"Was this in the master plan or just another afternoon at the beach? Where did these gods go when they were smashed into pieces, poor things? Does Aphrodite not still live? Is Venus dead? What happened to the Brazilian deities, the sea gods and the forest gods which the natives lived by? Were they banished from consciousness? Was Carl Jung on his high horse when he said we should carry the monastery within? How was it that Michelangelo and other devout Christians of the Italian Renaissance honored Christ and also the pagan gods which had been reduced to shards? How does that stance stand up theologically? Can we really have a foot in both or all camps?

45

"What cosmology were they living in? Was it that the Renaissance crowd didn't have the benefit of the Jesuits' prayer and exercise book? Did they believe in magic? Had the Church not yet put down its doctrine in the hard and fast vernacular so that every living soul would know the Truth and the Light? Was that blessed French priest and mathematician, who emptied himself of everything except thoughts for Christ, a prisoner unto himself? Marin Mersenne, right, who lived on boiled pickles and rancid fruit in his Parisian cell, dreaming of uncooked turnips? He spent a lifetime railing against magic, dreams and other beach scenes. But he was also called the father of acoustics, and it was rumored that he actually heard the music of the spheres.

"Did we not learn from the Council of Nicaea in 325 from whence all beauty came? Did not Trent do enough to purify and make uniform the religious spirit, giving out clear and splendid marching orders? What was reflected in the heavens when Constantine held his banner over the battle in the name of Christ? Do we not recognize the Holy Ghost when the spirit hits us in the face?

"What manner of man rescued soul from Christ, gave animals psyche, and personified a grain of salt, a blade of grass and anything else that moved on God's green earth? What manner of man gave images life, meaning and even a feminine spark? What manner of man repudiated a transcendent, ever-rising spirit in favor of a dank un-Christian soul that wanderer through the poetics of the moment, a downward excursion in the vicinity of Hades?

"My God, My God, why have Thou forsaken me?" the professor asked in wilting tones as he fell into his chair, holding his chest as if he were having a heart attack.

Colette heard movement, a rush of orders, and the sounds of an army marching. Professor Merkel was taken away on a stretcher, his hands raised in prayer or surrender. She thought the man was being carried off the battlefield.

Back at home, Colette imagined more Jesuits on the move, a tidal wave of theology in their wake, giving them air and keeping them afloat. The wind was decisively at their backs.

She would continue her journey under cover of night, heavy laden like a Jesuit following latitude lines supplied by royalty. For her voyage Colette would update her charts and infuse a fresh dose of longitude so she would not only know which way was up; she would know breadth, and displacement, and where time began.

Her voyage could take her through epochs and barren churches. She thought about her favorite Catholic writer, Flannery O'Connor, who lived most of her life on a small peacock farm in Milledgeville, Georgia, getting her theology through the eyes of the Southern grotesques who she saw in every church, barnyard, and waiting room. A character in her novel *Wise Blood* said, "The only way to the truth is blasphemy." Colette wondered whether she was taking the easy way, shooting from the hip, nailing poetic laments to the church house door.

Colette recalled O'Connor saying that she could never be a saint but perhaps a martyr if they killed her quick enough.

Colette looked beyond the horizon and could envision neither option. She marveled at O'Connor's ability to stake out hot-button theological issues with a strong dose of humor.

She wondered if O'Connor was spared the unrelenting visitation of dreams.

Chapter Seven

Colette woke a few days after Merkel's Brazil lecture with her father's cowboy voice in her head singing: "Drifting along with the tumbling tumbleweed." She saw this neither as a message from her father nor a sign from God but a reminder that she needed to record the details of a tumbleweed dream in the section of her journal labeled "Tumbleweed." She named her dream, "Prophets Transformed in the Parking Lot." Colette felt almost bloodied by the time she arrived at a final version.

She wrote that the dream began in a parking lot in front of a large Wal-Mart store in Texas. The cars that would be there were instead parked at a nearby drive-through mega-church. The sermon was taken from Yeats's famous poem "The Second Coming" and focused on the beast slouching towards Bethlehem to be born.

The parking lot did not remain empty for long. Men dressed in rags and wearing long beards began to straggle in. On closer inspection, it appeared the men were not wearing rags; rather, they were dressed in layer upon layer of old cloth worn in a manner that resembled folds. On even closer inspection, it was evident that each man was dressed alike, down to the disposition of the folds.

When at least fifty men had arrived, they began to discuss the Book of Job, sedately at first, finding quick agreement about the nature of Job, his essential goodness, and the tests that God had designed for him. Then the crowd became animated, talking much faster, arguing, and using their hands to make a point. As they spoke, the men seemed different. Some lost their beards. Some were now dressed in white gowns; others in black and blue. The mixture of colors became more pronounced by the minute.

The more they argued, the more different they became. They could agree on the goodness of Job and the necessary test from God, but why did He, all-knowing, fall for the devil's trick? What was the lesson here? Was God not yet fully formed and did He need Job to suffer before He could come fully into the light? Was Job's plight the price of God becoming conscious? Colette sensed the shift. The discussion was heated, respectful

48

and seemed to be going somewhere. It seemed that everyone had a point of view and was heard.

Yet as the conversation grew heated, workmen appeared in the parking lot, fashioning a mural for the prophets to enter. The prophets entered this work of art willingly, without dropping a syllable, until they transformed into part of the frieze and became silent, hands frozen in mid-air. To compensate for their loss, the artists-in-residence returned all beards to their original splendor and added greens, blues, and reds to their tunics, all of the colors of the rainbow, transforming them into vestments which felt rich and sacred. The scene resembled the Last Supper.

Once finished, the mural would be on display for centuries. To Colette, it was like the Machine God had finally entered from across the stage, directing the workers to fashion a frieze for the prophets to enter. Did they make a bargain by accepting even richer garments and colors for their silence and willingness to be frozen in time? Had an outside force, a Wal-Mart god or one from the mega-church, interceded in the interest of commerce and conventional piety? Was this dream her preparation for the Council of Trent?

Later that morning, Colette recited a shortened version for her mother.

"Isn't it going back a long time, Colette, dreaming about prophets? You know the priests and bishops have taken that over."

"This has really bothered me. It was like a parable or something."

"You mean like the feeding of the five thousand?"

"Yes, it seemed something like that."

"I don't understand. No one seemed to be holding a knife or a gun."

"Right. I mean scary in a different way. It felt like a message."

"It seemed to make sense. The prophets show up, have a nice conversation about Job, then they become a frieze. Be nice if we could all end up that way."

"You mean on the wall?"

"I mean being remembered."

"Thanks, Mom. You seem to get the hang of this."

"Just old-time religion, my dear."

Colette thought about her trip to the theological beach in Brazil, the long arm of the Jesuits, and Professor Merkel's wild class that ended with him collapsing in a heap in the front of the group. Because he clutched his chest, she thought he had had a heart attack, but smelling salts brought him back to life, if not to his senses.

The professor appeared to go a little astray towards the end of the class, bringing up the Greek gods, the early Christian idol smashers and probably the Furies. She had a hard time following him and would have to check her notes. Unclear as her memory was, there still seemed to be something in the air.

Colette thought it odd that she would travel halfway around the world and then dream about some old Jewish guys having a hot conversation in a Wal-Mart parking lot. For God's sake, she had never even been in a Wal-Mart store, and neither had her mother. She couldn't figure out the connection. Wal-Mart had cheap prices, so should she consider the biblical chatter in the parking lot down-market, as her English friends would say, or should she think of the product as low-priced and cut-rate?

Why the mega-church next door? She had never been to one of these either, although she had seen on television a Manhattan pastor named Dollar—Dollar Bill to his friends—preaching the prosperity gospel. Perhaps the church and the store had something in common. They were in the business of making money with commoditized, commercial messages. After you go to church and pay the pastor, you go to Wal-Mart to save money.

Colette didn't like her own flippant attitude, mainly because she was in unfamiliar territory. She thought that it was probably a good sign that Wal-Mart shoppers were at church because it gave cover, room and license to the prophets who seemed to come out of nowhere. She soon realized that the sermon was for her and not for the congregation at the mega-church.

Why the reference to the Yeats' poem about the beasts slouching towards Bethlehem to be born? If she remembered correctly, these were probably signs of the anti-Christ the poet saw after World War I, signs of horror and furor. Yeats saw this time as the beginning of the post-Christian period. God was dead, and the beasts were slouching towards Bethlehem to be born and to assume their proper place in the pantheon. Colette wondered if the dream had anything to do with the gnawing of the beast in her own belly.

She was conditioned to think about Armageddon because that sword had been over her head since she started Catholic school. Apparently Yeats had gotten the same message. Colette read the poet's words: "But now I know that twenty centuries of stony sleep were vexed to nightmare by a rocking cradle. And what rough beast, its hour come round at last, slouches towards Bethlehem to be born."

Listen to that, she thought. The words are almost one hundred years old, and they burn as much as they did in 1919. What if she brought the prophets into this circle of hell where mere anarchy was loosed upon the world? If they could handle the complexity of Job's plight, they probably wouldn't be tested too much by slouching beasts and the promise that some revelation was at hand. Wasn't the Bible full of this stuff, and didn't these guys get off on revelations? That was their bread and butter. They surely wouldn't worry about a few beasts slouching towards Bethlehem; they had likely met them somewhere earlier on some biblical byway populated by a requisite number of grotesques.

From what she remembered from the Bible, these guys were a little too polite for prophets. I mean, she said to herself, I didn't hear them talking to God and agreeing to sacrifice a son on God's whim. They just showed up in a parking lot. This was not exactly the same as descending from clouds or coming out of a whirlwind. Old Testament prophets always seemed to be threatening someone. The Wal-Mart guys just huddle, agree and leave.

Colette seemed to get inside her own conversation, imagining she was speaking in tongues while understanding the idiocy of the thought. She was suspicious of the capital "I" and was not happy to hear herself talking. She still wondered about Job and, particularly, why Job? And what about Yeats' rocking cradle? She felt that gnawing again.

She was grateful for the prophet dream but would have been more appreciative if it had a Brazilian flavor or a beach scene or two.

So the prophets show up, light up the room, then step out and become statuary, which to her looked like a scene from the Last Supper. It was beginning to seem like a game. Maybe they were hungry, bored, or tired. Perhaps they had heard enough; exegesis was coming out of their ears. Could it be that they had stumbled onto the truth outside of her hearing or in a place and time where her imagination failed her?

Why was all this childish religious verse taking over her mind this way? She wanted hardcore theology. She didn't mind Merkel's fun and games because at least he got somewhere. She wanted sturdy and resolute. Perhaps the dream was a caution, reminding her not to get too fanciful with theology as, at the end of the day, it was not an infinitely open argument. Brazil and the Jesuits lingered, but Trent was still there, almost untouched for five hundred years, watching over marriages and baptisms like a distant god.

Some mystery had slipped through her fingers and mind that night and ended up in some frame on some country house wall, implying in one breath the crucifixion, death and Resurrection of Christ. Why were the prophets so eager to be enshrined? Was Job's growing consciousness really a threat to God? Was hers? Or was this another round of inflation? At times, she thought she was losing her mind. It was time to see her psychologist again. Colette explained her concerns to O'Connell over the phone and scheduled a meeting for the next day.

"You don't sound like you are losing your mind, Ms. McGovern."

"That's what it has felt like, Mr. O'Connell."

51

"Can you describe the feeling?"

"I used to be able to keep religion at a distance and check in for baptisms, marriages and the occasional funeral. I was very happy. But what with this Trent project, I don't seem to get a minute's rest. I find it quite overwhelming. My dreams seem to be preparing me for the Council of Trent."

"Did you make that trip to Venice and Trent?"

"No, I went to Brazil."

"I didn't know Brazil was on the schedule."

"Just in my imagination. Professor Merkel spoke about the Jesuits in Brazil."

"Ah. I was sorry to learn about his fainting."

"I haven't seen him for a few days. Is he okay?"

"Yes, I think so. He's taking a couple weeks off. Any reaction to Brazil?"

"Professor Merkel was great. We had a lively discussion about the Jesuits projecting what was unresolved onto the Indians."

"How do you feel about that?"

"I understand the history and context. It seemed like an old story; the dark side of Christianity."

"That bothered you?"

"Not just that. It's all the images; the tumbleweed of images."

"Tumbleweed?"

"I use that term in my dream journal. It suggests a lot of dreams, too many at times."

"Are they similar to your dream about Pope John Paul?"

"Yes, I guess so. It's the religious thing in general. The dreams seem like a tutorial. They seem to be opening me up."

"To what?"

"I wish I knew. Perhaps it's the Trent project and all the dead stuff I'll have to dig up. That's why I need help."

"Understood. Now you sent me a summary of your dream about prophets in the parking lot. It seemed a very organized, revelatory dream. How did you feel about it?"

"Actually, I was a little annoyed. I had just come off this intense session about Brazil, and that night I get prophets in the parking lot. I figured it was payback for enjoying those beach scenes so much."

"I'm not sure dreams work that way, and you probably shouldn't be so hard on yourself. Not all dreams are immediately explicable."

"That's what bothered me. This dream seems so straightforward. Fifty or so prophets show up in an empty Wal-Mart parking lot, bearded and scruffy. As they discuss Job, they become more differentiated. When

52

finished, they step into a frieze with the feel of the Last Supper. They go home and I'm stuck with the story."

"Yes, it does seem straightforward. Have you been reading or studying Job?"

"Two years ago I had a class about the Book of Job."

"Are people around you talking about Job?"

"My mother occasionally refers to Job's patience."

"Right, that is how most people remember him. Let's ignore what it means for a moment and focus on why this dream bothers you."

"I guess I didn't want the dream, and it doesn't mean anything to me other than that these prophets have the answer, and I don't. I feel stuck in the middle of a religious puzzle that demands answers."

"Was that it? You had the dream, and they take away the prize?"

"Well, I hadn't thought about it that way. I was a little uncomfortable. I get enough of this from my mostly male lecturers during the day; at night, I expect a little compensation for that. It wouldn't hurt for a few angels to show up."

"Do you really mean that?"

"I'm not sure. Perhaps I should just ignore the dream."

"People do that all the time and are no worse for wear."

"Then why should I bother?"

"You know, Plato and the unexamined life. And some have told us there is a certain divinity in dreams. And Jung said we learn a lot when we dream. I'm still curious about your reference to men. Did the prophets seem foreign or strange to you?"

"You could say that. I just didn't like them. I know that's an odd thing to say about people in a dream. And the dream seemed like a performance, as if the prophets were on the stage. There was certainly something theatrical in their costumes, movements and step into eternity. In some respects the drama seemed more important than the theology."

"It's an honest reaction. You don't have to like dream figures; sometimes they can be monsters or trigger something in you. Any triggers?"

"You mean my father?" She wondered what he would think about her abortion. "I don't think so. We were open and really got along."

"Any of your instructors?"

"I don't think so."

"Boyfriend?"

"You mean that hot soccer player?"

"Soccer?"

"Catholic schools can't afford football."

"Got it. Now has our boyfriend retreated to the showers?"

Colette diverted the line of questioning with some boyfriend jokes, thanked O'Connell for the helpful session and went home to bed. She thought about the prophets raising their voices, making a fuss, then settling into a frieze for eternity. In her revelry, she wondered if this represented the real story of theology. Make a fuss, put on those pretty clothes of differentiation then demur and get in line. Was the dream preparing her for the religious theater called the Council of Trent? And was she alone in the theater of her dreams watching old men change in and out of costumes while they walked the theological walk? Was there room for a woman in this pantomime? Was there room for her?

Colette fell asleep, thinking of rain, showers, and being under water. A dream came to her like an old anthem. It was raining and she felt the wetness over her swollen, pregnant body, sure that what she was receiving was an anointing. However, the suction that pulled her heart and soul through ducts, tubes and membrane layers reminded her less of God than of a construction scene where she was being hung, drawn and quartered. Colette felt she had lost something holy.

In the dream Colette was, in her mother's words, all sixes and sevens, a notation from somewhere, some cereal box or awful quiz show, which filled her head with what felt like cabbages and nonsense.

In the dream Colette saw Alfie and heard him sing sweet words like sugar and treacle, but she turned away, vomiting into a kidney-shaped dish held by a hand that didn't seem connected to a body. She wondered if it had anything to do with the booming organ market in Brazil because now Colette felt empty and lighter than air.

In her dream Colette heard a congregation of men on the other side of the hospital curtain. She heard her father, Father Stravinsky, the soccer player, and a number of prophets, speaking in tongues, mashing up a low Latin with high Bronx, sounding like nails on a blackboard. She longed for the soothing sounds of Alfie who betrayed her, but there was no time because the chorus of fathers got louder and more religious as gods were called into the conversation, and she heard more than one voice belting out Jesus, Mary and Joseph the way her father did, while others dragged in Zeus, Hercules, and Most High Athena or found their way into the zodiac and settled down on Capricorn as if it was the center of the universe, pushing onward and outward as if on a dare, boasting about Leo, Taurus, Pisces and Sagittarius and their angry and abiding role at the center of the heavens.

Colette sighed, heard the names and thought she had known these gods and knew that the gods had known her because she was here for the love of god, bleeding under the sign of Virgo, pushing away the martial advances and the petty incantations from the man without his head. She was wishing and praying and hoping for her father, her real father, to return, but all she heard was Latin from Father Stravinsky, drowning out human voices and the other fathers, beyond the prophets and outside of time, receiving at the speed of light the endless litanies from endless lips begging not to be led into temptation while she whispered, this is my body, given up for the remission of sins for those sons who do not have ears to hear and eyes to see. Thus she prayed and thus she bled, while patiently waiting for women to enter the pantheon and come out from that place behind the black curtain.

Chapter Eight

Colette didn't know which end was up, not because she was looking
through the looking glass, though that view might be an accurate
description of her life, high heels and all, but because she awoke with
Yeats on her brain, her mother in her heart and a hole in her belly. She
recalled her father saying little to his wife, as he did not really remonstrate
in the words of some Hallmark card, but touched her on the sleeve and
looked her in the eye as if he meant it. He was Irish, and God often
controlled his Jesus, Mary, Joseph tongue, but his wife ruled his heart,
even when she grew round and shorter and that old apron with hints of
lemon, tarragon and noticeably thyme suggested she came from another
place and time; and her ankles swelled, and she had to wear those large,
wide-strapped black shoes to make her way to church and the store. He
did not flinch when she wore the long, black dresses that almost touched
the floor, suggesting every day's a funeral and the darkness resided within.

Colette worried that her looking glass was leading her away from high
heels into that dreaded, dead-end, tin-tack alley the academics at her St.
Anselm's in the Bronx called Thematic Something or Other, meaning
theology, semantics, or some big idea found in some high-brow research
journal no one read or cared about. Was she becoming a Fellow and one
of them? She laughed, and then she resisted.

Along with thoughts of her father and mother came the poet Yeats, who
might have been the only Irish poet who understood women, especially
older women, though she would be forgiven if she found at times in his
lyrical thump signs of an unrepentant priest.

Colette could almost hear her father recite to his wife the poem, "When
You Are Old." She could imagine him speaking to his wife in the
language of Yeats: "But one man loved the pilgrim soul in you, and loved
the sorrows of your changing face." Colette thought this was one of the
most beautiful lines she had ever read and kept the poet by her bed and at
the worry end of the looking glass. "How many loved your moments of

sad grace," she asked herself. Colette was holding on to her poetry for dear life.

Colette felt Yeats's beautiful, lyrical language falling by the wayside as she walked toward Professor Gleason's office where she would provide an update on her Trent project.

"Morning, Professor Gleason."

"Ms. McGovern. We are here to discuss the Trent project?"

"Yes, Sir,"

"Have you made any progress?"

He wore a gold band on his right ring finger. She wondered whether this signified his marriage to God or some earthly creature. Her mother's hands showed more wear.

"Mainly background; thinking about approaches. Professor Merkel gave an interesting lecture on the Jesuits in Brazil."

"Ah, Professor Merkel. He understands the literature. Was once an English teacher, you know."

"We had a lively class. He got me thinking about trying to understand Trent first through other stories and lenses before honing in on the actual event."

"You mean secondary sources? Interesting idea, but we must be careful we don't miss the forest for the trees."

She gave him a quizzical look.

"Let me explain. At the end of the day, Trent was about doctrine, right? And this doctrine has served us for centuries. It's all well and good to cite secondary sources for elaboration and to advance our understanding of Trent."

"But haven't we learned a lot since 1563? Professor Merkel mentioned the hundreds of letters that have only recently been translated. These were written at the time of Trent by Portuguese Jesuits in Brazil. Don't they provide new insights about how the Church expanded?"

"Certainly Ms. McGovern. I'm sure these letters enlarge the landscape but won't substantially change our theological thrust. You do know that Professor Merkel wrote novels? Not that there's anything wrong with that."

Colette hated herself for hearing something sexual in his thrust and told herself that he was no Alfie, and she hated herself all over again.

"How will we know this without looking?"

"Ah, Ms. McGovern, the Holy Father and the Vatican have every conceivable document under the sun; the collection likely includes the love letters from Brazil. Nothing really changes in the Catholic Church, just the tone. Isn't that what we hear in Pope Francis's voice? Hate the sin but love the sinner."

"I don't think they were love letters, sir. They seem to be about daily life and all that."

"Just a small Jesuit joke, Ms. McGovern; a little relief from the doctrine that rules our lives. One needs a sense of humor."

Colette didn't know if she was the "one," or Loyola, or the writer of love notes or the man married to the Church.

"Good luck," he said, while looking down at his shoe tassels, which seemed to move with his eyes. "We'll need an approved Master's thesis in about three months or so for a June graduation. I'd get right to the heart of the matter. Remember, the Trent teachings were declared Church doctrine, and any dissent was considered anathema and the person subject to excommunication. Of course, we've backed away from some of the harshness; tone and all that. But even I am surprised at the permanence of Trent. Maybe the Catholic Counter Revolution was actually successful."

"Another Jesuit joke, sir?"

His back was turned, and he was already out of the room.

She needed to clear her head.

Colette retreated to the library and thought about the Catholic novelist Graham Greene, who was a safe harbor whenever she got too deep into theology. She flipped through Greene's *The Heart of the Matter*, but it felt like a foreign country. The book was set in West Africa during World War II and showed the protagonist Scobie dealing with a cold wife, wharf rats, adultery and a rigid Catholic theology which entered the room when he received communion without confession, a mortal sin. He then committed suicide. The local priest had the last word about what goes on in someone's heart and the extent of God's mercy.

She was more comfortable inside Greene's *The End of the Affair*, about tangled love affairs during the London blitz and promises to God to behave if the love object was spared. He was, and good things began to happen, including miracles that seemed to occur right on the heels of the Machine God entering the room.

Colette considered herself a twenty-first century woman and did not want to be moved around on stage like piece of furniture which had no heft, design or purpose. She immediately regretted linking herself to furniture and considered it the doormat of a previous generation. So Colette, armed with a smarter, more modern theology, considered *The Heart of the Matter* too doctrinal, narrowly sexual, and somewhat chauvinistic, as it depicted a cold, sad, very Catholic British woman who forced her husband to have an affair. He popped too many pills because he had run out of rope, made worse because he took communion in the state of mortal sin. Only the deep documents of the Vatican would tell if this man remained outside of God's mercy.

In *The End of the Affair* at least the bombs were falling to keep things interesting; affairs were more exciting when the air raid warning sounded and the next door neighbor got whacked. Colette thought you can bring God into this equation, but when pressed, the Italians might suggest "Fortuna" as an equally resolute player. Greene reminded Colette that there was not a half-hog in this dance. It's either whole hog or you go home. She had picked up this phrase somewhere in the Bronx or in the Meat Packing District when spleen was something you put on a salad and not something you shared on social media. Colette feared her language was going south and becoming gentrified. She wondered how Greene would tell her mortal tale.

Her discourse on meat sent Colette to the school cafeteria for a salad with absolutely no spleen in sight. Ms. Aimes came up to her.

"Hi. I'm Colette McGovern. We're in Merkel's class."

"Oh, hello. Poor guy. I guess the class took everything out of him. I'm Rebecca Aimes. Pleased to meet you."

"Me too. I really appreciated your remarks in class. Very helpful for my senior project."

"Thank you. Are you researching one of the councils?"

"Yes, Trent. You?"

"That one seemed like a monster that I couldn't get my head around. I went with the First Vatican Council in the nineteenth century. So far it reads like one long catechism with the pope afraid of modernism, feminism and what's left of those pesky Protestants."

"I sort of regret not focusing on something more modern; you know, one that might impact contemporary issues. Trent is a bit of a mountain."

"Too late to change?"

"Yes, I think so. I just won't be able to do a frontal assault. I'll sneak up on it, looking for any feminine crumbs left on the side streets. Hope there's enough for a meal."

"That's what I say every time I get a meal here. The helpings get smaller every day."

"You're talking about the food, right?"

Rebecca laughed. "Yeah, but I just as well could be talking about the men and the instructors."

"The testosterone?"

"Sometimes it smells more like body odor."

"That bad, huh?"

"Yeah, when was the last time you dated a priest?"

"Not in recent memory."

"You're kidding, right?"

"That's my fallback position."

"I've taken a break from falling back."

"I know what you mean. From here?"

"Boston College."

"Good to keep them at a safe distance."

Colette knew that no distance was safe and that the Charles River and the heather bank might as well be in her back yard under the watchful eye of her mother. Alfie was a lout and no Cockney accent would save him from his fate. She really wanted to save the babies tossed in those Irish wells.

"Have you seen the movie 'Alfie'?"

"The old one or the remake?"

"The Michael Caine version from 1966."

"Don't think so, but I have seen the 2004 version with Jude Law. All I can remember is that he couldn't get an erection for at least half the film. He lived in Manhattan, so no one cared if he was gay. But that's what I came to see; I mean the erection. You a film buff?"

"Not really, though I'm studying this one for the film course."

"Probably beats Trent."

"I think so. I've been focusing on the Alfie guy in the film because he seemed like so many guys I know."

"Assholes, you mean?"

"Yeah, but with a cute British accent."

"Yeah, I fall for that kind every time."

Lunch was over and the women went their separate ways. Colette walked the college grounds and daydreamed.

She wondered about the new words that claimed their place in her life, like fall, feminine, theology and now Trent, which felt like a place where iron ore was extracted and mined from deep holes in a remote land. She heard harshness in the "T" sound that required tightening the jaw and putting the teeth together as if you were ready to do battle. The "r" helped a person come down off the battle ledge and required a very slight pause, perhaps a breathless rill before entering the vowel and the finality of the "nt." For the moment she would return the "o" to the word, making it fully Italian and therefore less dangerous.

The word "fall" was also coming into her life with increased urgency and when capitalized took on an additional threat. She well knew a fall within the vernacular, the skinned knee, the blood, the mother's curse and prayers. Her first really dangerous fall into the heather along the Charles River had wounded and sucked the life out her. She was beginning to understand the theology of sex. Colette would carry her wound forward, in her heart and in her mind.

60

Fed by a rough reading list, she might take the long, circuitous way to Trent, with layovers in Florence and Venice, to lessen the acidity already forming in her throat. She could visit Titian in the flesh and a get a blessed lift from his "Assumption of the Virgin."

She would look for women of the day who had seen all this in the flesh and might help her on her journey. She would load up her backpack with Bronx sayings and vulgarities to keep the evil spirits away. But sooner or later she would have to dip her toe into fifteen centuries of dogmatic theology and revisit prime movers like Original Sin, reimagining the first fall in Eden and all the falls that seemed to haunt the bachelor theologians of the Church.

There were falls and there were falls. Over the years she had heard a lot about "fortunate falls," mainly from tenured professors, bored priests, or would-be doctoral students about Adam's fall being fortunate in that he and the rest of mankind fell into knowledge and consciousness. She recalled from a recent class a Joe Blow going on about how man's coming into consciousness helped make God complete. Jehovah certainly seemed to be a bastard at times and went after Job with a passion. Mr. Blow suggested Jehovah must have been out of his mind; even a schizophrenic. The instructor was trying to be metaphorical, suggesting Jehovah was one-dimensional, seeing things literally and acting like a spoiled child, covering poor Job with boils. This was getting into dangerous territory and humor might save someone with a name like Blow. Colette couldn't quite figure out how her prophet's dream fit into a Joe Blow's theological landscape. The instructor had tenure and could say and dream whatever he liked. She had no such protection.

Colette had joked with her mother that she didn't go to bed to sleep; she went there to dream. Her mother waved her off but Colette was serious. Since she started the Trent project the dreams seemed to come nightly. More often than not, they seemed to be about theological issues, some of which she had never really thought about before. On many nights she dreamed she was inside a church. She had a nagging sense some failure or transgression was keeping her from participating in rituals.

As if on cue, Colette dreamed she was back in some cul-de-sac, familiar but with different markings, as if a new animal had been on the premises. The place was not soft, comfortable or feminine; rather, it felt like a cold ante-room to a church, and she would announce herself by scratching on the door, praying for admission. She was on her haunches, ready to pounce or submit; she wasn't sure. She didn't even know the secret code.

On waking, Colette realized that she was looking for a way out of this ante-room, Trent and her life. She recalled Polonius's quote in *Hamlet*:

"By indirections find directions out." She had no idea what Polonius was up to and why this phrase came to mind other than to remind her that perhaps she should have zigged when she had fatefully zagged.

She was glad Professor Merkel was also a novelist, and she still wondered why her thesis advisor disparaged him, sounding like one of those boring Greeks who put poets at the bottom of the food chain. Perhaps Merkel should have been at Trent in 1563; the outcome might have been different, more metaphorical and easier to wrap your head around. She laughed but still feared that Jehovah might be lurking there in the shadows, taking notes and taking names.

Rilke was there on the end of her tongue using his tongue to talk about transformation. Stop this transcendent stuff; go deep, go down, transform yourself. No picking yourself up by the bootstraps here. No Light Brigade fantasies in order. Watch that blossom on the cherry tree unfold and get inside the bloom. God is everywhere. You are smaller than you think. Easy for him, she thought.

Now she was daydreaming in the college library, vaguely recalling Carl Jung's writings on transformation which were out there somewhere in Polonius's shadow. She found Jung's *Symbols of Transformation*, last checked out of the library twenty years earlier. She hoped the digital edition lived. At five hundred pages that's a lot of transformation, she thought and wondered if she had enough time.

She also wondered if she had enough heart, stopping on page 31, as it had been marked with a sliver of tissue paper. Colette felt marginalized and out of sorts, so she took the easy way, focusing on the footnote which was underlined. Jung was speaking in six-point type about the Christ Myth:

> The documents that give us our information about the origins of Christianity are of such nature that in the present state of historical science no student would venture to use them for the purpose of compiling a biography of the historical Jesus.
> To look behind these evangelical narratives for the life of a natural historical human being would not occur to any thoughtful men today if it were not for the influence of the earliest rationalistic theologians.
> Thus the lives and deeds of the culture-heroes and founders of religions are the purest compensations of typical mythological motifs, behind which individual figures entirely disappear.

Was Mr. Joe Blow right about Jehovah? Did Jung find little room in his psychology for the literal Christ of Christmas and Easter? Would this play in Trent? Wasn't Merkel struck down after he boasted about bringing back the pagan gods as emblems of character, promising they would then live forever? Did he really say that the whole mythology thing was psychology projected into the heavens? Did he say that the Greeks, Egyptians and Babylonians had provided the model for the Trinity? Was the Vatican aware of this? What would Jesus say about this man who was probably writing a novel? What would Jesus say about her?

Exhausted from a day when she seemed to be besieged by memories of her parents, her punishing secret, dangerous words, tempting transformations and the growing burden of Trent, Colette fell asleep that night with an abundance of theology in her head.

She dreamed she was back in another ante-room, a dreamscape, watching a scene that might be in a Vatican garden or a more modest space. Francis and another man were with two nuns who appeared to be guides or interlocutors. All stood outside a building, waiting to enter. There was humor in the air, and Colette felt she could be seeing a "Who's On First?" routine. It somehow became clear that the two men were about to enter a monastery to learn who would be the next pope. The men pointed to each other and asked the nuns, but they seem uninterested. Once inside, the men were supposed to receive a sign regarding who will be the anointed one.

As soon as he entered, the unnamed man felt a change come over him, a sign. He felt pumped up, inflated, full of himself. He imagined he had been hit with a thunderbolt which moved him sideways. The man believed he was the anointed one. Power already radiated from him.

Then this inflated man traveled underground with Francis and watched him in silence as he administered to the poor and to people who looked like gargoyles. The pretender then announced through his tears and anguish to everyone that his companion was the true pope, but no one would listen.

An authority figure searched for the pope's name but couldn't find it. His companion wept some more and begged the official to look deeper. Finally, on the last page of the book, the official found the name of Pope Francis in small letters. The other man dropped to his knees, kissed the pope's ring, and, still underground, experienced the fullness of the holy man.

The nuns clapped in unison, but this small sound was drowned out by the movement of heavy, embroidered vestments and brocade shoes worn by the Princes of the Church who stepped high over chapel stones on their way to a coronation.

On waking, Colette felt overwhelmed by the humility and gentleness the Pope Francis figure displayed in the dream. Colette prayed that this dream would serve as her way into the Council of Trent where she would find the true spirit of the Church, understated, precious and forgiving.

She remembered Rilke's advice about life being an endless series of transformations. Colette wondered whether she had the courage to change.

Chapter Nine

Colette remained a hostage to her tumbleweed dreams which threatened to take over her life. She felt like a prisoner insider her head. She tried to imagine the dark, underground corridors at the Council of Trent where souls rested and deals were made. Colette thought again about her recent dream of Pope Francis, below ground and administering to the grotesques. Why was she dreaming these stories that seemed like parables? Were the dreams compensation for the Council of Trent, at least her idea of that council which had come from old books and an old theology which Professor Gleason cited when they met? Were her dreams just shards, broken off bits of herself, her moods, demons and failures? Or were her dreams also her prayers; unsaid, imagined and wistful, trying to find the light of day and perhaps the ear of God? Were her dreams her penance for that mortal sin? Colette felt that whatever they were, her dreams had her by the scruff of the neck. They were leading her.

That night a dream returned her to a church.

A priest invited Colette up to the front of a dream church largely empty of congregation. He signaled that she should sit with loved ones, but she did not know the three people there. The priest said her presence was requested so she could be honored for her work and dedication, but no words were spoken. The priest disappeared, and the altar was empty. She heard shuffling sounds at the back of the church, indicating the remaining parishioners were leaving. She noticed the statues of the saints and the Holy Family were covered as during the final days of Lent, but these statues were covered from head to toe in black and they wore blindfolds. There was no movement, sound or distraction in the church. The doors of the church seemed to slam shut hours earlier.

In the dream Colette sat in the first pew looking up at the altar, which was also covered in black, and she felt a profound sense of loneliness and loss. The carpeting leading up to the altar was covered in a black shroud. The lectern where the priest delivered the gospel and the good news was covered in a dark tent. The color seemed to have left the stained glass windows. They were just there, leaden and opaque with no hint of salvation or redemption. All the icons of her youth had been stripped away. No hints, no memories, no incense smells that could bring her back to life.

She looked up at the soaring church alcove and at the long oak beam which supported the roof and imagined songs and hymns following this trajectory, soaring like the spirit, looking for openings but falling on deaf ears and on a spent, barren land. She knew that there was a geometrical relationship between the height and width of the church, so on paper everything was in place. This empty church where the spirit would soar was architecturally pure. It would last another thousand years.

Still, she was in the first pew contemplating emptiness, scholastic spirits rising, and a darkening beauty. She felt an almost incomprehensible loss of soul, which was more than icons, vespers and layers of precious incense. She thought of the "Assumption of Mary" and how the artist was able to marry heaven and earth in love and revelry. In this dark place she found neither religion, nor love, nor meaning.

On waking, Colette didn't know whether she had suffered a dream, a vision or a nightmare. She sensed a loneliness and despair she had never felt before. Her dreams kept returning her to churches and religious scenes, as if they were teaching her a lesson. Her dream church seemed a place of profound despair. She wondered whether the dream was a warning as she got deeper into her Trent project. She tried to focus on her counselor's advice to see dreams as compensation representing her dark, shadow parts. Was it for her thesis, her sex or her sin? Her dreams seemed to come from a much deeper place. Colette increasingly felt her dreams were writing her.

She recalled her counselor suggesting that the religious images and themes in her dreams might be because "she was poking around a religion she had known since infancy but now she examined doctrine as a student with a critical feminine eye." Although O'Connell's remarks didn't take the sting out of her dreams or remove what seemed like a dangerous overhang, she nonetheless thought there was some truth in his remark. Colette vowed to hang onto those words for dear life and not let her night dreams rule her day.

She thought of Professor Merkel's seductive rant about the beaches of Brazil and laughed. She wanted to get out of her skin and her nightmares and follow the lines of latitude and longitude to discover new worlds. She heard her mother's voice: "Nice and easy does it every time."

Colette examined a map of Italy which was shaped like a perfect knee-high, winter boot for the fashionable woman. She was not sure why the old tale about the Italian boot had risen to such prominence in her mind.

Nor could she explain her fascination with Sicily being perched on the tip of the Italian toe. She tried to recall Loyola's Spiritual Exercises but could only remember the updated checklist for the modern woman. Colette wondered whether the desire to hang onto her Coach bag was another act of defiance.

Focus, she told herself. Enough of the silliness. She looked at the map of Italy again, focusing on the lines of latitude and longitude that might hold her gaze and keep her from going astray. Colette concentrated on 12 degrees east longitude, the imaginary line that seemed to almost cut through the heart of Trent far to the north and run down through heart of Vatican City, three-hundred miles to the south. She thought of the phrase her mother used a lot: "As the crow flies" and wondered whether the Council of Trent had its messenger crows that carried sacred gossip from the council to Vatican ears.

Colette studied the map of Italy and imagined the gentle breezes blowing in off the Tyrrhenian Sea warming the hearts in Rome. She looked north and envisioned a very cold Trent which appeared within walking distance of Austria. It seemed distant and forbidding, too far north for its own comfort. She could almost feel the stiff winds blowing down from the Dolomites and touching tongues at the Council of Trent, limiting words and freezing doctrine in place. Colette laughed at her thoughts.

While in her college library looking at a large wall map, a flat projection of the world on vinyl, Colette traced the latitude and longitude lines which would have taken the Jesuits the six-thousand miles from Europe to the beaches in Brazil. She recalled Professor Merkel's remarks about Indian breasts and genitals awash in the beach foam. She wondered whether such delicious postcard imaginings were a way to slow down her Trent project. She had told her counselor a week ago that she increasingly felt empty on the inside. He listened and suggested the Trent project might nourish her. Colette wasn't sure. The empty, lonely church of her recent dream was never far away.

Colette recalled her professors talking about Trent. Gleason appeared to see the council as a *fait accompli* with its bundle of infallible doctrines under lock and key at the Vatican. Merkel seemed more circumspect, spending far too much on Brazilian beaches under an unrelenting sun. She recalled Merkel fainting after referring to Trent and the old gods that were smashed to pieces by marauding Christians. Was that the price Merkel paid for imaging a polytheistic universe?

She would get to Trent but not right now. In her musings Colette had conjured up a Trent that seemed cold, hard to pronounce and a burden. She thought of her "Prophets in the Parking Lot" dream in which there was talk, disagreement and then a willful step into eternity. The rigid aesthetic and theology won the day. Was this the Trent story in miniature?

Colette saw Venice on the map of Italy, approximately one hundred and forty miles from Trent. Days earlier she had started reading *The Golden Book of Venice* by Mrs. Lawrence Turnbull. It was a historical novel about Venice published in 1900. Set in the late 1500s in Venice, the Council of Trent seemed to hang over this prosperous city state like an existential treat with a warning about doctrine and power. She knew the feeling.

Colette didn't know whether her vague views of Venice were informed by her professors' remarks, the Turnbull book or the flurry of late-winter ads on her Bronx television encouraging the Italian population of this New York borough to return to Italy before they died. The commercial was supposed to be a joke delivered by a jolly Italian grandfather who said "don't wait to be at death's door to come home." The Italian translation scrolled along the bottom of the television set: "Essere in punto di morte." Colette didn't find it funny but was fairly certain her Bronx neighbors would choose Venice over Trent in a heartbeat. That was where she would make her soft landing.

Venice called like a lover, she imagined, and she laughed at her own audacity. She had had enough trouble along the Charles River; the Venice canals should scare her to death. Colette studied her geography and realized that Venice was actually underwater and the situation got worse with every cruise ship which hovered on the horizon like an invading army. In her mind, this army was dressed in Bermuda shorts and polka dot shirts, cameras at the ready. She realized that coming in from the Adriatic would be too direct, taking her to St. Mark's Square in a flash to worship gargoyles and experience the long, slow lines of worshippers leaving the main cathedral.

She would come in from the north and east more or less, avoiding Trent, preferably under the cover of darkness. She might linger at the Venice city walls and try to decipher what sixteenth century astrologers saw in the evening sky. Not much, she figured, as Galileo was cloistered in Florence to the south, moving quietly between cities so the Vatican and its cadre of spies wouldn't put in Pope Paul V's ears suggestions of heresy, anathema, and excommunication. If there was a whisper campaign, Colette thought, it really had staying power because even in the twenty-first century the Vatican still talked about avoiding another Galileo problem. This time it was about a woman's body.

Colette was becoming a little uncertain of her geography and scheduled a session with Professor Gleason, explaining her decision to examine Trent through a Venetian lens.

"As you wish, Ms. McGovern, but remember the clock is ticking on your thesis. But you will find Venice interesting, full of wonder and remorse and with canals thick with the enemies of Rome plotting to bring down the Church. Be careful, however, because there is danger among the canals and on any given Sunday you can wake to the invading Ottoman Turks who haunted Venice for a century."

Colette was surprised by Gleason's remarks and said nothing. It sounded like a rant. She leaned back in her chair and watched her professor building structures with his hands and words as if he were handling clay. There he goes, she thought, holding up houses and institutions in the watery, shifting maze of canal-plagued Venice. Now Trent, the sturdy word again, fighting its Italian hope and modern promise, reaching back into mystery and time, imagining an edifice which was more than the catechism's simple line of Peter, the Rock, and foundation laws. Now antiquity talking, with Aristotle's take on light, heat and sperm, plus every scholastic comma and exquisite parsing, plus the dint of daily exhortations and prayers, plus the sacraments divine, plus the Jesuit's geometric godhead.

She wasn't sure where Gleason's remarks ended and her own revelry took over, heaping on bits and pieces of ancient texts which haunted her. Was Merkel somehow present? When she opened her eyes, Gleason was gone and she was alone in the classroom. She half expected the Ottoman Turks to show up. Colette hoped she hadn't fallen asleep during her professor's remarks.

"Get to the heart of the matter," Gleason had said on more than one occasion but still her mind wandered as she sat half-asleep in the classroom chair. Colette tried to forget Gleason's warning and thought about Anthony Trollope, the nineteenth century English author, who roamed around Venice and the world. She had read his work as an undergraduate and remembered him asking rhetorically how the Church-- an edifice on top of edifices-- could still be standing centuries later given the stench of burnt flesh of the damned that drifted over this watery city on a west wind from other city states guided by the ecclesiastical banner of righteousness. His question was asked late in the nineteenth century. Colette thought the same question could be asked in the twenty-first century.

Colette got to the heart of the matter and imagined she was back in Venice and St. Mark's Square, holding *The Golden Book of Venice* close to her heart with all the reverence she could muster. Colette decided that this novel would be her touchstone and guide, a way to help her better understand the Council of Trent, which was a dark shadow over Venice in the novel.

In *The Golden Book of Venice* the Vatican was an even greater threat. But the novel read like a romance and was soft at the edges but still another lens through which she could view the council.

Colette saw herself in Venice, waiting for the old gods to show themselves and compete for her loyalty. She recalled fourth century Christians, emboldened by Constantine, cutting off Apollo at the knees, Athena at the neck, and Venus at her rough-hewn crotch as if these gods just walked out of the Coliseum where the recently converted throngs gave all of them the thumbs down. Colette yearned for a repeat of the dream about John Paul sinking into the feminine earth with his lace tapestry and his body falling into a circle of peace. The dream Colette actually experienced felt more like her life talking back to her in the present tense. Nonetheless, she felt a genuine healing.

In the dream she was talking to a female doctor. The doctor said she had read some of the Colette's writings about the feminine, theology, and the absence of women at the Council of Trent. The doctor said, hesitatingly, that the coverage was biting and severe. The woman turned to Colette and showed a pained face. Colette thanked the doctor and said she laughed outrageously while preparing her remarks, as if the whole thing was a lark, a backyard chat session in the Bronx with a neighbor who was hard of hearing. She then burst into tears, crying uncontrollably, saying her remarks were not true, and she feared retribution. The doctor softened, smiled and approached Colette, placing her right hand over her patient's left breast, over the heart. The hand stayed in place for the longest time, as if the doctor was conducting a healing.

When she awoke, Colette remembered the dream and wept again because the dream seemed to capture her dilemma and her fate. In a way she felt the dream constituted a warning for her not to become too comfortable in her quest, relying on bombast and tricks with language and the mind. The way to truth was through the heart.

Days later, Colette returned to reading *The Golden Book of Venice* and was glad to see a fantasy Madonna rise from a black, flat-bottomed gondola with an iron prow and markings that captured every important island, inlet, and bridge in and around Venice. Of 10,000 gondolas in Venice, the beautiful one rose from the one boat that occupied Colette's imagination, parked, secured and immortalized right under her nose. The two oarsmen who lifted the beauty onto the quay as delicately as if they were delivering art fell back into the fog, silent and unnoticed. This was prelude; a time before rigid dogma set in. This was time, deliciously slow.

Then the language in *The Golden Book of Venice* caught up with Colette like a low Victorian drizzle in a Venetian vision, reflecting on a time past when there were only radiant skies, no ruin or decay, no conquering hands of man; only a splendid city of dreams. She was invited in by the author not as a critic but as a lover to witness in 1565 the changing culture of this serene republic, home to Titian.

The Council of Trent was still in the air, and philosophy was the mode in Venice for the serious as well as for men of fashion. Titian's "The Assumption of the Virgin" rose above the altar of the Servite convent where clergy and princes could agree on the sacredness and greatness of the Christian mystery. Author Turnbull left the line of welcoming cherubs and focused on other icons, cuts of stone and emblems scattered like leaves on the chapel floor. She then compared the stony rigidity of doctrine shaped by man from a little phase or truth with the grandeur found in the soul of man. Early on, *The Golden Book of Venice* hinted at the mischief the Council of Trent would bring to this Italian nation state. The author seemed to be suggesting that doctrine and Trent mischief would eventually damage the soul.

Colette continued to follow the narrative and felt that she was inside the story.

Many years later, as the sky took on a threatening pitch, the gondoliers gossiped, conspired, and engaged in their petty crimes. Unfazed, Marina of Murano, a living beauty, waited for her gondola, a dead sister's child in her arms. A Veronese artist on location remarked about the beautiful child. He also saw love and pity in the woman's face. He desired to paint her for the convent altar in the image of Madonna of the Sorrows. "I will paint thy face."

Fra Paulo Sarpi, head of the Servite Order, servant of the people and conscience of Venice, found consolation and pure thoughts in Marina's face. Her eyes were the last to be discovered. Sarpi had the final word: "Thy face is holy."

Marina stirred the heart of a nobleman named Marco, who begged the Venetian Senate to let him marry the commoner. They wed and later went to Rome with their son, who was blessed by Pope Clement VIII. The ruling princes feared that the natural order was being upended. There were storm clouds on the horizon.

Sarpi the Wise was reluctant to hear confessions since perhaps, as some suggested, in his heart he was an Anglican or a too-keen lover of science like his friend Galileo from Florence. The pope had tried to trip him up on his reading of Genesis, but the Inquisitor was not fluent in Greek and other languages. Fra Paulo, always the smartest man in the room, secretly thought that the Jesuits were using the confessional to pry state secrets from the wives of Venetian noblemen and send them by dispatch to the Vatican that seemed to know when the Turks planned to invade Venice and what printers were still issuing books declared anathema by the

Inquisition. More tales would come from the mischievous canals of Venice.

Colette continued reading. Venice felt some distress as Marina turned towards the Church and the nuns and away from her family. Colette thought this was Venice versus Rome in domestic miniature. Marco declared that the women of Venice were priest-ridden. "Marina Carina," he cried to his wife. She sank and she mourned; she prayed and she fasted, expressing a desire to travel to Rome to seek papal forgiveness and save the kingdom of Venice. Sarpi used all his wit, learning and wisdom to bring Marina back into the Venetian fold but failed.

Fra Sarpi was in and out of this fictional mist, sometimes as a savant and at other times a spirit. His fellow friars had been known to say under their breath "Here comes the bride" when he passed, hinting emotions resided in that heart, or perhaps he was engaged in romance, or more properly was the Bride of Christ, a union that would put him beyond gossip and concupiscence. His fellow friars loved and respected him, but still Fra Antonio was caught with a package of poison in his cassock destined for Sarpi's rare glass of wine. Danger still lurked.

Colette followed these twists and turns as they had taken her far away from her expectations. She understood the bathos and the sentimentality. Marina would go mad and take her entreaties to Rome in her head. Venice would keep the Vatican at bay through secular wit, a decent standing army and a fine navy. Sarpi would survive an assassination attempt to advise another day. With "Ave Marias" ringing out from vesper bells, Marina's child was feted in Venice, healing the city's wounds and signaling a bright future. The pope still grumbled in Rome.

Colette thought that the Council of Trent would cast a more substantial shadow over Venice. What was bothering her? Was it the creaking bones of an old form? Was it just the Victorian lens that gave an old story a predictable twist? Was it that the child in this tale lived in iconography while her own baby was abandoned in some dingy clinical anteroom? Was it that the author borrowed bits and pieces of the Madonna from the masters, put her in a Venetian palace and brought in the voice of God to direct this devout lady to her end, her family be damned?

Colette knew she was talking to herself. She was trying to find in some romantic Victorian text a clue, a hint, a backwards shuffle into meaning and understanding. Deep down, Colette admitted she had taken a side trip to Venice to put off her encounter with Trent, the city, the idea and the doctrine. Then she fell into the trap her most recent dream warned her about.

Colette heard vanity in her voice and felt inflation rising from her shoes. She remembered her dream about the supremacy of the heart and how bombast and the intellect would not advance the cause of her dream women at the Council of Trent. She felt ashamed of herself.

Colette was leaving her fictional Venice, experiencing one last vision of the Madonna, who was transformed by the weight of theology and Papal mischief into a whimpering lunatic taking an imaginary apology trip to Rome. Marina became the cross her family and state would have to bear. But this crucifixion was softened by the Venetian mists and the endless sounds of vespers.

Colette put the fantasy Venice aside and wondered about the cross she would be bound to bear. But that was only the half of it, as her mother might say. Much as Colette thought of herself as a twenty-first century woman, she feared she might have more in common with Marina than she would admit in public. She heard Jung's words about compensation and thought again about the dream in which the female doctor had placed a hand over her heart.

She imagined the latitude and longitude lines wrapping the earth had lost their way and became an indecipherable bundle of cords, strings and piano wires, confusing travelers and confusing her.

She thought about the Loyola script the Brazilian Jesuits followed as a matter of life and death. Colette knew she had to discover her script and her way. She was beginning to understand her script would likely be found, not on the wall of some dark doctrinal cave or in the watery Venetian lagoons, but inside herself.

That thought scared her to death.

Chapter Ten

"How was Venice, Ms. McGovern?"

"Do you mean the one in my head, Professor Gleason?"

Colette was still thinking of latitude and longitude lines gone astray.

"Now that's the proper answer I would expect from our full scholarship student carrying an academic load in religion, literature and psychology!"

"Thank you, sir."

She was glad he didn't mentioned their previous meeting, during which he seemed to be building with his hands and words Venice castles in the air.

"I take it the plane ticket didn't appear out of nowhere."

'No, it didn't, sir, but it might have been a blessing in disguise."

"Well, this is the right place to talk blessings. You mean you saved yourself a six-hour seat in steerage?"

Colette laughed.

"Yes, that too! I was actually thinking about how going to Trent or Venice might be a trap, at least before I fully understood the issues."

"I can imagine Venice being a trap or lure for the young, especially in the spring. Trent feels a little heavy. But that's not what you meant."

"No, professor. I have been reading about the poets and philosophers who loved Greece and especially those identified with the early Italian Renaissance."

"Very interesting observation, Ms. McGovern, but what does that say about the price of tea in China?"

"I don't know much about China. I just thought that paying too much attention to the literal, physical place early on might keep me from finding out other things. As I understand it, the Renaissance thinkers were attracted to the idea of Greece as much as the place."

"Things? I thought your task was to study the implications of the Trent doctrine in the present day. Might you not be going far afield?"

"Yes, sir, perhaps I am. It's just that Trent was more than four hundred and fifty years ago and there's been a lot of writing about the council during this period."

"You mean the Anglicans and the rest of the Protestant lot? But isn't that an old story, the Reformation and the various Counter Reformations. It's enough to make your head spin. A lot of things in our Catholic cabinet have survived rather well over the centuries. As you know, inspired doctrine changes slowly, if ever.

"Now, as you circle the Council of Trent, where might you be stopping along the way?"

"Well, I did a little circling of Trent through the eyes of a British female author, writing in 1900, from the perspective of Venice in the tumultuous years after the council."

"The author?"

"Mrs. Lawrence Turnbull."

"Well, the bull sounds very British. Was she an academic?"

"I don't think so."

"Her book?"

"*The Golden Book of Venice.*"

Gleason laughed.

"Sounds like a children's book, Ms. McGovern."

"Not exactly; it's a historical romance, I guess, that tries to capture the Venice-Rome power struggle. There's a Madonna figure that gets in the middle of it."

"I assume Venice won that round. Thank goodness the Church had the patience of Job. Onward and upward, I say. Let the Holy Spirit rule!"

"Yes, sir, but the story seemed to be about who had the right to rule a nation state. Turnbull did hint that the Church teetered on a rocky ledge. She did contrast cold doctrine with the immortal soul but you can only push this theme so far in a romance novel. The author seemed somewhat modern when she placed the soul of man above doctrine."

"Right, the old bogey men again. While I do encourage you to read widely, I would also ask you to place more academic weight on standard texts that have been well-studied and are part of our canon. I'm sure the Turnbull book was very enjoyable but fiction is fiction. And from what I remember, Victorian literature is pretty awful."

Colette laughed. "I understand. The book drips with sentimentality at times, but I was curious about how the Madonna as wife, mother, daughter and would-be saint would be handled in this melodramatic tale."

"And, yes?"

"As fiction, not very well. Her theology and psychology might be more interesting. But the ending is formulaic. It just got me thinking."

She couldn't explain her inner journey to Gleason.

"Any other planned detours on your way to Trent? I don't have to remind you that the clock is ticking."

"I understand, professor. I want to learn more about Fra Sarpi of the Servite convent in Venice during this period. He seemed to have access to the Trent Council papers from his work with the state. He was a bit of a legend. Sarpi was very shadowy in *The Golden Book of Venice*: a wise man, a mystic, a politician and a monk."

"Ah, Fra Sarpi. The Jesuits have heard of him. I think he had something to do with driving the Order out of Venice for a time. Yes, he knew the Venetian political game. Don't worry. We came back."

"The Venice book was not completely clear on that."

"I don't think many people read him anymore. Please keep in mind the sanctity of your sources as you go forward. If I remember correctly, Paul V burned a lot of Sarpi's writings, declaring them anathema. The rest of his writings were lost in a convent fire that is memorialized in a nondescript headstone which no one pays any attention to. Now any other stops along the way?"

"Nothing specific planned so far. I will probably look more closely at the Trollope book written in the late nineteenth century. He lived in Venice for a long time."

"I see. I'm sure the Council will stand up nicely to another Victorian writer of fiction. Please try to stay awake while reading it."

"I have also been thinking about reading Graham Greene again for a more modern perspective."

"I don't recall *The Power and the Glory* to be about Trent. Wasn't there a whiskey priest involved? I get his books mixed up."

Colette laughed again.

"So do I! It would be to get a perspective. And I'll probably stop at a few grave markers along the way, checking for fingerprints."

She wasn't trying to be funny. She simply felt an urge to resist Professor Gleason's Trent summons, a place brooding in its literalism. But that wasn't really it. Liturgy had been hitting her in the face for years, and she finally had a chance to slow it down and roll it around in her fingers, the way she would a pencil. Not true, she said to herself.

Colette wasn't sure why the Trent project was becoming so heavy and so personal. She had dreamed a lot in the past but never about religious matters. Now she seemed to be dreaming nightly and her dreams were almost always about religion. Sometimes the dreams opened up her heart in ways she hadn't experienced before. But now her dreams felt like warnings, suggesting she might be getting too close to certain issues for comfort. She was uncomfortable with the sexual nature of some of her dreams, particularly when doctrine was involved.

Colette had long worried about whether she would get caught in the Madonna trap, a worry that began with her mother telling her to be a good girl and the nuns reinforcing that sentiment with a vengeance. She recalled all the religion classes about beautiful female saints, including St. Therese of Avila who was said to have inflicted mortification on her own flesh. The nuns had a field day with that. Then along came Alfie, and she went underground to bury her dead. After that she went to Venice and got more than she bargained for.

She might have said, out of the frying pan into the fire, if she wasn't caught in some post-Venetian trance and reluctant to reframe her mother's words. At home, Colette felt a gathering unease.

The dream came to her unannounced, perhaps as coda and retribution. Surely Aquinas could not have such reach.

Colette had been thinking earlier about getting with the program. The dream gave her more than she bargained for.

A bird, perhaps a sparrow or a finch, was walking around a cutaway vagina, moving towards the clitoris. The woman, who had very large genitalia, was barely awake and nibbling on fruit. The images seemed scary and foreign to Colette.

A baby in a basket close to the woman had fruit in its mouth and was surrounded by fruit. Colette sensed she and other hands took the swaddled child to the altar for a double High Mass. The music and the light faded over the child, silent in his nursery. Somehow she knew the child was a boy.

Colette woke and shuddered at the pornography that had visited her in a dream. Serves you right, she said to herself. You had your fun with that fantasy Venice trip and begged for the feminine underside. Now it's biting you in the ass and hitting you in the face. Take that for compensation.

She was sure she didn't actually say these words, which were not her language. Colette sensed that these thoughts, uttered in language that she might have heard on the No. 1 train in the Bronx, were full of stuff and unrepeatable nonsense, as her mother might say. Shadow stuff, Jung might have said.

She went inside her prickly vision, as if she were looking through a fence or fingers held tight against the light, wondering why some fantasy cutout version of her sex would be shown to her in the middle of the night in more poetic detail than she could possibly imagine in the daylight. Even with her favorite mirror, she could not have imagined birds on a vagina prowl.

Colette didn't really know the difference between a sparrow and a finch but must have seen them sometime pecking away in her stamp-size back yard. In the dream they walk around in a cutaway vagina that was pink and too outlandish for the wall in her OBGYN's office, as they moved towards the clitoris. The physiology in this dream sequence confused her, as if she were looking at her sex upside down, inside out and a little out of kilter.

The woman with very large genitalia was dozing and eating fruit in a rather aimless and unselfconscious manner. The dreamer repeated the word "voracious" a number of times and was not sure whether she was speaking about sex, appetite, or some huge unrequited hunger.

Colette thought about the Madonna and child and flinched at the thought of a very sexual Mother Earth visiting her in a dream. If she was repressing anything, she was doing a very good job. Maybe there was no portrait here or psychological tic. The woman seemed to be about abundant generation and appeared to devour what she generated. She was wide open and let nature in.

The presence of the child bothered Colette both inside and outside the dream, and she fought the literal straightjacket she so often found herself in. Let the dream go, she told herself, and she did, staying within this display of abundance and satiety.

Colette had joined other willing hands to take this swaddled child to the altar. There was no sense that this represented an offering; it appeared to be the end and the beginning of a celebration. The child was not on some ancient slab waiting to hear from the gods. The child had come from largesse and a grotesque fertility, as open, necessary and inevitable. Colette heard the sound of an archetype taking shape before her eyes and taking her back, taking her down.

She also heard choral voices from another time celebrating with equal vigor a double High Mass. The voices were separated by a curtain in a church alcove, first as a low even tenor, then rising to alto. For a time the tongues blended in beautiful ancient Latin but then grew louder, rougher, with both sides of the curtain fighting for advantage. She could imagine being there on the first day of Babel listening to the civil, melodious sounds coming from the various tribes arriving from the compass points. Then the sounds clashed, weapons were drawn, and babble took over.

Colette was fearful and wanted to retreat from this front line territory where sex, theology, and linguistic swagger were at war inside her head. She was looking for a way out of this prison of a dream.

The way out didn't come easily. For days she was a slave to the vagina dream, drawn by wonderment, fear and her own prudishness. She couldn't get it out of her head. Colette thought about this festival woman often and attempted to frame her in a less dangerous narrative.

She thought of St. Hildegard of Bingen, a 12th century modern woman who advised popes and bishops and, though living in a nunnery, wrote a treatise on sex. In her view the strength of semen determined the sex of a child and the love and passion involved determined the child's disposition. Colette recognized Aristotle in the background but marveled at how much this largely cloistered nun seemed to know about passion and sexual delight from a woman's point of view. Colette thought that the nun who might have been the first sister to publically describe a female organism seemed to be more open to these matters than she was. Colette didn't know whether to laugh or cry. Still, this remarkable woman was a product of the 12th century and for all her gifts, found that sexual desire was the work of the devil.

She found some relief reading about Hildegard's visions that were rich in Latin, choral voices, angels and the Feminine Divine. The abbess considered the visions a gift from God and they informed her writings, poetry and art for a lifetime. Colette was disappointed that some contemporary experts on the subject suggested Hildegard was actually suffering from migraines. She read that feminists took issue with that diagnosis, arguing that it was common to describe historical women visionaries as suffering from mental illness. After all, she recalled, Joan of Arc was considered crazy. Migraines might have been an unconscious way of dealing with the Catholic Church. Abbotts and archbishops readily listened to Hildegard when they believed she had received a vision from God. Colette could imagine that the abbess was able to separate her nighttime visions from her daytime theology, which could have been written by Augustine. Bachelor theology continued to cast a long and psychologically dangerous shadow over the next one thousand years.

Colette desperately needed to escape her raw vagina dream and an abbess who wrote about female orgasms and had visions of God, if only to lower the temperature a little.

In that spirit she decided to spend a weekend at the Bronx Zoo and the Bronx Botanical Gardens, looking to balance her dream narrative with animal and vegetable life. She studied the animals that ate life. She tried to give the vagina woman some whole life under a ripe moon. She added bits and pieces from her journal that seemed to fit. She did her best to keep Venice out. And she kept Hildegard at a distance.

Colette did her best to reimagine the dream as a gift.

Then she wrote in her diary.

Woman

The woman waited patiently for animals to appear.
First the groundhog eating
Trees she wore for comfort; then the deer
Chewing on her forest dreams like cud.
Barn swallows pick gnats from her silver hair
Barred owls envied the field mice she devoured.
The woman had dropped her book and curled
Around a back porch stanchion like a snake,
Eyes on the moon. Gradually she was
Open to everything. An old dream
Looked for a home: a yellow finch
Walked around a cutaway vagina.
The woman large of genitals slumbered
While eating fruit. A baby in a reed
Basket was nearby ready to be placed
On an altar. Having giving birth
She was sharp as a scythe
Ready to cut the meadow in two.

Colette wanted to throw up, sickened by her own slippery romanticism
and desire to get away from the uncomfortable memes that visited her in
the middle of the night. So she wrapped the vagina woman in the faint
cloth of nature, borrowed from books and her visit to the zoo, and
produced some sentimental mush. She was ashamed of herself.

Colette tried to invoke a psychological process called "amplification."
She would take the dream and, by focusing on the dominant image, move
the dream forward. This time, she imagined a heavyset female neighbor in
the Bronx, lounging on a porch and wearing a smock which was dotted
with peacock symbols. But there was no vagina in sight and Colette
couldn't conjure one up. The woman was feeding the birds and the
squirrels. She was also feeding herself. No fruit in this instance; rather a
large bag of potato chips.

If Colette hadn't been so troubled, she might have laughed at her failed
exercise in creativity. Colette wasn't looking for perfection; just a story
line that wouldn't keep her up at night. Was "amplification" what
theology was calling for? She heard the lie within the lie. She was
searching for the feminine and a vagina showed up, large, plush and pink,
hitting her in the face. You wanted abundance, girl, she thought, and
that's what you got. You got what religion repressed. You got what you

repressed. She thought of the dream child celebrated at the altar with a nurturing presence. The child looked like her at that age.

Colette remembered a teacher telling her about the difference between a plot and a story. A plot might be: the king died and the queen died. A story: the king died and the queen died of grief.

Perhaps she had been given a plot and couldn't resist creating a story. That was only the half of it, as her mother might say. She tied the vagina woman in a bow and surrounded her with meadow animals. She left the child on the altar. But now it was all about her. Birth had sharpened her edges and probably her wits. She could now cut the meadow in two.

Colette didn't believe this manufactured tale for a minute. She wondered whether the dream was simply a gift from her unconscious, a reminder that sex, life, birth and abundance were reasons for joy and celebration, though how that played out in a double High Mass was unclear to her. Perhaps it simply represented the joy, extravagance and over-the-top nature of the dream. She thought of her dream about Pope John Paul II in which she was turned away from the altar. In comparison that dream seemed restrained and theological. In contrast, the vagina dream was pulsating with unrestrained libidinal energies. Doctrine seemed to take a back seat to sex, life and celebration.

She also wondered about possible relationships between the vagina dream and the Council of Trent. Colette hated herself for thinking about the centuries of vaginas the councils had tried to police. Nonetheless, she knew Aristotle, Augustine and Aquinas and a legion of scholastics had spent lifetimes in theologically pure, joyless and biologically incorrect studies of female sex organs which became doctrine, morality and prayer. She thought about the virginal Marina of Venice who seemed cut from Virgin Mary cloth, a character who might have been created by any second-rate theologian in a monastery perched on a cliff high above the Irish Sea.

Was this what the dream meant by her cutting the meadow in two? She felt her heart pounding, knowing this would not be a conversation she would be having with O'Connell. Colette recalled Hildegard who, remarkably, also wrote about medical subjects and wondered whether the abbess would consider the vagina dream a gift from God or the work of the devil.

You can run, Colette thought, but you can't hide.

Colette thought that it might have been a less painful meditation if she had gone back to the Greeks with at least a nod to Demeter, the goddess of Mother Earth, or better still Artemis, goddess of the hunt, childbirth, wildness and virginity. At least these fables offered room to maneuver, hide or even mark time. This was myth to get lost in. And she heard no church door slamming shut.

For the first time in years Colette got down on her knees and, in a schoolgirl pose, prayed for a release from dreams. She prayed to St. Theresa, her father's favorite saint, to free her from these punishing dreams, to keep theology at bay after she closed her eyes. She prayed for forgiveness for not delivering her own child to the altar with a gracious and innocent heart. She prayed that the weight of that sin would be lifted from her.

Her prayers were not answered.

A few nights later Colette dreamed she had been bequeathed half a church with a truncated communion rail and an altar that seemed within inches of the congregation. She felt this fractured space would not be suitable for full religious services. Looking beyond the pieces of a fallen church, she noticed an expanse of Italian marble, like a coliseum, waiting for occupation, like art, begging to be studied.

She felt some sadness about the limits of prayer, if that's what it was. Perhaps she was unable to dream a full church with a dedicated congregation. That notion seemed to capture her faith. These limitations concerned her, but she was intrigued by the field of Italian marble almost out of view. Was this another possible place for worship or a new field for mischief? She imagined the faithful moving beyond the remnants of a church and their comfort zone to the marble field where they could reinvent themselves. She sensed in the distance were new words or worlds, adjacent and unused.

The next morning Colette thought about this dream and recalled her prayers to St. Theresa a few days before. She wondered whether her prayers had been answered after all.

Chapter Eleven

Colette was glad that the weekend was over and she was back at college, meeting with Rebecca Aimes to chat about their thesis projects. Trying to be lighthearted, she mentioned the Madonna trap.

"The Madonna Trap!" laughed Rebecca Aimes. "Sounds like something the nuns cooked up."

"I was actually thinking about art," said Colette

"You need to see someone."

"No, not that. No real men in the picture. I just read this romance novel about love in Venice, and before you knew it, the Madonna figure was in league with the pope."

"That doesn't sound much like a honey trap."

"The honey left early, I guess. After the vespers made the rounds, Madonna dumped her husband and kid and fantasized about saving the papal kingdom."

"Colette, that doesn't sound like much of a tale."

"Yeah, it's not. I'm adding a few bells and whistles just to make the thing palatable."

"Why Venice?"

"It's on the way to Trent."

"Worth the visit?"

"I told Professor Gleason that I picked up a few ideas and themes. It is really a silly book. The Madonna practically walks into the picture frame. I was hoping for a little more angst and pain and perhaps a little more sex."

"And?"

"I recall that once she touched her husband's face. Or was that his hand? That's about as nasty as it gets. Nothing below the belt as the kid was conceived in the dark, like I was, I guess. I had read that some pope or theologian rated body parts according to their sinfulness. I think hands were blessed; intimate body parts, not so much. I think there was actually a medieval how-to book on how to avoid the inner thigh. Our maiden passed the test. She did embrace the man tenderly at one point, but that was a ruse to get him to reveal what Venice was up to with the Vatican."

Colette was half-tempted to mention her vagina dream but was reluctant to bring it into the daylight. Hildegard had now retreated into the mist.

"Sounds like a typical historical fiction."

"Right, but you'd think after two thousand years we'd find better employment for the Madonna other than being assumed into heaven and carrying the weight of the world's virginity. I guess that's what we get when we keep bumping into mystery. Maybe Venice didn't get the word from Trent."

"It sounds like they weren't interested or were too busy chasing off the marauding Turks," replied Rebecca.

"I can understand why," said Colette. "I'm looking for the vague and the mysterious, you know, the transcendent, and all I find is a pouty woman walking her virginal strut into art."

"Aren't you being a little hard on the lady? After all wasn't she in the image of the Mother of God. Are you going there?"

"Are you?"

"What do you mean?"

"The First Vatican Council, your project."

"Colette, it's a project; just another paper. I like the subject, but I can't reinvent history."

"Exactly, Rebecca. I think that's my problem."

"Nothing a little getting laid wouldn't correct, my dear."

Been there, done that, that, that, she said to herself. But her options were becoming a little clearer. Rebecca suggested she get laid. The next stop on a fact-finding journey would be her mother, who was watching "As the World Turns," a good choice at two o'clock in the afternoon. The daughter needed some comfort, and the mother reluctantly gave her a few minutes during a commercial.

"Your project getting you down, honey?"

"I guess so. So much to do, so little time."

"That's what your father used to say."

"Guess he was right."

"That Trent thing?"

"Sorry I ever heard the name. It doesn't even sound Italian any more. Sometimes I feel like I'm stuffing a Thanksgiving turkey."

At the moment, food was the farthest thing from her mind.

The culinary reference caught her mother's full attention.

"Turkey?"

"Yes. I keep stuffing the dam thing before I go to bed, and in the morning it seems to be a bony carcass again, all skeleton and wrinkled skin."

Colette didn't know where these cooking references were coming from. And she didn't know much about turkeys.

"Maybe you should see Father Stravinsky. He went to a good school in France. What's it called? The Sorbet or something? Like the fruit drink."

"It's the Sorbonne, Mother. And yes, it's a good school."

It was a week later that her mother coaxed her into attending Father Stravinsky's 10:00 a.m. Sunday Mass. Colette felt some peace hearing the old refrains that meant little but tugged at her heart like a nursery rhyme.

She was certain that her mother had planned the event for some time. The priest said Mass, walked back down the church nave ahead of the congregation, and then stood at the church door to greet the faithful. By the time Colette arrived in the back of the pack, she noticed that the priest was wearing a Yankee cap which must have been hidden under his cassock or provided by a handler. She recalled Fra Antonio hiding an envelope with poison in his cassock, waiting for an opportune moment to slip it into Paulo Sarpi's wine. He was apparently one of the plotters sent by Pope Paul V to silence the man who was becoming anathema to the Vatican. At least that was the tale she encountered on her medieval rounds.

While she was ruminating on her medieval text, the priest who was wearing a cassock with what she thought was St. Andrew's cross in commemoration of the saint who was crucified at an angle rather than dishonor Christ, held out his hand.

"Thanks for coming, Ms. McGovern."

She waited for the rest of it, the finale, but nothing came. It felt as if she was sleepwalking but still noticed his very prominent nose.

"Your mother said you were studying Trent? That's a very important council."

Her eyes lit up and, given the key word, she could now string more than two thoughts together.

"Yes, father. It's taking a lot of my time."

"If I may say so; go easy on yourself," the priest said in a soothing voice, reminding her of a song her father listened to.

"Let me tell you a little secret. We did most of the important councils in a week at the Sorbonne. Bam, Bam, Bam, and before you know it, you're at Vatican One and Two."

She heard or thought she heard wham, bam, thank you ma'am, and that didn't seem like a laundry pickup or a Sorbonne cheat sheet. She heard a bigger BAM but knew the priest was not talking about the Brooklyn Art Museum where they regularly discussed the price of tea in China. Who was that showing up now? Was it Gleason, Merkel, or that handsome gondolier from misty Venice?

"Thank you," she managed to say. She wanted to say Trent was like peeling an onion; there was always another layer and then, another.

The priest was moving on. "Well, nice to meet you. If you ever want to chat about the councils, please give me as call. It seems like only yesterday that I was walking through those dusty halls. But it's a beautiful Sunday. Enjoy and God Bless."

"See, I told you so!" her mother said on the walk home. "Isn't he handsome and a Yankee fan to boot?"

The Yankee cap bothered her a little. It was like an end-of-Mass prop to reveal to a congregation more interest in baseball than religion. Don't be a bitch, a voice cautioned her; the man tried to be nice. Maybe he has a bald spot. He is a little on the short side. Funny he would show up sporting the same St. Andrew's cross that was in one of her fantasies. What was it about dying sideways?

That was her problem, one of them which had her seeing red, especially at the end of the month. Add a splash of red at the end of a cassock or in that threatening night sky and she was already in the medicine chest. Colette would have been delighted if this was just about a clash of symbols, a subject she had wrestled with in one boring class after the other. As long as they showed up on schedule, were painted the proper hue and hinted of rosemary, she would not be kept up at night. But take the same pot, with the same ingredients, throw in a little theology, mix in some power politics, and overlay them with a mischievous God and the ecclesiastical trappings, and you've got more than your basic Irish stew.

It was the mashing up that was getting to her. She was minding her own business and having a nice chat with the priest in a Yankee cap when some friar with a fistful of poison showed up to threaten the order of the day, just like in a scene from "As the World Turns."

Perhaps the priest was right. Get off the Trent turkey trot for a few days and take a memory walk down council lane, as a guided romp in a museum where man's hand in the side of theology was frozen in time and held in place by the unchanged text. If it was good enough for the Sorbonne, it should be good enough for her.

At the door of her local church she had looked for traces of the Bull she had posted, mimicking Luther, and saw only the dregs of paper that had been apparently ripped from the door. The vulgarities had been scrubbed clean. She wondered if Father Stravinsky had read "Chanting the Feminine Down."

She would take the priest's advice and walk humbly through tradition. Colette would become part of the narrative that flowed from her lectures,

86

readings, musings and revelries. She would embrace the stories rising out of mist and take the spirit and legends of the Apostles into the daylight of reflection and belief. She would settle on firmer ground in Nicaea and Constantinople in the fourth century and wrestle with the Trinity and the divinity of Christ. She would recite the Nicene Creed from these places with the piety that she once practiced by rote.

Colette spent a week studying the role of Constantine in legitimizing the Church and the early Church councils, including the Council of Nicaea. She reflected on her readings, intent on making this Church history her own, if only to better prepare her for Trent.

It was the year 325 and she imagined standing with Constantine, who had invoked the Christian God before a battle and as victor reestablished the Holy Roman Empire in His image. There was trouble in the land. Theology was bumping into theology. The Father and Son have been called down from the heavens and a battle was brewing. The fracture lines between east and west were already appearing in the sands of Asia Minor.

With the emperor, Colette heard coming out of Alexandria the talk of the elder Arius that Jesus was not God because he showed emotions, grew in wisdom and age, and died. She heard Christ was not always eternal; there was a time when He was not. Arius, soon a heretic, argued that the Son was of a different substance than the Father. She wondered when the council would get around to the mother. The Trinity would have to wait.

The emperor called an ecumenical council, and the Nicene Creed was born, clarifying for all time the relationship between Father and Son. Colette was slowed by words such as begotten and tried to fight her own way back into unintended birth. She reminded herself that this Creed was the least she could believe, the rock that the Church still rested on.

Colette pushed on to the Council of Constantinople in 381, learning that the highways were populated with galloping bishops and that followers of Arius were stoned to death, torn to shreds or sent to prison. Heretics could be saved if a Christian would breathe three times into the mouth that had defied God.

Now she was at the Council of Ephesus, Asia Minor in 431, listening to Nestorius, Archbishop of Constantinople, say that scripture spoke of the humanity of Christ so the holy virgin should be called the mother of Christ and not the mother of God. He said this was not my godhead but my Body, broken for you. Christ's sweat, hunger and sacrifice which belonged to the flesh were to be adored because they had taken place for our sake.

As Colette read about Nestorius being declared a heretic and banished to a monastery, she wondered what would have happened if this view of the humanity of Christ would have become doctrine. Would there have been a place for women along the fault lines that were getting deeper in the sands of Asia Minor?

Colette pushed on past Ephesus on the Aegean, arriving just in time to learn about the Temple of Artemis and other lesser known shrines and temples destroyed by Christians at the earlier urgings of St. John Chrysostom and supported by the emperor. She heard this saint of both the East and the West moving beyond the intellectualism and theology and blessing the poor and disabled. This is my Body, said the hermit, holy man, and revolutionary. She saw hospitals in Constantinople that this man built.

She also heard him raging against feminine dress, rouge on the high cheeks and lush Mediterranean lips. She saw signs of the Madonna rising, though still covered in mystery and divine maleness, ready to be elevated to Virgin and Mother, growing out of shrines and temples into new shrines and temples. The blessed displaced Artemis and her dogs of war and hunt; they rid the form of hunting rage and wild virginity, in time taking on the lush blues, reds and greens from Titian's hand. Now militant monks enforced the Roman order.

Colette was called back to doctrine and text. Patriarchs of Constantinople and Alexandria battled over belief. How can Mary be the Mother of God when she bore the baby Jesus? How can I worship as a god a baby of a few months? Some were declared heretics; others were exiled. She learned that Jesus could not be too much of a man or too less of a God. She felt there was a war going on, a raw battle over the Body of Christ.

She would visit the shrine to Mary at Ephesus, attended by thousands of women who placed ornaments and households icons to be blessed by the Virgin. Their needs and desires rose like prayers to the ears of the council which heard their plea. The Godhead would remain intact. Constantinople and Rome squabbled over the graves of martyrs, seeking different gods. Divinity was everywhere underfoot.

She was underway again, pushing through Carthage, bowing to the goddess Astarte, high priestess of sexuality and war in that old Mesopotamian pantheon, walking over the remains of children thrown on funeral pyres to stave off the dangers coming from the Mediterranean Sea. Still she traveled north up the boot, weighed down with sinfulness and grace, listening to the ascetic scold Pelagius, the Celtic monk who did not believe in original sin, wagging his finger at Italian noblemen who took many mistresses in addition to their wives. Slave girls were lined up at the outdoor marketplace to be picked over by pagans and Christians alike. The monk continued to scold, and God remained in hiding, theology intact.

She looked for Artemis and Aphrodite, for Venus and Athena, in the heavens, on the sides of cliffs and in favorable seas, but found these gods who had visited revelers nightly with the rages and wonders that occupied the human house had been replaced by text, medieval, ethereal, and patriarchal. She knew that Constantine had sent poets to hell for writing falsely about the gods.

She heard the councils speaking in one voice, a vesper, a prayer. This is my Body, said the priest, and she recognized the language as coming from a very old and a very new place, placing her sex in a rule book untouched by time. Behind the monks who were destroying ancient temples was an endless sea of even more militant monks waving Virgin Mary banners and denouncing that corrupt den of vipers that was between a woman's legs. The Celtic monk declared that women had learned their manners at a brothel and men were no better than maddened stallions. Colette felt all this in her belly.

This is my Body, she heard again as she was being shaped, shipped, cleaned and blessed on that altar behind another black curtain, midwives still checking centuries later whether her hymen was still intact.

She heard the monk's anthem about the whore of Babylon and heard a prophet telling her that death entered the world through sex and passion. She wept watching the faithful Christians at the Council of Nicaea castrate themselves for a place alongside the angels and to be closer to Christ.

She recalled another wedding ceremony with Hymen showing up with garlands on his head and a flaming torch in his hand, bearing wishes from Dionysus and Aphrodite for a marriage rich in abundance. Then the scene seemed to fade and Hymen became silent. The flute dropped its notes and the dancing stopped. She felt herself running out of country and language, still hemmed in by an old text, weighty and threatening.

Colette sensed that she had lost herself in the story of the early councils and took a break from these reveries and readings. As she sat in the college library surrounded by piles of books and manuscripts, she realized that there was no easy way in and out of theology; few well-marked signs that might show her the way. She recalled Father Stravinsky saying he breezed through the councils in a week. What was she doing wrong? Did she lack the seriousness and the spine to take these romps through Church history? Should she be more of a penitent and a pilgrim?

Colette was unsure. She wanted her Trent project to be a romp, but it was becoming a burden. At times Trent seemed like a threat. It seemed that whenever she opened up theology, she also opened up herself and became softer and more vulnerable. Her research seemed be turning her inside, out. Her dreams that she prayed would end continued in torrents. In her mind they came in direct proportion to her background research for the Council of Trent. Colette didn't know whether she should take this as a warning or the price she had to pay for what her father called "poking the bear." She had a strong sense that during her study of the early councils she more often than not came down on the side of the heretics.

She got no peace on the night she ended her study of the early councils. The dream seemed to outrun her reverie.

Colette dreamed she was in front of a college class in a non-descript auditorium which held a few hundred students. She might have been in this place before. She said I am glad to be back, to see familiar faces again, and to talk about theology. "What do we say about something," she said in the dream, "that was so beautiful, so wonderful but was still killing people in the streets? What do we say about that icon you carry in your pocket or purse, the very thing that had been known to have the power to cause wars? Will we worship that too? Will we build an altar around that majesty? Just where do we go to find god?"

Colette was just getting warmed up. She took a watch cap from her head and wondered in passing why she was wearing it. She thought of the word "watch" and then let it go, vowing to return to the question. She was waving her arms and becoming very emotional. She tried to stand, but her legs felt wobbly. The dreamer gripped the table in front of her.

On standing, she looked the students in the eye and fumbled for her prepared text. She knew it existed somewhere because she remembered preparing it. She looked in her bag, under her chair, and in the thin air in front of her but found nothing.

She was losing her audience. Some faces seemed to be frowning; all seemed less friendly. One man who turned away showing his silhouette had the face of a gargoyle. The dreamer saw in this outlined face a huge question mark, starting at his skull and running down his neck.

She moved on, deeper, looking for signs and wonders, marks or hieroglyphics, as if stumbling from one dream room to the other. She was now inside an apartment in a man's dormitory. The place was dark but not threatening. The place was compact with a bunk bed and storage space. The man communicated from the dark side of the room, showing her pictures of angels and Jehovah-type figures which might be found in a church's stained glass windows, but in this case the images were on plastic sheets or acetate. They seemed like rough versions of an original and badly weathered.

She heard the man from the dark say these images are for you, or they are you, or would you find a way to frame this art? His words were mixed up as if he were talking through an underground bunker.

Still she traveled, deeper as through tumbleweed, passing well-known faces to which she could no longer place a name. She saw texts. One appeared written in Celtic with decorative edges; the other in a mix of tongues. She noticed stacked letters and directional signs, as if they were showing her the way. She was stopped in her tracks by what looked like Korean characters in block lettering with arrows pointing in every compass direction. She thought she heard the sound of sex coming from inside a tent.

Still she traveled, even deeper, telling a fellow traveler that she could detect low tire pressure in his car simply by looking at her own dashboard. He asked: was she out of her mind?

Chapter Twelve

"Thanks for seeing me on short notice, Mr. O'Connell."

"Certainly, Colette. It sounded important. What's going on?"

"Someone told me I was out of my mind."

"A friend?"

"I don't really know."

"Then an enemy perhaps?"

"Sorry to be so confusing. It was a voice in my head; you know, in a dream."

"Okay. That makes more sense. Any context to this person's remark?"

"The remark came at the end of a night of wild dreams that I experienced after a review of the early Church councils. Actually, I thought I was going out of my mind dealing with all that dogma."

"Why the hurry?"

"Well, my parish priest Father Stravinsky said when he was at the Sorbonne, they pushed through the early councils in a week. I tried to follow his advice."

"Congratulations. Learn anything?"

"I learned how much I didn't know. It's amazing what they were discussing fifteen hundred years ago. It seemed like black magic and often incomprehensible."

"You didn't understand the text?"

"I had trouble staying with the text; it seemed like a hammer. It felt like books and manuscripts were overwhelming me. So I wandered off with some of the prophets and complainers."

"Why the wandering?"

"I guess I was looking for a good story. Or I was looking for images that would hold my attention. As a matter of fact, the guy in my dream accused me of telling him stories."

"We'll get to him in a moment. Can we talk a little more about why reading about the councils might upset you?"

"I think I've been trying to get to Trent and something always gets in the way. There always seems to be a detour."

"Like Venice?"

"Yes, exactly."

"Have you been?"

"As I mentioned to Professor Gleason, I just went in my head, reading a proper nineteenth century novel about a Madonna figure living in the shadow of Trent."

"Worth it?"

"It just reminded me of how Madonna is presented at different times and cultures."

"That seems useful. Did you pick up anything from the early councils?"

"Well, it's hard to even read around the edges without getting a sense that the Church was basically anti-feminine. The Church seems to have spent the last two thousand years shoring up a male hierarchy. So much time was spent arguing over the Immaculate Conception and all the rest that seems like myth and nonsense to eternally define the female. It seemed pathological."

"That's a strong statement."

"I know I should keep an open mind, but the early Church fathers seemed to have been very interested in celibacy, virginity, sexless marriages, castrations, sexless cohabitation, and so on. I know Augustine was a loud voice in these matters. But it seemed so negative, equating sex with sin, based on the Garden of Eden myth."

"I understand. I assume this was one aspect of the cult of the Virgin, building up the divinity by de-emphasizing the human. Augustine, with help from Aristotle was part of this frenzy. Virginity and celibacy had seats in the front of the church."

"That's a good way to put it."

"And keep in mind that the early councils were still in the throes of the end times. No need to get married if the world was coming to an end."

"I guess!" she laughed.

"Anything else about your side trips through Church history?"

"At times I felt as if I was following an army of monks who were tearing down pagan shrines and temples. They seemed particularly enraged at the goddesses."

"That's an interesting image. Why the monks?"

"I'm not really sure."

"Anything else?"

"Sometimes I felt I was wandering in the desert picking up shards of broken icons from between my toes."

"Another startling image. Were the monks to blame?"

"I don't really know. The battles over a paternalistic theology were murderous, with women always paying the price."

"That's powerful. How did it make you feel?"

"I'm really angry and pissed off, if you don't mind my saying so. I can't eat or sleep. Do you know that in the early Church adultery was a crime if practiced by women? A misdemeanor or something for men meaning, I guess, they could still go to communion. And one reason given for not having children was to keep them off the dung heap or whatever you call it in Greek. We're talking female babies here who were put out in the elements to die. And don't get me started on some bishop who told the midwives to inspect the hymens of virgins who were sent to a male household for their protection. Then we are given Mary, who gave birth without her hymen being broken, without afterbirth, without any mess. It was nuts. It's killing me to read this. Just who was writing these rules?"

Colette wasn't sure how much she said to the psychologist. She wasn't sure if she told him about being behind that dark curtain again, this time with Alfie dressed in a cassock made of sackcloth and looking like an old threatening monk. She didn't know whether all this talk about large and small virgins, in the air and in her head, came into the healing room, which was beginning to sway like the auditorium of her dreams, gargoyles to the left and right of her. She didn't know if she mentioned the vagina dream. She didn't know whether her nightmare child came forth.

She did know the psychologist was out of his chair and patting her on the arm. "Are you all right, Ms. McGovern? Can I get you some water?"

"Okay."

"I thought you were going to faint."

"What happened?"

"You became very excited talking about the monks, shattered icons and women's issues. Then you began to speak at a faster clip and leaned back in your chair with your eyes closed."

"Sorry."

"No need to be. This has really affected you."

"I probably take it too seriously."

"Of course, it's a serious subject."

"Another thing. This doesn't feel like history. I just read about religious fanatics destroying ancient temples in Palmyra in Syria calling them idolatrous. And women are being accused of polytheism and are being raped. This language sounds very familiar. The ISIS thugs seem like just another bunch of religious fanatics and misogynists that have been roaming the Middle East since after the birth of Christ. I met some on my travels."

"Yes, it does. Now how are you feeling? We can pick this up at another time."

"I'm okay, overstimulated I guess." She regretted the word immediately.

"Okay. Now what about that guy who said that you were out of your mind?"

"His remark came at the end of a string of dreams, and I'm not sure how they are related."

"Perhaps I can help."

"Well, the first one was about being in front of a college class speaking about the danger in theology. As I was getting warmed up, I looked for my notes but couldn't find them. The students became angry. One man turned his face away. He looked like a gargoyle."

"My goodness. No wonder you are upset."

"Thanks. Sometimes it's little easier telling you than writing in my journal."

He didn't pick up on that.

"So what do you think was the text you couldn't find?"

"Trent?"

"You must be feeling better. Is that a joke, Colette?"

"Not really. It might be that my reach is exceeding my grasp, as my mother would say."

"I see."

"Or maybe I should just keep quiet until I learn a little more."

"Possibly."

"Or maybe the subject is just too big to get my head around."

"I suspect that isn't the case. Now do you want to talk about another dream?"

"I was in this bunker-like place, and some guy in the shadows showed me images of angels and gods printed on large sheets of plastic. It looked like they came from an old, perhaps abandoned, church."

"See any connection to the other dream?"

"Maybe this guy in the dark was giving me the text or the image. In the first part of the dream I'm looking for my notes but can't find them. Maybe they don't exist. Maybe he was giving me the real thing."

"Does this torture you?"

She didn't like the term at all.

"Not torture. I'm upset that I'm having this story go on inside my head. It's like something had taken charge."

"And who or what might that be?"

"God." Colette couldn't say it without laughing.

"Well, perhaps not, but something had a hold of you. You might remember that Jung called anything that subdued his conscious will and took control over him a neglected god."

"The Council of Nicaea left a lasting impression. Jung's gods seemed to be everywhere, taking control of my will. My recent dreams seemed to be a maze. I felt lost. "

"For good reason Ms. McGovern. Theology seems to be bumping into psychology and playing out in your dreams."

"Maybe I am losing my mind."

"I don't think so."

"It feels so heavy, threatening and theological."

"Perhaps you should slow down and not proceed with this forced march through council history. Perhaps theology would have less of a sting if viewed from a distance."

Colette wasn't sure. She felt what had stung her remained in her body and under her skin, ready to sting again if she crossed the wrong theological divide.

"Ms. McGovern, you might recall Jung talking about the autonomous psyche when it comes to dreams and visions. Does this make sense to you?"

"That there was some autonomous part of me generating these nightmares?"

"I haven't heard that word nightmare before. Is that what these dreams feel like?"

"They feel like someone is holding a gun to my head and saying you had better take notice."

"That's strong language."

"That's what it feels like."

"Then we'll have to find a way to take some sting out of that command."

"I would like that."

"It's been a long day. Anything more you want to discuss from that dream string?"

"I wrote in my journal that it was a tumbleweed dream, meaning rolling out of my vision and not very clear. At times it feels as if I'm in a drama."

"That's a nice way to put it. Any images that you remember?"

"I think I was looking at a book or manuscript. On one side, I saw words that seemed to be written in Celtic. I have looked at *The Book of Kells* online. My father had a Gaelic dictionary which belonged to his father. I decorated my poem 'Chanting the Feminine Down' with images from the book."

"And on the other side?"

96

"It was just a lot of languages thrown together. I wrote that it looked like a mix of tongues. I thought I detected block Korean letters from which radiated directional signs to all corners of the compass."

"Do you read Korean?"

"No, sir. There's a Korean deli in my neighborhood that I have been going to for years. I recognized a few symbols and know the difference between Korean and Chinese calligraphy. The owner's wife had shown me how to draw a few characters."

"Excellent. Any idea what all of this means?"

"It's very confusing to me. The Celtic could be a reminder of one of the scolding monks I met during my travels."

"I didn't know that. Was the dream monk scolding in this instance? I mean, did it feel like that?"

"No, there was no emotion I could sense. It was as if this book was the text and held what I needed to know. It wasn't presented as the last word, but it had that kind of feeling."

"Good. And the Korean?"

"I just don't know. I don't visit the deli enough for it to stay with me in that way. The characters were quite large and seemed more formal than what I have seen in a store sign. Plus there seemed to be borders around the characters. You know, like I was being told to take notice."

"And the directional signs to all compass points?"

"It just felt like that. I recall some arrows were straight while others seemed bent or broken."

"Broken arrow? What might that mean?"

"Might they mean the wrong direction or a faulty path or something?"

"Very good. Go on."

"That it was intentionally confusing."

"Why?"

"It serves me right," she said, mimicking her mother.

"Does it?"

"I don't know. Perhaps I've been pressing too hard, and the psyche is saying, slow down a bit."

"Well said. If so, should we assume this is for your psychological health?"

"At first I thought it was to shut me up."

"Who or what would want to shut you up?"

"God," she said nervously.

"Remember that Jung called those forces that changed his life for good or ill, gods. You might want to differentiate between these psychic forces and a transcendent God?"

Colette wasn't sure. She felt strongly that the flavor she tasted in her dreams was very theological and hovered over her like a very large and threatening "G."

"I guess reading about a half a dozen councils over a few days would be enough to produce a headache."

"Yes, indeed. Now, any other items you want to talk about before we end the session?"

She said yes to be polite, but did not go down into that dark underground bunker with images of an angry god and cherubs patiently waiting for the virgin. She did not go to that other place, another bunker and another time where she gave up life. Colette felt she had spent enough time underground.

On her bus ride home Colette recalled the patient and enduring love displayed by Penelope who waited all those years for Odysseus. She thought of Molly Bloom ending her circular journey through Dublin on that June day with a beautiful and immutable "yes."

That night she wrote in her journal that the "way to Trent is circular, through history and time."

Colette wasn't sure she believed her own handwriting.

Chapter Thirteen

As Colette returned to her study of the Council of Trent she tried to stay with Molly's bloom, a patiently radiant mountain flower on a ledge overlooking the Irish Sea, reaching for peace and safe harbor. During the day, try as she might, Colette felt that peace slipping through her fingers.

In the quiet of that evening when she was alone in her bedroom Colette imagined she heard voices rolling in with the waves and clouds. The voices became louder and shriller. Colette heard the gods, her professors, feverish monks, and her mother framing the last incantation. The beach filled up with medieval texts, angry scrolls and parchments fresh from the pulpit. Old languages weighed down the sea and banished the small gods to the outer rim.

That night Colette dreamed that she was at some rail hub in Frankfurt, Milan or Rome, waiting for her luggage and looking for her mother, who was older, wearing a veil over her head and face, as if she were going to church, back in time when everything was covered.

Her luggage was on a train parked at a distance between sand traps and steel pylons. She had a vague sense of no man's land and would rather not experience the pain. She wanted an easy way out, perhaps blaming her mother or her Mother. She looked down from the train platform and cried out desperately for the woman she had known all her life.

Colette was knocking on train windows and pulling at train doors, as if she deserved entrance. The actor Robin Williams showed up in one frame looking and sounding very much like Mrs. Doubtfire and reprimanded her for the way she was manhandling the luscious oaken doors on this fast train from Edinburgh which carried 80,000 passengers a month. Colette touched the oaken grain with her hand, glad to finally be on solid ground. Mrs. Doubtfire suggested that she take a look at the new train engine. "It's a thing of beauty, my dear, modern to a fault. She cuts through the air like butter."

She thanked him or her and said that such an experience would be too much for the heart and tapped her left breast with her right hand, feigning weakness. She then walked away from the scene, pleased that she had not been found guilty or taken on too much baggage at a rail junction with tracks going in every direction. She had a vague memory of bent arrows posted on some deli in the Bronx, telling her in a foreign tongue that she had been learning in her sleep where to go or not to go.

Colette was half-awake and half-asleep. She remembered her travels, her dreams and the warnings from the Church councils. In her reverie she heard voices coming off the sea. They were getting louder, appearing to fight for her attention. "Don't hang around Nicaea too long," said a voice long on advice. "It's a fool's errand and they are making it up as they go along."

"Walk through these epochs like a walk in the park," said a priest in a language that was a cross between French and Croatian.

"Please don't float your boat in too many rivers at once, Ms. McGovern," said the man in a bow tie who looked a little like Carl Jung. "Practice doesn't always make perfect."

Now a louder voice came from beyond the sea, familiar but still dark and distant. She imagined Professor Merkel rising from his Jesuit couch, scooping up the beach gods in Brazil, and redistributing them on pagan altars wrecked by monks along the train tracks of her dreams.

That was where she wanted to go, backwards and down, until she was able to fill out the pantheon with her own moods and wretched desires. A battle was at hand. What came first, she wondered, and could not complete her profane thought.

In her reverie Professor Merkel lost some of his charm and daily wit. He now pounded his chest and tossed Latin phrases at her as if he were Jehovah issuing thunderbolts. The phrases seemed to refer to sin and redemption. She resisted him and felt her direction away from battle was backwards through wet sand.

The professor grew louder as if he were on steroids. Colette imagined him getting down on his haunches, looking like a lion. This naked figure with veins showing through his haunches and an existential dream on his face reminded her of William Blake's Nebuchadnezzar, the Old Testament prophet who built Babylon to celebrate his pride and majesty, placing himself above God. Then the prophet lost his mind and was sent into the fields to eat grass like the oxen. He returned to his senses when he looked to the heavens and saw God.

Colette entered this vision as if it were a catechism, resisting Blake's wild raging which suggested Jesus was the Imagination. She lingered on the prophet's bird claws and the eagle feathers which covered his body. He had the eyes of a madman. His lips were curled in perpetual curse. "This is not my Body," she whispered in the wind.

Colette was not sure that anyone had heard the confession she held in her teeth and crushed with her mouth, as if she had learned something from the false prophet after all.

Colette felt she was losing direction and becoming lost inside her own head. When she became lost, she usually returned to her tumbleweed journal with its psychological leaps, weird dreams and outright nightmares. She had fallen into the trap of thinking she could balance theology and her dreams, with each balancing the other out. She hadn't fully anticipated all the double talk and innuendo that filled one's head after midnight. And why hadn't she paid more attention to the little people who Jung said represent our tics and repressions and cause us mischief? Otherwise, why would Robin Williams as Mrs. Doubtfire show up on that Edinburg Express talking about a shiny new engine? Talk about going off the rails! That's where Colette felt she was located; on both sides of the rails looking for her mother, Godot, or some raging prophet coming from Blake's beautiful mind. Who was it who said I was out of my mind? She asked the little people: haven't we been here before?

Colette would turn and turn again, looking over the old texts that promised direction and piety; one more stab, one more opportunity, one more conga line. Her weekend in Venice now seemed like some kind of sop, white bread in milk, becoming mush and leaking memory. It was a way to appease her conscience, a demonstration she had spent her time at the ramparts. But that sentimental weekend now seemed like a self-exacting bribe, taking much more from her than it would give.

Colette recalled Professor Gleason jokingly suggesting that, since the Venice book didn't work out so well, she should read *The Recognitions of Clement*, a romance written in the early part of the third century.

"It's a hoot," she remembered him saying while wondering whether adults really spoke that way. "It's the last time there was any real romance in this old, cold church."

She figured he was speaking of early Christian romance and not some modern steamy version. The romance was in the fictional haze that took some of the bite out of scripture. She was right. After a quick reading Colette learned the book was about Clement finding his soul while tagging along with St. Peter for a few hundred pages.

Colette scheduled a meeting with Professor Gleason to discuss the book.

"So you got around to reading it?" Gleason asked, apparently surprised anyone would take his advice.

"Yes, sir; a quick reading. One last stop on the way to Trent. I was looking for a little less fiery theology and a bit more piety."

"That's an odd word even for a distinguished graduate student to use. Where did that come from?"

She wasn't about to take the professor on a trip through her demons.

"I probably wanted an easy read and to get away from heavy theology. That will come soon enough."

"We can't escape that fate. Now, any reaction to the Clement book?"

"Just really curious. It's so easy to read. I don't know whether this is due to later editing and multiple translations. The version I read was very well done."

"No one really knows how many hands the manuscript had passed through. We don't really know who Clement was. Some think the character was based on the first century bishop of Rome or a compilation. It has remained a bit of a fictional curiosity."

"Why is that, professor?"

"As you noted, it was well written and edited and seemed too modern for a time when Christians were just crawling out of the catacombs. They hadn't yet reached the Dark Ages."

"Yes. And I thought about the form. Picaresque, I guess, what with Clement, Peter and company traveling through Syria, Palestine and Judea, I think."

"Good point, but what does that have to do with the price of tea in China?"

"Probably nothing! The form and the changing locations might take some of the sting out of the theology discussions. They go on and on and at times seem circular."

"That's pedagogy for you, Ms. McGovern. By indirections find direction out."

She was thinking "asshole," what with him digging into his Shakespeare file, but then remembered doing the same thing herself.

"Anything here float your boat, Ms. McGovern?"

Colette might have drifted back to Venice and got lost in the canals.

"Well, even if you don't believe all the theology talk, the points are well argued. I assume the author or authors read Greek and knew Plato and Socrates. St. Peter sounded like he'd been coached by the Greeks."

"You may well be right. I assume Clement was familiar with Greek."

"Yes."

"Are we talking mainly about tone here? I recall the book covering all the usual bases—free will, the nature of evil, the divinity of Christ and all that."

"Yes, sir; I think so. But it seems more than tone. The arguments between St. Peter and Simon Magus, a somewhat mysterious heretic and magician, I guess, are not particularly one-sided. Peter won out in the end, but Simon made some really good points."

"Such as?"

"Oh, the ability to really know God. Why would God create a world where evil existed? And why didn't Christ save himself from the cross?"

"Good questions. But I think they have all been fully answered over the centuries."

"I understand, professor. The outcome of the story is telescoped, but there is some tension and a lot of back and forth."

"Don't we know how the story ends?"

"Of course, but Peter doesn't automatically shoot down Simon Magus by accusing him of being a heretic."

"Right, that is the form of the book, the back and forth. Perhaps the third century camp followers were more inclined to sit on the edge of their seats."

"I wasn't on the edge of my seat but was a little surprised about how much leeway the author gave the heretic. He pressed Peter a lot."

"I think that's why they call it romance fiction. Some of the sharp theological edges have been smoothed out a little."

"At times I thought Simon Magus was getting the upper hand, particularly when they were discussing polytheism. It's probably my imagination, but at times I thought the author wanted the heretic to win."

"Isn't there a term for this type of literary criticism, Ms. McGovern?"

"The intentional fallacy or something?"

"Yes, reading too much into the text. But no harm done. We all do it and this book is a perfect candidate. Don't worry; the issues were decided a long time ago."

"I did think the book devoted an extraordinary amount of space to idols, paganism, and mythology."

"Why do you think Clement did that?"

"He was pushing monotheism with very exacting arguments. By this time I guess the emboldened Christians were tearing down the pagan altars and shrines."

"Quite right. Paganism and idol worship stood in the way of the march of Christianity. There is some evidence that the pagan shrines were losing their constituency by this time. And the emperor approved, you know, making everything legal."

"Actually, I laughed when I read some of the descriptions. St. Peter and others were denouncing paganism in ways that suggested they might actually believe mythological stories. The tales about the pagan gods seemed more compelling than much of the Christian story, at least in image and detail."

"That seems a little far-fetched. I know this is Christian fiction, but Clement still had an axe to grind."

"I'll have a closer look at it. I do recall St. Peter's almost erotic discussion of Jupiter committing adultery, patricide, incest, infanticide, denouncing these mythic activities while describing them in great detail."

"Interesting take on the psychology of mythology. Our friend Clement, whoever he was, might be a stalking horse for repressed Christianity. Why don't you revisit these key points? After wrestling with this heretic, you should be ready for Trent."

"Yes, sir," she said, knowing she was stalling. But there was more, something almost erotic about the way St. Peter ticked off the temptations new Christians faced, but without too much fire and brimstone. The book might have been banned at another time.

For a closer look at Clement, Colette traced the author's path through Judea, Palestine and Greater Syria, following him on his wanderlust and listening to Peter who seemed to have the patience of Job and a mind clear enough to look into Plato's cave, shadows and all. She was sustained by all the names, characters and demons she had met during her catechism classes in the Bronx. Colette settled into this fiction.

Clement resembled Sisyphus pushing a rock up a hill, acknowledging that he too was tied to an old geography and existential angst. What about life after death, the dust-to-dust refrain and the darkness of oblivion? Colette sensed more despair in these remarks than she had found in her vintage catechism.

She heard talk of creation and gnats and elephants in a liquid swirl, a homeopathic soup, and imagined creatures resting on the inside of caves. The vicissitudes like the Flood and the Exodus come and go, with all the predictability of an ancient tale, but there was still a shadow which was dragged through the proceedings. Deals were made, and transactions were completed. Moses allowed idol sacrifice for a while as long as only one god was worshipped at a time, thus cutting evil in half.

She was in the land of fantasy and heretics. She was where the old land rose and the heavens descended. Peter engaged Simon Magus, the heretic, in a balanced conversation, as if they were at the beginning of a sparring match. As she read, Colette underlined passages and made notes in the margins of the book.

Simon was married to Luna, so his waxing and waning were already established. He boasted to the congregation that he was a magician. He could dig through mountains and pass through rock. He could free himself when imprisoned and change his countenance. He could make beards grow on little boys. He could make new trees and new sprouts. He could change himself into a sheep or a goat. He could render statues animated. He could throw himself off lofty mountains without harm.

His mother Rachel conceived him as a virgin, and he pretended to be a man. He could create a boy out of thin air. He could turn air into water and water into blood. He could speak with the other gods in the heavens, known and unknown. He could carry water for the old, provide food for the sick, and care for the dying without them knowing he was present. He could die again and again in the spirit and return always in the flesh.

He was not Peter's Christ who came in war, at the point of a sword, declaring a martial religion, while feigning meekness. He reminded Peter not to speak of peace. He said there are many gods, but there was only one incomprehensible god, and he was the god of all others. He said everyone can become a god, not by conquest or avarice but by acknowledging all the gods in the pantheon who contain parts of man. There was one Body and we all remain a part.

Peter remained guarded and polite, reminding Simon of the primacy of the scriptures which informed us that it's the devil that seized our imagination and filled our head with images of false gods who roamed the heavens in their debauchery and idleness.

Peter accused Simon of being an idol worshipper bowing down to a dangerous polytheism sent in his dreams and opaque visions. When he was so caught up in his inner, devilish world, Simon couldn't hear the word of God. For this he needed a sixth sense and without divine intervention he would remain lost in his debauchery and earthly, animal senses.

Colette seemed to get closer to the text and heard Simon and Peter more directly.

"Peter, you speak of my heart and my soul, places you cannot truly understand, not even with your all powerful God and the heavenly sixth sense you claim. I remain a servant of the all-powerful God but am also disposed to use my mind and imagination. Can you and your followers say that? Can you imagine regions far away that we cannot yet dream of?"

"Simon, you speak of dreams again, as if they are a divine revelation. You don't seem to recognize they are delivered on the serpent's tongue as if directly from the Garden of Eden, where dangerous knowledge was defined forever. Don't you recall Jeremiah's warnings about dreams? You look down and tell us you are imagining your feet and shoes on the same land where the serpent squirmed. You lack vision, Simon. In that spirit I implore you to look up, as I do, to the heavens, the seat of God's perfection and angelic presence. We are instructed to raise our eyes to the Lord, the God of joy and our youth. Be patient, Simon, and we will pray for your heart.

105

"My dear heretic," Peter continued, "the imagination is fallacy, a temptation to the wrong path. You have your eye on the evil ways of man and find purpose in that unchristian land. From whence comes evil, we ask, other than from lax faith, unreason and an insufficient belief? God is the author of good, not evil.

"Simon, you are like the magician who opposed Moses. You believe in theatrical miracles, raving about mountains dancing, statues walking, and brass dogs barking. You are acting like a pagan, confusing signs and wonders. You speak about God but fill your soul with erratic and perverse religions that are all lost in the mirror of time. You follow the banquet flute and the wayward harp into error, listening to your inner dance. You claim like some mute prophet that what men suffer are really their gods. Do you not see this as heresy?"

"You are eloquent, Peter, and I hear your entreaties. I hear your arguments that you pile up like tree branches and mud in constructing a new hut, hoping everything will stay in place no matter the fierce winds. Will your God protect our huts and our persons when the wind rises? As I have said before, Christ could not deliver himself from the cross. What say you to that, Peter?"

"I say that this gift is the miracle which you do not see and will not understand. How can you, Simon, a heretic and a magician, know this eternal truth when you still speak of stone dogs barking and a wind that whispers directly to your private ear? You lack the words to speak and the ears to hear the truth. You seem not to know that the one true religion was the source of all modesty and sobriety."

Colette felt she was inside a narrative that was inside a vision, a strange map which might have been laid over Palestine by a medieval alchemist. She read that Peter stayed on the high line, winning the rounds and sharing in the cheers of the attendant congregations who had been warned of the outcome. Simon Magus protested that a militant Christ who came in anger and war was leading a house divided. He repeated the butcheries found in the bible.

Peter returned from yet another land, older and fiercer, having seen a cunning serpent grinding his teeth and rubbing his forehead. It was as if the apostle had been refreshed from his time in the desert living off nettles and cactus hair.

"Remember, my souls," says Peter, "that Zoroaster was Ham's first magician who gave us the Tower of Babel. We have learned that all wars, rapes, and plunder come from idolatry. Do you not see this? Melt your useless images, Simon, and give any remaining value to the poor or cast them into the sea to be washed clean through eternity!"

Peter continued. "I do not mean to insult all history. Egyptian idolatry was more reasonable because it helped men govern. But paganism had an enormity that has touched every land as far as the eye can see. We cannot travel even a day without finding these devilish icons underfoot.

"We stand in awe of the heavens because the motion of the stars is in accordance with the wisdom of God, not some idolatrous act. We stand with the Greeks in believing the atomic theory and insist every loose atom in words, every speck of dust, every wayward seed that man gives up in the praise of God and children is in the hands of the divine. We live in a world of correspondences blessed by the creator."

The text told Colette that Simon wandered around Palestine, Antioch and Syria, one step ahead of Peter's congregation, denouncing the holy man and changing faces and shapes and finally casting his evil wares into the sea. Though vanquished, Simon the Magician hovered over the narrative like an unseen god.

Colette imagined talking to the characters in the unfolding story at the center of her vision, unsure of the salutation. "Do you say, Peter, that princes of the world are like adulterers who corrupt the minds of men, violating, seducing, and turning them away from love of the true bridegroom Christ in favor of unsavory lovers?"

"I have said that, based on the Scriptures," she imagined Peter responding.

Colette was lost in that sea of princes, lovers, adulterers and bridegrooms. "For the love of Christ, where does this passion begin and end?" she asked.

"What you ask is what the scriptures have revealed. In the beginning was the Word, and in the end is the Word," Peter answered.

"Nothing in between?" she asked.

"There is nothing but truth between God's firmament and the souls of men."

Colette imagined a shift in time and tone, with other voices coming into the room, begging for attention. It was if she heard fiction piled on top of fiction. She heard someone say, "Don't get me started on astrology," and thought it couldn't be St. Peter but was wary of opening the night door to others.

She returned to the text and listened to Peter's words. Colette might have drifted into a dream.

"We know astrology is a trick and a fantasy. So much depends on whether Mars is in a certain position in relation to Venus, and Saturn is looking on without the good stars taking notice. Venus in conjunction with the incestuous moon produces women that are ready for agriculture and even more manly work. They are eager to commit adultery with whomever they please, using no delicacies, no ointments and no feminine robes. They might as well be dwelling in Aquarius, acting like men."

Colette sensed that Peter was trying to manage and inflate the conversation, but in her reverie she heard Professor Gleason at the margins, dropping bits and pieces into the narrative. Gleason seemed at home in this old-style theological romp. Colette imagined she was back in the classroom, listening to Professor Gleason update his students.

"Consider the Brahmans, who were peaceful, committed no murders, didn't worship idols, eat animals or follow the stars to avoid cannibalism. I grant sometimes they would murder and eat strangers. The good stars don't prevent these men from marrying their mothers, sisters and daughters."

Gleason continued. "Understand that evil came from the inharmonious conjunction of elements, usually fed by lust. That was why adultery was so prevalent. Consider Saturn and all his whoring and incest. There are people who erect statues to this god and pray to him every day, thus making mockery of the one true god."

"This is the folly of paganism, is it not?" said a male voice in the crowd, "This is why polytheism should be banished from the earth."

"By root and branch, it must be taken out," replied Gleason. "The wicked and the profane gain ground daily. Today we have the wicked and obscene Jupiter, a parricide, an adulterer, a practitioner of incest and people proclaim him publically in songs and poetry. He married his sister, for God's sake! I cannot understand why they venerate him and execrate the one true god."

The friendly voice in the crowd continued, "These are the habits of the tender and simple minded. The poets helped with this folly, did they not?"

"Yes, Orpheus deceived men into thinking they were stars, trees, animals, flowers, birds, and fountains. He was a very dangerous man. So was Ovid, who was banished from Rome by the wise Augustus.

"We know that fables debase piety," Gleason continued. "The poets told us Mercury is speech, Juno is charity, Minerva is courage and Venus is lust. We know enough about the soul of man to know that this condition is not our Truth. Leda still committed adultery with the swan and Zeus, disguised as a bull, with Europa; then the world changed forever.

"These silly tales should be pushed into the sea. The zodiac is mischievous architecture. It should be crushed to dust beneath our feet."

Colette imagined Simon Magus showing up in an attempt to counter Gleason's reading of mythology. As soon as Simon Magus opened his mouth, he sounded very much like Professor Merkel, who could be standing in front of her class.

"All glory to God but the zodiac is not real! It's an image and an idea. It's part of our mythology. It represents the contents of our collective soul. It is a mirror in which we can reflect our manners and inclinations; our successes and failures; and our lusts and benedictions. It is the full range of our pathologies and desires. The zodiac is as real as the circular, star-struck wanderings of our damaged souls. The zodiac is the place where our ungodly imaginations can run free and create anything under the sun. We live our lives in the mist."

Colette half-expected the heavens to open and for Merkel to be stricken as he was earlier.

With every remark Gleason sounded more like Peter. "Ah yes, dear friend, a habitat for false gods and the debased Christian behavior you describe."

"So, Professor Gleason, we will have no poetry, dreams, astrology, mythology, symbols, personification, images or metaphors? So we will kill everything as if it's the serpent in the grass, forgetting that the serpent also represents wisdom? Will we pluck the imagination from our souls as if we are plucking a chicken? We will be unable to build correspondences between things except by invoking a cold and strained belief that was given birth in Aristotle's brain and made more dangerous by Aquinas. We will lose the very things that make us human. You will lose the middle ground of fancy. You leave us with nothing but your old, cold allegory."

"But, my dear Merkel, the Christian mystery is as old as man."

"But it creaks, sir, like the sound of your knees when you walk."

Gleason responded, "Isn't that a little below the belt, father?"

"Yes," replied Merkel, "but isn't that precisely where Clement, Peter, and all the gods have been hanging out for centuries, just below the belt? Saturn and Jupiter might get a hard-on, but then it's over. They rape someone else. For us, there seems no release; no hard-on. We keep beating that dead horse."

Colette felt as if she was falling back onto a low altar among the beasts and fornicators and those at both ends of buggery. Just what had she given birth to? She knew Mars and Saturn were in the mix. In the foreground, she imagined two Punch and Judy shadows in black dress, pawing at each other as in pantomime, probably waiting for the devil to show up as dictated by the script. Who said the God of one era became the devil in the next?

She reflected on her vision. Clement took center stage followed by Simon Magus and Peter and then the three retreated into the mist under the banner, "Happy Ending." Was that a theological joke? The Jesuits in clerical garb and wearing large crosses nudged the others out of the picture. It was as if this strange fiction was chasing its clerical tail. The actors left scattered on the biblical landscapes piles of mythology, theology, and psychology, mixed up and forbidding. They had picked through all the references to lust and ungodly pagan sex in the heathen zodiac and recast in language that might have been found in a fraternity house, in a horny Jesuit seminary or in some ante-room at the Council of Trent.

Colette sensed some force or power had taken over her words and her mind, conjuring up pornographic scenes as ripe as her vagina dream. She vaguely recalled Jung's feeling-toned complex where raw, primitive energies from the unconscious were triggered, spawning images she could hardly imagine.

She felt the weight of centuries on her back, all the battles waged for the perfect god, and the visions upon visions that filled the blessed texts. Did someone really say that the Blessed Trinity was as real as the Babylonian gods that served as the model? Did Emperor Charlemagne know this when he embraced the Trinity in 796, putting it at the center of the Holy Roman Empire? Colette, unable to comprehend this mashup of gods, fictions, allegories and tall tales, collapsed into precious sleep, praying for a way out of her nightmare.

Colette dreamed she was invited into the temple to make music with a god. The music resided on the page like a poem, going down the language tree until all that remained was a spot on a barren floor. A voice told her to listen and pray until she heard the angel choir. She demurred and decided to leave the church and seek new clothes and adventures, hoping the spirit would touch her in time to utter something sacred.

She found no peace. She wondered why a pagan dream hauled Apollo up marble steps to an altar on Good Friday morning with the female choir in pursuit. Apollo was tied to the cross, smiling. He shook Colette's hand.

She watched and then joined the bloody mob. They chanted from beyond the grave: "Why was god so willing, stumbling and falling on the way to his death? Why did he have flowers in his hair?"

"Does the crucifixion ever stop?"

On waking, Colette thought the question about the crucifixion sounded very personal.

110

Chapter Fourteen

Colette looked for ways to enter the city of Trent, treading old paths and walkways, looking for signs and markers. She remembered her readings about the founding of the pagan city, as if it was just another story, just another myth.

The catacombs opened and the good souls came, disturbing the living, and raising the dead. They came on the west winds carrying pieces of scripture, righteous in geography and power. They came with the following seas, full of pagan sounds, chamber pots and servants fearful of the devil hiding in bowls. They came down from church doors and from oaken forests where prophesies had been written and received. They came from the hearts and minds of kings and princesses who were conversant with the mind of god.

They came down from the Dolomites carrying images of Neptune and the Celtic water god wearing Vatican ruffles and Italian finery. Those in front of the parade carried the Trent flag with a screaming eagle stuck in the middle of a yellow and blue sea. It looked as if they had picked up old coats from the rack outside the classroom door. Others might have stopped by the gym that served as a theater and found costumes that had been used over the years for Peter Pan, Richard III, and probably Macbeth.

He's back, she thought and pulled herself out of the fog of Syria and Greece and back to the classroom to see Professor Merkel leading what looked like a cross between a Halloween parade and the lumpish end of a religious pep rally after all the miracles had been revealed, plundered and released.

Merkel wore a satin curtain over his shoulders and a four-corner bishop hat which might have been a lamp shade. The miter held in his right hand might have been a shower curtain rod. He wore bright red shoes and might have had a touch of rouge on his cheeks.

Behind him were a dozen male and female students, strutting down the aisle dressed in theatrical scraps and throwing kisses to fellow students who reached out to touch them as if they were celebrities. She heard what she thought were strains of "Ave Maria" and "Onward Christian Soldiers," but the strains quickly became Madonna's "Like a Virgin," driven into life by the quickened dance steps of the raging pilgrimage which was waving brooms in the air as if they were on fire.

The grand marshal led this throng, walking backwards as if he was entering the field of play, whistle in his lips, ordering temps and contra-temps. As the accordion group reached the front of the room and collapsed into one another in a giggling frenzy, Professor Merkel announced with his whistle that the parade should come to a full stop.

"Ladies and gentleman, welcome to Trent, a once rollicking pagan city that rediscovered its greatness resting on the shoulders of the Council of Trent, held from 1545 to 1563! This magnificent event charted the course of the Roman Catholic Church to this very day. So let those dates burn in your brain.

"And while your brain is working, please find a place for the Italian Renaissance, which was in full flower a half-century before the Council of Trent and sowing the seeds of a new world order. The Italian Renaissance had the audacity to celebrate the feminine in art, life and literature! Understand that those stern men in Rome wearing frocks and banging on tables with their crucifixes didn't like what they saw in Florence. These men imagined the Whore of Babylon and might as well have been looking in the mirror. We will meet her shortly."

Colette had filtered out the marshal music, gave a perfunctory nod to the "Ave Maria," then went inside Madonna's "Like a Virgin," traveling with the singer back to Venice in that wicked gondola while the drums at the baseline took her through the Madonna/whore territory. The singer went on her cathedral rant flashing her fishnet stockings in the direction of Rome. Colette had trouble imagining herself in fishnet stockings dancing to the music and menacing the Vatican.

"Please welcome the Whore of Babylon!" said Professor Merkel to the assemblage.

Professor Merkel wore a Halloween mask smeared with swatches of blues and greens and was decorated with costume jewelry that might have been purchased at a discount store. Madonna no longer hovered near the baseline; she was replaced by the Jesuit singing something in Latin which her mother might hum over the kitchen sink.

Merkel removed his mask and presented it to his students. He asked, "Why is this lady coming to class today?"

"You wanted to celebrate your return from the dead?"

The voice came from the back of the room.

"Now, that would appeal to my vanity, my dear soul. Isn't there enough of that contained in this disturbing archetype?"

112

"Trent is a little boring so you wanted to bring in a character from Netflix," the voice answered.

"I didn't know that, Mr. So-and-So," Merkel said, using her mother's language. "We will yet make you into a serious student of this council. Now who is this woman, and what does she have to do with Trent?"

"The Roman Empire was considered the Whore of Babylon by many, and then the Vatican assumed the position."

Colette heard snickering and laughter. The student who made that remark was wearing some kind of uniform.

"We will not digress on positions, Mr. Luther Martin, missionary or otherwise. That would be too delicate. But we should ask why all this stuff about whores, bridegrooms, and prostitutes when we are talking about our Holy Mother the Church? Isn't it a little unsavory?"

"Professor Merkel," said Rebecca Aimes, "the Book of Revelations seems to equate the Whore of Babylon with the pagan Roman Empire, mentioning the seven hills and all that. She was the mother of all harlots."

"Right you are, but why do you think these metaphors have been used throughout the ages by Dante, Luther, Calvin and others to slime the Catholic Church?"

"The Church was an easy target what with the Crusades and the selling of indulgences?"

"Right you are Ms. Aimes but why this charged, sexual language of the marriage bed to describe Church doctrines or its folly?"

"As I said, the Church was an easy target. And it had appropriated the language of marriage such as brides and bridegrooms of Christ, putting virginity and celibacy on twin and equal altars. These are charged metaphors, and I suppose it's easy for opponents to slip the negative whore stuff into the conversation. What seems even more charged and dangerous was when Plato compared a woman's uterus to a living creature that gets angry and Aquinas tied the female sex to Original Sin. Wasn't there some weird gospel about Christ coming to undo the work of the female, including lust, birth, and decay?"

Professor Merkel responded. "I think Jung refers to an Egyptian apocryphal gospel about Christ redeeming the feminine, but good point. Anything else?"

"There were gods and there were gods," said Colette. "The Romans came with their god Neptune and named the place Tridentum, the city with the three teeth. There are three hills around the city, and soon the Trinity would appear, destined to demonize and replace the gods who had come before. Perhaps in this context the other woman is always the whore. I guess every new doctrine bites and has teeth."

Colette thought she sounded like a priest.

"Quite right, Ms. McGovern. Thank you for putting your teeth into that delicious piece of history. That's progress for you. Onwards and upwards! The old gods are displaced because they represent our lower forms. Please remember that the Catholic Church is psychologically correct because it represents the higher forms."

The classroom was quiet now; Colette could detect some orthodoxy in the air, pushing this way and that way, looking for advantage. She had glimpses of Professor Merkel donning and removing masks, first the Whore of Babylon, then the Celtic water god, then Neptune, a Jehovah lookalike, trident in hand.

A number of students had picked up the Neptune motif and seemed to be dressed exactly alike, suggesting they rented their costumes at the same place. Colette waited for some huge secret to wash over her, delivered by Poseidon, Merkel or a timely vision that would help her get body and soul into Trent. She watched the troop exchange masks and high fives, piling their costumes in the corner as if they were really only rags.

Was this the pantomime after all, devilishly arranged by the professor and his band that conspired just outside her earshot? Was this the scene that would complete her, the archetype that would fill the ache that had wounded her?

She would not have been surprised if one of the student stragglers put a match to the pile of costumes which was already taking on new life. She noticed the mask depicting the Celtic water god on the hastily erected altar. Colette saw items that she was sure were in her purse such as a mirror, hand cream, and eye shadow.

Colette was walking back through history, certain that Professor Merkel had designed this retrospective as a dramatic tutorial in answer to her prayers. The battle lines were drawn in a familiar pattern; a simple priest from Florence took on the whore of Babylon.

"Welcome to the Bonfire of the Vanities," said Professor Merkel, without mask or trident. "Can you smell those fine Italian embers smoldering?"

There was no response.

"All right, the next time we'll burn this place down. A little imagination wouldn't hurt. Now, please, why would we pay attention to some crazy Dominican burning books and art about fifty years before Trent?"

"Because he was a crazy priest burning stuff?"

"Sure enough; Girolamo Savonarola gained attention for his deeds, but why did he become such a cult figure? You must have read some book or seen some movie or other about this crazy guy."

"I read Tom Wolfe's novel by that name, but I don't remember any crazy priest."

"Yes, correct. He just used the title as metaphor."

"Let's set the table. This friar turned priest thought he was a gift from God and in the vanguard of a new righteous church. The Catholic Church was beginning to look like the Whore of Babylon. He recruited a bunch of young thugs who patrolled Florence looking for women in short dresses, men kissing, and any forms of buggery.

"For a while, the Church looked the other way and secular officials were threatened by his rabid following and success. He campaigned against every sin in the book and even some that weren't written down, such as smiting this, and smiting that, and smiting as you like it. Full of himself, he organized a huge bonfire on February 7, 1497, and burned art, mirrors, cosmetics, dresses, playing cards, flutes, ancient manuscripts, artwork, paintings and sculptures.

"That's the basic story line. This is Renaissance Florence, for Christ's sake. Why in God's name did it happen there? What do you think, Ms. McGovern?"

Colette felt that she was looking through a mask fashioned out of doctrine and astrological signs. She wanted to get to Florence, but her mind wandered back to Palestine and Peter, who was half in love with Jupiter's sex romp through the zodiac. But she would find her way back.

"Professor Merkel, I have been reading that third-century novel supposedly written by Clement."

"Oh yes, *The Recognitions of Clement*. Odd book to take down from the shelf. Talk about a long and blessed life!"

"Well, it was in digital form. I was surprised there was such a thing as early Christian fiction."

"Yes, it's remarkable in many ways; the candor, I mean. I don't really know how much the translations improved the original. But can this take us to Florence and to Trent for that matter?"

"I don't know. There was a lot of dogma, but it wasn't so dogmatic. I was struck with how candid the discussions were and how sensuous Peter was when discussing the sex habits of the Roman gods. It seemed a little bizarre even for early Christian fiction."

"Yes, indeed. What are we to make of that?"

"Sounds like repression to me. Or just a natural reaction to what was considered pagan excesses."

"Correct on both counts. Doctrine and theology tend to harden over time. One can understand this taking place in Palestine or Judea in the third century but could the same thing take place in Florence a thousand years later? Keep in mind Michelangelo was in Florence doing some of his most important work at the time."

Colette listened to the conversation roll on. Maybe the crazy priest was considered more important than Michelangelo? Well, the artist was expelled from Florence during the height of Savonarola power. Wasn't Michelangelo gay? It was no wonder the man left town. And what about that Egyptian Christ sent to redeem the feminine? Merkel's "apocryphal" seemed like another line of doctrinal code.

She imagined mirrors surrounded by other mirrors on a funeral pyre, fed by the cries of Latin zealots, reflecting light and heat and carrying images of female babies placed on top of a dung heap and set on fire. Colette shuddered.

Rebecca Aimes responded. "What Savonarola did in the presence of such art and refined culture was pure madness. He must have been pathological. He wanted to kill what makes us human."

"Bravo, Ms. Aimes. Excellent! That is precisely the heart of the matter. Our crazy priest was waging a war against the imagination or anima, the feminine principle."

"Didn't he die for his sins, Professor?" asked Luther Martin.

"My goodness, the man with the missionary position made a joke. Yes, indeed. He died for his sins. That's the archetypal view and fits as he always imagined himself nailed to the cross. I think he wrote a book with crucifix in the title, *The Triumph of the Cross*. At the end of the day, he believed his own press releases and dreams. Seems he went on a mythic journey to meet the Virgin Mary in heaven, presented her with a crown fashioned by Florentine artisans, and in return Mary predicted a glorious future for Florence, perhaps even replacing Rome as the New Jerusalem. I should add that there's a long history of weirdos who summon up the Virgin Mary and the like in their dreams to make a point.

Colette felt guilty.

"That didn't sit very well. Savonarola upped the ante and said he would prove his revelations by walking through fire, but he got cold feet at the last minute. Then it rained and everyone got pissed off. It was the first trial by fire in Florence in hundreds of years, and it was like the population missed out on a hanging. The priest cancelled Carnival and replaced bawdy songs with devotionals. What's a city to do for recreation? Yes, exactly; they would call for a burning!"

Colette stayed with Merkel's fast talk and glibness until it wore her out. She enjoyed the way he slipped in and out of doctrine, as if changing his skin. Sometimes she didn't know which spots were real and which ones were painted on for effect and disguise. His romp through the Italian Renaissance seemed like a high-wire act but with very little at stake.

There was an eruption which in context seemed about as dangerous as a monk picking his nose in public.

"He was hanged and burned at the stake along with two of his colleagues. His right hand was said to twitch just before death as if he was blessing those who were cheering and fanning the flames. He suffocated before the flames could reach him, disappointing his audience again. But the faithful had gotten a taste and would not let it go for centuries."

Colette heard Merkel drone on at his whimsical best. "Before long Savonarola was resurrected. Luther found in him a forerunner of reformist language, especially in matters of faith and grace. The Dominicans brought him back to life as the pious devotional figure. Some thought he was the best hope for the Church before the Reformation. Keep your fingers crossed; there's still an outside chance this guy will become a saint."

Merkel was speaking, but Colette could have been listening to Simon Magus in another key: "I can walk through mountains and cause rocks to change their shape. I am god of the trees and tundra. I cause life at the atomic level. I am wind and universal remorse. I cause havoc and clocks to wind down. My temptation is to take hold of the spirit and to soar. I will take every thought for Christ in drawing rooms and in the ether until the end of times. I make boys out of air and girls out of ash. I am the wood that carried the crucifixion."

Merkel was winding down, joking about the apocryphal and where Trent fit into the scheme of things. "Stay with Trent, my friends; don't let Neptune drown or swallow you. Stay true to the faith. A story comes to life only when it is bathed in blood; everything blessed is a recapitulation of Golgotha."

"There was a time, a very old and dangerous time," he continued, almost as a prayer, "when stories became myths and myths the core of ritual and regret. Hear the plot and hear it well. A Trent city chorus in 1475 said that a Christian boy Simonino was murdered by Jews who drained his blood for use in baking Passover matzo. The accused were tortured and burned at the stake. This was a blood libel, archetypal and ancient, and almost impossible to expunge.

"The Church knew that this was a lie early on, but the spirit was afoot and magic in the air. Altars and shrines sprang up around Trent. Simonino became a cult; his artifacts freely traded outside churches and in the marketplace. Miracles were reported. Simonino was venerated across Europe and could claim at least one hundred miracles, more or less. He became the patron saint of kidnapped and tortured children. In 1758, the Jews were cleared of this crime. In 1965, Simonino was removed from the saint's calendar, though he might still be on denominational milk cartons.

"The boy still lived in etchings, woodcuts, marble relief, and cemetery friezes sometimes as a character out of Dickens, Little Boy Blue, or a cherub floating just out of reach. This was a time, a very old and dangerous time, when image became memory and memory art."

Colette thought Merkel was talking directly to her when he said with a flourish: "You must be tortured like Savonarola if your soul is to be moved. You must tempt the burning tree."

She felt that she was back inside the fantasy battle between Merkel and Gleason, which was inside mythology and inside psychology and wrapped in a suffocating theology with no apparent way out.

Chapter Fifteen

Colette dreamed that she was in the rear of a deserted Catholic church. A man was following her. She thought of the word "skulking." She seemed to recognize the man and said "I know you." He held a very old bible and other items she couldn't make out. The man remained silent as she looked him in the eye and tried to confirm his identity. She now noticed that he was holding religious items in both hands outward towards her like a fan. Colette identified prayer cards, candles, and pictures of saints.

She was confused and struggled with the difference between identifying him and identifying with him. Deep down, she understood that the man was a messenger, carrying icons she was familiar with.

She stayed underground, dreaming that she was in a churchlike setting with an unadorned altar presented to the dreamer at a sharp 30-degree angle. She climbed this steep path with the help of unseen hands. Once at the summit, she heard triumphant church music in the background. The dreamer was not sure whether she should leave or stay for the ceremony. She felt deeply conflicted.

Colette remained underground, desiring to wear a yarmulke, so she checked with a Jewish friend to see if this was possible. The friend disappeared and left her wondering whether it was time for her own rituals, costumes and practices. Colette had the strange sense that she was in mourning.

On waking, Colette recorded the dreams in her journal. She wondered what new and fresh rituals might come from her study of the Council of Trent.

Later, she spoke to her mother.

"You want to be a Jew?" her mother asked.

"No, Mother. I had a dream about wearing a yarmulke. I asked a Jewish friend whether it would be okay."

"Do you have Jewish friends, Colette?"

"Mother, of course I do. But that's not the point. Anyway, this was a friend in my dream."

"So, what's the point?"

"I feel brain dead with all this Catholic stuff. Maybe I just need a break."

"Then go to Atlantic City."

"I was hoping for Venice."

Colette was trying to make a joke and immediately regretted it. She recalled the price she paid for that journey.

"When you're rich and famous," her mother replied. "I saw George Clooney in a gondola in Venice. He got married there. So why the Jewish dream? Don't you usually dream of popes and safe stuff?"

"Mother, it doesn't work that way, except if you're George Clooney. Last Easter night, I dreamed you died at the hands of a homeless man and wild dogs. Talk about a nightmare."

"What a horrible thing to dream! My own flesh and blood!"

Colette laughed. "Oh, Mother. Everything is not personal. Remember Mrs. Carlucci down the block. Recall she died last Easter? The dream could have been prompted by her. Plus I read the obituaries regularly."

"But she was not your mother."

"Oh Mother, oh brother. Please think of me for a minute! In the dream I had to spend all that time with the local coroner sorting things out, then making arrangements with the funeral home. It took up most of my night. Thank goodness I left before the formaldehyde was pumped in."

She immediately regretted her last remark.

"That was a pretty detailed dream. Awful."

"Mother, dreams aren't literally true. You play with them, and see where they take you."

"Sounds like the lottery."

She was running out of dreams and didn't believe her own advice.

"Mom, one more, please! How about this? I dreamed that I came across an accident scene and found a young woman, naked, outstretched on the road, badly injured and bleeding from head, face, side and buttocks with a crowd surrounding her. An elderly man shouted instructions from a distance, telling her to get up. I brought a garden hose with a flow of clean water and bandages. I washed her and wiped away the blood. She seemed to be coming back to life."

"That was awful, Colette. It reminded me of you. Please be careful. It could be a premonition. The bible warned against this of kind thing. We should leave dreaming to the prophets."

"Mother, in the dream the woman was a stranger. I had never seen her before. She looked nothing like me. And the wounds did not seem to be very deep. Actually, I think this was a Good Samaritan dream just like in the bible. I came across an injured person. A crowd surrounded her but did nothing. A man called out instructions from a distance, ordering her to get up but without any real feeling. I responded with Christian kindness. You see! Dreams can have a simple moral and a happy ending. I'm sure the young woman is okay now."

Her mother stared with her mouth open and didn't say a word. Colette felt horrible and knew her showing off had upset her mother. She felt worse having to lie about the meaning of the dream.

Colette put her arm around her mother and said, "I love you. I'll try to do better with my dreams."

"That's okay, honey. It's all very strange to me. I'm glad you were able to help that poor girl."

"Sure, Mom. There's no reason a dream can't have a happy ending."

Colette felt that Merkel had opened her up by leap-frogging through Church history. Then the dreams seemed to enter her open wounds, perhaps to replace all the blood Colette imagined she had lost when the fetus was sucked out of her. She had a strong sense that the woman lying naked, outstretched and bloody on a street corner with wounds to her hands, feet, legs and side, as if she had been crucified, looked, felt, and appeared to be very much like her.

When she next met with O'Connell, he asked, "Why the crucifixion theme?"

"I guess my response is why not? In the dream about a traffic accident the woman had marks on her hands and feet as if she had been crucified. It's been a heavy dose of religion inside and outside of class for a couple of weeks. I enjoy Professor Merkel's classes, but he is very dramatic."

"Meaning he keeps your attention."

"Yes, he does, most of the time. This might seem crazy, but sometimes he sounds like other people I've read about recently and could even be speaking in their voices. On one recent occasion he sounded very much like the heretic Simon Magus. I realized I was daydreaming or imagining this, but sometimes the voices seem to take over."

"You understand disassociation, right?"

"Yes, I do, but I don't feel disconnected. Sometimes I feel too connected, too involved with the subject. Maybe Professor Merkel was channeling Simon Magus or channeling me. Maybe he's speaking in tongues and all that. Maybe the two men are just saying the same thing. Professor Merkel at times sounded as if he would be more comfortable in the company of Simon Magus than with the crowd at the Council of Trent."

"I understand. I can feel the weight of these interlocking narratives in your voice. Can you describe the discomfort you feel?"

121

"Yes, I feel discomfort, but it's not personal. He's a great teacher and the wearing of masks and dressing in costumes is a provocative way to talk about the gods and get inside theology. Merkel's theatrics help a lot. I get that, but ..."

"But?"

"At times I sense some invention in his remarks."

"Are you talking about facts or style? You said he was theatrical."

"I recall Professor Gleason once describing him as a novelist, as if that explains everything."

"It might explain some things."

"In terms of delivery, you mean?"

"Perhaps. Novelists just see the world differently."

"I realize that's true. I get a little confused when religion, myth, psychology, historical figures and the kitchen sink are all thrown together into some kind of instant soup. I realize some of this is play on the professor's part, but when I dream I seem to pay a price for this theatricality. I bleed. Then it's no laughing matter. Does this make sense?"

"Yes, very much so. This is heavy stuff. Do your dreams reflect this soup?"

"I dream a lot about entering churches, climbing altar steps and trying to decipher religious signs and icons."

"That sounds very normal and probably healthy."

"Sometimes the religious icons and signs seem dry and predictable, as if the meaning has been squeezed out of them."

"By you?"

"By the dream itself. You know, sometimes these dreams about religion just don't seem nourishing; they don't seem moist."

"Moist?"

"I read it somewhere. I think it suggests psychological health. You know; the ability to grow."

"And you don't feel that you are growing?"

"I am learning a lot. I have never been so overwhelmed by a college project. I just worry about walking around the same old statues in a decaying church looking for meaning. Sometimes it seems like I'm beating a dead horse."

"Is Trent hanging over you? Is Trent the dead horse?"

"A little. I'm just circling it, waiting for a way in. Trent seems so heavy and forbidding. I feel Trent is becoming dangerous. So I'm probing the perimeter. But even the early councils seem a little like war, with enough doctrinal disputes to kill for."

122

"I sense your pain and discomfort when you are walking around a deadly, dangerous carcass."

Colette laughed more than she had in weeks. She appreciated O'Connell's levity and his ability to round out her narrative. Her mother might say he was keeping her from going off the deep end.

"Do you have friends or fellow students you can talk to about this?"

"I feel comfortable with Rebecca Aimes. She's very smart. I've learned a lot from her."

"That's not the half of it," she heard he mother say.

"Glad to hear that. Perhaps I can add that you seem to be carrying a weight. I mean, all this theology, all this stuff. It's a weight. You know, it's a masculine weight."

"I can't help but feel paternalism in the dogma. When the feminine shows up, she is on an altar constructed and approved by clerics and theologians and watched over by an all-seeing, all-knowing God."

"I don't mean to move beyond my competence. I am no theologian. It's just that our theology is masculine, no matter what Jung said about the doctrine of the Assumption being the most important religious event since the Reformation. You have to decide whether that is a burden."

"I definitely feel that in the language and the structure of the Church. I think it's becoming a burden. I don't sense the Assumption has benefitted women psychologically. But Titian's masterpiece still speaks to me."

"Perhaps you should handle the text as historical and not as some revelation."

"Is that what I've been doing?"

"I'm guessing. You take your work very seriously."

"Thank you. I mean to. But how do I handle text as text, Trent as Trent, and dogma as dogma and not be influenced?"

"You'll be influenced, all right. But some distancing might be helpful. The doctrine is not going anywhere. It's a little late to rewrite that script."

"Is that what I've been doing or fantasizing about?"

"I don't know, Ms. McGovern. You are smart, serious and committed. Why would you accept a fixed, archaic male hierarchy?"

"I'll try to dream about that, sir."

"That's a righteous coda to the session," said O'Connell. "Let's continue to talk soon about the weight of your dreams."

"Thank you," she replied, sensing that her dreams might be both her salvation and her curse. Wasn't her soul supposed to speak to her in a feminine voice? Or did Church doctrine speak to her in a male voice--her animus--which showed up inside her dreams? Colette had trouble doing the math that seemed to be pulling her apart.

She vaguely remembered a class about Jung's conjunction of opposites or the joining of the thinking and feeling aspects of the psyche. She also recalled that Jung explained this union with alchemical metaphors. At the moment, Colette considered these metaphors a little fanciful and instead imagined some large caldron in which bits and pieces of the collective psyche were brought to a boil, probably at the hands of some theologian. During the cooking, the heavy masculine doctrine settled to the bottom while the feminine elements, including feelings, soulfulness and Anima herself, drifted into the air as vapor and were then bottled as Virgin Mary breath, just another male fantasy, a brand and another indulgence. What was at the bottom of the cauldron built churches and justified wars.

Colette felt that she was fighting her own wars on all fronts.

She left O'Connell's office thinking about the heavy masculine church, the weight of her dreams and why Trent was turning her inside out. She was exhausted and wanted to hide, so she made a beeline for the first private space she could find, the ladies' room, where Rebecca Aimes was talking to herself.

"Next time, I'm coming back as a man," said Rebecca Aimes, watching herself in the bathroom mirror curl her blonde hair around a right index finger. Colette turned away from the mirror.

During one of Merkel's lectures Colette had imagined rescuing her cosmetic pack from Savonarola's Bonfire of the Vanities but not before cursing the damaging effect of fire on blush which was essential to her cavernous high cheeks. Differentiation was not only something found in a philosophy books. It was on her face. All grace to my face, her mother might have said.

"I'm with you, Rebecca. I might choose a young Alfie, but not the one who has trouble getting erections. I've had enough of karma."

"Isn't he the one you told me about? The asshole?"

"Yes, that's the one. As my mother says, turn around is fair play, whatever that means."

"What's good for the goose is good for the gander," said Rebecca, laughing. "Why do mothers always take over when we're in the bathroom?"

"We let our guard down and they know it. They know when we're most vulnerable. I don't know squat, to coin a bathroom metaphor. They just seem to know when we need a good talking to."

That was enough to send the conversation into high gear.

The two women bandied about their future roles as soldier, sailor, priest or spy and why the mischief in the eye. Colette was now open to all possibilities. A man might have said she was pumped up, estrogen there for the taking. Only her nipples twitched.

124

That night Colette dreamed that she was a robed warrior, a samurai; her hair was pulled back in a ponytail and a knife rested between her teeth. She steadied herself on this medieval stage holding up a mirror that Savonarola had not yet crushed, praising her own beauty and steadfastness, awaiting the emperor's command.

The command came and the samurai was transformed into a roly-poly Michelin Man, wide-eyed, bouncy and looking around for a villain to subdue. The warrior found his mark, circled him like a snake, and as they rolled down a hill of heather, put him in a full nelson and leg scissors. Without as much as a how-do-you-do, the warrior slit the man's throat with no obvious blood spatter or venous wounding. The chant the dreamer heard in the background was a guttural and primitive version of "Who Let the Dogs Out."

Colette awoke to clean hands and the sense that she had participated in a highly stylized, murderous dance directed by forces outside her control. She felt a deep reverence for the archetypal forces that had stirred her up and banished other icons to the periphery of this pantomime. She looked for some sectarian language that would carry this blessed, watershed moment, but all she could find, parked in that special ether of her own making, was a fast food commercial, "We Have the Meats!" delivered in the deepest male voiceover belonging to an actor who had already left the room.

For the first time in a long while, Colette felt fullness in her belly.

Chapter Sixteen

Colette said to her small Trent study group, "I'm not here to visit shrines and watch someone die over and over again, waiting for the ending to change. Don't you know that's the definition of insanity?"

Colette felt that she was showing off and wanted to pull back her words, which must have come from some minor Victorian romance novelist or a dream she half-remembered.

"If you ask me," Luther Martin responded, "the whole damn thing is insane. We have princesses, nuncios, theologians, Vatican secret police, blood letters, money changers and the whole nine yards in and out of Trent for what, eighteen years, bitching and moaning that it was too hot or too cold or they weren't receiving some princely stipend or bribe on time, and just what the hell did they come away with?"

Colette would have to ask Luther about his name.

"They came away with what became the modern-day prayer book and missal. These still exist in a similar form today. A lot of our rituals about marriage and the importance of family came from Trent. We have a lot to thank these blood letters for."

She was pleased Murphy Braun, a priest in training, had a sense of humor. She wanted to go somewhere with his name, turn it around a few times and find other forms, but now was not the time or place to play with brawn, brain or brown.

Colette felt at home in this study group and hoped it would provide some protection from the doctrine that seemed to be overwhelming her. She was pleased that at least two other people were poking around Trent, even though for them the council wasn't a thesis project.

"What's your take on Trent, Colette?" asked Luther. "Professor Gleason said you had been studying it for a few months."

She would have to ask him about his military fatigues and why he was sporting a tattoo of a beast on his right forearm that could have come right out of William Blake or Yeats. Colette thought about the beast slouching towards Bethlehem to be born. She hoped this study group would hatch something less ominous.

"Yes, I have. Trent seemed such a big event and had such ramifications for so long, I figured I would take it slow, look around, visit Venice, and focus on the back story. Of course, I am keenly interested in the impact the council had on women."

Colette was surprised by how sensuous her language sounded.

"In a way, Trent is an old, worn story that has been regurgitated for centuries. The first Trent manuscript was written about fifty years after the fact and seemed to be based on a mix of pique, gossip, threats and power politics. Later we get some hagiography, an Anglican screed, and Trent recast in the middle of a Venetian Madonna-whore fairy tale."

Her two study companions laughed. They looked at each other, perhaps wondering if they were on the same page.

"That was great, Colette! Now I see why Gleason sent you in our direction. I understand there are many angles and points of view. But at the end of the day wasn't Trent really a power struggle between a line of popes and the European powers? You know, the Church versus state thing?"

"That is exactly right, Luther. France, Germany and to a lesser extent Spain were engaged in a political dance with the Vatican during these decades. By 1545, Lutherans had a substantial foothold in Germany, but the emperor didn't want to go to war with the Vatican for fear of domestic repercussions. France was Catholic and had its own agenda. For nationalistic reasons Germany wanted an agreement with Rome."

"Politics was just the context," responded Murphy. "Trent was about a great religious struggle. It was an answer to the Reformation, though a very late one at that. Trent was really about the battle for the souls of people. I would put doctrine at the center of any discussion."

Colette was tempted to sway to the music as she hummed to herself: And this way and that way, this way and that, retracing her footsteps among the carnage that gave birth to Trent.

"And what say thee, Colette?" Luther asked, sounding a bit like Clement, who might still be kicking around Palestine, looking for sinners and new ways to bury the dead.

"Certainly doctrine would be at the center of any discussion," she replied. "But my research has suggested that elevating doctrine to a level of the one truth has consequences. Look at the effect that crazy priest Savonarola had on the feminine. We're still paying the price."

"Is that a fair characterization? Savonarola was fighting against excess and wantonness," said Murphy Braun. "The Mardi Gras in Florence was a scandal."

"Sounds like he was kicking some ass," said Luther.

"He was a smoking gun," Colette said, trying out her martial tone. "Savonarola was one of many trying to stamp out the soul of man and woman, sometimes with his own boots. The Vatican was only different in degree. The Inquisition and manuscript burnings started centuries before Trent in response to an old fear."

"You mean the Church feared for our immortal souls?" asked Murphy.

"Yes, the Church saw that as a danger, but there were deeper fears. The Church had long feared ancient literature. Pope Pius V called the printing press the devil's work. Rome was suspicious of poets, artists and public recitations and lived uncomfortably alongside Renaissance artists. Rome was even more suspicious of the feminine form. This is an old itch that goes back to Aristotle.

"I realize I might be showing my biases here. The focus for my thesis is on the influence of the Council of Trent on the feminine in the Catholic Church. I am also paying attention to counterweights to Trent, especially the mythology, art and rudimentary psychology that flourished during the Italian Renaissance. I get the sense that as the Church matured, if that's the right word, the feminine became more frozen in time and theology."

The study session seemed to have become academic and the participants drifted away. Her Trent was becoming clearer.

Colette reflected on what more she might have said.

She recalled Trollope's book about Pope Paul V and Fra Sarpi, the Venetian friar who had written about Trent and was a mysterious but influential figure in the years after the council. She recalled saying earlier to Professor Gleason that Trollope took a long, unsentimental Victorian view of Trent and could still hear the Vatican shaking in its boots three hundred years later. Trollope must have been hearing things.

Colette raised some of these issues when she next met with Gleason.

"Professor Gleason, I think the Council of Trent was not that concerned with the Protestant Reformation."

"That is something of a novel reading of the event. What brought you to that conclusion?"

"From what I've read of Trent, the Protestant concerns didn't get much of a hearing."

"That is true, but wasn't it mainly because Rome didn't want to give them the notoriety?"

"I suppose. I don't know what a psychological reading of Trent might look like. Didn't the Church ignore the obvious; especially the selling of indulgences and the like, knowing that after Trent, one way or another, the priests would have to clean up their act? I can't remember where I read

128

this, but surely no Church official thought the old corrupt ways could continue indefinitely."

"I'm no mind reader, Ms. McGovern, but we're getting a little far afield. We remain a fact-based organization. What is your source for this view of Trent? Our friend Trollope?"

"Yes, he had the benefit of time and a perspective. He seemed to think that the doctrinal matters resolved at Trent were like black magic to the modern mind. He suggested that the real danger the Church perceived, even on a subconscious level, was modernity. Trollope wrote that at the time of Trent the Church still had men who created treatises, folios, volumes and encyclopedias and, with the printing press, they became obsolete overnight."

"The Church was not completely stupid. She adapted rather well to the printing press."

"I understand, Professor Gleason. But the Church's first response to the printing press was banning books. Some books were banned even before they were published. I read that more manuscripts and books were banned in the decades before Trent than in the previous century. Trent struggled with this and a new Index was published in 1564. I also read that the Index of Prohibited Books survived until the 1950s and included almost every fiction and non-fiction writer of consequence for centuries. One of the last books put on the list was *The Second Sex* by Simon de Beauvoir that pointed the finger at the Church for its role in institutionalizing misogyny."

"I don't know the number of banned books," replied Gleason. "It was an unsettling time, with many people believing the world was coming to an end. The Calvinists and Anabaptists played into this theme. People were doing desperate things. The books added later were part of a moral advisory."

"I do wonder why Trent reads like a long catechism class taught by very unruly teachers." Colette was surprised by her own language.

"That's a strange way to put it. What exactly do you mean?"

"It's just a feeling. As you know, there's no definitive work about Trent, one that is based on full access to Vatican documents. The books I've consulted about Trent seem to reflect a particular age and seem full of biases. The book by Sarpi in the early seventeenth century and published in England seemed to be based in part on sources who actually attended the council, but even this book seemed politicized."

"Perhaps the truth about Trent is in the outcome, Ms. McGovern, the modern day Church?"

"Perhaps, Professor. Every writer I've read had an angle and an axe to grind. In moments of levity I've wondered what Trent might sound like if it was made into a musical."

Colette didn't know why she was opening herself up this way. She had seen the *Book of Mormon* two years earlier but there seemed more to her outburst. She recalled a recent dream in which she was armed with a cutlass and in the middle of a fantasy fight to repel borders on a pirate ship. It seemed like a scene from the "Pirates of the Caribbean," except in the rigging above the melee was a framed holy book. She seemed to be fighting for the right not to read it but at the same time it seemed out of reach.

She heard a voice cautioning her: "Nice and easy does it every time."

"Now you are really going off the rails."

The phrase sounded familiar, as if Mrs. Doubtfire was in the room.

Colette sensed that she might be stuck in the middle of one of Jung's complexes which contained enough energy to blow up the Council of Trent. She had to slow down. She wondered whether she was fighting back. Colette almost laughed out loud remembering the fantasy exchange between Merkel and Gleason fed by Peter's version of the old gods fornicating in the heavens. Fuck it, she thought, and blamed the Bronx for her vulgarity.

"I'm not suggesting an actual musical be made, though the *Book of Mormon* is popular, probably because it replaces the theological hammer with a sing-along. I saw the play and thought it was great. But think about it. You have the basic historical story line with the popes in the middle and France, Germany, and Spain all squabbling at a distance but sometimes out in the open. For the eighteen years of the council, with its stops and starts and interruptions for the plague, low water in the reservoir, or lack of funds, the religious and secular powers probed each other's strengths and weaknesses. They threatened each other, created buffer zones, bribed neighboring states, raised the ante and thrust their chests out but were careful not to go too far and upset the apple cart. That's the eighteen-year dance."

"Go on."

"Then we have all the intrigue at the council, the backbiting, the deals, the ceremony, the rituals and the endless lip service to the concerns of the Protestant reformers. By no stretch was it a brokered convention. Rome cooked the books and dominated the attendees so that there was never really any doubt that the Vatican's agenda would be approved. The council didn't really deal with the furor over indulgences or the marriage of priests or other hot button issues. They swept them under the rug. The delegates rarely ever read the final doctrinal proposals before they were voted on. It was a sham. So we either go straight to the Greek formula or bring in the Monty Python crowd, who at least would give the impression that they actually attended Trent. They are able to speak perfect Medieval Latin on the first try. They even look like those nuncios from Milan or perhaps Venice. These guys can dance, tell jokes and preach at the same time."

"Harsh words indeed, Ms. McGovern. You should know that the Monty Python crowd had a lot of fans among the priesthood who can occasionally celebrate its own failings. Now, just out of curiosity, where does the idea of musical come in? I haven't found much to sing about in your remarks."

'It's a work in progress, Professor. I'd go back to the old stand-by, the Greek chorus. Anyway, the Greek chorus comments on the action, pointing out dangers, subtleties, unintended consequences, karma and the like. The chorus made for a much more interesting play. Otherwise, everyone would have left early."

"I understand the Greek chorus. So our Trent the Musical will have a Greek chorus that provides theatergoers with the inside story of Trent, whatever that is?"

"I'm still working on that. Maybe the chorus would voice the views of those who were not heard at Trent. I'm still looking for female characters that could play this role. Maybe Mrs. Turnbull shows up in her proper English accent warning Venice about the pirates, funded by the pope, who were breaching the city walls. Aphrodite would be welcome. Perhaps Artemis could attend with the Virgin Mary who replaced her and took over her altar at Ephesus?"

Colette was not ready to invite to the musical stage the very feminine Pope John Paul II of her dream, slipping delicately into Mother Earth and chanting the feminine down. She immediately dismissed any mention of her vagina dream. Perhaps Pope Francis would show up in his cloak of humility.

"Then, maybe one of the Monty Python gang participates in a duel with the nuncios over the question of the Virgin birth with very broad swords. Perhaps he battles three theologians, tied together in one body, about the Trinity, blindfolded and with one hand tied behind his back. After a decisive victory he exits stage left singing 'I must confess; I'm a Muttering Nuncio,' in perfect Medieval Latin."

Colette imagined Carl Jung walking across the stage, muttering and shaking his head, looking for the feminine in Christian theology. He finally admitted the Assumption really hadn't worked out in the way he had expected.

"In addition to the Monty Python bunch, who's on stage?"

"Protestants, sir. Lutherans in particular. Who knows? Martin Luther could show up after being granted safe passage. Perhaps we'd bring in some of the Greek gods if we could reassemble the shards of crushed icons. Perhaps Clement could make sure Simon Magus got equal time. The two of them still seem to be hanging around the neighborhood."

"There are at least six popes turning over in their graves. You might recall the standing ovation given at the Council of Trent when participants learned Martin Luther had died. I believe an abundance of wine was shipped in from Vicenza and Verona for the celebration. If you intend to take Trent the Musical to Broadway, keep in mind that Luther was a raging anti-Semite, a self-proclaimed prophet and probably out of his mind. Any more suggestions for your chorus?"

Colette almost said that Luther learned all his anti-Semitism from the Catholic Church, but refrained. She considered inviting on stage all the popes who claimed the Jews killed Christ. She wanted to suggest Jesus for a bit part but decided no one would recognize him.

Colette recovered her footing. "Perhaps we could hear from the Jesuits who were converting Brazil during the time of Trent for another perspective."

"And what might that be?"

"As Professor Merkel explained it, Brazil was perceived as the New Eden, fleshy and natural. Doctrine trampled the feminine all over again."

Colette was dying to mention the *Book of Mormon* missionaries in Uganda and General Fucking-Butt-Naked and his plan for female genital mutilation for the entire village because he feared the clitorises would rise in unison and destroy him. She thought of the missionaries filling out their religious narrative with characters like Darth Vader. Was it Jesus who appeared in the play and called a missionary a dick?

Was all this drama also found at the Council of Trent and in early councils, in medieval tones and shades, in the mysteries and the miracles that became dogma and cudgel, understated, divine and dangerous? Just what happened to all the women in the village?

"The good man certainly knows how to bring drama to the occasion," said Gleason.

As if on cue, Professor Merkel walked into the room and broke into song.

"Damn their torments, damn their lies; we will see the people rise!"

Colette and Gleason exchanged glances indicating confusion and the fear that someone else was writing the narrative.

"I take it that cameo was not in your script, Ms. McGovern?"

"No, sir, though I could have sworn the correct words were 'damn their warnings, damn their lies.' I guess he must have heard us talking."

132

The Greek chorus and the musical were running out of steam, and the participants backed away from one other, wary as if they were actually standing at the barricades of *Les Miserables*. By now, Professor Merkel's cameo might well have been a mirage, though Colette was still struggling with the words "torments" and "warnings" and settled on the fact that they both could be saying something about her or Trent or both. Everyone seemed to be setting up barricades—the popes, the Jesuits, the princes, the theologians, St. Peter, the crazies, and those yet to be driven out in the open. Then they filled their songs, slogans and doctrines with scripture, piety, and eternal damnation. She would have given good money to see the Monty Python troupe storming the beaches in Brazil, shedding their swords, boots and underwear as they stumbled into the New Eden and a conga line of breasts, speaking Latin like natives and baptizing in newly named ocean inlets everyone who came into their line of vision and had trinkets to trade for this indulgence.

Gleason had said he was glad that she was having her fun. "It's always easier to walk around the edges of a burning building than through the heart of the flames."

Colette kept coming back to the heart of the matter, with the meanings shifting as she moved back in time. She had just read that when some men lined up at the wrong barricades, they had their hearts cut out. Eleven Anabaptist men had their hearts cut out during the Munster Riots in 1530. She wondered what that specific organ had to do with a theology that claimed that baptism was an adult affair. It was a little easier to understand why an Anabaptist bishop had his tongue cut out and his hands cut off; then he was beheaded. She wondered what organ she would have to give up for her sin.

Colette was at the barricades again; Munster was the New Jerusalem. She read that one thousand adults were baptized on the first day. A rival bishop was killed, and his genitals were nailed to the city gate. Welcome to Zion, home to polygamy and unrelenting orgies. Public nudity was allowed. We will end sexual shame forever. David chose fifty wives who would give him many lives. All believers were priests.

Colette thought of other imaginary worlds she had traveled to, all the New Jerusalem's that had appeared along the way. At the moment she needed some relief from hide-bound theology and went to William Blake's "Marriage of Heaven and Hell" for another voice. The poet offered his own mythology.

"The ancient poets animated all sensible objects with the gods and imagined the divine in woods, rivers and mountains. Then a system called priesthood was founded. This took the gods out of nature. Then the priests pronounced that the Gods had ordered such things. Thus men forgot that all deities reside in the human heart."

William Blake was fond of the Book of Numbers: "Would to God that all the Lord's people were prophets."

Did the man know about Munster? Had the poet visited Trent as well as the New Millennium? He seemed to have understood the nuncios. Was Professor Merkel, who collapsed after saying something similar, channeling Blake?

Colette now understood why the Catholics and the Lutherans cut the hearts out of the Anabaptists. She also understood why some Ugandan war lord shoved the Book of Mormon up a missionary's ass.

Didn't the Ugandans have the last laugh, revealing they knew all along that the Mormon stories were metaphors and not literally true? This was the musical's punch line.

Had they been visited by Jung's small, vexing gods who usurped control over their lives? Would they have laughed at Trent doctrine which would have become part of their sing-along, a joyful version of her still unscripted "I'm a Muttering Nuncio"?

Despite all her bluster, Colette no longer felt like laughing. She had seen a headline in the New York Daily News about a female politician. "Nevertheless, She Persisted," it read. She had seen women at her college sporting tattoos with this headline.

Colette had an image of herself walking through Gleason's burning building while feeling the newspaper headline being burned from her lips, head and heart.

God help me, she thought.

Chapter Seventeen

Colette had a dream in which she was opening an oversized textbook. Her gaze fell on the first sentence, which was about the Virgin Mary. The line was more like a series of keywords than a free flowing sentence with the words Virgin and Mary appearing somewhat askew, as if ripped out of context. Thick slices of what appeared to be the breast meat of chickens were spread out unevenly at the top of the page. She thought the meat looked very red and brown, as if it had been out in the sun too long. She struggled to discover inside the dream the connection between a reference to the Virgin Mary and the red meat that appeared on the page, rotting before her eyes. Colette thought that she could be ripping words out of context and combining them to form new meanings. She wasn't sure if the blood red meat was the result of her "cooking" or a running commentary on the last few months. She wondered whether her approach to Trent was like chasing red meat that seemed rancid and indigestible, and whether this dream was a warning: if she continued to "rip apart" doctrine and theology, the net result would be dead meat and carcasses. She tried hard not to think that this dream had anything to do with her abortion.

Colette adorned the Virgin Mary dream page in her journal with dozens of question marks, exclamation points and other marks of exasperation. She slammed her journal shut and hurried to Professor Merkel's class. She had a feeling that her dreams were increasingly finding their way into the daylight.

She wasn't entirely surprised when Merkel walked into class wearing satin slippers, a weathervane on his head and a blood red bishop's hat tucked under his right arm. And if the man had started singing lines from the incomplete "Trent the Musical," she might have joined him.

When he got closer, she observed that the weathervane was anchored by a black skull cap. The professor remained quiet for a few minutes as if waiting for someone to offer an opinion or observation. No one did.

"Now my Trentonians, let me ask: Which way does the wind blow?" With that, he nudged the weathervane into circulation and recited: "Round and round it goes and where it stops nobody knows!"

Then he broke into song which borrowed a tune from "HMS Pinafore" with new words: "The moral of this story for one and all, if you want to get the clarion call is ....is what, Mr. Luther Martin?"

"We need to know which way the wind blows."

"Bravo to the man who carries the Protestant Reformation daily! Now which way does the wind blow, dear sir?"

"It depends, Professor. Weather vanes and compasses have to be compensated for the earth's magnetic field if they are to be true. There could be a fifteen or twenty degrees difference in some places."

"Bravo, again! I presume you didn't learn that in philosophy class. Where, pray tell?"

"When I was in the Army, sir."

"And Semper Fi to you, sir, in my very best Latin."

"Thank you."

"Now that we know which way the wind blows, what the hell does that have to do with Trent?"

"Based on my readings about this historical period, 'compensation' seems a good word. There seems so much going on at Trent, so much confusion and points of view that we have to find a way to balance all that self-interest."

"Interesting, Ms. McGovern. Now what about the self-interest?"

"Germany and France wanted a hand in the agenda. The various popes wanted to control the proceedings. The smaller delegations wanted a voice. And there seemed a genuine desire throughout on the part of many, at least outside of Trent, to address the concerns of the Protestant Reformation."

"To Mr. Martin's point, where's the compensation? How can I keep my weathervane pointing true north?"

"The compensation comes in the form of course correction, sir. We entertain various points of view. People have been writing about the Council of Trent for hundreds of years. We consider all these views, balance them, and come to our conclusions."

"But, Ms. McGovern, don't we have the official Trent version? Didn't Pope Pius IV declare the doctrines agreed on at Trent to be infallible teachings of the Church and declare that those who didn't agree were heretics and preachers of anathema? Attendees could not even change a syllable in the manuscripts. Are we flirting with anathema?"

Colette laughed and waited unsuccessfully for a chorus to join her.

"Yes, sir. We have the official Trent version that seemed to have been rushed out the door without being fully read by the attendees and given immediately to the pope for his approval. This sounds like bad fiction. Some accounts suggest that he rewarded nineteen of his supporters with appointments to the College of Cardinals and other goodies."

"So the fix was in?"

"I think Pope Pius IV got the results that the other popes who reigned during the council pushed for. The demands of Germany and France to address concerns of Martin Luther were ignored. Protestant attendees didn't even get a vote."

"And how was our dear friend Martin Luther treated during these proceedings?"

"The council hated and wanted to kill him. They are still cheering his death," said Murphy Braun.

"Poor thing. Now let's get back to Ms. McGovern's suggestion about compensation. Mr. Luther Martin, does that pass the Army smell test?"

"Yes, sir. I think it does."

Merkel removed the weathervane from his head and pried off with his fingers the skull cap which seemed to be attached with glue. He put on the bishop's hat and confirmed in the bookcase glass that it was the correct three fingers above the brow, offering a military salute to prove he was right.

He turned smartly towards the class and asked, "Who am I? Don't stand on ceremony. Fast and furious, please."

Three distinct voices from the back of the classroom responded to the professor's demand in turn. Colette listened.

"You could be a bishop or a cardinal."

"You look like New York's Cardinal Dolan without the gut."

"With the satin slippers, you look a little like Fra Sarpi, that monk who wrote the book about Trent. But he was much shorter. A midget, I heard. Wasn't he excommunicated? I heard he was gay. I heard he was in a convent ménage à trois. I heard his cute red slippers were beatified."

Merkel took everything in and continued.

"Stay focused, my good and generous souls! Look for patterns and sleight of hand. Be aware of what the professor has up his sleeves."

Merkel seemed to be painting a picture with his hands. He motioned for two female students to come to the front of the class. As they shuffled forward, he described the pantomime the students were to be engaged in. He begged the class for a willing suspension of disbelief.

"My dear Trentonians, please look for a touch of Titian in this scene which these beauties and I are about to act out. A little background, first. This imagined painting, which we have studied, is of Pope Paul III and his

137

grandsons, painted just in time for the opening of Trent. That was 1545-1546 to the uninitiated. The Pope was a real hack job, fathering four illegitimate children and putting his grandsons in high Church positions."

He motioned for the two female students to come alongside him.

"Welcome grandsons Allessandro and Ottavio to center stage. We also need some craggy faced gentleman to sit in for Pope Paul III. Luther Martin, you will do for our craggy pope. Hold that vision."

Two young women joined Merkel and were given cardinal hats retrieved from the waste paper basket. Luther was given a cloak, miter and some kind of skull cap. The women took positions on either side of the newly declared pope, one looking on menacingly behind him, the other showing a little too much leg. Colette imagined she was seeing things and formed the words, "holy shit" which took her back to the Crusades and the solders covering their faces and bodies with papal shit. Everything was beginning to make sense.

"Well done," Merkel said. "We now have the unholy Trinity. And I have satisfied the number one requirement of my pedagogy: push 'show and tell' to its obscene limits in order to hold your blessed attention. Hold that vision! Hold that thought!"

Merkel rolled an easel to the front of the classroom and unveiled with a flourish a large reproduction of the actual Titian painting, as if he were opening a museum.

"What shall we call all this art and all this folly?"

"An embarrassment of riches," said Murphy Braun,

"Bless you, sir. You have a future in a world that wears long black gowns! But why the two decidedly unequal depictions of Titian's masterpiece?"

Colette saw that the three models were becoming restless and probably asking themselves the same thing.

"You wanted to remind us that art transforms and brings out what makes us human in all its guises."

"I hope you smoke, Ms. Aimes, because you are dead on, and you get the cigar!"

"Thank you, professor," she replied.

Merkel continued. "Please keep your eyes on all that is sacred and profane in front of our eyes. Watch the colors change, the faces twitch and justice prevail.

"Notice Allessandro in his cardinal's dress and hat, right hand splayed as if he is in prayer or going to cut the old man's throat. The knife would be hidden in the cassock. And the younger, ready to pay benediction to the old man. For my money, the kid is showing too much silken leg and is a

138

bit of the dandy. I would hazard we can't trust that man of the expensive cloth."

For effect Merkel moved the knife in the hand of Allessandro's stand-in towards Pope Luther Martin's throat. The class burst out laughing.

"Better if you laugh at this pope's extravagance, improprieties, graft, opportunism, and impiety. No offense Mr. Martin! Laugh at the indulgences he sold and the scale of his theft and corruption. But follow your eyes and not your nose. Look at the truth and redemption in this portrait. See Titian's cunningly complex art showing an old but imposing pope surrounded by sycophants. He was still center stage and steely. Contemplate his white shroud, the clock and hints that time was passing. Doesn't his face tell you he knew all of this?

"This is Titian's genius; this is the pope's genius because he set Trent in motion, disease-ridden and contagious to be sure. This old man was the father of the Council of Trent because he still carried the smell of Rome burning in 1527 in his rather large and prominent nose and, old as he was, took notice. Talk about smoke and mirrors! Stay focused on the art of the Catholic Counter Reformation and let the dogma that will now come by the hundred weight fall at your feet as necessary entreaties. Now let me count the ways and stipulate the admonitions."

As Professor Merkel prepared for his next remarks by doing knee bends and a few jumping jacks, Titian's models quietly returned to their seats, casting off their clerical garb as they walked and bowing dramatically to their classmates who applauded.

The professor took a few deep breaths and continued. "We have come to the Council of Trent, virginal and in the raw. We have been summoned by his holiness with the big nose. Please open your ears and let the blessed doctrine pour in. Listen to my soft melodic invocations which are delivered to you with wit and purpose and through the glass, darkly. Mirror, mirror on the wall, why do we stumble before we fall?"

Colette almost fell out of her chair hearing all that mirror and glass talk from Merkel. Had he been reading her mind? Had he too been circling Trent like an outcast, poking holes in the perimeter?

Professor Merkel began.

"Don't be caught up in the sanctimonious chatter from the Trent halls that among Catholic priests hardly one can be found who is not a notorious fornicator. Please do not dwell on the fact that incest, masturbation, homosexuality and bestiality were declared heretical and anathema, with rape yet to be mentioned.

"Do not put yourself between Pope and emperor, who were squabbling about who could hold the chalice and in what hand. To be sure, dwell on the mystery and not the transaction. Stay with clean hands and hearts. Do not align yourself with those who would find heresy in the wine spilled on the altar cloth.

"Do not side with those reformers who desire vulgar tongues delivering the Mass or demand lascivious songs, noises and screeches in the presence of the Redeemer.

"Be wary of those who say the Mass is simply a commemoration; that vestments are incitements to unworldliness; and that water should not be commingled with wine. Remember that the Council of Basel denied the cup to Bohemians. Remember, he who demands the communion cup cannot be Catholic.

"Do not walk in the shoes of the Bishop of Sequoia who has said of Trent that nuncios did imitate unskilled physicians who gave lectures or anointed with oil a mortal disease. Do not use language idly. Do not needlessly decorate your words with descriptions when the Church fathers have given us solid, weighty, and unpoetic language with which to frame our thoughts.

"Do not be misled by the Bishop of Sidonia's use of gratuitous metaphors when he said the Pope should himself be reformed because darkness could not be taken from the stars except if it were removed from the sun. Beware of those who think themselves co-equal creators and gods, even as they speak rubbish.

"Do not side with the Lutherans who in their primitive mentality can't understand the difference between adoring Christ and venerating the saints, as we learned from the blessed bishops at the Council in Nicaea in 787. All praise to the image; all praise to the artist!

"Do not dispute Pope Leo X's infallible wisdom in banning books that had been read for one hundred, two hundred, or five hundred years or the Inquisition's righteousness, declaring that the world already had too many books. It is better to forbid a thousand books without cause than to permit one bad apple to get through. Reflect on the damage the apple had already caused.

"Do not resist the divinely inspired doctrine that says it is perfectly acceptable to go to war over Original Sin, sacred relics and masturbation.

"Do not travel with those who argue that women were not given a place at Trent, and we had to wait centuries before the Virgin Mary was put on the agenda and given a place in our hearts. Do not break bread with those who say the Doctrine of the Immaculate Conception was a centuries old myth created by crazed, celibate men and intended to deny the flesh and demonize sex.

"Do not exaggerate the Trent doctrine that stated man could only violate someone else's marriage but not his own, while his own marriage

140

can only be violated by the wife to whom his has given riches, children and safety.

"Do not hold up to ridicule the Trent doctrine that, when referring to the push for married priests stated, 'If anyone says that it is not better and more godly to live in virginity or in an unmarried state than to marry, let him be anathema.'

"Do not mock our blessed brothers, the guardians of our special morality, for declaring the face and hands honorable, the arms and chest less honorable, and the thighs and sexual organs dishonorable. They were merely taking their cues from the wise Aristotle and our blessed Church fathers, Augustine and Aquinas, who advised we keep our eyes and senses focused on the spirit rising to the Godhead and not on the flanks of someone in heat.

"Do not embrace the Venetian Friar Sarpi and his friar hacks who called the Council of Trent an Iliad of outrage, when his books are filled with pagan gods and goddesses who copulate on weekends as well as holy days and therefore have been consigned to hell."

Colette felt that she had been listening to a quick-paced rendition of the Ten Commandments served up with the "Thou Shalt Nots" collected over a lifetime and bits and pieces of the Trent narrative which had been dragged out of a reluctant class. The mention of the Virgin Mary reminded her of those words spilled and broken on her dream page in a pool of blood and sediment. Aphrodite broke into her reverie and the goddess became co-mingled with the other elements on the page, serving up a dish of love and remembrance. Colette wondered how many more goddesses needed to be killed.

Merkel, who had sat in a chair in the front row of the class after his oration, stood up and appeared to be looking for his Titian stand-ins.

"Now where were we before getting sidetracked with Titian's parade and that delicious volley of Trent dogma?"

No response.

"I don't blame you for falling off or falling away. Sometimes I do go on. I must remember to take my meds and remember my dispensations."

A few snickers.

"We were talking about compensation," Merkel continued. "Trent was a long time ago. Over the years, there have been a few books on the subject, including at least one with the Vatican's blessing. As we have learned they all seem to be uneven and biased in one way or the other. How do we balance the various views?"

"Professor Merkel, about your remarks on Trent. You seemed to level a broadside against Trent and certain doctrines. At the same time your remarks sounded like a listicle; you know, an Internet meme designed to attract a lot of clicks. This is a list as a thematic structure."

"Thank you, Ms. Aimes. You mean I am finally current, trending and clickable?"

"I guess you are, professor. But my question is: was your list to get our attention or a statement about theology?"

"My list, as you put it, was to get your attention, wake up the Trent crowd, bring you to images, underscore the danger in theology, encourage you to think for yourselves and remind you that we tend to shape and revision the history of religion to our purpose. In other words, history is a kind of fiction, even Church history. The bible can be considered a fiction written and rewritten by a thousand hands, seen and unseen, most with an axe to grind. My prattling should not be viewed as the one truth. Does this help?"

"I think so. Thanks."

"I'll have to think a little about listicles. I suppose the Beatitudes would be an example of this form: Blessed are the poor in spirit for theirs is the kingdom of heaven."

Colette thought she might have another musical in the works.

"Professor Merkel. Can we get back to Rebecca's question about the central contribution of Trent?"

"By all means, Ms. McGovern. Please proceed."

"I felt a little lost when you provided your listicles; some seemed to present straight dogma. At other times, your tone seemed slightly parodic."

"Quite right! As I mentioned earlier, this was intentional, a reminder of the theological hammer and of the fiction we call gospel truth."

"Can you explain what you mean by the fiction we call gospel truth?" asked Colette.

"I'll try," responded Merkel. "We know the gospel truth in the bible resides in the eye of the beholder. Some hear the voice of God while others hear fiction, sometimes serious, sometimes laughable but fiction nonetheless. Of course, this deadly divide is not funny. You have studied the many wars fought over doctrine. The blueprint for the modern Catholic Church that was produced at the Council of Trent was developed after centuries of blood and unchristian mayhem. The last witch was burned in Europe the year Jung's grandfather was born.

"I should add that I am not using the word fiction simply in a narrow literary sense. Rather, I mean fiction to represent the torrent of images, symbols and metaphors from the unconscious. So I also mean fiction in the psychological sense.

"But let me try to approach the question from another angle. As the story goes, our dear friend Sigmund Freud, the father of all pathologies, acknowledged in an interview that, although people saw him as a scientist, he was really an artist by nature. He called his case studies fictions and noted that his books are closer to works of the imagination than treatises on pathology. He won the Goethe Prize for Literature."

The class remained quiet, and Merkel seemed to sense they weren't with him.

"Okay, let's look at it this way. We have heard a fair bit about Trent as dogma, listicle, politics, and the like. I rained down on you a series of dogmatic listicles, some that Freud might have enjoyed, to simulate the Zeus, thunderbolt effect. Remember my blessed attention to show and tell."

Luther Martin broke the silence with a loud "Semper Fi," and the class seemed to relax.

"Okay, back to Freud. We learn in the same interview that Freud really thought he was writing novels. So what, pray tell, in terms of language would be the difference between a novel and a scientific paper?"

"The language itself, Professor," responded Colette. "The novel is an imaginative act, rich in symbols and imagery. The scientific paper is based on observable facts."

"Exactly. Now why would Freud embrace the form of the novel?"

"Perhaps he needed or wanted more freedom," replied Rebecca. "He was writing about the psychology of people and their darkest secrets. Perhaps he needed somewhere to hide?"

"Nicely put. Thank you. What do you think Freud was hiding from, Ms. Aimes?"

"In another class I studied Freud's seduction theory. Early in his career he considered sexual abuse reported by his patients, mainly women, to be true. Later he changed his mind and considered these reports fantasy."

"Now why would he do a thing like that, Ms. Aimes?"

"I'm not sure. He didn't get much support from his colleagues. This seemed to be the patriarchy talking. I had read he was a fan of some weird doctor who treated excessive menstrual bleeding by operating on the woman's nose. It seemed absolutely nuts. I also read that he moved away from real world issues, the wounding. He seemed eager to get to Oedipus and that full family fantasy tale."

"Thank you, Ms. Aimes. Very nice indeed! As you might know, Freud had been accused of making changes in his letters and case studies about the seduction theory to support this shift in opinion and perhaps to support that crazy nose doctor you mentioned. So what are we to make of these juicy tidbits about fiction and revised text?"

"Well, what you and Rebecca described seemed like a cover-up."

"Thank you, Mr. Martin. Covering up what?"

Rebecca replied.

"Perhaps he was unable to separate the trauma from the myth. Perhaps he was too much of a literalist. A teacher said that Freud perceived memories as if they were items in a cauldron, waiting to bubble over. Memories remained personal for him."

"And for Jung, Ms. McGovern?"

"I read a Jung quote that goes something like this: 'What we don't face consciously comes back as fate.'"

Colette paused to reflect on her own fate and then continued.

"I've read that Jung was more in tune with the deep archetypal energies than Freud, though Freud obviously embraced myth. Perhaps Jung was able to see more fully both the wound in a story or a memory and as well as the archetypal, unconscious dimensions.

"Myths are perspectives, Professor, ways of seeing," continued Colette, reciting words she must have heard while knocking around with Clement in the Holy Land or while eavesdropping on her professors.

"Brilliant, Ms. McGovern! Now let's bring this baby home, which means the Council of Trent. Who would be more comfortable at Trent, Mr. Freud or Mr. Jung?"

"Based on Rebecca's remarks about Freud and the patriarchy," said Colette, "I think Freud would be more at home. I've read that Freud's interpretation of dreams was allegorical while Jung's was metaphorical. This seems close to the Church's teaching on images in general. I read somewhere that Freud's movement was linear, rational and masculine while Jung's movement was circular, symbolic and feminine.

"Also, Jung was very conscious of the lack of the feminine in the Church and understood that a masculine godhead lacked archetypal roots in the feminine, with all due respects to the Doctrine of the Assumption."

"Ms. Aimes?"

"I agree with Colette. I think Freud's theory of hysteria, though later retracted, could have been articulated by Aristotle or the Church Fathers. The remedy for girls who masturbated frequently and had painful menstruations was to operate on their noses which were thought by Freud to have an intimate connection to a woman's sexual organs. What packing the nose with cocaine had to do with sex, I'm not sure. Freud seemed to fit in nicely with 2,000 years of celibate and religious eunuchs who have had a pathological interest in women's sex organs."

"Ouch," said Merkel, taking the words out of Colette's mouth, and then he recovered.

144

"Yes, indeed, Ms. Aimes. Thank you very much. Freud might have made a few friends at Trent when he suggested 'coitus interruptus' was the very basis of neurosis. Don't get me started on penis envy and Freud's view that having a baby would overcome that disability. He sounded like the priest who said sex before Communion will ruin a mother's milk."

Merkel's voice trailed away, as if he were trying to find his way after his romp through Trent. Colette heard him say something about the fire next time, Florence, and "wait until we get to the nudes."

Colette had looked around the room, anticipating that the sex talk would bring the class to life, but it was as if the class had been looking at an old black and white movie in which someone who looked like Freud was playing with sex toys found on some doctrinal high street. Echoes of her more provocative sex dreams were showing up in the middle of a classroom discussion led by a Jesuit. She felt trapped somewhere between Freud's slippery text and Jung's psychic energy field. The Church Fathers might have been directing traffic.

That night Colette dreamed that she passed eight or so nuns who were standing at a bus stop. She stopped, waved, turned towards the nuns and was ready to say hello when she realized they had become mannequins.

In another dream she entered a church and joined two men in a pew. One man said he didn't dream much the night before or his dreams were light. She said that dreams should be heavy, weighty and punishing so that they left their mark.

Colette woke in a cold sweat, certain that her body and soul contained all the marks she could possibly absorb.

Chapter Eighteen

That same night Colette awoke from a dream in which an older man told her, "Whatever else happened, or whatever was said, I will hold you in my heart." She felt the dream was personal, heartfelt and ritualistic. As she hurried to Merkel's class, she prayed that the voice she heard in the dream belonged to her father.

By the time she arrived at class, Merkel was going back and forth with Luther Martin about being stuck at the railroad station at Trent. Colette immediately conjured up memories of Robin Williams, Mrs. Doubtfire, and all the times she seemed to be going off the rails.

"Okay, Mr. Martin, I'll play this delicious game. The train will leave shortly. Now that we have Freud, Jung and a bunch of nuncios wrestling over the theology of sex, mythology, and blah, blah, blah, until they are blue in the face, what about the rest of us stuck in that one-horse town called Trent and looking for a little R&R? Where do we go?"

"We go to the local bath house to see Freud, Jung and the nuncios dancing around in their knickers, getting their feminine on."

"I've seen the preview, so no thank you my friend," said Merkel.

Colette didn't recognize the voice making the joke.

"Well, we could take a Roman holiday," said Luther Martin.

"Can someone get us closer to the mother lode?"

"Perhaps we go to art," suggested Rebecca.

"Perhaps we do, Ms. Aimes."

"But what about theology?"

"Good question, Mr. Martin. Theology is still very much with us. I am trying to get inside that fiction called the Italian Renaissance, for a peek and consideration, a little counterweight to Trent. We might ask if this art is indeed a healing fiction, a psychology within itself; or, as one psychologist suggested, a case history within a polytheistic pantheon. I am also trying to see art within Jung's energy field, as Ms. McGovern put it. My so-called 'gospel truth' is no more sacramental than Liar's Poker, a game of small change and big laughs. No forced conversions, I promise."

Luther laughed and Merkel continued.

"So we know the straight-line dogma coming out of the Council of Trent. But were there issues hanging fire? Ms. McGovern?"

"Perhaps they were the things we don't see? In your discussion of the Titian painting of Pope Paul III you suggested that we keep an eye on art, sleight of hand and the changes in light and texture."

"Please, go on."

"The remarks about sacred art in the Trent books I have read seemed to focus on the usual: fear of idolatry; how to venerate sacred images, etc. The remarks were heavy on threats and warnings about icons exciting people to lust and lasciviousness. Talk about a theological hammer."

"Bravo, Ms. McGovern! Well said. This was, as you might say, a mere listicle at Trent, but the discussion of images appropriate to a Christian vision was wrought with implications. For example, could we depict the Virgin Mary engaged in a sex act?"

Colette was tempted to reveal her Virgin Mary dream, but it felt it was too moist. She was not ready for a discussion of dead meat. She didn't like the way this was going.

"We looked at this theme in an art history class," replied Luther Martin. "There have been lots of parodies of the Virgin Mary; the concept seemed to beg for parody. I recall a 1996 painting by a Nigerian-born artist titled 'The Holy Virgin Mary.' It was an oil painting with glitter and elephant dung depicting a black Virgin Mary. It caused a stink, as they say."

"Thanks, Mr. Martin. I recall seeing it at the Brooklyn Museum of Art. Quite sensational really and considered an outrage. I think someone tried to deface it. However, the crowds were enormous, and that tells another tale."

"You mentioned that the Virgin Mary was begging for parody. Please explain."

"I simply meant that the concept is open to parody, as in the Madonna song, 'Like a Virgin.'"

"Right. Sorry to mix my metaphors, but is this a dead-end street? I mean the Virgin Mary is the Virgin Mary, now and forever. Recall that Jung said we view these mysteries symbolically. He said that Mary's elevation satisfied the archetype."

"Professor, perhaps that's precisely the point. Perhaps what is hanging fire are concepts out of reach. I mean they are not part of our consciousness. Mary is the part of the divine architecture and not part of my psychology. Perhaps she's a concept more than an archetype meant to fill out a patriarchal Trinity. And didn't Jung say that the Trinity was not psychologically accurate? In your Trent parody didn't you say this doctrine was an old myth brought to life by crazed old men eager to deny the flesh?"

"Good, Ms. McGovern. Jung referred to this filling out as a "quaternity," adding elements to the godhead like the feminine and physical matter that the Church had repressed. Remember that fairy tale about evil being the absence of good. Go on."

"I'll try. It seems to mean that the theology we have after two thousand years was written in stone and fossilized. It has an abstract, ethereal notion of the feminine. How can it be otherwise when you add the weight of scriptures, received wisdom, scholasticism, patriarchal symbols and particularly the history of papal infallibility? Pius IV declared the findings of Trent infallible without even reading them."

"Ouch. If you don't mind, can we focus on the theology of all this? Are you saying, Ms. McGovern, that theology is outside of us in a way, perhaps transcendent, onward and upward, heavenly and all that?"

"I'm not sure. I recall a writer who differentiated between the soul and spirit, with the spirit being a Christian notion that, as you mentioned, had a transcendent, other-worldly feel to it while the soul is associated with the human psyche and expressed in dreams, nightmares, visions and the like. Image-making is the central task of the psyche. I think Jung said that."

"Beautifully said. Everyone please hang onto the elements in this intriguing thread. Can we take Ms. McGovern's narrative to Trent? Is there a place to hang this hat? Mr. Martin, I see your hand."

"We discussed that Trent issued a decree on sacred images. But it wanted some oversight, if that's the way to put it, over the types and way images were used. I liked Colette's discussion of spirit and soul. But I don't see how the Church would or could police art. I mean, look at all the beautiful Church art."

"Anyone? Ms. Aimes?"

"I'd just add that the infamous Bonfire of the Vanities was a response by Savonarola and his band of brown-shirted thugs to what was considered the excesses of the Italian Renaissance. That was about fifty years before Trent."

"But didn't Trent make moot this gross response to the images associated with art and the feminine? That was then. Didn't the council make another Savonarola highly unlikely?"

"I don't know, Professor," Rebecca Aimes replied.

"Ms. McGovern?"

"As we have touched on before, the Trent view of images, as in earlier councils, seemed more political than psychological. I think Jung pointed out the lack of progress on this subject even before Trent. I recall Aldous Huxley writing in 1945 that Trent focused more on historical time and not on the transcendent functions of religion. In any event how does Rome legislate the way my psyche interacts with an image?"

"Might someone build on Ms. McGovern's incisive remarks?"

"I think the way to look at this, Professor," said Luther Martin "was that Trent affirmed the relevance of sacred images in the Church. That differentiated the Catholic Church from the Protestant Reformation. But I sensed that, with all the talk, sacred images reflected a doctrine of differentiation and was more about policy than art."

"Thanks for the remark and context, Mr. Martin. You have a point. There was only one Savonarola that we know of, but there was widespread concern during the early Italian Renaissance that art was becoming too sensual and secular. When you have a chance, have a look at Antonio Pollaiuolo's 'Battle of the Ten Nudes,' a spectacular engraving from 1465 that looks like an old Roman work about gladiators except they are much prettier. Like Michelangelo and others at this time, Pollaiuolo studied cadavers and got the human form absolutely right. Talk about raising the dead."

"Why do you think the available Trent documents say little about the Church's concern about the whole canvas and not just the images?"

"Good question, Ms. McGovern. I probably haven't read as widely about Trent as you and your classmates, but my guess is that the attendees were rubberstamping what earlier councils had said about the difference between adoring and venerating an image. As you mentioned, Jung said something to this effect. To Mr. Martin's point, others have suggested that this was more about Church politics than art. A psychological reading might put the war inside the heads of clerics and theologians and not on some distant altar. Some might call this religion; others might call it pathology.

"As I intimated, early Renaissance art made the Catholic Church nervous due to the downplaying of religious themes and an emphasis on the subjects that might please the patrons of the arts. Look at Botticelli's 'The Birth of Venus,' painted for the Medici family. Venus is naked on a sea shell, a rather unusual depiction at the time even if you take into account the pagan hangover. Think about the borrowings from Ovid's 'Metamorphosis' and a statue of Aphrodite from Cnidos, which is now in Turkey, I think. This is pagan and classical myth coming together in a voluptuous Venus, and that scared the hell out of the Church. Add a little decadence to that mix, and you have that crazy Savonarola and his punk brigade on their anti-feminine rampage.

"Now is the time, the very best and perfect time," Merkel sang to some melody, "to get inside the Vatican's head. We are thirty years, more or less, before the smallish clerical conga line and hangers-on made their way to Trent, which to Rome was a foreign country with a German pallor. Don't unpack your bags just yet.

"Now think about our friend Luther—not dear Martin here—who bumped into a Dominican friar who was selling indulgences out of the back of his friar wagon by the hundred-weight. Luther was so pissed that he nailed his Ninety-Five Theses to the church door in 1517. In 1520, Pope Leo X got around to ordering Luther to retract all his writings. When the man refused, the Pope excommunicated him and banished him from the various lands. So that was hanging fire big time over the Vatican's head. Hold that thought.

"A few years earlier, Michelangelo, who had been busy with the Sistine Chapel ceiling, escaped Savonarola's wrath by getting out of town. At the four corners of the spectacular Creation painting are images of twenty male nudes called Ignudi, the Italian word for nude. The nudes have been described as a blending of classicism and modern superheroes. The nudes are muscular, athletic and beautiful, some with a distinct feminine appeal. Many are frontal views with full nudity. Some are surrounded by acorns that looked very much like penises or in the Tuscan slang, pickle heads."

Colette thought she saw that look again, with Merkel crawling up the Brazilian beach in the direction of Indian breasts and a brand new Eden.

"So, knowing what we know about Trent and the Reformation stew, what do you think worried the Vatican the most: Luther's doctrine or the human body? Is it luscious Venus with the flowing hair hiding her sex; the homoerotic gladiators who lumber through their graceful moves, Michelangelo's pretty boys on display above the Pope's head or Luther's scripture-based bible thumping?"

"How many Italians do you think saw Venus hiding her sex, Professor?"

"Ah, Ms. Aimes, good question. I think most visitors were more than happy to see Venus in her natural form. Of course, there must have been a few cardinal codgers praying that the sky would fall or others more than happy to look at disgusting male nudes."

"Professor Merkel, did the Council of Trent give the Church cover to push against nudity and sexuality in general? I don't recall much about this subject except the use of religious imagery."

"Excellent, Ms. McGovern. There appears some truth in what you say. Rome was feeling a bit puffed up after Trent. The Jesuits were in ascendancy and anxious to do the Pope's work. There were a lot of hacks around who would paint by the numbers. And there were enough art patrons who winced at nudity and bulging, cavernous pickle heads. We would call them Calvinists. Perseus and Andromeda might still show up on a canvas, but they were about as sexually enticing as Professor Merkel or that plastic adult toy shop on the edge of town. There was the requisite skin, but the images were a little elongated, which influenced perspective. No pickle heads and no cigar!"

The few audible snickers told Colette that few wanted to imagine Merkel on that canvas.

Luther Martin interrupted the silence. "Professor, I vaguely remember the Church's opposition to nudes got silly at times. Could you explain that?"

"Certainly, Mr. Martin. The Church always gets silly around nudes. Having old white men making policy about the flesh hasn't worked very well in two thousand years. You might have in mind Michelangelo's 'The Last Judgement,' commissioned by Pope Clement VII and completed around the time of Trent. The painting was criticized early in the composition by some in the Vatican with one official saying it was better suited to a tavern or a public bath. Michelangelo was pissed and put this guy's face on Minos, the god of the underworld, adding donkey ears because the Vatican official was such an asshole. But the Pope demurred, saying he didn't have jurisdiction over hell, winning praise as far as the Ottoman Empire because this was the only time His Holiness made a joke during the entire sixteenth century. Catholics are still raving about this one-time event. We are still waiting for word from Rome on jokes uttered in subsequent centuries.

"After the painting was finished, a couple of nuncios, a smattering of cardinals and the requisite theological guy from central casting got their clerical knickers in a twist when they learned that All God's Children in Michelangelo's 'The Last Judgment' waited for the final judgment in the bloody nude. And as we all know, dear souls, this is by definition, scriptural inspiration and the long-arm of the scholastics was wrong, sinful and, yes, anathema. The official reason was that Trent condemned nudity in religious art because lasciviousness was to be avoided and images could not incite the viewer to lust. I'll let you imagine the unofficial reason.

"With the Trent wind at their backs, these keepers of virtue hired Daniela da Volterra to paint over the nudity. He got an unfair reputation for being a prude but won widespread attention for his special talent in painting over pickle heads and other sexual organs. I think the term was breech-maker, though that word doesn't translate well from the Italian. Being too big for one's britches was another thing entirely. Or huge, as they say on the street. Dick-head was not yet in the lexicon.

"Fortunately an art-loving cardinal had someone paint a copy of 'The Last Judgment' on wood. The restoration was based on this 1549 painting. The original wasn't restored until 1993, and we can only wonder how many pickle heads got in the way of this restoration or resurrection.

"Volterra was also told to cover up two of his creations, a painting of St. Catherine and St. Blaise, whose positions on canvas were considered unseemly. Translation: they looked like they were having sex. This was a repainting as much as a cover-up. As the prudery quotient increased in the seventeenth and eighteenth centuries, further coverings were added. It's not that the human form completely went away in response to the Church's Counter Revolutions against Renaissance art. There were still nymphs strutting around the stage with plenty of neck, the occasional breast and hint of a nipple. But the figures tended to be a little out of perspective, a far cry from the meaty Renaissance stuff. It was like looking at sex through a clerical lens, conical in shape; promising everything, delivering nothing."

The class gave Merkel a round of applause.

"Thank you very much, thank you very much," he responded, sounding like some celebrity Colette couldn't remember who offered an elongated, theatrical thank you.

Merkel slid two fingers under his clerical collar as if trying to let in a little more air; then he continued.

"Ms. McGovern, you asked moments ago if Trent gave the Church cover to push against sexuality and nudity. The examples I offered suggest that the Church took every advantage of the so-called authority that came from the council. But Martin Luther and his cronies were pushing from the other side. This crowd would become the new thugs who roamed through churches, smashing statues and images. The Church wanted the high ground on this, arguing, we have such an exalted position because of our tradition of scripture, perceived wisdom and the scholastic gang. That's a pretty imposing trifecta which has withstood frontal attacks for centuries.

"And by the end of the sixteenth century, we started to see large paintings as altar art as well as restrained sculptures and wood carvings. While the so-called Trent standards weren't uniformly effective, they produced results and tempered art. There were very talented outliers such as Caravaggio who painted in 1606 "Death of the Virgin" which depicted Mary's death in extreme naturalistic, human detail that was in line with Loyola's idea of deep intimacy with a religious subject. Iconography was out the window.

"At the other end we have a collection of mainly old white men trying to influence the style, content and purpose of art. The same old men had fingers in the money pie and financial connections; they could feed a starving artist. Who was the guy who said money rests comfortably between the spiritual and the worldly? It worked nicely during this period.

152

Now what happened when an artist or a population is forced to conform to a dubious standard? Anyone?"

"You could have a revolution on your hands," responded Luther.

"You could be right. Let me be clearer. What do you call what the Church had done?"

"Religion?"

"Mr. Martin, I see you still have your sense of humor!"

"What the Church did was a misuse of doctrine. The Church had neither the tools nor temperament to dictate the standard for art and creativity."

"Yes, Ms. McGovern, you have a point. Now what do we call the Church's actions? They might call it protecting the flock. You would call it …?"

"Repression or suppression," responded Rebecca Aimes.

"Good. And what happens when you suppress or repress something?"

"It pops up somewhere else."

"Where, Ms. McGovern?"

"Anywhere. Underground. On the black market. In another town. In the Caravaggio painting of the Virgin Mary you mentioned. Or, as Jung suggested, as our fate. As I understand it, suppression suggests a more conscious decision while repression is a more unconscious act."

"Nicely put," replied Merkel. "Can we hazard a guess about how this might play out psychologically at Trent and elsewhere?"

Colette answered. "Thanks. I suppose we could think of suppression in this context as a largely conscious decision to create a narrow doctrine about the veneration of icons as distinguished from adoration. Repression seems a more neurotic response to art, images, the anima principle and the feminine in general and is largely unconscious. The Church knew this territory well. But this account is too neat and tidy. At the end of the day doctrine was often enforced at the point of a sword or at the stake. Doctrine could and did kill. How an image was received became a matter of life and death. How the image was received and perceived resulted in centuries of madness that is still hanging fire."

"Well-said and well-done, Ms. McGovern. Thank you for your take on that fascinating, pulsating and dangerous zone where theology and psychology collide, a territory we must all walk through. And there is no better time than now."

The professor opened and closed a large bible with an exaggerated motion, as if he were looking for the last word. He air-kissed the red cover.

"Amen, I say to you. Amen! I'm off to Disney World. If you want another angle on this feverish image worship, I suggest you spend a few

153

moments at the Second Council of Nicaea in 787, which was a very good year. It was positively medieval yet had the stench of Trent. The attending bishops were dressed to the nines as if they were ready for a wedding or a burning. Don't you love those guys in tight, embroidered, lace vestments? As the song goes: 'Lots of fun at Finnegan's wake.'

"And while you are in lovely, welcoming Nicaea, please play close attention to what the gathering said about the positively huge difference between adoring and venerating images. This was the central theological issue of the day and caused more schisms, conflicts, wars, mayhem and gas that you can shake a stick at.

"See you soon. Bye, bye!"

Professor Merkel exited stage left, red satin shoes not making a sound or leaving a trace.

Colette felt like she had gone on another world theology tour with Professor Merkel and, in keeping with her recent dream about the Virgin Mary, it felt like a "red meat" theological rampage. She recalled Merkel's breathless recitation of "Trent the Listicle," wondering if it would replace her vague version of "Trent the Musical." She thought about the theological hammer and wondered who or where it would strike next.

She tried to think about icons, Titian and a dream in which legless beggars put their scavenged gifts on lower altar steps. Colette hungered for beauty in all things but felt she was being ushered down narrow byways, watched over by holy men holding signs that might have said, "This way to soul."

That night Colette dreamed about sending a letter to a bird. On waking, she wrote what she remembered and filled in where the hunger was: "Shall I send a letter to a bird that fell from the sky in the center of my eye, in the middle of a dream or in the movement of a stream? Will it carry all that I whisper, wonder and reveal? Will it give credence to everything I feel, in the image, in my soul and in what my dream beggars leave with the tug at my sleeve? Will I write, will I say at the dawn of every day, I believe, I believe, in what I sketch and what I weave."

Chapter Nineteen

After Merkel left the room on his promised trip to Disney World, Colette returned to the library, to her dusty medieval texts, the heavy tomes, and the Greek and Latin bibles that were impenetrable to her. The latter served mainly to anchor the room in the past. She wanted all this knowledge and history to seep into her pores and help her understand the mysteries. She wanted this wisdom to take over her tongue and influence all she would write in her journal.

Colette felt she was inundated with scholarly articles that described the significance of the Second Council of Nicaea in the eighth century. The authors referred back to the apostles, forward to Trent, and then landed in the modern Catholic Church, as if everything had been divinely inspired and approved. The history of the Church was an unbending line, straight and emphatic, as is it had been drawn by the hand of God.

She read that in 726 there was a volcanic eruption in the Aegean Sea and the Emperor saw this as a sign of God's anger over the veneration of icons. Byzantine soldiers who were iconoclasts roamed through Constantinople, plundering churches, smashing idols and throwing the pieces into the sea. The soldiers chased the papal representatives out of the city. Monks were murdered. Relics of dead saints embedded in altars and shrines were removed and burned. Battle lines were drawn. The council had to be moved to Nicaea. About three hundred bishops attended as well as a handful of non-voting monks and clerics. Those who had plotted against the council because they saw the devil in icons recanted and were given a seat at the table.

Colette sensed in the seven sessions that made up the Council of Nicaea that the world had come together for a time; East and West; Orthodox and Catholic. But there were hints that Emperor Charlemagne was whispering in the ear of Pope Hadrian I, who called the council. Fingers were pointed. Did the Muslim abomination of any representation of the human form fuel this movement or were followers of St. Paul who loathed the human body responsible for the hatred of religious icons? Colette felt she was back in some catacomb with the walls marked with signs and arrows telling her to move this way and that way. She recalled her dream that was filled with directional arrows and Korean iconography. The dream seemed to suggest that her psyche was at war with herself and she was directionless.

Colette searched among these shards of history, the threats and chest-thumping, the image-breakers and the righteous, and was stopped in her tracks by the words of St. John Damascene, an eighth-century Syrian monk and priest who wrote "Apologia Against Those Who Decry Holy Images," a document that played an important role at the Council of Nicaea in 787. Two decades earlier he had been declared a traitorous worshipper of images.

St. John's words seemed poetic and archetypal. For him, images were central to life, a mirror of creation. He wondered in an almost modern style why worshippers who had benefitted so much from the saints would return to a time of fear, as if they had not picked up the courage offered in the words of Christ. Colette heard a psychology in his voice. He scoffed at accusations of idol worship. Christians were a new breed and had passed the stage of infancy, reaching the perfection of manhood. The world was made visible through images, whether through statues, a canvas or our imaginations. He referred to the Trinity that was captured faintly in the images of the sun, light and burning rays. At times she thought she was reading poetry.

Colette heard the saint say that the mind and soul were places for the production of images. The mind and soul were also places to preserve memory and the past. Take away the ability to produce images and man would be out of harmony with God who gave us this capacity to imagine and describe within his laws.

In St. John's words Colette heard in the eighth century an enlightened discourse on the difference between a flat, one-dimensional allegory and the richness of the image and symbol. At another time, Colette might have said that she had died and gone to heaven.

She stayed with the holy man and his range and complexity of mind. St. John reflected on the difference between worshipping God and venerating the saints. He derided those who despised matter by falling into the Manichean heresy. This was an act of will, a projection that disregarded natural law. St. John argued that we proclaim God through our senses and particularly our sight. An image was a result of our consciousness not unlike the relationship between words and the listening ear. He counseled his readers to either do away with the worship of matter or become an enlightened man who knows too much to fall for devil worship of images. This man knew that he venerated what the image symbolized. This man knew that the honor given to an image harked back to the original.

Colette felt in a state of wonderment hearing St. John put a loving and modern face on biblical verses. He warned his readers that if they gave up images on account of the law and ecclesiastic tradition, they should also keep the Sabbath and be circumcised. She felt these words carried an anti-Semitic sting. The saint continued: Observe the old law and no profit will come from Christ. If you do not venerate images, you do not worship Christ. She sensed that his voice was rising and taking on a sharper edge.

The devil still worked the perimeter. St. John recounted the story of the devil who promised to stop tempting him with dreams of fornication if the cleric would stop venerating a statue of the Virgin Mary. In these medieval words Colette heard hints of a very modern psychological lament, "Maria Cross," where women and the cross were joined in a sexual and theological tangle. Was she in Graham Greene territory again? Why did sex always seem to be a part of that doctrinal triangle?

Colette could almost forgive St. John for lapsing into medieval liturgy. He appeared in good Catholic company when he placed so much emphasis on how the devil of fornication was being used to prevent the worship of Mary. The veneration of images was a greater evil than illicit fornication.

She was taken in by his poetic cast of mind and how modern his thinking seemed to be. He was writing eight hundred years before the Council of Trent. St. John reiterated that banishing images reduced our mind to a blankness and stupidity. After all, images make the invisible, visible. Why did his language seem more modern than anything she had read about Trent? Colette recalled her remarks in Merkel's class about suppression and repression as they related to venerating icons and now realized her conclusions were primitive and flat compared to St. John's account more than a century earlier.

With visions of a smart and benevolent saint in her head, Colette felt ready to dig into the documents about the Council of Nicaea. After a few hours she felt she was in another, unfamiliar country. She imagined a midnight journey into an antique land where the Patriarch declared that no miracle comes from that stone or icon sent from the savage mind of Simon Magus, the fire-breathing heretic, who fashioned young boys out of mountain breath and made trees appear in full bloom on the rocky, inhospitable land of mountain goats.

Colette returned to the heavy, academic articles about the Council of Nicaea, making notes and adding question marks, but found she was daydreaming again and hearing voices that seemed to be coming from the mist she was trying to penetrate.

She imagined three hundred bishops at Nicaea sitting in a divine circle mumbling about the Trinity and reflecting on two circles that shared the same center, one inside the other.

The voices she heard were loud and clear, coming together in what seemed like one threatening chorus. It was as if these words were already enshrined inside her head, coming from a different place and time, familiar and distinct. Colette followed the voices in her text, in her mind and in the air, tracing every word with her fingers.

"Forget the wild stories of the poets and the pagan tongues," the assembled collective said. "Ignore the scribble on those icons showing the way out of Rome and a thousand godless cities, leading the populace astray.

"To those apostates who accuse us of worshipping an icon or relic as we do our God, we say: Use your God-given talents, use your facilities, study the language of this land, which is Greek, and once you have acknowledged your ignorance, crawl back into your mythological cave, praying every hour to God that you may be forgiven for your ignorance, stupidity, and despicable excesses of imagination.

"For these false prophets of unreason cannot know, because they are not touched by the Spirit, that the Greek language, also given by God, has a range of words that describe and differentiate worship of the Godhead and the veneration of images, a distinction that would not confuse a ten-year-old boy in Athens or Sparta. We know from the scribes and translators that *latreia* refers to worshipping of the Most High God and *proskunesis* refers to veneration of the saints.

"Is it any wonder that God has provided for us at this council language that comes directly from the Holy Spirit and for that reason is divinely inspired and irrefutable?"

Colette heard the heavens open and imagined Zeus or Jehovah hurling thunderbolts down on the righteous who gathered at the Council of Nicaea. St. John had retreated with his sublime psychology of the image and the idea that the act of veneration also takes place in the imagination. The attendees at the Council of Nicaea had lost the arc of the holy man's loving heart.

The three hundred bishops seemed to join the muscular chorus, adding their anathemas to the litany of offenses that seemed to grow with the saying. She tried desperately to imagine the Monty Python troupe at the head of this parade, if only to lessen the sting, but was shouted down with a vengeance she had never experienced before. The words she heard seemed to come from an archetypal place, old as time and very familiar, as if she were at Sunday Mass.

"To the foes of Christianity who are the image breakers and deniers, and the wily serpents among us, we declare them Anathema.

"To those who don't show proper reverence to worthy and venerable images because they pay more attention to their sinful and wayward hands and feet and improper thoughts: Anathema.

"To those who declare images are god or, Heaven forbid, gods, as if plucked from the pagan pantheon, a black star in the devilish night: Anathema.

"To those who call the statues above our altars idols because they do not understand that these associations add nobility and wonder to the image: Anathema.

As Colette heard the next pronouncements, she tried desperately to determine their source. The language and syntax were familiar, as if she was listening to priests through the confessional curtain. She recalled what Jung said about the shadow: "The thing a person has no wish to be." Then the voices took over.

"We will stay clear of filthy lucre in accordance with our divine canons. We will suffer every unclean thought for Christ, honoring his suffering on the cross, death and resurrection. If we do stumble and fall in some unmentionable sexual congress, we proclaim that we will take absolutely no pleasure from that unclean act. If so, we will twice receive the curse of Anathema.

"If we inadvertently look too closely at a woman's face or God forbid her breasts, sensing a heat and modest gathering in our loins, we will declare even in the public square: 'I have sinned exceedingly in thought and deed.' We are Anathema.

"If we are wintering in our cold rooms, lonely and intemperate, and fall victim to our own flesh and commit the monstrous sin of Onan and spill our seed, an act expressly condemned by the Fathers of the Church, we are anathema, knowing we have committed an affront to nature and Divine Law.

"If we wear those red satin shoes instead of those made from the hides of beasts; if we wrap our necks in colorful scarves which obscure our collars; if we fiddle with embroidered cuffs rather than practice penance; we have become an obscenity, making ourselves into an idol so we can be worshipped by others as well as ourselves when we stand like a peacock in front of that dangerous mirror; for all this, we are Anathema.

"If we become the village gossip and even worse take the sins offered during the holy sacrament of confession, inflate and round them out like fresh bread to be served for our amusement in the town square, we are Anathema."

159

Colette immediately sought shelter and protection from this bombardment of anathemas and her time in what felt like a confessional. She had the faintest notion that she had heard or dreamed these priests and wondered what that memory had to do with her search for the feminine. She had a feeling that these voices came from the same place as her vagina dream.

She buried her head in the medieval texts, academic journals, and an array of bibles. All books were open on the desk in her library study room. Had she been reading the texts, recreating the Council of Nicaea as if she were on a walking trip with Clement in the Holy Land? Had she been reading the words on the page or adding metaphors to the text, heating it up as Merkel and Gleason had done in their Punch and Judy dance? Or were the words delivered into her mouth, as if they were scripture, final and unassailable?

Did the Council of Nicaea miss the meaning, metaphor and soulfulness in the writings of St. John Damascene? Was the distinction between adoring and venerating images just a case of neurotic projection, a war inside the heads of holy men and played out across the bloody centuries? Was the sin of the clerics the inability to understand metaphors, the language of correspondences and the workings of the soul? Did these holy men literalize the image and lose its essence in their moralistic tongue lashings?

Colette turned and saw a reflection in a glass book case. She did not recognize the woman staring back at her. Her hair seemed to be on fire; her eyes were half closed. She had one last vision of the Council of Nicaea, showing nuns and monks at the council seating at opposite ends of a large hall, separated by an armed guard. They were not allowed to eat together. They could not wear any colorful clothing or sing or say any words that might have come from the dark side of the moon. The images that Colette saw in her revelry looked like stick figures in a morality play wandering across an almost empty stage. She had a faint notion that in this allegory she had conjured up there were at least two of the Seven Deadly Sins—Pride and Lust—in what looked like Neptune masks and shower curtain shoulder wraps.

She tried to remember St. John's world of image, symbol and delight which was as beautiful as the soul of God's creation. Colette sensed that St. John's world of images were as much about the creative psyche of man as the right relationship to the icon. The images were not just out there; they were inside of her, ready to be transformed. She remembered Jung's words about image being psyche. She recalled the religious voices at the Council of Nicaea raining down anathemas on the unbelievers and placing images on the holy altar as if they were flat and one-dimensional. The council showed her the way of the spirit and she kept falling back into her dreams looking for soul.

Colette imagined herself moving inside text and doctrine. She highlighted sections, underlined phrases and looked for words that would bite and break through. Despite the threats from Nicaea, she found herself looking for angel words that would speak to her soul.

Colette fell asleep in the study room while praying for comfort and relief and on waking recorded in her journal a dream she had about being in a restaurant that felt like a church. A hint of instruction seemed to be in the air.

The crowd grew quickly, and she was worried about whether the restaurant could feed the attendees who might grow into the thousands. She imagined the feeding of the five thousand with five barley loaves and two fishes and, although she didn't explicitly see these items on the menu, she was quite sure that there was a miracle taking place before her eyes. The dreamer felt in the presence of God.

The dream revealed Walt Whitman reciting poetry, Mae West engaged in burlesque, and the rest of the throng seemed to be praying. Colette didn't know how, but she detected in the congregation prayers that came directly from the heart, even when the lips were barely moving.

Into this theater of prayer walked a diminutive Jewish man who she thought looked like the prophet Jacob. She didn't know how she knew. He was carrying the Talmud with some difficulty, finally getting to the front of the procession. The man, who seemed to be in a trance, said to the crowd in a loud voice: "I am singing my ancestry" and proceeded to do so in a language Colette didn't understand.

The crowd grew silent. Those who knew the words joined in and those who did not moved their lips, perhaps certain that their prayer would be a righteous gift from the heart.

Colette woke from this dream still feeling the heavy burden of theology and still moving her lips, as if to find the right prayer. But she was grateful that the dream reminded her of the gift of charity and the miracles of the heart. These blessings, too, came from an old and honored place.

She still saw the Council of Nicaea through a glass darkly.

Chapter Twenty

"You must have had a nightmare, my dear."

"Why do you say that, Mother?"

"You were screaming in your sleep."

"Really? Anything in particular?"

"I heard a few goddamns and Jesus Christs. It's that Trent thing, Colette. It's getting to you. You need to take a break."

"You're probably right, Mom. It has me by the scruff, as Dad would say."

"Your father's still right. It's been months, dear. When will you be finished?"

"Just when I think I'm done, something else pops up, like another council."

"Didn't Father Stravinsky say he did the whole thing in a week?"

"He must be smarter than me or had better teachers."

"Anything you want to talk about, Colette?"

"You mean the dream?"

"Sure, about anything."

"I had a long and weird study session about the Council of Nicaea during which I might have been declared a heretic. I was up to my neck in old books and manuscripts which also had me by the scruff.

"Then I had this dream about being in a restaurant or a church, the feeding of the five thousand and a Jewish guy who was singing about his ancestry."

"Christ, Colette. I see what you mean."

"Don't worry, Mother. The dream must have been sent to balance the Council of Nicaea and that damnation stuff. The dream was quite pleasant. I wondered where the thousands would get their food, and images of the five barley loaves and two fishes came up. I didn't see them; I just felt them."

Colette felt that neither the food nor the miracle was for her.

"There was some strange stuff including Mae West, Walt Whitman, and other people I couldn't make out, who seemed to be lip-synching or trying to find the right words. Then the Jewish guy went to the front and started chanting about his ancestry in a strange language. Maybe Yiddish or Hebrew; I couldn't tell. But everyone seemed to sing something along with him or be with him in spirit. That part of the dream was quite beautiful."

"Where did Mae West come from? She died before you were born."

"They just show up, Mom, like Walt Whitman. He's been dead more than a hundred years, and I don't really like his poetry."

"Maybe he was there as punishment."

"I hope it doesn't work that way. I'd be in real trouble. For now, I'll just concentrate on the feeding of the five thousand and the happy Jewish ending."

"That is one of my favorite miracles. I mean, Lazarus was all right, and who can argue about the changing water into wine? But feeding the hungry! I've heard the number might have been as many as twenty thousand people following Jesus, though every priest I've heard had a different figure. Father Stravinsky said we should concentrate on the actual giving rather than the twelve baskets of leftovers. He probably learned that at the Sorbonne."

"Mother, I should hand over the Trent project to you. I like your biblical analysis."

"Not on your life, Colette. I wouldn't touch that Trent thing with a ten-foot pole. It's killing you."

Her father again.

"I'll be all right, Mom. I just have to figure out what that Jewish guy who looked like the Prophet Jacob and carrying the Talmud was doing in my dream and why was he singing his ancestry."

"You are not thinking again about becoming Jewish are you, dear?"

"Well, it crossed my mind. This Catholic stuff is becoming a real pain in the ass."

"Now, Colette. It's not right to mix swear words and religion."

"I know. What would father say? I'm sorry. I'll just think about the feeding of the five thousand and leave it at that."

"Father Stravinsky pretty much told us a few weeks ago he didn't really believe in hell."

"Thanks, Mother. I feel better already."

"He said hell is really in our heads. You know, like a guilty conscience."

"Maybe I'll become Jewish. I don't think there is a hell in Judaism. Come to think of it, I don't think the Jews had a Council of Trent. I understand they argue constantly over the interpretation of scriptures. It seems very healthy."

"Poor things. I'm so glad the Catholic Church has agreed on one meaning for all the gospels and epistles and we can read them again and again and never get a different version. The feeding of the five thousand or twenty thousand always has the same happy ending."

Colette went to her mother, embraced her and kissed her on the cheek. "Mom, I know the church means a lot to you, especially after Dad died. Once I get done with Trent, I'll be a regular."

Her mother smiled as if saying, I should live so long.

Colette left her mother in the kitchen and went to her bedroom to reflect on a night of dreams. She was trying to figure out how she went from Professor Merkel's class about Trent, to her bizarre and at times unconscious romp through the Second Council of Nicaea and finally to a Christian parable with a Jewish backdrop. Colette was haunted by the recurrence of Jewish themes in her dreams. She couldn't let the thought go.

Colette thought again about the prophets in the Wal-Mart parking lot. That was the last time she had dreamed or even thought of anything faintly Jewish. She did find many examples of anti-Semitism during the Protestant Reformation and Catholic Counter Reformation, but they seemed like footnotes to the real action. Had she been missing something? She recalled the awful piece Martin Luther had written about the Jews. She regretted not telling Gleason that Luther had learned his hate from fifteen hundred years of Church history.

She wondered again about the thin Jewish man who looked like Jacob. She had forgotten that the celebration in the restaurant which felt like a church was a little farcical in the beginning, a cross between "American Idol" and a quiz show, and she couldn't figure out for the life of her what the connection was. There was frivolity in the crowd and a lot of lip-syncing. Yes, there was an extravagance; a theatricality to the dream. Mae West and Walt Whitman weren't behaving exactly as wallflowers. They seemed to have their lines, and everyone seemed to speaking over the other person. But that was theater with the pouting of lips and the wearing of masks. It felt like a script which would eventually give way to the real action and meaning.

Was that it? Enjoy a little song and dance and side drama, pig out on the food which seemed to miraculously appear or at least that was what she imagined. So far, there was no harm done. Colette reminded herself that throughout the dream, even when people were playing the fool, there was a religious sense and a feeling God was present. This was a feel and

164

intuition, and perhaps a prayer rather than a solid presence. She also reminded herself that it seemed no less real.

The diminutive Jewish man who looked like Jacob seemed to become more important every time she looked at the entry in her diary titled, "I am Singing My Ancestry." In the Talmud he was carrying thousands of years of Jewish law and rabbinical teachings under his arm. Under his arm, she repeated; it was all right there for study and reflection. Colette thought that this was the right way to carry the past.

She imagined the catacombs and Vatican vaults full of banned books, leftover cosmetics, mirrors and high cheek rouge from Savonarola's anti-feminine carnage. She saw legions of clerics shuffling between Antioch, Carthage, Nicaea, and Trent, hustling indulgences on village greens, running through rosary beads as if they were on fire, and hurling the curse of anathema at any poor soul who got in their way.

How did she know right away that this man was a Jew? She couldn't remember if he was wearing a yarmulke. She thought he was. Then she remembered an earlier dream in which she asked a Jewish friend whether it would be all right for her to wear a yarmulke. Just what the hell was going on? She had not reflected earlier on this being a skull cap for Jewish men. Had she been around priests too long?

She kept coming back to the Talmud, which she saw as law and tradition. She remembered the dream about prophets in the parking lot showing up in rags and having earnest and heated conversations about the meaning of the Book of Job. She had come to love that dream because it unfolded like a tapestry and seemed to offer a simple allegorical reading which anyone could understand. She thought of her mother and the feeding of the five or twenty thousand. The simple story line touched her, a reminder that she had been knee-deep in theology.

What was singing an ancestry, anyway? Colette could sing a few bars about her Irish ancestry, but it wouldn't make much of a song. The Talmud suggested he was singing his Jewish ancestry, including history, prophets, laws and rabbinical teachings. Perhaps the heart mattered more than language. Perhaps those with a good heart understood him. She didn't like that interpretation.

What was the connection between the miracle of Jesus and singing an ancestry? Was this the Old Testament and New Testament in miniature, all over again? Colette didn't think so because there was no competition or tension. The singing seemed like a coda to the feeding, though that didn't make sense to her. Was she or should she be feeding off both religions? Was she compartmentalizing everything to do with the Trent project and making too much of what really was a fixed Vatican parade populated by nuncios and prelates who were on the take?

She was becoming fatigued from looking inside her own head. She would have to talk to O'Connell. She thought about praying to take some of the sting out of her dreams, but the heart-felt language of her youth was beginning to feel like an old theology born thousands of years ago.

Sometimes Colette thought she was looking for god in all the wrong places and recalled an earlier dream she called, "God in Every Junk Yard Solo." She remembered the dream as being simple and lovely. The dream stayed with her because, in its focus on what was holy and what was prayer, it appeared to reveal a fundamental and radical Christian message.

Colette opened her journal to this dream and read the entry about the sounds of a beautiful women's chorus coming from a nearby church that seemed to be for women only. The dreamer was listening through a stained-glass window which felt like a membrane. She reached the vestibule and positioned herself behind a group of young girls who were to receive their First Communion. With difficulty, she moved towards the altar where she found numerous hand-made gifts, some very large. On the bottom altar steps were tokens such as empty wine bottles, broken pieces of window glass, trinkets, small denomination coins, and colored bottle caps. Some of these items were arranged as if they had fallen randomly from a kaleidoscope. Other items appeared to be placed artistically on an old rug and a piece of ragged, bloody cloth.

These items seemed more suited to an outdoor bazaar than at the foot of an altar. They appeared to be discarded bits, perhaps discovered on the street, in the junk pile, and in the rubbish bin.

Her journal notes stated that these found items have been placed as a lowly offering at the foot of the altar. The dream felt as if there was majesty and holiness in these offerings. The First Communion ritual was a central part of the dream, but the modest offerings on the lowest altar step were imbued with their own kind of ritual and remembrance. Reflecting on the discarded bottle caps and the throwaway coins, she felt that she was in the presence of something holy.

Colette noticed an entry in the margin of her journal: "This might be your vanity talking." She reflected on that entry and decided the dream didn't feel that way. Colette didn't feel she was in charge or directing the dream. It was as if she were in service to the dream. She was an observer.

Colette was moved by the choral music, the stained glass, the communion procession, but those seemed like old rituals. The tokens were gifts left on the altar steps and therefore imbued with wonder. She sensed a certain order in the relationship among the chorus, stained glass and communion girls. Was this about hierarchy?

She wondered whether her dream about being in every junk yard solo would be declared anathema by the three hundred bishops sitting at

Nicaea. She hadn't really thought about why she had included the word "solo"; it just came out of nowhere. Did she mean solo as in alone or solitary? She did not know but thought the discussion might raise some interesting questions about the Trinity at Nicaea, Trent or any other council.

She was fooling herself. She remembered the rulings of anathema raining down on her at Nicaea, real or imagined. Her dreams would be declared anathema. The tokens at the foot of the altar would be declared anathema because they would be seen to revile and dishonor venerable images on the altar. The tokens would be declared anathema because her journal entry suggested these items had a godlike presence or feel.

What if she could eat the forbidden fruit? What if she would stop fooling herself in trying to pick the theological shards out of her dreams and poetry out of her journal notes, hoping the relevant parts remained meaty, fixed and meaningful? What if she would cease trying to reimagine theology from the ground up? Would St. John Damascene be in her corner?

Colette walked and she talked, ducking Trent, mountains of litanies, and bundled anathemas as if they were the plague. She walked away from her junk yard dream and into a poem which she would not be nailing to the church house door.

God in Every Junk Yard Solo

A stained glass membrane
Filters feminine choral voices
From a medieval chamber.
I wait in the vestibule
For an anointing.
Those with flowing blonde hair
Hiding cassock and stole
Enter first
Then lugging golden bowls
The washers of feet
And finally legions of young virgins
In communion dress.
The church door appears
Neither open nor closed.
So I must begin the ritual again.

Outside the carnage:
Amputees, lepers and whores

Some on rollers
Supporting their stumps
Others wiggling at ground level
Through urban filth
As if crawling out of the earth.
All jealously guard offerings
Taken from the town dump
And spread over oil-stained rags—
Bits of shattered eyewear glass
Coke and Pepsi bottle tops
Plastic necklace beads
Blue and green paper stars
Wedding confetti
Coins from every nation on earth
Sprinkled on top of gifts,
Each display varied and particular
Arranged in a crude circle
In the shadow of the holy place.

I wait for the begging hands
The mutterings of the infirm
The tugging of the legless at my trouser cuffs
The ritual stumbling of the blind
The one-penny thunder in the orphan's cup
The sister traded over into sin.

Not a word
Just the dry-channel
Pull of a man's stump
Conducting his circular prayer
Around his junk yard altar,
A tribute slow and painful
Enough to be repeated
By those of us
Just learning to walk.

Chapter Twenty-One

Colette felt that she had spent years circling Trent, listening to the bombast, and reflecting on how many angels could really dance on the head of a pin. She concluded that this was the perfect way for the Pope's emissaries to end a council session and send everyone scurrying towards the door. She wasn't sure when the theological question ceased being a matter of intense religious scrutiny and actually became a joke, a response to another ponderous day at the office. She thought it might have something to do with the Gregorian and Julian calendars but realized, once you bring a pope into the discussion, anything might happen. She might as well be looking for directions in the zodiac.

Colette was hearing the old authoritarian grammar, the subject/verb construction delivered with fist and finality. Some words like God, the Virgin Mary and the Trinity were parked above the line as if they were exhortations to be noted and worshipped. The words below the line, the adverbs and adjectives, represented a danger and a warning not to load up the main line with descriptors, the honey words of excess and metaphorical flourish because this was the road to perdition and idol worship. And she had been down that road before, a route right through Nicaea.

Colette now understood that Trent was a place and an idea, a fantasy and a religious rite. Was the council also a fiction? The Council of Trent was fed by all the councils that came before and established the rituals, dogmas and sacramental life still found at her Holy Angels Church.

She had studied the ancient texts and listened to the Church fathers. Colette had imagined and sometimes dreamed that she trudged through the Holy Land behind ravaging monks and new Christians, walking through the shards of crushed pagan statues, searching for the feminine. She had read the books about the Council of Trent. She could recite the council's liturgy in her sleep. She often did.

Colette could easily imagine the male voices at the Council of Trent were speaking in Latin, slow and ponderous, as if delivered from the head without the intrusion of lips, tongue or heart. She heard no flesh in these words, no emotional component. There was no soul. The words were weighted down with earlier councils and scholastic brutishness which had taken decoration out of language and thought. She had listened earnestly for a woman's voice at Trent. She now knew every session by heart, listened in on the idle chatter and joke-telling in the corridors.

Colette heard the subdued blasphemies and the occasional cursing of the Pope. She saw muscle displayed and the vengeful pens. She watched ritual and decorum revealed as predictably as the bends in a bishop's chasuble. She watched the caravans of theatrics, the processions of pampered and perfumed men wearing garments made famous in some medieval fashion show, and the self-absorbed prelates carrying the mirrors Savonarola hadn't crushed. She observed the comings and goings, the conclaves within the council, the petty squabbles exaggerated for effect. But she never saw, or sensed, or smelled, or heard a woman except in mentions of marriage, consanguinity, and women living at the edge of man's authority. St. Paul sometimes showed up, reminding all that virginity was the preferred choice, but to escape damnation, marriage would be acceptable. There were those scholastics in the room checking whether the hymen was still intact. Aristotle, Augustine and Aquinas found the devil in a woman's womb with virginity the sinless cure. Colette knew that if she had shown up at Trent in the flesh, she would be guilty as charged.

Colette recalled the quip from an instructor who suggested that all history began as tragedy and ended as farce. Some of the Trent documents she had read sounded like satire. Puffed-up clergy and willing functionaries compiling thunderous lists about the sacraments, the communion wafer, priestly celibacy, and the ever fractious Trinity, all sanctioned by the Pope who invoked eternal damnation and other injunctions, which sounded like both satire and farce. She could still envision Trent the Musical, but the play would have to take into consideration the drownings, the burnings, the hangings and the strangling that occurred in the shadow of the council, sanctioned and complete, like a recessional hymn, courtesy of Rome.

She realized that she would have to lighten her theological load, if only briefly, to gain perspective. Colette frequently went to her dream journal when she wanted to escape the weight of thunderous doctrine. She was reminded of a recent dream in which she was driving around in circles looking for a church. Every time she stopped for directions, a familiar face said turn this way or that way, this way or that. As she drove, she noticed a large lake to her left. Every time she seemed to get closer to the church, the water level of the lake would drop. By the time she found the church, the water in the lake was down to a trickle, and cars were driving across it. She then noticed the church doors were chained and padlocked. There was no water, no religion and no escape.

She assumed that her vague notion of finding a church had resulted in a cost, a loss of water, moisture, and sustenance. The padlocked doors seemed to confirm that suspicion. Was she looking for sustenance and moisture in all the wrong places? Was Trent the padlocked church and meaning and spiritual nutrition were to be found elsewhere? Where were the moisture and the meaning in a hanging or a burning?

Colette later read a story about the battle between the Franciscans and the Dominicans regarding the Virgin Mary, with the former taking the official Catholic Church's position and the latter ascribing human traits to the Virgin. Apparently to make a point, the Dominicans in Bern, Switzerland, contrived an image of the Virgin that was so managed by machinery, as to move, speak, groan, complain and give audible answers to those who addressed it. It did everything but give birth. This, along with a bleeding host and other like inventions, so influenced people's minds that in Bern, the Papal bull and the Franciscan doctrine were meaningless in light of the Virgin's miraculous traits, at least until the Dominican contrivers were detected and were burned for heresy.

Colette assumed that this was a rant by the anti-papal faction, a thrice-told tale, which bestowed considerable wit and daring on the monks in a period allegorical piece, Virgin machinery included. Or it could have been true. She recalled reading about another Catholic plot in Paris to tempt people into sin. Apparently, beggars were placed in key parts of the city and asked for alms in the name of the Virgin Mary. If you didn't contribute, you were an apostate, imprisoned and perhaps burned at the stake.

From what she had read, the burnings at the stake were meant to be an introduction to hell on a small and manageable scale and also a social event that attracted huge crowds. Suffering depended on which way the wind blew and with what severity. Who was the philosopher who said you can't move small enough? She wanted to move small, take a few theological leaps, and look for a little Trent, religion in miniature that might be a modest reflection of the muscular work at the council. What was the shadow side of all that breast beating and foot stomping by clerics, nuncios and legates who were all singing from the same punishing hymn book?

Martin Luther was afoot. William Tyndale had published the first English edition of the New Testament in 1529 which immediately became contraband, with Sir Thomas More leading an effort to buy copies and burn them before distribution. Tyndale was declared a heretic, strangled and burned at the stake. What was a graduate student to do with these events that hung over the period like a curse?

The more Colette read about the history of the Catholic Church in sixteenth century Europe, the more she wondered why attendees at the Council of Trent seemed oblivious to the violence taking place in its name. The Council of Trent was too tidy, too predictable and far too orderly for the times.

Colette thought about sixteenth century England and small art that held such religious horror. She consulted her library's extensive collection of woodcuts and photos of woodcuts which emphasized religious themes. Among the collections she found woodcuts that depicted the burnings, hangings and drownings, all carried out in the name of God around the time of Trent.

Colette imagined she was at Smithfield outside the London wall, the historical home of Bartholomew's Fair, medieval duels, tournaments for knights and the King's jesters. This was also the great horse market.

She examined a series of woodcuts that provided an aerial view of Smithfield. In place of the weekly market was an oval fence that kept in view a thousand spectators. Some were gossiping; others seemed to be looking intensely at the center of the oval. Children played with balls and sticks in the foreground, half in the scene and half out. Horses appeared to rear up out of nowhere as if they had been provoked from behind, somewhere beyond the curtain. They were stylized and manicured like chess pieces. Most wore tournament headdress, suggesting something important was afoot.

Colette examined other woodcuts and noticed more movement, more physiology and the curves of animal flesh. They seemed more modern to her. Dandies in stylish hats were littered among the waiting crowd. The scene was more festive, and even the horses appeared to notice. She noticed a few soldiers on horseback ringing the crowd. The dogs that have been on the periphery were more skittish, now showing their teeth.

In the background, the buildings that framed the market were in in full view. Tournament banners adorned the prominent towers. Small groups of people were huddled on the porticos and abutments of buildings. At the center of the buildings a modest stage had been constructed for royalty and other dignitaries. Some views suggested they were mainly women with veils covering much of their faces. Other views suggested a lively, mixed crowd displaying arm movements and interest in the pending tournament. Two or three ladies hid behind fans.

Some views revealed dark clouds and a threatening sky. Bolts of lightning appeared to be descending on a church in the center of this small art. Others showed at the heart of the woodcut more ominous shading, anticipating behavior that might be expected from attendees at a festival. Pairs of women continued to hug each other.

Inside the oval depicted in the woodcut was a portable, wooden pulpit for Bishop Shaxton, who would give the benediction. Scattered around the areas were men preparing bundles of faggots for the fire. A soldier stood forever at attention, enforcing the peace. At the center was a woman naked except for a shift. She had her hands together in prayer. The woodcut indicated others tied to the stake, but she was the one who the spectators were watching. Everything was stopped in time.

Colette wanted to stay with the apocryphal and faintly merciful but couldn't ignore Trent's shadow which was everywhere in the Smithfield marketplace. The woodcut read: "The Description of Smithfield with the order and manner of certain of the council sitting there at the burning of Anne Askew and John Lascelles with two others, a priest and a tailor."

Colette added to her knowledge gained from the woodcut. The burning at the stake was on July 16, 1546. Askew was so broken from being tortured on the rack in the Tower of London she had to be carried in a chair to her execution and bound to the stake with iron chains. She had refused to confess, embrace Catholicism or name names, so she was burned slowly, not having the option of strangulation to ease her death.

Colette wondered whether men heard, whether Trent heard, the sound of burning flesh and the language of Anne Askew's examinations at the hands of her Catholic Inquisitors as the council opened. She wondered whether the male historians who reported the martyr's torture and death captured her voice, tone and authority. Was she punished for leaving her husband and children and demanding a divorce based on scripture? What about the historian who played up her inherent womanly weakness and suggested that she was a weak vessel of the Lord? Was the martyr punished for satirizing her male antagonists for their grasp of theological issues? Was she murdered because she was known around London as the beautiful preacher who attracted a following of influential and like-minded women? Was she sacrificed because of her fine mind? Was she burnt to death because she was a woman?

Colette felt that she was a long way from ancient stories about women who outwitted men and sometimes even the gods. The story of Anne Askew, filtered through centuries of questionable male sensibilities, seemed a naturalistic horror story in any language with the martyr being the only woman recorded to be tortured on the rack in the Tower of London to the grisly pleasure of her torturers. Colette was now outside of myth and inside a theology that would literally pluck out her tongue if she did not believe in the presence of Christ in the host.

Askew's martyrdom also fed the Protestant Reformation and centuries later became an important allegory and, in the middle of the nineteenth century, found its way into the Protestant Sabbath Schools in America courtesy of "*Female Martyrs of the English Reformation*" by Charlotte Elizabeth, published in 1844. If the book was meant to be an easy Sunday read, Colette had never been to catechism. She found this account of pain, suffering and religious mendacity to be a horror story. Askew's plight was made more severe by her pluckiness, knowledge of Scripture and wit during her numerous inquisitions. Colette could hear the martyr's torturers making jokes about the female form as they laid her bare and open on the rack until her joints pulled apart. Were they looking for the organs that Aristotle and the scholastics shamed as they diminished the feminine?

A member of the Privy Council told the martyr that "A woman has no more business with Scripture than a sow has wearing a saddle." Her response: "My lord, a sow has as much business wearing a saddle as an ass does wearing a bishop's miter."

When asked about a passage of Scripture, she replied, "I would not throw pearls among swine, for acorns were good enough."

When the Bishop of Winchester demanded more direct answers, she responded: "I said I would not sing a new song to the lord in a strange land."

When an inquisitor at Sadler's Hall asked whether she had said she'd rather read five lines in the bible, than to hear five Masses in the temple, she responded, "I confessed that I had said no less. Not for the dispraise of either the epistle or gospel, but they only did greatly edify me and the other nothing at all. As St. Paul doth witness in the fourteenth chapter of his first Epistle to the Corinthians, where he doth say: 'If the trumpet giveth an uncertain sound, who will prepare himself to the battle?'"

The bishop asked her about confession: "St. James sayeth that every man ought to acknowledge his faults to others, and the one pray for the other."

He asked her what she said to the king's book. She answered that "I could say nothing to it, because I never saw it."

He asked her if the spirit of God was in her. She responded: "If it was not, I was but reprobate and cast away."

He asked her if she did not think private Masses helped departed souls. She responded that "it was great idolatry to believe more in them than in the death which Christ died for us."

Then the Lord Mayor asked her if a mouse who ate the host received God or not. She made no answer but smiled.

The Lord Mayor reminded her that Saint Paul forbade a woman to speak or to talk the word of God. She replied that she knew Paul's meaning as well as he, which was, a woman ought not to speak in the congregation by way of teaching. Then she asked him how many women he had seen go into the pulpit and preach? He said none. Then she said, "He ought to find no fault in poor women, except they had offended the law."

The Lord Mayor became quiet.

"Why so few words?" another of her tormentors asked.

"God has given me the gift of knowledge," she answered, "but not of utterance. As Solomon says, 'a woman of a few words is the gift of God.'"

Colette heard in the martyr's voice, even one that had been shaped by centuries of men and bathed in suspect hagiography, a narrative that would have found a fitting home at Trent. She could almost hear the nuncios stomping their feet at the audacity of this martyr who so boldly and accurately cited Scripture. Anne Askew had said to one of her Inquisitors that neither Christ nor the apostles had put anyone to death. Colette thought that the Council of Trent could have used a touch of this sanity and wisdom. She wondered how many women and children the assembled had murdered.

She counted scores of women who were burned at the stake in England alone during the Council of Trent, including mothers, wives and daughters, the blind and the infirm and those who might have missed Mass. Colette was in over her head and asked Professor Merkel for his advice.

"Well, Ms. McGovern. So you have been looking at religious events in England around the time of the Council of Trent?"

"Yes, Professor. And thank you for seeing me on short notice. I've been surprised by how little attention the Council of Trent gave to events occurring at the same time in other countries, including Britain. As you know, I've been struggling with Trent because I actually think the French and Germans were right; that it was an illegal council and something of a fraud."

"Now hold your horses and keep your hat on! These are serious charges."

"Yes, I know. I haven't put them in writing yet. I'm just feeling my way."

"Nice and easy does it every time."

Colette heard her mother talking.

"Thanks. I've told you that I'm trying to view events occurring at the same time as Trent to gain perspective. You helped a lot with the Brazil story. I've looked into the Council of Nicaea for a perspective on the treatment of images. I've read various books that anticipate Trent."

"Professor Gleason is your thesis advisor, so his advice is also important. For my sake, the more perspective the better!"

"Thank you. Along those lines, I've been studying the female martyrs burned at the stake around the early and middle years of Trent. Pictures of woodcuts based on these burnings are shocking."

"That's interesting. Why did you cross the Channel, so to speak?"

"To tell you the truth, I wanted to get away from Trent, metaphorically speaking."

"I don't blame you. But you should be careful about drawing too close a parallel between the two events."

"Yes, that's what I'm struggling with. For months I've been listening to the heavy, threatening male voices coming out of Trent, usually under the threat of divine retribution for heresies."

"And what are you hearing in Merry Old England?"

"I'm hearing the heavy, threatening male voices, usually under the threat of divine retribution for heresies. The accent is different."

"They sound very much alike. Why is that?"

"I don't know if they are reading from the same script. It was written in Rome, so I suppose I'm answering my own question."

"Yes, the author is correct, but the historical context is worth examining."

"In England you mean? There seems a savagery to these burnings. It was almost like a national psychosis."

"You could be right. England was a Protestant nation under Henry VIII and then Bloody and very Catholic Mary came along in 1553. She was the real zealot. The repression of Protestants was severe. Everyone seemed under suspicion for the slightest infraction."

"Like not going to church?"

"Exactly," replied Merkel. "There were spies everywhere. Henry tended to take out the clergy. Mary went after the tradespeople. The number of butchers, bakers and candle stick makers burned was incredible. It staggers the imagination that there could be this level of insurrection among the trade groups. She must have thought they were a secret society making candles and shoes to use against the crown."

"The same was true of women," said Colette. "Nearly sixty were burned during a short period. Some like Anne Askew were well known and targeted for their public views. But there were also maids, handicapped women including a blind girl, and I don't know how many children. The woodcuts show children being tossed into the flames. A 19th century book about female martyrs reads like a endless parade of men but mainly women burnt at the stake for not believing in the communion host. It seemed murderous."

"England in the sixteenth and seventeenth centuries was particularly hard on women for sorcery, murdering their husbands or offenses related to the coinage of the realm. But Bloody Mary conducted a witch hunt, to be sure."

"It was just a feeling," Colette responded, "but I sensed something deeply anti-feminine in all of this and more than the usual stuff coming out of the Church at the time. There seemed to be a rage and a hatred of women in these actions. They seemed to fantasize about the devil being inside women's wombs. Anne Askew's tormentors seemed to take pleasure in pulling apart her joints and sexual organs. It was so bad the Lieutenant of the Tower of London refused and complained to Henry VIII."

"I understand your point, but it's not easy to psychoanalyze a period in history. Every country goes nuts from time to time. Few countries in Europe did not embrace the burning at the stake and related savagery. Pathology was in the air and had been for a long time. In Germany in the early seventeenth century hundreds of midwives were killed, accused of using sorcery and killing infants."

"But, Professor, why the sexual frenzy? Why the focus on the women and reproduction? Why this hatred of women and sex? "

"A psychological reading might suggest that the scholastics, with help from Aristotle, deeply feared the feminine and in turn demonized it. There seemed some intellectual vagueness to a doctrine like the Virgin birth which might have been born from hearsay, gossip, ancient myths, rewritten bible verses, and some old woman in Ephesus or wherever, claiming Mary's hymen was intact. Once the Church elevated virginity and celibacy as co-equals, the confessional was going to be a very busy place."

Colette wanted to stay out of the small, dark room, so she changed the subject.

"Doesn't it seem a little odd that Queen Mary would go to war against women in her country?"

"The newly converted are always the worst. She brought Catholicism back to England with a vengeance. It is always about power, money and allegiances. Rumor has it that Bloody Mary blamed her false pregnancy in 1555 on God's punishment for tolerating heretics in the land. Her inner chamber spread rumors that she only had gas pains. You can probably take that with a grain of salt. But they did throw a lot of babies on the fire."

"Maybe she was taking out her anger and disappointment on those poor fertile women?"

"Bloody Mary was a bitch—add the appropriate rhyme—and her name was on a lot of English lips by the end of her reign. It rained for years, and the people blamed her and the Pope. This would cut deeply into the burgeoning tourist trade. Then the famine of biblical proportions hit the land, and the country saw this as the price it paid for popery."

"These actions seem petty, anti-feminine and institutional," Colette responded, not really knowing what to say.

Merkel replied.

"The Church had been going after women for centuries, usually with trumped-up accusations of heresies, sexual sins, witchcraft and the like. If you have the time and inclination, have a look at Marguerite Porete, who was part of the beguine movement of wandering nuns in medieval Europe. She was burned at the stake in Paris in 1310 for heresy. There's a good bit of evidence today suggesting she was burned because she was a woman."

Colette had no stomach to witness another burning, so she nibbled at the edge of history, understanding that the beguines were independent women serving the poor and operating outside of Church authority. She discovered at her college library Marguerite Porete's *The Mirror of Simple Souls* in digital form, first published around 1296. She wondered what this female mystic would be mirroring across the ages.

Colette immediately fell into the medieval poem, the allegory, the personification and the feminization of language, particularly the pronouns. God the Father was described as a woman and as a mother. Souls were described as female and the Intellect was considered feminine. Colette realized that this inversion of pronouns and other language was not unusual in mystical poetry and allegories, but she was taken in by the ease with which the poet used the theme of Romantic love between same-sex pairs, mixed sex pairs and other pairings along the social strata to personify spiritual love. This was Porete's way of saying that the soul could never be really described by words. A person received mirror images, reflections and mere hints of the divine soul.

Colette neither read nor sensed any heresy in this beautiful poetic language which placed the "sweetest Love Divine within the Holy Trinity," though she did detect the danger in the author marveling at "Those who are governed by Reason and Fear, Desire, Work and Will, and who know not the grand nobility of being ordered by nothingness." Porete went further and described, allegorically, two churches: the Holy Church Little that was based on reason, ritual and dogma and the Holy Church Great, the place for freed souls. The ultimate love of God outweighed the teachings of scholars, theologians, priests and other religious.

Porete wrote with humor, bombast and a poetic expansiveness that seemed modern for the time. She reminded her readers that everything we say about God is "more like lying than speaking the truth." Colette found candor and humility in these words, as well as danger. She thought how courageous Porete had been in stating in her poetic way that we no longer need to reach God through penance, scriptures and rituals since these activities are optional if not useless.

Colette was left with her own desperate imaginings. She nursed a vague and unreasonable hope that her mother would show up out of thin air to comfort her and feed her. She felt under fire, sensing her forays backwards into Trent and across the English Channel looking for martyrs and some compensation did not provide the clarity she desired. She was looking for the feminine anywhere she could find it, in the sly epistles of Anne Askew, the relics of ash, and the bloody leavings of a Bloody Mary.

Then she was introduced to Marguerite Porete who was burned because she turned her back on the patriarchy of the Church, arguing in her medieval poetic tongue that there were many other ways to God, more feminine, more personal and more joyous. Colette had a sneaking suspicion that her sin was being independent, a poet, a mystic and a woman. The cleric who announced Marguerite Porete's death sentence sounded very modern in his remarks delivered in Paris, May 31, 1310: "Still she persisted in this state."

Colette read about Marguerite Porete's trial in Paris. The men in attendance started with the usual prayers and charges of heretical depravity. They reminded the large crowd that Porete "had remained contumacious and rebellious about these matters." The mystic was offered a sentence of greater excommunication but she persisted in her work and refused absolution. The Church officials handed her over to secular authorities to be burned at the stake. The woman was said to have displayed "many signs of penitence, both noble and pious, in her death."

Trent would declare Porete's teaching on faith and good works to be anathema without knowing her name. Colette reflected on the two hundred and thirty six years between the murders of Anne Askew and Marguerite Porete. She recalled Aldous Huxley writing that religions which paid most attention to history, pseudo-history and fixed doctrines were the most violent. In one of her classes Colette learned that the religious wars, Inquisitions and Crusades had taken tens of millions of lives. She felt she had witnessed the death of at least two of this number.

After so much death and violence against women, Colette prayed she would settle into a peaceful sleep.

She dreamed she was next to a crib admiring a beautiful baby. Colette wanted to pick up the baby but someone who appeared to be a priest cautioned against it. She learned over the crib and was shocked to see unlit candles coming out of the child's eyes and the head and body covered with garlands.

Colette woke in a cold sweat and sobbed deeply, fearing the dream suggested the child was indeed a child of God and wrapped in garlands, ready for sacrifice. In her midnight dread it appeared as if the child was on an altar or was the altar with candles provided by the priest to represent light and vision. Colette feared that the dream might be about what she was sacrificing on the altar of Trent: her baby, herself and her sanity.

In spite of all her travels and research, her communing with the ancients and the council fathers, dreams still came, as if they were establishing another theology inside her heart and inside her soul.

She thought of Anne Askew, spread-eagled on the rack in the tower of London. She thought of Marguerite Porete who died with piety and nobility while burning to death.

She recalled being behind that curtain and seeing her cold reflection in a steel surface.

Chapter Twenty-Two

Colette was thinking about beginnings, middles and endings, a structure some nun taught her to help organize thoughts, words and deeds. Over time, she became confused when the same nun told her that in the Beginning was the Word and the Word was with God, and the Word was God, a construction that threw an earlier clarity out the window.

She had listened to her theology instructor wander down Greek alleyways mumbling about the Word being in the nominative case or maybe a predicate, hanging there waiting for attention. From what she remembered, all these linguistic roads led to the Trinity. The cloud over her head reminded her to stay with the small "t." Colette had to acknowledge that the nun had had some success because some bits of doctrine seemed always to sneak in unannounced when she was trying to get her head around the Council of Trent and the byways that led to and from Trent, that old Celtic and Roman city with Neptune rising. And what exactly was the definite article, she wondered; was it the real thing?

The more she tried to plant her feet four-square in the present, the more she seemed to retreat, spurred on this time by the classroom comments weeks earlier by Professor Merkel.

"You should really have a look at St. Augustine's *Confessions*. Keep in mind that he wrote the book when he was the bad boy of North Africa in the fourth century rebelling against God and his mother, if you know what I mean. It's Oedipal, if you ask me; the classic Freudian trap!"

Merkel continued. "Fast forward to 1336, and we have Petrarch climbing some mountain in southern France and, through luck or divine intervention, opening Augustine's *Confessions* to a passage about the depths of the soul, memory and the imagination. That was the beginning of the Renaissance. If you don't believe me, look it up."

She did: Book X, Chapter 8 of *Confessions*. She read the words of Augustine.

"How great, my God, is this force of memory, how exceedingly great! It is like a vast and boundless subterranean shrine. Who has ever reached the bottom of it? Yet this is a faculty of my mind and belongs to my nature; nor can I myself grasp all that I am. Therefore, the mind is not large enough to contain itself."

When she next met Professor Merkel she asked him whether this quote was the essence of Augustine.

"Yup," said Professor Merkel, responding to her question. "This is the big one. Petrarch found in Augustine references to soul, memory and images. More important, Petrarch was not just blabbing about returning to nature and growing corn pones in an idle meadow. The spark he found in Augustine confirmed to him that soul was separate from man and the source of the imagination and image-making."

"Why did it take a thousand years for this insight to come to light? People had been reading Augustine for a long time. And didn't he share Aristotle's anti-feminine views?"

"Good question. Augustine was a product of his time. His views about women now sound like dangerous nonsense. He also emphasized Christianity's transcendent function. Aristotle had his back and probably his front too. Perhaps the Dark Ages had to come and go. The psyche was probably restless and felt neglected with all that melancholy, self-abuse and denial of the feminine. You've read about the early councils where imagination was wrapped in altar cloth, wet towels and allegorical blinders. Then Florence came along and the uninvited lady showed up at the dance. Anything could happen. And what happened was the Italian Renaissance, a period unmatched for its soulfulness. And keep in mind, despite his insights, Augustine embraced a distinct, separate spiritual path. He needed Petrarch to complete his thought and give it depth. For Petrarch, the descent into soul was the key insight. There's the Renaissance in germ."

"But we're not talking about a new religion, right?"

"Right. The Renaissance wasn't a new religion. Petrarch and others were discovering Greece—not the actual country but the idea of Greece, and its polytheism; all those nasty, randy gods in the zodiac."

"The Church didn't mind?"

"The Renaissance was an unadvertised eruption, coming out of that soulful ooze. We can see from the Renaissance artists and poets that they were quite comfortable worshipping Christ as well as honoring the mythological gods. The latter provided an imaginative perspective: the soulfulness. But this was dangerous territory because the Church had been railing against daemons forever. The Renaissance crowd must have known deep down that Catholic theology was already becoming a straightjacket and a bit of a drag. Think about it. Much Catholic doctrine seemed like childish nonsense until transformed by art."

Colette thought about Titian's "The Assumption of Mary."

"But this period wasn't all peaches and cream, right, Professor? I mean there were wars, plagues, feuds, mythical virgins who spread sexual poisons and diseases; so death was everywhere."

"I don't know about those mythical virgins but, yes, death was everywhere. Artists contemplated death because it served as an inspiration outside of theology. We can thank the Greeks for that. Pathology is all it's cracked up to be."

"I worry about opening up another front, Professor. I finally retreated from Trent and have been desperately trying to get back home, in a manner of speaking. My mother is ready to toss me out of the house."

"Don't cross your mother, whatever you do. Trent will make more sense if you know a little more about the Renaissance and what the Church was running away from, if only unconsciously. Or mainly unconsciously! The Italians were big on mirrors and as we know are still admiring their delicious past. Those folks love looking at themselves in the mirror and then dreaming about their reflections. It never ends."

"What am I reflecting or mirroring, sir?"

"All the gods in the mythological junkyard, Ms. McGovern."

"I beg your pardon?"

She had been to that place before.

"No need. Just a hint of my failed Jesuit wit. Try Boccaccio. He wrote about famous women who were all over that junkyard. Some have called his work smoke, mirrors and lots of brothels."

"Professor, I don't fully understand. I recall Boccaccio hanging out in some fine Italian mist. He sounded like an Italian pasta sauce or some nineteenth century opera singer. Was he also a priest? Sometimes I think I'm going out of my mind. Should I be committed?"

"That would help, Ms. McGovern. That would help."

After meeting with Merkel, Colette took the weekend off, mostly sleeping, before settling in to read Giovanni Boccaccio's Famous Women, now advertised as one of the first books in the west in which a version of the modern woman appeared.

She recalled the Professor Merkel telling her that she "deserved a break today and a Roman holiday to boot. Let the Council of Trent drift for a while in its suffering orthodoxy and perpetual dullness. You are certainly well-traveled with those fanciful trips to Venice, Trent, and London. And I almost forgot Brazil. Loved that beach scene! Florence will likely be your cup of tea."

"Is it likely I will encounter the Virgin Mary, sir, among the famous women?" she remembered asking him.

"She is safe in her temple and will be well cared for until her coming-out party in the nineteenth century. By then, this archetype will have been frozen in time, and the world will be celebrating a very cold virginity. Muck around for a bit among the shards of pagan icons from the days of old when Constantine let the hammer down. Walk backward gingerly and give thanks to God as you move through those heavy seas of orthodox theology. Let your imagination run wild. Please stay away from the marauding monks."

Colette regularly checked over her shoulder for the monks. And she felt that her imagination had been running wild for some time. She wanted to slow it down. She read Boccaccio's *Famous Women* slowly, taking in all the stories of the mythical heroines, reflecting on their successes and failures, and their wisdom and humanity. She was taking notes and taking names in her journal.

Colette could readily imagine a chorus of women dressed in long silk tunics and, shielded by a membrane that allowed their voices to be heard, to sing their ancestry, down through the ages, down through time. They sounded sweeter than angels.

Boccaccio provided the marching orders. Colette read along with him, making marks in the text that would find their way into her heart. She stayed absolutely true to his words, moving her lips in wonder as she read.

Boccaccio praised his teacher Petrarch for writing about famous men. The student expressed surprise that so little attention had been given to women who had accomplished great things. He suggested that women, because they are softer by nature, should be praised even more than men for their accomplishments. His focus would not be on the righteous Christian and Hebrew women who prepared themselves for everlasting glory. Their die was cast. Their everlasting repose in the bosom of Christ was assured. He would travel with the pagan women who had a keen desire to seek the fleeting glories of this world, whether through sex, bribery, and even virtues that are worthy of the blessed saints.

Boccaccio's women lived by wit and invention. The Sicilian queen Ceres invented agriculture, tamed oxen and was elevated to goddess by her people. Minerva, the goddess of wisdom, invented the chariot and the number system. She also invented a way to extract olive oil. His women seemed ready to take over the world.

Colette felt early on that this was becoming her story, too. She would read, write and re-imagine the various pagan tales.

In *Famous Women* they came: a bumper crop of women, large enough to provide a sitting congregation at the Council of Trent. By the numbers they came, beginning with first mother Eve who experienced the frequent pains of childbirth and suffered the grief that tortured the mind at the death of her children and grandchildren. Colette felt that Eve was more human than the poet imagined. She was old and tired from working in the vineyards and eager for the end of her days. The poet let the first mother go to her rest, passing over the heat, cold and other sufferings associated with leaving the Garden. Her grief seemed greater than her first sin.

Colette continued to enter these stories. A hundred or so famous women displayed cunning, daring and duplicity which would shock a Christian sensibility. The poet presented these women through the lens of history, memory and myth. He didn't offer excuses for the shifting personas and fictions which provided cover and possibilities. He scolded, he praised, he wandered and he sighed.

Colette imagined that Boccaccio was speaking directly to her when he introduced Semiramis, Queen of the Assyrians, who, after her husband died, disguised herself as a man to hold onto power. She took the persona of her young son Ninyas and assumed control of the army, winning battles and accomplishing more than many men. The moral within the tale suggested that leadership spirit was more important than a person's sex.

Colette thought that these words should have been spoken by the nuncios at the Council of Trent.

The tale continued. After Semiramis conquered many more lands and won a place in the memory of her nation, she became a victim of the flesh. After a great struggle she was overcome by sexual desire and had sex with many men, including her own son. Boccaccio, serving as his own chorus, referred to this as a beastly crime.

Undeterred, Boccaccio continued his tale. The queen executed men after fornication to hide her crime. Some say she invented the chastity belt to be worn by other women in the household so they would not compete with her for lovers. To legitimize her unholy acts, the queen announced free love throughout the land. Perhaps she opened brothels at water wells and on the edges of towns. At long last, her son killed her because he could no longer endure the incest or the thought of his mother bearing his children.

Colette wondered how women of the 14th century might have reacted to this fantastical tale, perhaps the second fall of the feminine after Eve. She remembered Peter's lustful descriptions of sex acts among the Greek gods in *The Recognitions of Clement* and her professor's accompanying theater. Then she smiled, glad to be safe inside the drama.

Boccaccio continued his travels. Colette made notes as the author wandered through Libya, Babylonia, and Thebes, meeting virgins, warriors and fornicators looking for stories and redemption among pagans or written in the stars. Many of his fantastical tales pointed directly to the feminine heart.

Boccaccio wrote about the dutiful wives of the Minyans, who remained nameless due to the negligence of writers, arrogant males or the mischief of fortune. Their husbands were men of quality who traveled with Jason and the Argonauts. But history also reported that these noble men became misguided and arrogant, thinking their blessings were due solely to their own actions. They became boastful and prideful, lusting after power. Driven by hubris, they plotted against the state. Blinded by their self-importance, they made childish mistakes and were soon discovered, imprisoned and sentenced to death.

Hearing of the sentence, their wives hatched a plan to free their husbands. The women dressed in poor mourning clothes went to the prison to say goodbye to their husbands. Once inside, they exchanged clothes with their husbands, who left the prison without being discovered. The author assumed a happy ending and reflected on the courage, wit, and duty found in the hearts of these women. There was no greater love than a wife laying down her life for her husband. Would men be just as selfless?

Boccaccio wrote that these brave and loving women were really men in the best, most honorable sense and the puffed-up Minyan youth they impersonated were like actors in a drama. He spoke of traits, proclivities and strength of character that the male Minyans lacked. At times he was severe, invoking manliness as an ideal for women, thus covering his tracks.

Colette read and enlarged the author's words. "We speak of what resided inside the hearts of these brave women which became animated by love when their husbands were in peril. We speak of the spirit and soulfulness of these women who are emblems of what is best in the human spirit. We speak of the ability of these women who used Christian charity to thwart the state. We speak of an abiding unselfishness the women displayed in taking on the personae of the opposite sex to save the lives of those they loved."

Colette sensed that despite Boccaccio's stern moralism displayed throughout the book, he seemed to be really fond of women. She thought that the men at the Council of Trent should have been filled with his understanding, charity and forgiveness.

She was hearing voices again and imagining herself in different places and times. She read Boccaccio's comments about the moral failings of his famous women even with all their successes. These were large and small warnings to satisfy his audience. He was his own chorus. On a whim and as a way to make things more interesting, Colette invited the Council of Trent to assume the voice of Boccaccio's inner chorus. In her fancy she thought that the men of Trent would get a taste of these pre-Renaissance tales, and she might see Trent in another color. Trent needed to know the world was changing and so was the role of women. So she gave Trent voice and she gave Trent words. Colette didn't know whether this was art, folly or another version of the cul-de-sac that she encountered so often in her dreams.

She soon found out, when her imagined Trent chorus went after Boccaccio.

"Oh, listen to the poet twist the sexes of our most gracious Minyans for nothing more than his dubious storytelling, gain and petty fame. What has man wrought?"

Boccaccio appeared not to notice and proceeded to honor Ilia, a Vestal Virgin, who had been forced into the temple by her brother so she could produce no heir to oppose him. But fate intervened, and she became pregnant, giving birth to Romulus and Remus, founders of the city of Rome. For her sin of fornicating inside the sacred temple, Ilia was buried alive in accordance with ancient law and her children were exposed to the elements but were saved and suckled by a wolf. Though her body was covered with earth, her children guaranteed she would live in everlasting glory.

The Italian author continued to comment on his own tales, writing that the death of the Vestal Virgin was a worthy tale indeed, and it was difficult not to stay with this well-known lineage, following the tantalizing threads into myth. But it was more important to reflect on the poor girl being condemned to what was little different from a nunnery. This was a common occurrence of the age with young girls being sentenced under the veil of religion to the nun's cell. Fathers have done this to save the costs of dowries for their daughters. The man was likely to say among his intimate circles that his virgin daughter will pray for his business and help him get into heaven, God willing. This is nonsense, wrote Boccaccio.

Colette paraphrased Boccaccio in her notebook.

"We know that an idle woman worships Venus and envies public prostitutes. We know that nuns, on witnessing a wedding and admiring the bride's dress and abundant trinkets, feel a great sadness, cursing their parents for putting them in such a predicament, never to taste the fruits of the marriage bed. They dearly wanted to escape this imprisonment and, we blush to say, taste the sexual pleasures that have been denied them."

Colette felt great satisfaction in recording Boccaccio in her own words and wondered how a thirteenth century artist could sound so modern, two centuries before the Council of Trent. Her chorus responded.

"This myth-maker we heard, this writer, this golden voice of story-telling surely offended both the gods and women by his raucous accounts that suggest he had spent too much time in the company of Bacchus, drunk and without virtue and with a tongue the shape of a serpent's head and just as deadly. How dare he sully the names of our virtuous sisters by making them the adulterous clay of his wretched fantasy?"

Boccaccio remained quiet and his *Famous Women* now focused on Greece and sang the praises of Leaena, a prostitute, but only after asking the indulgence of virtuous women and famous queens who might be reading the book.

The author noted that virtue can be found everywhere. Even the rays of the sun are not made evil when they come to rest on dirt. Virtue found in prostitutes can shame evil queens. His tale is short and true.

A tyrant king in Macedonia was murdered by two young nobles, Harmonious and Ariston. Leaena was implicated because of her closeness to the nobles. She was tortured but refused to answer because she might hurt others, valuing friendship above all else. The severity of the torture increased, and the woman feared she was losing the strength to resist. So she bit her tongue in half and spat it out. This noble act denied her tormenters the answers they desired. He who said that women keep silence best when they are ignorant did not know this prostitute.

Colette waited for the chorus to respond but heard nothing. She continued to follow Boccaccio in his travels.

Boccaccio left Greece and returned to Rome, having heard the stately voice of Roman matron Veturia who was desperate to save Rome and her son Coriolanus, named for his battle prowess. Some slight angered the son, and he raised an army to take the city. The ambassadors came, suing for peace. Priests genuflected before the warrior son but to no avail. Finally, Veturia and Coriolanus's wife Volumnia arrived with a small army of women. The son bursts into anger, accusing his mother of being in the enemy tent.

Veturia scolded her son, reminding him that the soil he stood on was the land where he was conceived. She suggested it was better that she had not given birth to him in the first place. She reminded him of his children and their lives as slaves should he lose his war.

In this tale feminine wiles rule the day. There are tears, embraces, groans, prayers, and the beating of breasts. Coriolanus's heart was touched as never before. His anger subsided, and his respect for his mother grew. He pulled his army from Rome.

The city built a temple in honor of Veturia so that she could be worshipped through the ages down to the present day. From that time when women passed by, men should rise in their honor. Women were permitted to wear purple dresses and receive inheritances.

The author wrote that other voices were heard in the kingdom. Colette knew that Boccaccio was balancing his tales and keeping his enemies at a distance. She thought that the grumbling the author recorded sounded very modern. She returned to her text, as if writing her own fictions.

"The more ornamentation a woman wore, the less wealth her husband enjoyed. Not only was it a woman's world but men had become feminine, gently walking in the shadow of their wives who were heavily laden with jewels. The men whined and mumbled about their wretched lots. Time has not lessened women's tight hold on their prerogatives. Men who call themselves slaves only bend the truth a little."

Now she heard both Boccaccio and her Trent chorus moaning about it being a woman's world where men might as well wear dresses as they fade into the earth while the wives squander their inheritance. Colette could almost imagine the women dancing on the graves of the deceased.

Colette was having her fun. She could imagine Boccaccio, a little annoyed at the growing power of women, throwing his hands in the air and waiting for fortune or fate to intervene. In the background the Trent chorus sounded much more ominous, mumbling something about the end of the world.

Boccaccio continued his tale.

Flora, the Goddess of Flowers, was a wealthy Roman woman and also a prostitute. Some say she used up the beauty of her youth with misdirected young men in the city's brothels. She gladly took the riches from these simple-minded men who during these wanton excesses were not thinking with their heads. This is a common curse that affects the male species.

Stories come through time and memory; sometimes through a mist and at other times over grains of sand left with faint footprints after the sea retreats. One story had survived that puts another face on the goddess.

A temple custodian was bored and played with dice on the marble floor. To add some conflict to the game, he decided that his left hand would represent himself and the right, Hercules. The stakes were modest. The custodian would get dinner and a girl if he won. If not, Hercules would receive the same treasures. Hercules, no slouch in fierce combat, won and the custodian gave him a dinner and Flora.

The tale hangs, almost out of reach. Flora slept in the temple and dreamed Hercules had lain with her. He said that she would be paid by a man as she left the holy place. As if by magic, she met the young, wealthy Fanitius, who fell in love with Flora and took her home. She stayed with him for years. When he died, she became his heir and very rich. But this was not the end of the story

Flora was without child and, as her days drew shorter, she contemplated her legacy. She would leave her wealth to the people of

Rome and, using financial wit, decreed that the interest of the sum of money would be used for public games on her birthday.

Colette read that the celebrations also included lewd acts, circus movements by naked prostitutes, and jokes about the oldest profession. These carnal activities tempted spectators to fornicate on beds of flowers, thus honoring Flora every time they reached the height of pleasure. The citizenry, so taken by the Floral Games, loudly reminded the politicians that they should not dip into Flora's interest fund for wars, political spoils, or family payoffs. They demanded that the games be held religiously every year. The Roman Senate, stung by what message this pornographic carnival sent to the world, came up with a political fairy tale. Flora was a goddess after all. She was Boccaccio's fiction.

Colette thought about the sexless, repressed, fantasy Venice she had visited and the vagina dream which continued to haunt her.

Her imagined Trent chorus couldn't restrain itself.

"We are almost mute by this elevation of whoredom to the level of state craft. May the gods drown you in the sea of your lies and fables from the Dark Ages."

Boccaccio continued to push through the haze and mist of history with Colette close at hand.

A young Roman woman appeared; her name, husband and history have been lost. Her mother had also been touched by ill-fortune and was imprisoned and sentenced to death for some unknown crime. Feeling sorry for her, the guard decided to let her die from hunger.

When the daughter visited her mother in prison, the guards made sure she was not carrying food. They didn't realize the daughter had recently given birth so she had enough milk in her breasts to feed her mother for days. A guard stumbled onto the truth and was surprised by the daughter's love and sacrifice. This tale finally reached the city council that released the mother from jail to honor her daughter's devotion.

Boccaccio wondered, if the ancients bestowed an oaken crown on a man who saved a citizen in battle, what crown could we offer a daughter who had saved her mother? He wrote that there was no plant that could provide leaves to honor so unselfish an action.

Colette fell into one last tale, the story of Marcia, a Roman maiden, virgin and artist. The noblewoman painted a self-portrait on a tablet while looking in a mirror. An etching based on this tale was used on a 16th century Italian edition of *Famous Women*. Colette wondered if this was what Merkel was referring to when he spoke about mirrors reflecting images over time. Was this lady showing the way to the Renaissance?

Colette heard the rumblings of the chorus fading in the distance. She closed *Famous Women* but sensed that the spirit of Boccaccio still traveled among the one hundred women with piety and a fierce pen, inviting readers to amend or delete passages they were uncomfortable with. He still resided comfortably within his own fictions. She did too.

She imagined moving in and out of mythology and random tales, adding asides and footnotes, and bringing in a personal chorus for emphasis. She wasn't always exactly sure where the text began and ended. It was fluid, open to history and inflation; it was full of characters who marched through time leaving few footprints but huge memories.

Colette felt that she now could tell the story of Flora the Prostitute a hundred times, each with a different flavor, because it put gods and humans in the same narrative and offered a fantastic tale that provided a lens or a perspective.

She searched for the right words and flirted with psychology. Flora was also an archetype, filled with lust, cunning, nobility, vanity and humanity. She had a wicked sense of humor, leaving a well-funded, freakish procession of prostitutes and circus clowns who would move to the sounds of street-level fornication.

Colette thought about her whirlwind fantasy journey through the Aegean and laughed at the liberties she had taken, moving in and out of myth as if she were a goddess. The stories shifted under the weight of Boccaccio's editorializing in a nod to the righteous, her own fantasies, and her imaginary Trent chorus trying to uphold the reputation of Church. How much of this was generated inside her head was unclear.

Colette was sure she had entered the prison with the unnamed and unknown Roman woman who gave breast milk to her mother, saving her life. In a way, Colette felt that the facts of this fable had also saved her life because the tale was small, human and vital.

Colette was growing weary of large themes and the panoply of gods who could amaze and destroy in the same sentence. She was also weary of her own stops and starts, re-imagining Trent and camping out on the periphery. She felt lost, passing and counting time. She remained deeply troubled that Boccaccio found an unorthodox feminine virtue in his pagan pantheon, while two hundred years later religious zealots burned women at the stake. If the gods were watching, they didn't make a sound.

Chapter Twenty-Three

"How was Florence?"

"I don't think I actually landed there, Professor Merkel. We mainly spent time in Greece, Rome and other ancient lands."

"We, Ms. McGovern?"

"Boccaccio and I. I was just tagging along, looking at his famous women. He was my guide. Sometimes I got inside the narrative."

"We all want to be at the head of the class. So, did Boccaccio shed any light on the Council of Trent?"

"I think Trent could use all the light it could get. Frankly, I'm shocked that the Council of Trent didn't pick up on what Boccaccio was writing about. If they did, the attendees might have had a greater appreciation of women."

"And what was that, pray tell?"

"In some follow-up research I read that Boccaccio in his earlier works was a bit of a misogynist, a bit of a scold, but in *Famous Women* he presented more complex women in a much greater range of life activities."

"So why the change of heart?"

"I had read that Boccaccio was older. Perhaps Petrarch was whispering in his ear. Perhaps more important was that he wanted to get out of the Middle Ages and away from the Christian overhang. Humanism was threatening to break out. He presented Eve as human and beautiful and Adam was left out in the cold. The Virgin Mary didn't even show up; nor did the saints."

"Yes," replied Merkel. "He was right on the cusp with his teacher Petrarch between the Middle Ages and the Renaissance. Any other hints of this transition between epochs?"

"Well, he seemed to have a lot more fun with myths, poking fun at the ancients. He was very patient with the Juno cult but still called the goddess overrated, as if he was trying to take some of the air out of the old tales. It seemed like Boccaccio was taking these wild myths and turning them into a kind of history."

"Please continue."

"As you know, in Boccaccio's earlier works women were often presented as sexual demons and temptresses, a narrative consistent with the Church's view of sexuality and libido. In *Famous Women* he pulled back from this harsh tone and relentless moralizing. He seemed more interested in developing characters."

"But *Famous Women* is still populated by randy goddesses."

"Certainly the lady shows up from time to time but more often the famous women displayed characteristics that involved the heart, such as love, compassion and charity. I guess the focus was on conjugal rather than erotic love. And there seemed less emphasis on the role of fortune in people's lives."

"Is this a feminist book, Ms. McGovern?"

"I think it points in that direction. It feels feminist in the sense that women's wit, courage and selflessness so often rule the day. I sense little of the Christian shadow here."

"So what are we to do with these stories?"

"I must admit Boccaccio sucked me in. At times I seemed to be inside the narrative. I imagined Boccaccio's occasional scolding was coming from the Council of Trent. A few more hours and I would be writing my own stories."

"Please go on."

"I realize Boccaccio didn't give up completely on his mythical license and tells the reader he's all about tall tales. But it is human nature and the feminine heart that takes center stage."

"So *Famous Women* is more about human behavior than famous women doing what they do?"

"*Famous Women* might be considered one of the first studies in feminine behavior."

"Please continue that thought."

"I'll try. At times the characters seem like stick figures but the conflicts they endured were real, such as when a daughter breastfed her dying mother. Characterizations like this seem almost psychological but this is just a feeling."

"Feelings also count. Now back to Trent if we can. Imagine you're attending the council and have been asked to address what the Church might learn from *Famous Women*."

"I think they would toss me out in the street. I got an earful while reading Boccaccio."

Merkel laughed. "Humor me. Imagine this time around there are a few nuncios, prelates and what-nots that had left the Dark Ages and knew deep-down that change was in the air. I'll join you in the colloquy. Keep in mind that I might drift in and out of the conversation. Trent has become a huge responsibility, and we are hearing many voices. You will still have Boccaccio in your ear."

Colette began her presentation to the imagined council crowd that was becoming increasingly familiar, glad her professor allowed for some levity.

"I have just come from Florence, and I think the council should be cognizant of the writings of Boccaccio, especially *Famous Women* which celebrated the lives of a hundred famous women culled from myths and pagan tales."

Merkel tried to disguise his voice by speaking through his hands.

"May I ask, dear and honored lady; do you assume to offend our ears with talk of pagan legends and foul deeds? After all, we stand here in the presence of the one true God."

Colette continued.

"Honored brethren: while Boccaccio did not go to the saints for examples of virtue, the women he presents represent an array of behaviors that would not offend your august presence."

"Proceed then with care and discretion."

"Very well," she responded. "Boccaccio, Petrarch and other artists in the fourteenth century borrowed from the Greeks and mythology to enrich their stories."

"But, dear lady, are you not talking about polytheism and a zodiac full of strange gods? Do we not risk our souls being contaminated by these heathen gods?"

"Gentlemen, these stories were fiction or tall tales as Boccaccio told us. The ancient goddesses and other women of high station were ways to celebrate women for their character, wit and cunning, and at times their superiority to men. The author re-imagined these figures to give them more depth."

Merkel turned to his left and right, pretending to whisper in a concerned manner to the nuncios at his side.

"Honorable lady, the Church has long celebrated virtuous women and virgins. We have the Blessed Virgin Mary, the ultimate example of gracious and selfless living."

"Gentlemen, Boccaccio tells us early on that he would look to this earth and the fallen. He found virtue in women who overcame adversity and shine in what you might consider Christian character."

Colette could see Merkel shuffling his feet and showing pained expressions on his face as if he was really at Trent. His voice was getting edgy.

194

"I hear there are many whores among Boccaccio's women. Shall we let them too into the council?"

"Honorable gentlemen, I suspect there are as many prostitutes who walk the streets of Trent and other cities you are familiar with. Boccaccio often had a harsh tone towards these women, but his heart also opened for the least among us. He was concerned about the way women were being treated. He condemned fathers for imprisoning their daughters in nunneries."

Merkel now sounded like Boccaccio's chorus. Colette wondered whether he had read *Famous Women*.

"He spoke that blasphemy and heresy?"

"Yes, he did and with some power. He said fathers put daughters in nunneries without their consent and expected them to pray for the fathers' business and everlasting life. He wrote that fathers did this so they didn't have to pay marriage dowries."

"Do my ears deceive me, dear lady, or am I hearing a monstrous blasphemy against our Catholic fathers?"

Merkel looked around, a little more furtive this time, motioning with his hands as if asking for a time out. He hands formed the shape of a hastily arranged "T." Then he made the sign of the cross.

"Does the lady have anything to add?" Merkel asked in a strained voice.

Colette replied. "Boccaccio suggested that nuns who looked on the marriage ceremony and saw silk dresses and pearls hated their fathers for denying them the marriage bed."

"Surely there can be no more of this horror."

Colette persisted.

"Boccaccio wrote that the nunnery was better off with fewer nuns rather than being inhabited by those who think night and day about smuggling young men into their bedrooms for carnal pleasure. May God bless the honorable and devout nuns!"

"May God bless the honorable and devout nuns," Merkel replied, as if out of habit.

"Amen to that," he added.

"Not ready for prime time, sir?"

"You or me, Ms. McGovern?"

"Me, of course, sir."

"We'll probably have to cut out the piece about the nuns. Very sensitive subject. Maybe tone down the sex stuff. Most of the attendees had spent a fair bit of time in the confessional and knew everyone's dark little secrets. Rumor has it that they shared details about sexual sins with the Pope. Mainly women, I'm sorry to say, because the guys were in the bars. That was Venice's big worry, if I recall. Put that out in public and you can raise a standing army in days and more than a fistful of florins. But let's not move too far away from piety. Going to bed with any of the Seven Deadly might get you in trouble."

"Thank you, Professor Merkel, but I'm no longer sure whether I should go this way or that way, this way or that."

"I can appreciate the sensitive line that you walk, trying to please both the soothsayers and the naysayers. I suggest that you continue your presentation to the council while I take a short Roman holiday, if you know what I mean. As always, I can hear everything with my luscious membranes and have the memory of an elephant."

"Certainly, Professor. I can hold down this fort and find the right language for the attendees. I will work very hard to stay out of the confessional mode. I'm glad Boccaccio is close at hand."

"That is a consummation devoutly to be wished, Ms. McGovern. And if you remember who said that, please give me a holla. Ta, ta for now!"

Colette waited for the trumpeting to come from either the wilds or some celestial hangout, but she received few vibrations. Merkel's voice had merged with a Greek chorus somewhere in the distance which was fading like a low prayer. She felt Boccaccio's presence in the hall and that she had been touched by God.

She conjured up the Trent attendees again just beyond the mist and continued her practice run.

"Honorable Sirs: Boccaccio didn't excuse women's lack of piety, but he celebrated their gifts, often showing them smarter and more able than men. He showed many instances where women were superior to men."

Colette heard the chorus inside her head and felt it punishing her heart.

"Yes, we seem to remember the good Christian poet informing us that the world was indeed owned by women, and it had become a woman's world where they could wear trinkets and grow rich from their husband's inheritance."

The voice seemed to come from a distance. Was she answering her own questions?

"Kind Sirs: Boccaccio sometimes sounded like a grumbling husband who was unhappy with his wife's progress. I think he offered these observations to appease men. The man had a sense of humor."

"The poet probably had a wife at home nagging him. But where is the nobility in this tale?"

"Honored Sirs, Boccaccio offers a hundred tales and many are about female compassion and piety. I leave you with just one:

"Paulina Busa, a noblewoman from Canosa di Puglia in southern Italy, welcomed to her house 10,000 wounded, naked and hungry soldiers, injured when Hannibal crushed the Roman army. She gave them shelter.

She brought in a doctor to tend to their wounds. She nursed, fed and clothed them. Busa provided weapons to those in need and money when they were ready to depart. She remained there to care for new arrivals who had heard about her compassion.

"Boccaccio reminded us that the ancients praised Alexander, king of Macedonia, for his generosity, but much of what he gave to others he had seized by force. She gave freely from her legal inheritance. The poet told us that gold exists to be used for the common good. For her generosity, compassion and selflessness, he placed Busa above Alexander in the pantheon of good deeds.

"The poet did not use the language of the gospels, but he might as well be talking about Christian charity. I wouldn't be at all surprised if he would recommend sainthood for Busa. It has remained the lot of women to care for a world ravaged and destroyed by men.

"You scoff at women taking over the world and stealing the inheritances of men. That's a man's tale told for his own satisfaction. *Famous Women* is a book about Christian charity, and I'm surprised that the poet did not include Christ in his volume. After all, Christ's mission was to preach love, charity, virtue, and compassion, and Boccaccio makes clear that these are primarily female virtues. I am not the first to suggest that Christ was like Hermaphrodite, son of Hermes and Aphrodite, who as we learned from Ovid entered a union with a nymph combining male and female characteristics."

Colette was in a feverish state and her imaginary audience from the Council of Trent now became the perfect crowd to which she could speak completely from the heart. She might have been defending her thesis which existed only in her head. The nuncios might be invisible, but she had met them all before and knew them well. Boccaccio had already provided her with the text.

"Desist with this blasphemy and heresy!" her audience demanded.

She continued.

"*Famous Women* is an allegory about the strength and piety of pagan women. Boccaccio wrote that the saints were not good examples because they are focused on the afterlife. Men of the Council of Trent, you have focused on the saints and the Virgin Mary and ignored the heroic and pious women who are under your noses. You ignored our God-given imagination. You ignored our hearts."

The Trent voices Colette now heard seemed to be coming from her own lips, fed by all the old texts she had been reading for five months. She was on both sides of the argument.

"You have gone too far! Your words are anathema and heresy! You are excommunicated and forever placed outside the community of the faithful."

Colette did not relent.

"Dear Sirs, I am only telling you stories that are well-known throughout Italy and the world. I offered you parables."

Colette imagined the anger growing at the Council of Trent and took comfort in the knowledge that Professor Merkel might have returned.

"Parables be damned! You insulted Christ and the Virgin Mary. You joined man and women in an ungodly, pagan and abhorrent way. What you have said is an utter abomination."

She continued her argument.

"Kind Sirs, I told you fables that the ancients taught us. They are not real. They just provide a perspective on the past. They are food for the imagination. They are tonic for the soul."

"There is no salvation for you, dear woman. May God strike us dead if we do not utter this sentence: By the grace of Jesus Christ, his saints and the cherubim and seraphim, by the holy blood of the martyrs, by the honored dead in repose with the Father, the entire Trent congregation sentence you to eternal damnation in the relentless fires of hell!"

Colette found strength in Boccaccio.

"Would you rather hear the tale, dear sirs, of women being tortured and burned at the stake for their beliefs? Do you recall Marguerite Porete who was burned at the stake in Paris in 1310 for imagining a feminine God the Father? Do you recall during the time of Trent that Anne Askew was burnt at the stake in Britain because she was a woman?

"Was Boccaccio not a more devoted lover of womankind than either the Vatican or this very council where women don't even exist in the mist? They are invisible except as receptacles for what Aquinas called the male seed implanted without lust, that physical reenactment of divine disobedience."

"God damn you, woman!"

She heard a chorus of "Amen."

"Too far, sirs, too far?" she asked, out of words and out of air.

"You can go to hell!"

Colette felt her head exploding and recalled collapsing in the classroom. When she awoke, it was dark. She sensed all her research from the last five months seemed to come pouring out of her mouth, as if it was actual doctrine. For the first time she was able with the help of Boccaccio to look at theology through a feminine lens. It excited and overwhelmed her. Colette had no doubt that if the nuncios were in the classroom in the flesh, they would have excommunicated her and sentenced her to death.

Colette felt open and exposed, her body stretched out over time, memory and theology, as if she was Anne Askew on the rack in the Tower of London, her joints pulled out of their sockets and her mouth fixed in eternal pain. She felt that the men in the Tower and at Trent were focused on her womb.

She could still hear the chorus in her head, endlessly announcing her final sentence. Somehow Colette felt complicit in her own sentencing.

Chapter Twenty-Four

The night after her imaginary classroom session with the Council of Trent attendees, Colette dreamed she was fussing around in the vestibule of a church. She dearly wanted to use the word "back" but seemed compelled to stay with the Latin. She was fidgeting, taking note of the collection boxes, the baptismal font and stacks of missals. She heard a celebration in front of the church but sensed that she couldn't participate or at the very least was waiting for instructions.

In time, a priest appeared in a somewhat shadowy form and pointed to a staircase that appeared to have just been built out of unfinished lumber. The priest said that she should climb the staircase and proceed to the other side. She pointed out that there was no path, no structure and no sign. It would be like walking through thin air.

The priest assured her that it would appear to her as she crossed. She followed him as he climbed the stairs and walked across to the other side but after stepping off the stairway, she fell into an inverted funnel that had a textured and organic feel to it, as if it were alive. She felt as if she were inside a giant parsnip which had been hollowed out. As she fell, she told someone who was close to her: "I am going to hell."

The scene shifted and Colette talked to someone, perhaps her mother, about a big upcoming event which could be a marriage. When she pushed for more details, the other person said, the future was in the hands of an angel and she would understand in time. Colette said she knew the song and sang: "She walks, like an angel walks." She held out both hands hoping to touch the angel but found only air.

Colette remembered listening to her father singing along with Dean Martin and Frank Sinatra and their version of "My Kind of Girl." Colette recalled her father mimicking the singers as they made faces when they sang off-key, "She cooks like an angel looks."

She was glad to wake from her parsnip hell with a memory of her father who seemed to be drifting away from her. She was hoping that the angel dream was a way out or compensation for her falling into hell, but it gave her Sinatra and Martin, who were from another world. You can't take a joke, she told herself.

She wasn't ready to leave her father just yet. She laughed when she remembered how he would slip into another angel song, "Pretty Little Angel Eyes," when he was bored with the singers and wanted to counter their antics. She laughed again when she recalled him trying to hit the high notes, chasing eternity, heaven above and probably paradise. He was never able to reach those heights but enjoyed it all the same, rewarding his attempt with a cold Coke.

"Was that you singing, Colette?" her mother asked. "It's been years since I've heard you sing. Wasn't that one of your father's favorites?"

"Yes. I dreamed about an angel and when I woke, I found myself singing Dad's angel song."

"That's beautiful, dear. Did the angel bring good tidings? Angels are messengers, you know."

"I hadn't thought about that, Mother. A woman said something was going to happen, and it's in the hands of an angel. And that I would understand in time. I sensed it might be about a marriage."

"Colette, you didn't tell me!"

"No such luck, Mother. I didn't get the sense it was like a regular wedding."

"Maybe a spiritual wedding. Father Stravinsky called Christ the Bridegroom of the Church and that we are all married to him."

She tried to imagine Christ walking like an angel walks. Both thoughts sounded a little creepy.

"Are you planning to be become a nun? That would be a spiritual wedding. Come to think of it, you are looking drawn, thin and nun-like these days."

Her mother was making a joke, but Colette didn't find it funny.

"No, Mother. I've been reading about families who forced their daughters to enter the convent so they would not have to pay for the wedding."

"Now dear, you know your father put away some money for your wedding when you're ready. Anyway, I don't think you could sit still all day and pray."

"Thanks for the vote of confidence, Mom."

"Okay, I'll drop the marriage thing. How are you? I haven't seen you for a few days."

"Oh, out and about. I'm trying to put the Trent project to bed."

She felt uncomfortable with the reference to bed.

"That Trent thing! You should have left it dead and buried. You haven't been eating or sleeping right since that project started."

201

"I know, Mother. A couple more weeks should do it. Trent seems less important now than a month ago. But I couldn't have come to this conclusion without digging up a lot of dead bodies."

Her mother crossed herself.

"Now, my dear; we must be careful with such words what with your father's body not yet cold a half mile from here."

The reference to her father's not-yet-cold dead body always won the argument and the day. Colette hugged and kissed her mother, who smiled sweetly.

She would not tell her about falling through an inverted parsnip into hell, though she didn't feel the temperature rising. She seemed to remember that the inside of the parsnip had rings that could have been veins or markers. She thought of Dante's "Inferno" and recalled that the entrance to Hell was called a vestibule with a sign that read "Nowhere." From what she remembered, the sign meant the people in the vestibule had refused to make choices in life; they would be awarded neither praise nor blame.

She picked through an old volume and stopped at a few pages that were marked. She couldn't remember why Hector, Homer, Ovid and other pagans were assigned to Limbo rather than the unbaptized children she heard so much about in catechism class. Dante's Hell was full of pagans and mythical creatures. He made room for at least seven popes. Simon Magus, the sorcerer, was perpetually baptized with oil and fire. Other soothsayers and fortune tellers had their heads twisted backwards so the tears ran down their backs and over the creases in their buttocks. Where would Boccaccio be?

Colette thought that Dante's description of the whore Thais could have been fit reading in the anterooms at Trent. "Repulsive and disheveled tramp, scratching herself with shitty fingernails, spreading her legs, while squatting up and down."

She entered her own fiction and wondered what circle of hell she might have landed on in her trip down the parsnip tunnel. Surely she had earned a place among the lustful, gluttonous, avaricious, or the wrathful?

Colette remembered the recent classroom fantasy exercise during which the imagined Trent assembly accusing her of heresy for telling stories about the pagan gods and goddesses. She had a few more things to say, and she said them to herself.

"Dear Sirs and Holy Men: I am doing nothing more than the honorable Dante did in using myths and pagan tales to tell his stories. Did he not add richness to his narration? Did he not capture prurient interests? Did he really believe Epicurus should be sent to the Sixth Circle of Hell as a heretic because he loved temporal happiness and denied the soul's immortality? Should this advocate of fine dining and white tablecloths be subjected to eternal burning, so severe that the poet claims some lands on earth can hear this daily torture? Does he belong in the same company as Pope Anastasius II who in 497 allowed a heretic to take communion? Surely he is not in the company of the thief and the blasphemer who shaped his two fists like figs, in the Italian tradition, and raised them above his head, saying, 'God, this is for you!' Should not a man who says 'fuck you' to the Most High be burned at the stake every day before and after his death?"

Colette feared, as a blasphemer, she would be placed in burning sand, supine. A usurer would receive the same punishment but be in a crouch position while a sodomite would wander endlessly in the burning circle. She would have to do a thorough self-examination before admitting to flattery because that sin would forever immerse her in excrement. Colette had walked in circles many times before, so she figured she had already paid the above-ground price for being a hypocrite.

Dante's *Divine Comedy* was said to be the last book of the Middle Ages and represented the culture's last underworld, dark, circular and punitive. Colette was having her fun, lining up the grafters, slanderers, and falsifiers and having them sit back-to-back in some treacherous muck, scratching their leprous sores. That was the easy part, perhaps a way of quieting the voices which kept coming out of Trent, first as pantomime then as nightmare, hunting her down. She had studied enough psychology to know when something was a figment of her imagination or when she was engaged in displacement, substituting a new angle or perspective when something becomes dangerous. "You can go to hell" definitely got her attention.

Colette wondered about the priest who encouraged her to climb the stairway and literally walk across air. She tried to place him again. He looked a little like a priest she had known from her childhood. Father Butler was short, thin with craven features due to smoking two packs of cigarettes a day. Years later, her mother told her that when Father Butler stopped drinking Irish whiskey, he started smoking heavily. Parishioners were so pleased that he had stopped drinking that they didn't dare say anything about his smoking.

The dream priest was thin, short and had a hint of a craggy face that might have been covered by a veil. At this point, the distinction between the dream and her re-imaginings was not entirely clear. She responded to the priest's dress and authority the way she might have as a young woman. He said only a few words and pointed to the route. But he did demonstrate, walking up the stairway and across the chasm. It was not as if he were leading her astray.

She thought about being in the church vestibule and worked hard to keep at bay images of Dante's entrance to hell and the signage about "Nowhere" because that was where she seemed to be living at the moment. Colette recalled other dreams in which she desired to join a service or a celebration but was held back for some reason.

She heard another voice inside her head. It sounded like a cross between her professors, her mother and her psychologist. Was it her conscience talking? It said: "Will you stop confusing theology with mythology or whatever the hell you call it?"

It was as if she were listening to herself think and talking to herself at the same time. God help me, she prayed. But the voice or voices in her head continued.

"Let me put it this way. You or whoever was hanging out in the back of the church looking at the poor box or old missals appeared lost. The guy who looked like a priest arrived and suggested that you should climb the staircase and walk through air. He might be a priest, an undertaker or the custodian. He could be up to no good or a god; who knows? Anyway, since this was a dream, this guy could also be a Trickster, the god, spirit, animal or demi-god who possesses secret knowledge and plays tricks. Cartoon characters, such as Reynard the Fox, often play the Trickster. Do we have a foxy priest or a priestly fox on our hands? Remember that Reynard was French, and that in itself lowered the trust index.

"The priest climbed the staircase and walked across air. You followed him and fell into an upside-down parsnip that you imagine was hell. This was no Garden of Eden. A theological reading would suggest that you lacked the grace, virtue or balls to follow the priest. Therefore, you must be lacking. Monthly stipends and regular attendance at Mass can buy back what's missing. Centuries ago this would have been called an indulgence."

Colette swore that this was the right side of her brain talking, drumming up all the theological data and psychological bits it could find.

The voice continued inside her head.

"To go a little further, someone could be telling you not to pay so much attention to priests or religion in general. You are conflicted, probably because of your religious training, your parents, your project and that memory you're been running from. Even the word Trent seems like oversized luggage that will weigh heavily on your back and cost you exorbitant fees as you move across borders. You need a vacation."

The voice that now sounded a bit like Professor Merkel with cartoon bluster had run out of steam, so she settled for comfort food, conjuring up the voice of her father singing "Pretty Little Angel Eyes," straining to reach the a cappella and to rhyme heaven above with love. "I love you so; I'll never let you go." He was something.

Even after all her travels and fantasies, Colette still believed in angels.

That night Colette dreamed she was in a family setting, listening to voices that seemed vaguely familiar. There was tension in the air. Colette felt that her remarks about history and the importance of the feminine were being ignored. She heard the word "patriarchy" and the word seem to grow and fill the room. A man entered carrying a crucifix. He said to her, "You have lost our confidence." Colette responded with anger and finality: "It's over." The man replied: "It's never over." Then he opened a door and descended into the basement with his cross on his shoulder.

On waking, Colette was sweating and her heart was pounding. She tried to push away the thought that the man in her dream looked like her father by recalling the role of the Trickster in dreams. It didn't help. But Colette was confident that in the dream she had signaled that she would not descend with the man and would not follow his way of the cross.

Colette recalled another, earlier dream about a crucifix. In the dream she had received a full-size, white mahogany crucifix in the mail. She recalled telling someone that you never know when a cross might come in handy. In the dream the statement sounded like a joke.

In the daylight it sounded like a prediction.

Chapter Twenty-Five

"Have we finally put Trent to bed, Ms. McGovern?"

That word again. What was it with priests and bed, dead and bread? Focus, girl, she told herself.

"Not completely, Professor Gleason. I've studied most of the early councils. I have done a lot of reading around the early Italian Renaissance, especially Boccaccio. I dipped into Dante. I recall delivering a few remarks at the Council of Trent, metaphorically speaking."

"Rewriting history, Ms. McGovern?"

"Oh, no, sir. Professor Merkel suggested that I sharpen my thinking by imagining an exchange with the attendees."

"Ah yes; the power of the imagination! How did that work out?"

"I mentioned Boccaccio and his stories of righteous pagan women who performed Christian acts and in some instances were very saintly."

"Any response from this imagined congregation?"

"Yes, sir. At first they were polite, but the more stories I told of these pagan women, the angrier they became. Boccaccio's chorus complained about women taking over the world, and I said he was just another guy moaning about the progress women were making. And this was in 1361 or so."

"So the imagined council members actually heard and responded to your questions? That is quite a feat, Ms. McGovern! Was this through mental telepathy or was it a case of divine intervention?"

"From what I remember, neither, sir. Professor Merkel agreed to be the interlocutor during the exchange, delivering the council's response to my questions."

And did Professor Merkel coach you, Ms. McGovern?"

"No, sir. Not really. He was mainly a stand-in for the council. He might have challenged me to rephrase or sharpen my questions."

"How sharp did you get?"

"Well, my questions especially about the feminine in the Church must have gotten a little sharp because the council declared I was a heretic."

"That's not as bad as a burning at the stake. But what made the council so angry?"

"I think it was my mention of Jesus as a hermaphrodite, sharing female and male characteristics. I did mention something about Aquinas considering women a receptacle for male sperm. I meant no offense."

"And where, pray tell, was Professor Merkel during this delicious exchange?"

"If I remember the conversation, he was there for most of it. I think he needed a break and decided to leave the room for a while. He encouraged me to continue."

"And did you?"

"Yes, sir. It was amazing how much the Trent attendees sounded like Boccaccio's inner chorus."

"I see. Please go on."

"I tried to explain that the reason Boccaccio wrote about pagan women was they were more interesting than Christian women who were guaranteed heaven. I might have said Dante did the same thing; populate hell with a lot of mythic, pagan souls because they were interesting and instructive."

"Was the council amused?"

"I don't think so. I tried to explain that mythic stories or pagan gods were not true in the literal sense. Like parables, they provide another perspective, a way of seeing. Dante and Boccaccio were Christians, of course, but I think they were equally interested in a popular narrative that provided new ways of seeing."

"New ways? I thought the Church had laid out the one true path centuries earlier?"

"I understand. I think these early Italian Renaissance writers were able to embrace both Christ and the Greek myths that were the center of the short-lived Neoplatonist movement."

"Ah, Plato. The Church had embraced Aristotle a long time ago as the man of science and reason. We don't mind poets and storytellers as long as they are respectful of our history. But more on that in a moment. How did the session with the council end? I understand Professor Merkel took a break and you were obliged to deal with the nuncios and other delegates on your own? I take it Boccaccio was still by your side?"

"Yes, sir. I felt Boccaccio's presence at all times, but I did hear other voices. Perhaps it was my imagination or I was channeling Professor Merkel. I had a sense that he actually came back into the classroom. I had read so much about the Council of Trent that it seemed relatively easy to answer my own questions."

Colette didn't know whether that was meant to be a joke.

"I heard council members getting very angry, telling me to go to hell and God-damning me."

"That's a harsh sentence, Ms. McGovern. With your exhausting research into Trent you might well have been summoning the dead. Or, with Merkel in and out of the room, you might have been imagining things. Boccaccio would be pleased that you dug him up and took him to Trent."

"Everyone is telling me that Trent is taking me over like some weight or beast. So maybe I have been digging up the dead. I understand the psychology of that. Jung might say I'm caught in a complex and wrestling with the beast. It's like I'm giving birth to something. The council has gotten to me and affected me psychologically. I've had more than a few sleepless nights. And the dreams come like tumbleweeds. One of my friends said I had been 'Trented.' It sounded like I might have been on the receiving end of a drive-by shooting."

Colette regretted mentioning the dreams.

"I sympathize with you. Theology can wear heavily on us all. We have years of indoctrinating at church, then we're sent out into the world and perhaps find another narrative. Anything else you'd like to tell the council?"

"Will you be the interlocutor?"

"All right, I will wear my theology hat. Please proceed."

"Honored assembled: Trent is so close to Florence where Boccaccio and other early Renaissance figures lived. Why is there so little of the spirit of Florence at Trent?"

"That wasn't the compelling issue of the day; Luther and the Reformation were."

"But Dear Sirs: The Council of Trent constantly thwarted attempts to address the concerns of the Reformation, especially in regard to the behavior of clergy and the sale of indulgences."

"We understand your question. The council was well aware of the concerns of the Protestants but decided not to address them head-on, so these forces would receive no political advantages. The council was very aware of priestly abuses, the sale of indulgences, and issues relating to a bishop's residency."

Colette no longer knew whether that voice was coming from 1563 or the present day. The words could have been spoken at any moment during that run of time. She would drop the honorifics.

"More than a century before Trent, Boccaccio displayed tolerance and sympathy for pagan women and goddesses. The pagan veil seemed to be a way to address the psychology of women. Why was there so little discussion of women at Trent except as property or devil?"

"The council was rich in mentions of the Virgin Mary, the ultimate mother and daughter and wife. The Church holds Mary as the ideal matriarchal figure."

Colette responded. "Aquinas wrote that the sanctity of the soul remained even when the body was violated. He also wrote that women who were raped likely betrayed a proud and contemptuous bearing, and this was a way for them to learn humility. Does the council still hold with Aquinas?"

"Dear Soul: we hear a little of Boccaccio's ravings in your lascivious question. We have come a long way since our saintly Aquinas instructed us eight hundred years ago. The Virgin Mary has grown in stature and importance through the endless prayers of the faithful and the infallible acts of our popes."

"The council decided that the representation of sacred images in churches and other places was acceptable as long as the images were not lascivious and were consistent with Church teachings. How did the council expect that to be enforced?"

"The Holy Father shared his wisdom with his flock. The Church expected the proper restraint from artists so that they would not be tempted by depravity. This is when we pray for the wisdom of the Holy Spirit."

The voice was either reading from a catechism or mocking her questions. The interlocutor was changing his stripes. Colette tried again.

"I was still wondering about the Italian Renaissance and why Trent paid no attention to a force that was literally in the council's backyard."

"In truth, Trent was closer to Germany's backyard."

"I was wondering if the council was aware of Marsilio Ficino, who was considered a Renaissance Doctor of Soul?"

"Wasn't Ficino a short, ugly humpback who lived in Florence? Didn't he believe in astrology and practiced homosexuality under the guise of Platonic love? Didn't he believe that the practice of alchemy could help ward off the plague? That midget was a real piece of work."

"He did study astrology and made a fuss about being born under the influence of Saturn. It was in the air. The Italian Renaissance was open to everything, trying to throw off the straightjacket of Aristotle."

"Wasn't the humpback accused of practicing magic by Pope Innocent VIII?"

"Yes," Colette replied, "but the Church often accused people of heresy and witchcraft. Ficino was cleared."

"That's nice for him, but there is no seat for him at Trent. We'd be a laughingstock."

"Ficino spoke of the World Soul that is inherent in the material world. The soul belongs to the elements and non-human animals. The soul is responsible for the growth of rocks and trees. Soul is in our dreams and imaginings. It is alive in everything. Image-making is the path to soul."

Professor Gleason began his litany of soul talk, as if it were a contest.

"The soul is immortal," he said. "It is the mind of God, transcendent and the spark of ineffable spirit. The soul is height, elevation and ascendancy. Soul is the inexorable movement towards the Light. Soul is always spirit rising relentlessly to the Godhead."

Colette felt Gleason had taken her to the summit of a mountain, as if he were introducing her to a god. She felt like a foreigner in this thin air and fought to get back to ground level. She prayed to Ficino and Boccaccio to be her guides, to take her down into her indecision, her pathologies, her fears and her melancholy. She prayed to be taken down into her dreams and nightmares where her guides have told her that soul resided. She asked Proteus to be by her side, helping her find direction through her blunders, errors and vanity. She asked St. John Damascene to let her enter the vastness of soul he imagined.

Colette felt like a long exhaustive ceremony was over. All the words had been spoken. The council had rained down its thunder. She vaguely remembered seeing in a vision Gleason and Merkel engaged in their Punch and Judy exchange, mimicking the prophets and heretics of old, getting their knickers in a twist.

Colette and Professor Gleason went to opposite corners of the classroom. She slumped into a nearby chair, as if acknowledging defeat. She heard the professor shuffle out of the room without saying another word.

Colette felt as if soul, bloodied and bruised, had left the building, along with her interlocutor and the rest of the council crowd, though the final summons still lingered in the air. The exchange with Gleason might have been written on the council walls or buried in some unmarked archive of her brain, ready for service. The text was familiar; some of it wooden, all leading to the theological cul-de-sac she had visited many times before.

She left the college and went home, slipping in the back door and past her mother dozing on the couch and into her bedroom. She did some breathing exercises and tried to meditate as O'Connell had suggested. She thought about praying again, but that seemed to raise her pulse rate. She tried to sleep, but the weight of centuries seemed to fall on her, pinning her in place.

Colette, half awake and half asleep, was on the move again, looking for company, ideally a carrier of Renaissance soul and a companion on her journey. She thought of Dante, Beatrice his spiritual prompt, and Virgil, sturdy guide and honorable man, even though he was a pagan. Colette could hear her interlocutor say she was no Dante nor was the rest of that crowd. I know, I know, she said out of habit.

She had her eye on Dante, who was wandering, circling downward, past the inhabitants of hell, some floating in their own shit, witnessing the lustful and the gluttonous, living their sins eternally. There were stories among the ghosts walking here, and Dante interrogated some of them who remained curious about what was happening in the light of day. Who was still in power, who had been murdered, and who was the next clergy to join in their wretched circle of avarice?

The descent had the feel of a very dark catechism with its listing of increasingly wretched sins laid out in impeccable Italian rhyme. But it was deeper and more complex than that. For her, the place seems ancient, cold and mythological, populated by the pagan gods and fantastical beasts long in service to the underworld. Nonetheless, despite the poet's fears and reversals, the direction was always upward. Beatrice remained nearby, and Paradise was just around the corner.

How to contain the wanderings? Trent seemed to be in her rear-view mirror, sturdy as an old dictionary that projects its weight. The final document would likely contain sixteen hundred years of doctrine, interpretation and conceit; one thing piled on top of the other, polished over time, enough to take on a well-practiced sheen.

How to contain the wanderings? Colette thought of the fantasy tit-for-tat exchange she had with Merkel, Boccaccio, or the man in the moon. She was no longer sure if she was in on the joke. Colette had learned to listen to her voices. For all the times she had heard the word "soul" mentioned in church, class, or alleyways, it always seemed vaporous, like the breath against the window that immediately disappeared. She was almost relieved when she learned that some philosopher had said the soul was located in the pineal gland in the center of the brain. Despite being so specifically anchored, the soul continued to drift upward into the vaporous world of the spirit.

She was on the move again, looking for company, waiting for a vision to come. She imagined in a field of poppies, daisies, and forsythia, Persephone and her friends playing on a bright summer day under the watchful eyes of her mother, Demeter and Zeus looking down from the heavens. The scene was filled with love and laughter.

Persephone decided to bring a flower to her mother, choosing a narcissus. She could not know that flower was her father's wish. Immediately, the earth opened, and Hades appeared and abducted the maiden in his golden chariot. On her way to Hades, she could not utter a sound.

Demeter searched for her daughter without success and soon abandoned her duties as Goddess of Grain. The flowers died, and her mood grew dark. In her grief Demeter wandered, stopping at a fountain where the distraught goddess met four females who took her home. Their parents offered her shelter and care. In return, Demeter cared for their son. She decided to thank the family by placing the child in the fire every night, thus assuring him immortality. The family could not understand this offering and sent Demeter out of their house. That brought back the goddess in Demeter, and she showed her true self to the family. The family asked for forgiveness and promised to build a temple in Demeter's honor.

When she remembered her lost daughter, Demeter was full of rage and demanded that Zeus find her. He had sent Hermes to look for Persephone. Hermes reported that he was shocked to find a very happy Queen of Hades. Persephone greeted new arrivals and helped them find their place in hell. She missed her mother but was attached to Hades.

Hades took in Persephone's sorrow and comforted her. He gave her pomegranate seeds. He would miss her, but her mother should be honored too. Then she climbed inside Hermes's chariot and was returned to her mother. The flowers were joyous on Persephone's return, but Demeter knew the daughter she gave birth to was gone. The mother recalled Zeus's declaration that for Persephone to return home, she must be pure as the maiden Hades took. But with the pomegranate seeds staining the daughter's lips red, she had tasted the fruit of sexual life.

Persephone returned to Hades and with each spring came back with the flowers that bear her name, telling the story of rebirth. When she left in the fall, her mother mourned and waited for spring. Persephone was pleased to guide those in Hades to the next phase of their lives.

Colette reflected on how many times she had ambled through this myth, bathing in the archetypal spring flowers, watching with anticipation as the earth opened up, and still wondering how you give immortality to a child by putting him daily in a fire.

Colette laughed at her CliffsNotes literalism but remembered that the rape scene always bothered her, though she knew various Greek and Roman writers interpreted rape to suit their fancy. The word still stung.

Colette remembered that the Renaissance embraced Persephone as a guide who welcomed the dead to Hades. Colette had read that the rape should be seen as an initiation, moving the daughter from a natural life to a psychic life. But why did rape show up so often in art, myth and creation stories as that act of war on a woman's body? What happens when the "Rape of the Sabine Women," the "Rape of Lucretia" and the rape in Shakespeare's "Titus Andronicus" are repeated, celebrated, recreated and reimagined over time, distance and centuries? What happens when those frightful images were married to an ancient theology and served up on proper doctrinal plates that sucked all the generational pain out of this endless archetype of suffering?

This is my Body, Colette repeated over and over again, traveling with that blessed promise into the mist. What am I avoiding? She now felt as if she had been playing at the edges of hell, that wretched metaphorical playground of her mind. Did someone say anteroom? Did someone say there's a price to pay for your pride, young lady?

That night Colette dreamed she entered a vast space that looked like a museum with nun-like statues of the Black Madonna covered with hoods so their faces were barely visible. They were looking away. She then entered the interior of a palace entirely fashioned out of gold. She saw a gilded altar, gold plated organ pipes and piles of loose gold coins. The dreamer felt as if the world's gold had been melted down to create these religious icons, bedposts, living room furniture, picture frames and tinted windows. She felt no sense of prayer, worship or God.

She found no spirit and no soul.

Chapter Twenty-Six

"On the road again, Ms. McGovern?"

"Yes, sir."

Colette vaguely remembered her Boccaccio/Trent romp with Merkel. It seemed like a long time ago, anchored somewhere in the mist.

"Where to this time?"

"I spent a little time with Dante but never ventured far from Florence."

"That's the only way to get close to the Italian Renaissance. It was a fantasy, you know. No need to travel there."

"As in fable, Professor Merkel?"

"As in fantasy, in the psychological sense: a lot of imaginative work; new forms of art, rhetoric and expression."

"I'm trying to get my head around the influence, if any, the Italian Renaissance had on the Council of Trent."

"Will this be with or without interlocutors?"

"Without," she replied.

"Okay. Some fence posts: a lot of well-known artists, including Dante, Ficino and Michelangelo, were hounded, threatened and expelled by the various popes for their work or opinions. That's a place to start."

"Was there something about the Renaissance and the arrival of Neoplatonism that got in the Vatican's craw?"

"I don't know about the craw, but the essence of Neoplatonism and reliance on Greek myths was, well, anathema to the Vatican if you get my drift."

"Was it about the gods, the polytheistic beliefs?"

"Yes, of course, but it was more. The Greek and other cultures of the time had a close relationship with death and celebrated it in rituals and in their temples. Then Christ came along, was crucified, and descended into Hell that some folks call Hades. Then Christ rose on the third day. The man killed death in a way and immortalized the Resurrection. Jung said Christ became Hell, a statement with psychological overtones. Fast forward two thousand years, and we have some folks calling Hell a state of being, an extreme alienation from others. Of course, scholars can find this modern sentiment in Jesus's words. But old mythologies die hard. For centuries the Apostle's Creed has been going on about Christ's descent into hell. We probably have the Council of Trent to thank for that. Choose your poison."

"Thanks, Professor. I understand that the Christian narrative, while it might go through Hell, always gets to Easter Sunday. But what happened to all those creatures of the underworld that Dante and others gave us? I mean, they don't just go away, right? They don't just disappear?"

"Exactly, Ms. McGovern. The old ghosts don't just disappear, no matter how much the Vatican wishes it were so. I mean Christians could smash all the pagan icons and destroy their altars, but mythology was hard to slay. So if you change the basic story line, you change the game. This was a huge victory for the cause."

"A victory in a sense that it destroyed more than the gods of the underworld?"

"Yes, in a way. Christianity repopulated Hades with the various demons, especially Satan. The devil still walked the land, tempting us. This was a hangover from the early Christians, who were getting messages from their unconscious. Still do, really. Religious literalism and fundamentalism will be the death of us. This is why you can find dinosaurs in Noah's Ark theme parks mainly in the South."

"But Hell just didn't disappear?"

"Not at all! It has survived in our curses and exclamations, as in 'Go to Hell!' Oh, it's still there in a sentimental way. Christianity has sanitized and Satanized Hell."

"Why were Ficino and others so keen to bring back Platonic philosophy and all it entailed? Why the interest in Greek mythology?"

"Few people in Florence at that time could read Greek, so they depended on translations. Plato opened to artists and philosophers new, imaginative and rhetorical worlds."

"And the Greek myths?"

"Greek mythology seemed to resonate with our friends in Florence. I'm not completely sure why. By some measure, Michelangelo, Dante and the rest were living during absolutely horrible times. There was the plague, crazy popes, murders, incest, patricide, banishments, poisonings and all the stuff we read about in Shakespeare's Italian-based plays. It was bloody awful."

"How were they able to open up to this new world of the imagination? You'd think they'd have been running for their lives."

"That seems logical, but there was something about the Italian Renaissance that allowed these figures to accept and embrace all these horrors of the day and still create art and live amazing, imaginative lives."

"Was there anything in the Greek myths that fed their daring and their art?"

"That's a good question, Ms. McGovern. The myths were rich tableau grist for any artist. We know Boccaccio wrote about pagan women because they were more interesting than the saints. Dante had his religious cosmology right, but he met a lot of pagans during his wanderings."

"So the Renaissance was attracted to the storytelling?"

"Yes, but there also seemed to be a psychological pull."

"As in the story of Persephone?"

"Yes, her movement is downward toward transformation and service."

"So, Persephone didn't mind being a tour guide in Hades?"

"Yes, Hermes did find that was indeed the case. She was helping souls, for Christ's sake. But this was a violent transformation away from parents and home to all sorts of shit, no doubt."

"You are moving away from myth and story to what, psychology?"

"Brilliant, Ms. McGovern! Yes, at least I'm attempting to do that. I believe our friends found in Greek mythology, with its focus on going down, death, and soul and image work, a completely new perspective. This might be an answer to the earlier question about how these guys could create such beautiful stuff when the place was going to hell in a handbasket. That's precisely it."

"Professor, could you talk a little more about this attraction to depth or the pull of the underworld?"

"Sure, consider the basic Christian cosmology, reiterated at the Council of Trent. You had God in his heavens and, presumably, all is right with the world. The biggies like the Trinity were still there. Also, there's a long line of popes, including a fair number of thieves, murderers and swine who showed up for our merriment. The long scholastic tradition was in place with sixteen hundred years of rituals, weird handshakes, councils, side deals, indulgences and party hacks. That's a lot of stuff to move off center stage."

"But the Church's movement is up, correct, towards heaven and away from a hell that has been conquered?"

Colette vaguely remembered the soul-versus-spirit food fight with Gleason. Trent the Musical had faded.

"Up is the only way for the Church. Heavens, steeples, prayers and alcoves are all up. The body will fade into pure spirit."

"But forces pull us down? Death pulls us down?"

216

"Yes, but keep in mind that death and hell have been conquered by the Resurrection."

"Then why would the Church even worry about the likes of Ficino and Dante? The institution had everything going for it."

"I've long thought the Church wanted a total victory. I mean this in the political, theological and military sense. At another time we can chat about religion being war. That said, I think in the Renaissance artists they saw a philosophy or a topology that could be a real threat to the Church. They were comfortable in the middle ground of fantasy where the daemons lived."

"In the polytheism?"

"Yes, but the Church fathers for all their subtlety didn't get either the Renaissance or the Italian take on the Greek myths."

"They were more than stories?"

"Exactly, but more than that. We think Ficino and friends embraced these myths because they provided a new way of seeing, an angle, and a subtle and perhaps subversive perspective on the way they were living and dying. While the Church biggies were digging around the mythical underworld looking for the bones of old deities, the Renaissance magicians were having a conversation with their souls. What did the soul want; how can I serve it?"

"Was the Church's concern mainly with polytheism or this new way of thinking?"

"Probably both. We know Savonarola around this time was holding his Bonfire of the Vanities. Recall that the priest was burning everything he could get his sticky fingers on that had to do with art, the feminine, cosmetics, theater, and raucous pre-Lenten celebrations. He was probably at the extreme as he ended up at the stake, but his concerns were generally shared by the Vatican and clergy."

"Were there other elements in this new way of thinking that bothered the Church?"

"Of course. In addition to embracing myths, polytheism, and aspects of the Greek cosmology, the Renaissance thinkers were interested in the interior life of man, and how this is expressed in dreams, visions, nightmares and the like, the very things the Church had been saying for years came from the devil or the daemons. The Church didn't want people examining their subjective selves, their interior lives. It embraced the old warning by Jeremiah about interpreting dreams. That's what priests were supposed to do. The denial of the middle ground of fantasy where Plato's daemons resided was central to Christian psychology. This repression was central to the Christian allegory.

"I think you know that during the Council of Nicaea in 787 images were embraced in a very narrow sense. This is the difference between allegory and symbolism. Perhaps the Church wanted to have its cake and eat it too. In actual practice, Church doctrine outlawed individual symbol formation. This was the real war, even if fought unconsciously at times."

Colette responded: "I remember that St. John Damascene had a complex, soulful view of images but the Council seemed to flatten out his view. It doesn't sound that much different from the Church attempting to control the images in art even to the point of covering up crotches and nipples on paintings."

"Ah, yes, the difference was in degree," Merkel replied. "Dreams are very personal, and the Vatican couldn't control a population of dreamers by edict. I don't think it was only about the dreams. The Renaissance opened up our personal space and what it meant to be human. It enlarged the notion of soul and tied it to our imaginings. And sometimes these images are perverted and grotesque. The unconscious is messy. This seemed to be the psychology behind the Church's opposition to individual symbol formation.

"As one writer remarked, 'in my symptoms is my soul.' That's a hell of a statement, if you think about it. There was an 'inwardness' to much of this and an appreciation that self-understanding and soulfulness could be found in pathology, in those dark, moist and messy holes that mark our psychologies. And this was more than the humanism of the Renaissance which was much talked about. It's that downward movement into death."

"Phew! Thank you very much for that. So polytheism was a minor issue?"

"No, I don't think it was minor. The Church had spent its entire history and a war chest beating into everyone's head the One God, Three Person sing-along. That was a very big deal; the movement toward monotheism and all it entails. Any threat from polytheism was considered an existential threat and was taken very seriously by the Church."

"Other than in the works of art, does Renaissance psychology, if I can put it that way, linger?"

"It depends on who you ask. There's a field called archetypal psychology that finds value in the imaginal, mythological universe the Italian Renaissance provided."

"It's based on myths? That doesn't sound very scientific."

She remembered Merkel's remarks about Freud's storytelling.

"Well, yes and no," replied Merkel. "Central to archetypal psychology is the image, dream and interior life. These images are often carried by myths and the endlessly repeated archetypal ideas or figures that shed light on the human condition."

"This sounds a lot like Carl Jung?"

"Yes, indeed, and some who came after him more fully made the Renaissance connection. This was because they could move a little farther from the Christian pull. Jung got to this place by a different route; he didn't get here by waltzing through the Italian Renaissance. He got his sea legs in some nut house in Switzerland."

"The inmates were painting the walls of the asylum with excrement?"

"Close. Jung paid attention to utterances, dreams, and nightmares; to the patients' pathologies, I suppose you could say. He realized the importance of the image to understanding psychic life. After his break with Freud and his own meltdown, he came to the conclusion that image was psyche. His recently published his *Red Book*, written a century ago, is an artistic, visionary, dream-filled account of his descent into his unconscious. This was his journey into his psychological hell."

Colette remained silent. That territory seemed dangerously familiar.

"I understand that his family was very conflicted about publishing it, as the scientist was overwhelmed by the dreamer. Jung spoke about being seized by his visions, which he acknowledged as the unconscious activation of an archetypal image."

Colette nodded.

Merkel continued. "The *Red Book* is worth a look because the book is a very emotional, graphically expressive and symbolic look at Jung's descent into himself and his hell."

"This seems to be a different Jung than the one I'm familiar with."

"Well, yes and no. It was the transcendent aspect of Christianity that he struggled with. He associated the Christian religion with light and consciousness. Christ had overcome the darkness and the underworld, precisely where Jung would go for his psychological insights."

"Sounds like the end of the story."

"Perhaps, but Jung would likely say that the stories, like the gods, will be with us forever. When you have the time, appetite, itch and patience, have a look at Jung's *Symbols of Transformation* and you'll get some of the tension on this score. The book is a bloody beast, but he is eloquent at times."

"I opened a library copy once. I read a critical footnote about the historical Christ. The book seemed dust-covered and rarely read. Is this about polytheism?"

"In a way, yes," Merkel replied. "Jung wrote something to the effect that the world had not only lost or been deprived of its gods, but it had also lost its soul."

"Did Jung mean we were becoming less psychological?"

"Yes, Ms. McGovern, you've hit the nail on the head! He wrote in the Transformation book that even modern science had great difficulty in vindicating the soul's right to existence and making a credible argument that the soul was a mode of being with characteristics that can be investigated."

"Is this because we're data-driven and suspicious of what can't be replicated?"

"I wouldn't put it exactly that way, but I guess you are right. By becoming less psychological, Jung probably meant we were becoming literalists, looking for the quick answers. Thus the footnote about the historical Christ you mentioned. Jung suggested that our habit of inventing personality cults and heroes was part of this development."

"Did he see Christianity as a cult?"

"He used the term, but I don't know if it had the same connotations it has today. He wrote that the efforts of rationalistic theology—big shout out to Augustine and Aquinas—to preserve a personal Jesus as the last and most precious aspect of the divinity that we are no longer capable of imagining were in keeping with this tendency to create the cult of the hero."

Colette remembered her father singing along with the Johnny Cash version of "Your Own Personal Jesus." The words were on her lips: "Someone to hear your prayers; someone who cares."

"I'm not sure I follow you on this," she said to Merkel, pulling herself back from memory.

"Understood. Jung is very dense at times. It's part of the culture's move away from introspection and self-awareness. He can also be a bit of a scold, reminding us that man has never really loved the visible God. They do not love him for what he appears to be, a mere man, because if the pious want to love humanity, they just have to turn to their neighbors or enemies."

"Huh?"

"Correct response. Jung says that we want the literal hero and cult God, but our actions suggest that we neither love this god nor that neighbor. His point was that the religious figure can't be a mere man. It had to represent, psychologically, the archetypal contents of the collective unconscious, which is the archaic heritage of humanity."

"We seem to have traveled a long way from religion," remarked Colette.

"Yes and no. Jung never quite took off his religious hat. He seemed to view Jesus symbolically, mythically or psychologically. He wrote that the reason why Jesus' words have such suggestive power is that they express symbolic truths that are rooted in the very structure of the human psyche."

"I don't remember learning that in catechism class."

"I think that class has long been a morality play, a trumped up, allegorical reading of biblical tales."

"Is this another cultural lament from Jung?"

"I suppose so. He suggested that the guardians of symbolic truth, namely the religions, have been robbed of their efficacy by science."

"This sounds like blame the messenger game. What about religion's responsibility?"

"Christianity didn't escape his scorn. He suggested that the insistence on bare bones dogma, ethics for ethics sake, the humanization of the Christ-figure, the idealization of the feminine, the denial of the reality of evil and the attempts to write Christ's literal life story are singularly unimpressive."

"It sounds like Jung attended every session during the eighteen-year Council of Trent."

"I think he looked at the early councils and their focus on symbol formation which he considered largely completed by Trent. Imagine that! The game was over. The council seemed to sugarcoat some of the more fiery stuff dealing with the marriage bed and the like. As you know, Jung had real concerns about the Trinity and the doctrine's psychological implications. For Jung the Trinity was psychologically incomplete because it didn't account for the feminine, matter or evil. Jung saw the danger when the symbolic underpinnings of religion were lost."

"Symbolic as in images, dreams, archetypes, and the like?"

"Yes, but primarily religious symbols that also resonate and represent living, breathing, psychological truths. Jung wrote that without a symbolic dimension, religion was bare dogma."

"And Trent?"

"That's your specialty, Ms. McGovern. An outsider might say that the nuncios, and the rest of the theological gang, took eighteen years to prove Jung correct."

"There were a lot of lists presented at Trent, lengthy, boring, unattainable lists."

"Yup, that's what the man is talking about. For Jung, Christ spoke archetypally and gave his mission a symbolic dimension."

"Can you give an example of how Christians turned away from this symbolic dimension or path?"

"May I offer an example from the pages of pagan sexual practices without being too graphic? According to Jung, sex played a major part in symbol formation even when the symbols are religious."

"Certainly, Professor. I'll hold my ears if the pagans make me blush."

"Very well. According to Jung, it's only been two thousand years since the cult of sex was in full bloom. He acknowledged that the pagans just didn't know any better. But he did emphasize that they understood in antiquity that the union with God was more or less concrete coitus. Accordingly, we can no longer pretend that the forces motivating the production of symbols have suddenly become different since the birth of Christ."

"Christ, Professor, if you will forgive the expression. That's fairly charged sexual symbolism. The early Christians wouldn't have known this, right? It would have to have been unconscious?"

"Yes, well put. Symbolic formations are usually unconscious. But let me read Jung's exact words on this. 'The fact that primitive Christianity resolutely turned away from nature and the instincts in general and, through its asceticism, from sex in particular, clearly indicates the source from which its motive forces came. So it is not surprising that this transformation has left noticeable traces in Christian symbolism. Had it not done so, Christianity would never have been able to transform libido.'"

"He's saying that the Church transformed an important source of energy? Maybe this had everything to do with the Church's view on sexuality, virginity and is related to the sexual abuse by priests. Maybe the Church never fully transformed libido. Maybe this is the reason the Church has long suppressed women? Maybe this is the reason behind the nineteenth century decision to declare the Assumption of Mary into Heaven an infallible doctrine? Maybe this is why the Church needed a blessed Virgin and an all-male Trinity? Maybe this is why we have no women priests? Maybe this is their fiction and their fantasy?"

For a second, Colette felt she was behind the abortion curtain.

"Very astute point, Ms. McGovern. No doubt the Church had long had a woman problem that can't be explained away by biblical tall tales. However, the global growth of the Church suggests that the basic message of Christianity still has a great deal of power, including symbolic power. But neither threats nor legislation nor thunderbolts from Zeus will completely contain libido and anima."

"Do you think Jung would make these connections?"

"Frankly, I'm not sure. Jung does say that some people profess to be shocked when he brings the most sublime spiritual ideas into an association with what they call the subhuman and carnal. Read sex! He said his job was to remind us of what archetypal and unconscious forces still rule our lives."

"And this is archetypal psychology?"

"Yes, you can put it that way. But for Jung, this was life and death stuff. He doesn't play around. Listen to him when he asks: 'What can a

222

rationalist do with the dogma of the Virgin birth or with Christ's sacrificial death or the Trinity?'"

"Goodness," replied Colette. "Jung would have paid a heavy price for saying that at the Council of Trent."

"Perhaps. Trent was sixteen hundred years after the birth of Christ. Christians had toppled the pagan statues but were still burning the witches, astrologers and magicians. The daemons of the middle ground of Renaissance fantasy became Christianity's demons in the doctrinal sense."

"Would it be safe to infer, Professor," Colette asked, "that the Council of Trent, in its focus on rigid dogma and the battles over the communion host and so on took some of the power out of the religious symbols?"

"Careful, Ms. McGovern. We must be careful about projecting too much onto the council and demanding too much from the weary souls in attendance. But Jung's position is clear. He writes that the Christian religion remains fresh when I am hearing Christ symbolically and paying less attention to repetitious dogma."

"I appreciate your remarks about libidinal energy. I keep going back to the Italian Renaissance. You've talked about the Renaissance artists who were breaking through old forms. Radical new ideas and books were circulating. It must have felt like a new world order on the horizon. All this in the Vatican's backyard and the folks at the Council of Trent seemed to think they were back in Nicaea in 787. You'd think they would have had more on their minds than preparing for battle over the difference between adoration and veneration, especially when that seemed to be a war they were mainly waging inside their own heads."

Merkel laughed.

"That, Ms. McGovern, is the question of the day! What was the source of this threat that hung over the Church like an existential god? Did the Vatican think that the Renaissance magicians and alchemists, if enough were burned at the stake, would just go away? Did the Vatican think that banning and burning books for about four hundred years would end the conversation? Or with a sixteenth-century run, did the Vatican figure it could outlast this Renaissance eruption, perhaps even cover it with suffocating dogma and sleight of hand? Or did all this pagan stuff just scare the hell out of them, and they were happy to hide behind their purple gowns? Or did the Church believe the rumor that there was going to be another Greek invasion all dressed up in Italian finery and ready to go? Or was the Church simply building a robust edifice to be prepared when the feminine showed up in full battle dress and declared war?"

"And this means, Professor Merkel?"

"Ms. McGovern, you should put on your walking shoes because you have some more traveling to do. You need to hear the Greek voices our friends in fifteenth century Florence were hearing loud and clear.

"But, before your journey ends, have a peek at Jung's *Red Book* which was written before he got stuffy and scientific. Jung encouraged all his patients to find their own symbolic expressions, their mythologies."

"It sounds very personal and dangerous," she said.

Professor Merkel was on his way out of the room.

Colette thought she was in familiar territory. She already knew that theology was that burning thing, her very own ring of fire.

Chapter Twenty-Seven

With Professor Merkel's remarks on transformation still ringing her ears, Colette returned to the college library, preparing for another trip back in time. Rebecca Aimes joined Colette in what they referred to as the Greek corner of the library, due largely to the presence of knock-off marble statues of Athena, Zeus, and Aphrodite with her breasts on full display.

"Up to your eye teeth in the Greeks, I see," Rebecca said.

Colette laughed.

"I'm just trying to offset the effects of that turkey Trent I've been feeding on."

"Well, Colette, Greek food is much better. Where to this time?"

"I'm trying to discover the Greek who was responsible for the Italian Renaissance. I know Renaissance Italians were all over Plato with their version of Neoplatonism, though I'm still pissed off at that Plato guy for demonizing the female flesh."

"Right. Plato did women no favors when he concluded that the uterus wandered through the body causing distemper. But the Italians seemed to be paying more attention to writers who came after Plato, who weren't on the Plato and Aristotle bandwagon when it came to the female body."

"I just spoke to Professor Merkel about Carl Jung and his views on the psychology of religion. He spoke about pagan libidinal energies that were channeled into Church rituals and the like. Perhaps the Renaissance saw some of these same energies in the Greeks?"

"I don't know," Rebecca responded. "The Italians were taking philosophical and mythological texts from both the East and West, though the Greeks seemed to be their main source. The Italians seemed to be looking for an imaginal place, perhaps because, as Merkel has mentioned, their religious and cultural containers were no longer working psychologically. Plotinus in the third century was very influential."

"I'm not familiar with him. What did he write?"

"*The Enneads*, a collection of philosophical essays that was assembled and edited by an assistant, was very important to the Florentines, especially to Marsilio Ficino who ran a philosophy academy in Florence. Plotinus is a good place to start."

Colette felt that she was making every effort to move forward in time and history, but each new step seemed to take her back and down into yet another mystery.

Her introduction to Plotinus was a photo of a bronze bust of a man with a nose that looked as if it was sliced by a sword. He didn't appear to be a happy man. When she learned that he was a vegetarian, the look made more sense. He apparently distrusted materialism, his body, as well as meat from animals. He didn't seem to have sex on the brain. He didn't seem to be the kind of philosopher Italians could learn much from.

She was wrong. *The Enneads*, completed in 270, seemed modern, unadorned and straightforward, with no apparent axe to grind or mention of Christianity that she could see. The book was lyrical, like a poem or a secular prayer without the damnation. She was taken by the eloquent language Plotinus used to describe how the ancients, who believed in the World Soul, brought down divine beings into shrines and onto altars, thus securing a part of a universal harmony.

Colette thought she was back in the metaphorical world of St. John Damascenes where image-making was presented as a soulful activity.

She read out loud Plotinus' words about where the soul resided, and why man constructed altars and shrines in nature.

"I think, therefore, that the ancient sages who sought to serve the presence of the divine beings by the erection of altars for shrines and statues, showed insight into the nature of the All; they perceived that, though the soul is everywhere tractable, its presence will be secured all the more readily when an appropriate receptacle is elaborated, a place especially capable of receiving some portion or phase of it, something reproducing it, or presenting it, and serving like a mirror to catch an image of it."

Colette felt like someone had just blown up the Council of Trent with its lengthy dictums on how images should be perceived, received, managed and expressed. Remarks that the attendees at Trent would surely have considered anathema to her sounded soulful and modern. Plotinus, wearing neither clerical garb nor mythological cloak, seemed to her like a scientist, or at times a psychologist, as he commented on how man's evil acts play out in the scheme of things. Ancient myths were part of the discussion, but they seemed more like referents and metaphors than facts to be worshipped. Images and their endless reflections and mirroring filled out the archetype and the world soul. She was not surprised that Marsilio Ficino curled up with this book at his Florence hearth.

226

Plotinus wrote that myths are our way of speaking. They are a representation of our discourse and carry a certain morality. He referred to Hermes with the generator organ always in an active position, even when the god was surrounded by eunuchs.

Colette laughed at Plotinus's description of Hermes always ready for sex while trying to sort out the details of the particular myth. She wondered how Hermes's "active position" would play in the Bronx.

She continued reading out loud Plotinus's words, sensing that they held more majesty when she heard them with both her ears and her heart.

"The souls of men, seeing their images in the mirror of Dionysus, as it were, have entered into that realm in a leap downward from the Supreme; but even then they are not cut off from their origin, from the divine Intelligence."

Colette contemplated the flow of Plotinus's language, unadorned, balanced, logical and pure. Questions were raised and answered with no bombast, rather understatement; a logician rather than a preacher. The universe balanced itself out; evil would be dealt with but not by way of thunderbolts or anathema. Zeus took pity on men's toils and gave them respite in due time, freeing them from the body so that they may come to dwell where the Universal Soul, unconcerned with earthly needs, had always dwelt.

Plotinus embraced the gifts from the gods, praising Prometheus, who had given us fire and the arts, and asked whether his brother Epimetheus, who lacked foresight and was unable to bestow positive traits on animals, had a place in an ensouled world. The gods arrived on schedule without fanfare or trumpets, taking their rightful places in the zodiac, offering image, vision and perspective to the gatherings below.

Zeus remained busy, ordering Athena and Hephaistos to create the first god in a human female form. She was to be a beautiful evil. This was punishment for humans receiving the gift of fire from Prometheus. They called her Pandora, meaning the all-gifted, and the gods provided seductive presents. Athena taught her needlework; Aphrodite taught her grace; and Hermes introduced her to a shameful mind. Prometheus warned his brother Epimetheus not to accept gifts from Pandora, but he didn't listen, having no foresight. She opened the jar and released evil upon the earth. It was not possible to escape the mind of Zeus.

For Plotinus there was a creation story and the movement of soul within this myth. The very nature of his universe was to "ensoul" the world and each other by building relationships and developing correspondences. Aphrodite and other gods bringing gifts added something to this formation brought about by Prometheus, who was forward-looking in the myth.

Colette thought that Zeus in Plotinus's language had a complicated view of the feminine, bestowing Pandora with grace, guile, skill, beauty, cunning, and evil intent and traits that were the handiwork of the gods. In ancient times, Pandora would have been considered a dangerous goddess. The Italian Renaissance might have seen her as a powerful archetypal force. Today, she would be called a bitch. With that insight, Colette laughed and thought that she might be getting the hang of it even at the eleventh hour.

The Neoplatonist introduced these stories with the ease of a poet, with a habit of making connections, comfortable that the pagan gods had a place in his pantheon. The cosmos received graces, gifts from here and there, from the gods of the Supreme and those other Intellectual-Principles whose nature was to fill with soul. This was probably the secret behind the myth.

Plotinus suggested that myths are stories that offer perspectives. He wrote that the reader can take the Pandora myth in a number of ways, but certainly it was "an account of the bestowal of gifts upon the Kosmos" that harmonized with the World Soul.

Colette recalled her discussion with Gleason about soul and wished that she had had a better knowledge of Plotinus at the time, especially of his cool demeanor and unheated language. The Greek could be as blunt and cold as any cleric she had read, but he could talk eloquently about happiness in the plant and animal world. He wrote that "Those that deny the happy life to plants on the ground that they lack sensation are really denying it to all living things."

After slogging through so much theology and sparring with real and imaginary audiences about doctrinal matters, she was glad to read someone who seemed, despite his stoicism to have a sense of humor, even if she had to travel back to 270. She laughed when reading his remarks about the movement of the planets and stars causing stomach aches, gout and bouts of palsy in the general population. The claim that Mars or Aphrodite could cause adultery represented the height of unreason. This was as close as Plotinus came to losing his calm.

Colette felt sure that she had traveled this territory before. Perhaps she was finally getting her mythology right.

Plotinus also had his fun with Hercules. He wrote that this god "of the heavens would still tell of his feats; but there is the other man to whom all that is trivial; he has been translated to a holier place; he has won his way to the Intellectual Realm; he is more than Hercules; proven in combat in which the combatants are wise."

As Colette read Plotinus, she recalled her recent conversation with Professor Merkel about Carl Jung and his *Symbols of Transformation*.

Jung said image was psyche and central to a person's soul-making activity. Colette sensed that she was hearing the same language and intent in Plotinus when he wrote that each soul has its own image-making facility which combined with memory that was not only remembrance; it was also a condition induced by past experiences and visions.

She read that "soul in man was some sort of composite. All affection and experiences have their seat in the soul." The soul may feel sorrow and pain and every other affliction that belong to the body, but the soul seeks the mending of its instrument.

Colette felt as if she had just prayed, not to some god or even to Plotinus; she just said thanks for a third-century reminder that the soul had the capacity to repair itself. Was this the answer to Professor Merkel's latest charge? Was this what the fifteenth century Florentines discovered in the Greeks? Was it an old but very new canvas with images at the center and man and woman responsible for their own soul-making in a world of referents, correspondences and metaphors where everything was connected and linked? Plotinus found divinity in man and in the images that came from the heart. For the Greek "all knowing comes by likeness."

She was drawn to Plotinus who referred to the soul as a wanderer in a metaphysical world. She reflected on his advice about the soul finding her own way. The soul helped in this task because it was regenerative. Every soul must know its history and be aware of its own movement. Colette was almost in tears when she read that the soul doesn't travel in a straight line but in a circle that turns, not on some external axis but on its own center. This movement reflected the path of the heavenly bodies which are like a choral movement, an eternal dance, and perfection. For Plotinus, a psychology of soul represented a psychology of the imagination.

Colette thought about her travels and wanderings which took her to so many holy places. She now understood that her journey was not just about Trent, though it remained a powerful anthem. Colette was not bold enough to think Plotinus had been her secret travel guide. She had been wandering in a world of ideas, exchanging gods for perspectives, looking for connections, metaphors and insights, sensing at times she was close to losing her mind.

The Enneads ended in love.

Of all the books Colette had read during her thesis project, the work by Plotinus seemed more modern, psychological and humane than all the others. She sensed a complexity in this third century masterpiece.

Colette recognized Plotinus's movement away from the flesh to the intellectual sphere but she heard no venom in his voice; she heard no denunciation of the female flesh and the role of women in society that was so threatening and dominant at the Church councils. For Plotinus, all affection and experience have their seat in the soul. When the soul is ready, it withdraws to its own place above passion and affections.

Plotinus reminded her that the soul needed love. The philosopher wrote that the soul is Aphrodite of the heavens, here, turned harlot; Aphrodite of the public ways: yet the soul is always an Aphrodite. This was the intention of the myth which told of Aphrodite's birth and of Eros born with her.

Colette rested and longed to reside in the troubled beauty of Aphrodite, drifting into that dream space full of longing and intent, navigating soul. She felt at sea, moving out beyond the promising circles of Plotinus and into the mist. She felt as if she were leaving something solid and becoming unmoored.

That night, Colette dreamed she was on a ship, in some vast stretch of ocean in Southeast Asia. She sensed playfulness on board with crew members putting arms through struts, inventing different shapes and sizes as they dipped their hands in seawater and feigned surprise. She heard: so that is what you do for fun in Asia!

Someone pointed to a raft that held a bull with two heads, each facing in a different direction. At times, the bull seemed to slip onto the raft surface and battle against itself with its hooves, throwing up water in a spray.

Colette woke, feeling that she was floating aimlessly in water. She thought about the two heads that seem to be fighting each other, at times in a comic manner. She remained in this dreamy, watery state for a long time.

When fully awake, she vaguely understood that the two heads might have represented different ways of thinking: the psychological, archetypal or the theological. She was floating in an ocean, often a sign of the unconscious. The raft was not seaworthy and took on a lot of water. Maybe she was not ready for her journey back in time.

She vaguely recalled the admonition in Exodus about worshipping strange gods, though the god in question was a golden calf and not a two-headed bull on a raft going nowhere. Was she going nowhere, first this way and that way, this way and that, with a stop in Trent, side visits to Venice and Florence, picking up a little gossip here and there? Then came her leap of faith like some Renaissance magician, backward to taste the emerging consciousness of Plotinus. She was sucked in by the beauty and opaqueness of his language, the lean metaphors, and his using the gods as archetypes, as ways of experiencing her own psychology.

She sounded like a lawyer, instructing herself. She needed help.

"A two-headed bull you say?" asked O'Connell. "Where did that come from?"

"I tried to wrap my head around it but thought I needed another pair of eyes."

"Any initial thoughts?"

"It wasn't my first thought, but someone could have been telling me I'm bull-headed."

"You mean chasing after the Trent question as if your life depended on it?"

"Yes sir, exactly."

"Well, are you?"

"Yes, I think so."

"Hold that thought. The dream is probably a little more complicated than about you being tenacious. Why the ocean and South East Asia for that matter?"

"I don't know. I've never been to or studied the area. It seemed foreign to me."

"Foreign. Hold onto that. Now the water must suggest something."

"I thought it might represent the unconscious, but that seemed too easy."

"Easy is good. How would that work?"

"In my research I'm digging around my own unconscious or maybe what Jung called the collective unconscious. I'm up to my eyeteeth in myths, fables and the like. I just read extensively in Plotinus, the Neoplatonist who referred to the vastness of soul."

"Your research is taking you both into yourself and into the collective. Does this feel dangerous to you?"

"Dangerous?"

"I mean dangerous in the psychological sense. You are turning over a lot of manuscripts and speaking to the dead in a way. And you seem to be spending a fair bit of time with the ancients. Then there's the Christian overhang, keeping an eye on you. That might be your shadow talking. You are looking for another path, and the Church could be pulling you back."

"Do you mean that?"

"I'm being fanciful to help the conversation. I'm sure there are some threads of truth here. Recall that your earlier dreams had a very distinct theological flavor. Pope John Paul tried to take you into the grave with him, figuratively speaking, to teach you something about the feminine and the dead.

"You remember that, correct?" O'Connell asked.

"Yes, very well. I try to reflect on all my dreams, but they are beginning to bump into my research and at times everything flows together, dreamlike. Do you know what I mean?"

"I think so. As I understand, much of the material you are dealing with is metaphorical or symbolic. This is language that carries a heavy charge and is similar to the stuff of dreams. I believe you mentioned reading Jung's *Symbols of Transformation*. If I recall correctly, that is a very heavy book with profound implications for Christianity. His questions about creating psychological containers to hold religious beliefs are still hanging fire."

"I recall Plotinus saying something along these lines," said Colette, "about containers to hold images and visions in the psyche. I can't recall what writer said Christianity no longer offered containers for the contemporary culture."

"You see what I mean. You have been traveling the underworld."

"Well, I did take a side trip with Dante through the Inferno."

"That's a journey worth taking! I just wanted to emphasize that you have been carrying a pretty stiff archetypal weight. This can come with a cost. But, if you don't mind, can we return to that after we figure out what that two-headed bull was doing on a raft in the ocean in Asia playing footsy with himself? Can you get us started?"

"I often feel adrift these days, but I don't see myself in the role of a bull, symbolically or otherwise."

"And why is that?"

"Well, it's usually associated with masculine themes like virility and strength."

"Right. Just for fun, why don't you put yourself in that role?"

"As a bull?"

"As holding the archetypal features of a bull?"

"I suppose I have certain strengths, though I don't know about the virility part. Some people have told me I'm a bull in a china shop."

"Good. We'll agree that bulls represent the male qualities you describe. And Jung has said that women project animus or masculine images. Would you say you are currently in a male domain?"

"You mean at school? Of course; I'm surrounded by priests and brothers. I seem to have spent a lifetime with all those Trent guys. My Trent excursions have been to find the feminine voice, you know, a little female company. Most of the women are pagans and are dead. I seem to be fighting with myself. And, as you know, my dreams are full of priests, popes, cardinals and a few prophets."

"Yes. It's hard not to draw that conclusion. What about the two-headed bull? Where does it come in?"

"Going back to what we discussed earlier: I am pushing myself into a man's world like a bull in a china shop. I search for the feminine and male doctrine holds me back."

"I'll take your mixed metaphors. Go on."

"I'm on a raft, drifting in foreign waters. I don't know which way to go."

"Is that true?"

"In a way. I have my fears."

"Okay, hold your fears and stay with the bull. Why the two heads?"

"It's like a two-headed monster or something."

"What was the bull doing on the raft, other than standing?"

"It seems like he was playing footsy or splashing himself or itself with its hooves."

"I'll give you the cartoon overtones here, but why the splashing?"

"The bull would ordinarily lock horns, but that is difficult to do under these circumstances. To really engage in a fight, the bull would have to be separated."

"So to lock horns, the bull would have to be broken in two. We are talking metaphorical dream talk here, of course."

"Sure, perhaps the bull represents the two horns of my dilemma, theology on one side and maybe psychology or the feminine on the other. For the two-horned bull to do battle or resolve the issue, one or both sides might have to be destroyed."

"Very nicely put, Ms. McGovern. Well done!"

"I'm not sure what I just said. Or rather I'm not sure what it means."

"You have your finger on it. I can't say for sure. Perhaps the balancing act you have been engaging in is not working or, as the dream suggests, you could be at a stalemate with a two-headed bull stuck on a raft in the ocean."

"I have attacked them?"

"I don't know. Have you?"

"I don't know either. If I could put it this way: Trent seems to be the big bull with large horns who knows his way around the barnyard. I mean, Trent has legitimized and more or less defined the Catholic Church for five hundred years. The theology is still masculine. There are still no women in the hierarchy. The women are all saints and out of reach. The teachings, especially the sexual stuff, still echo Aristotle and his notions of energy and sperm. Today I still hear the Vatican claiming all the doctrines under attack represent the implacable Word of God. But that's not what I heard rummaging through the early Church councils. Those guys seemed to be writing fictions that corresponded to their religious biases and perhaps neuroses. As my mother might say, all this seems at times like 'stuff and nonsense.' Despite all the setbacks, the Church won the Trent battle and many since."

"That's their battle. Maybe the bull on the raft is yours?"

233

"You mean I'm locking horns with myself? I'm playing footsie with myself? That I'm lost?"

"Are you?"

Colette wasn't feeling well. She needed a break and left O'Connell's office. She wasn't sure what she had been hearing. She was lost in the World Soul of Plotinus. Then she dreamed about a bull playing footsie on a raft in the South China Sea. She was deeply concerned about her conversation with the psychologist, about the neatness in dividing up the world. She was grateful for his help but wondered whether there would be a price to pay for this allegorical romp and splitting the image in two.

She recalled teachers who discussed the bull as a sacred symbol of the Egyptians. She also recalled a Spanish writer who suggested that life and love were dangerous, two-horned topics, no different than facing the bull in the ring. In her research she found a reference to a hollow metal bull in which heretics were burned to death but couldn't remember the time or place. Colette felt that she had been wandering in these danger zones for some time.

She remembered that in a class on symbols the instructor mentioned that a ship had long been considered a vessel and a symbol of the female sex organ. Colette had a hard time getting her head around being at sea inside her own sex and mind while a two-horned bull was playing with itself in plain view. She felt her body begin to shake and wanted to change the subject. She tried without success to think about pomegranates and the Brazilian beach scene.

Why were the old maps of the unseen worlds offered by Plotinus, Damascenes and Boccaccio so much richer and more soulful than all the pronouncements at Nicaea, Trent and the other councils that seemed to suck life out of the image?

Just why was she lost at sea? Why did she feel sick in her heart?

Colette remembered Jung's words about the gods becoming diseases when they do not receive the proper attention.

"Christ," she thought and hoped her mother was close at hand.

Chapter Twenty-Eight

Colette was moving in circles, drifting through tumbleweed, imagining that she was inside an archetype, promising meaning and possibly salvation. Her dreams consumed her.

Colette dreamed she was in a monk's cell surrounded by a dozen or so monks and priests who administered to her, putting holy oil on her hands and feet, and praying for her. She stood at the doorway of the cell and screamed through her tears, "I don't want to leave this holy place."

Colette continued to dream in fits and starts.

The walls of her cell were white; the shadows in every corner were demons who became a crone, a beauty, a cadaver and finally Blake's Tiger, who stood watch over her burning night dreams. Her bed was made of saplings and dry leaves. The sheets were reeds from the Nile. Holy men in winter frocks breathed on her zealously, as if she was on fire.

She was now on her way to Golgotha.

Colette dreamed of a badly bloodied Jesus on the cross. It was near the end. Right before his death he moaned—oh, oh, oh—from his head to his toes. He spoke from every muscle, organ and bone of his body. He died when the last sound left his feet.

Stalin was at Christ's feet, praising the way he died and joining the centurions in song. He ordered Colette to put the bloody garments in a canvas bag. She put in body parts, including the heart.

Colette turned and turned again, looking for purpose, hoping for meaning, praying to be released from her circular grave. She dreamed again.

A god spoke to the Colette, telling her that a man in her presence was dead. She got down on her knees, eager to anoint hands, feet and lips and saw his eyes moving quickly across the night sky. "He is not dead!" she proclaimed. "He is not dead!" she repeated, as if railing against the heavens.

A hand came out of the darkness and reached over her shoulder, covering the man's face with a sack. When she protested, the voice said: "No matter. The ritual must continue; everything to its time and season."

Colette dreamed that she was tied to the ground, to the earth, with leather straps anchored in soil. For a long time, she fought the upward pull, finally letting go. She felt as if she was dying and let her weightless body drift through vistas, clouds and stars. She passed murals of saints, an image of her dead father, and a hint of Christ. She believed she was in the presence of God and finally at peace.

The feeling did not last. The shadows she encountered in another dream laughed and groaned through their sores and carbuncles, warning her about the trap of piety and the gentle ascent through well-manicured lanes of managed clouds. The voices grow more pronounced. "You will be tempted," she heard, "to enter the Virgin Mary frame, with its bloodless and tearless birth, an anecdote built on a story that became an unrelenting legend, frozen by the pope's anxious cry of infallibility before the curtain came down on the scene."

Inside her dreams Colette continued to hear voices from another dimension, a mix of her professors, Trent outliers, and Renaissance revelers. The voices seemed to form a chorus that she might have heard during her travels, though much fainter.

"Do you, dreamer of dreams, not know the difference between the god of the spirit and the god of the soul? Did you not wonder why Clement, the Bishop, put in Peter's mouth the rich details about the gods endlessly coupling in the heavens? Why did his mouth find so much joy in this lasciviousness? Why so much passion when the pagan gods were being rebuked?

"You with the night eyes have watched the gods construct Pandora out of clay on orders of Zeus. Shall we also say this clay was just the stuff of earth and nothing else? Shall we argue that the gifts of intelligence from Athena, love from Aphrodite, and hunting prowess from Artemis represented more clay on top of clay—and no more? Does not the mirror we hold up to these gods reflect back lives and characters we have known? Was not this beautiful evil one more familiar to our households and imaginations than the lone Eve banished into the wilderness for eating the forbidden fruit?"

Colette felt bombarded with questions coming from all corners of her dream world. She was bewildered and sought relief. She ducked into an amphitheater where a pope, who looked like a parish priest she vaguely remembered, was jumping up and down, seeming to lead the congregation in calisthenics more than prayer. When the assembled appeared to match the level of the pope's enthusiasm, he raised his vestments and revealed

236

that he was wearing bicycle shorts bearing the logo, "Specialized." Then he did a wild dance and uttered a primordial scream, as if intent on bringing down the heavens.

The pope gave way to an old man with a white beard who appeared to be on his deathbed. Colette applied pancake makeup to his face with a spatula. She attempted to lower the man from a bed that was almost at the vertical, coming face to face with him in the process. She detected little life in the man. She continued to slide him down her body, feeling the weight in his trunk and getting a slight whiff of his bowels, as if the man is relaxing, letting himself go.

She understood that inside the dream she had been looking death in the face and had felt its weight. She had served as an undertaker, preparing the body for burial. She had smelled the stench of death and did not flinch; she thought it was normal. She felt blessed to be able to embrace his lower extremities and put her face close to the bowels which were letting go.

Colette wakened from her torrent of dreams curled up at the foot of her bed in the fetal position, holding onto her belly for dear life. She tried crying for her mother but no words came out of her mouth. She wept, remembering the dream about a badly bloodied Jesus on the cross. Colette felt complicit in his crucifixion and understood that picking up body parts and pieces of his garments was her penance and her cross. She sensed that she was in death or near death or with death, recalling with horror and awe the dream about bonding with the man as he slid down her body into the grave. Was it a god who said that the ritual must continue?

She barely recalled the voices that seemed to come from the chorus she had met during her travels. Colette felt that the pull of Plotinus, taking her into that safe, reasoned place, was being overcome by a heavy downward drag into dreams, nightmares and darkness, as if the last six months of her underworld travel were recapitulated. It was as if Dante was calling her to an accounting. What circle, she thought, was appropriate for a woman who has aborted her child?

Colette felt as if she were literally alone on that raft in the middle of the sea, being pulled apart as if on the medieval rack, stretched to the breaking point by the Tower of London crowd who would deliriously kill for their beliefs. She felt more alone than in any time in her life and sobbed deeply, muffling the sound with her sleeve. Soon the cries become so loud and the need became so great that Colette could no longer keep her anguish to herself. Her mother was by her side.

"My dear Colette, my heart, what's wrong?" asked her mother through her tears.

"Mom, I gave up my baby. I had an abortion. Forgive me. Daddy, please forgive me!"

"There, there, there," said her mother. "It . . . it will be all right. I love you, honey."

The daughter heard the pain, sorrow and hesitation in her mother's voice.

Colette's mother embraced her and rocked her to sleep while still sitting on the floor.

Colette dreamed that she was putting out chairs in a large, white, rectangular room. The chairs were oaken and heavy with slight curvature of the arms, suggesting movement. At the north end of this room was a large wooden throne that seemed to rise above all other chairs in the place. Colette reflected on the empty, vacant room waiting to be filled.

The man who was helping her to put out the chairs told her that everything had been decided; everyone was in agreement; there would be no dissention or dispute. Colette heard him say that the proceedings not yet underway were a *fait accompli*.

The man's remarks sounded short, focused and legal. Soon this rectangular space started to fill up with nuncios, prelates, bishops and princes who sat in the chairs around the perimeter of the room. She was reminded of the Council of Trent, except the assembled appeared to have entered a frieze which could be on display for an eternity. Then the pope entered, wearing a white cassock and a red shoulder cape. Since there was no dispute, there was no discussion. Not a word was spoken. The center of the room remained empty, as if the place had no substance and no soul.

Colette felt the condemnation in the hearts of the assembled. She said loud enough to be heard by the entire congregation: "This is my Body." Colette shuddered; then turned her back on the assembled, sensing she was repeating a ritual from an earlier time. It was as if she had awakened to consciousness in a still dangerous world controlled by the princes of the Church.

Somewhere deep within her memory was a vision of Pope John Paul II, who was chanting the feminine down as old squabbles about ritual raged on in the background. The holy man who was all heart slipped into a circle of peace.

She recalled the dream of Pope Francis administering to the grotesques in the catacombs while staying outside the trappings of power. Colette recalled all of the church dreams she had suffered and especially the scenes of the cold, soulless, and empty sanctuaries. She remembered the time that she had been turned away from the communion rail and was obliged to look on statues adorned in colors darker than Lent. She heard the shuffle of a thousand feet walking away from the church and walking away from her.

She remembered the Prophets in the Parking Lot, who differentiated themselves until ritual took over and they ended up in frieze, saying the same thing for an eternity. She thought of a soulful Jacob in the restaurant singing his ancestry as all in attendance seemed to join him in silent prayer. She longed to partake of that blessed food.

Colette remembered the padlocked church of her dream, which seemed to lack moisture, soul and heart. She now knew the padlocked church was Trent.

Chapter Twenty-Nine

Colette felt as if a load has been lifted from her shoulders. She had been to the Council of Trent and returned. Her project was near fruition. As if on cue, she saw Jung's *Red Book* resting in a wooden cradle at the main college library desk, as if it were to be viewed carefully like an antique bible. She opened the volume and found a medieval landscape full of snakes and demons, butterflies rising to the godhead and images of teetering cathedrals that she had seen so often in her dreams. The language on the scrumptious pages appeared to be a mashed up version of low Latin and even lower German, a convulsion that produced seductive mandalas which looked like her soul on fire. She followed Jung's brushstrokes, feints and diversions set in the stained-glass windows of his dreams until they faded like the grim images from her nightmares into the mist. Was this the cathedral that Merkel suggested she build inside herself? Was this the same nightmare landscape where Rilke was defeated decisively by his angels nightly and lived to sing their praise?

On the altar lip of this book she saw barely readable script which seemed to summarize her life: "We accomplish some of our greatest deeds in dreams. We accomplish nothing without a constant solicitation of madness. Take seriously every unknown wanderer in our inner world." Had she been reading the great man's mind?

Colette closed the *Red Book*, knowing that she was now even closer to home. In the distance Colette heard a soft voice: "What's it all about, Alfie?" She needed some help on the last leg of her journey.

She imagined a Virgil as her guide to uncover what had been repressed and scattered to the winds by devils, witch doctors and alchemists. The big words were gone, except when Piety and Chastity walked the stages in medieval morality plays in backwater towns across the Empire. Dreams about dungeons, snakes and beheadings had been sent to the madhouse where they could be written on prison walls and ignored. Poets became the laughing stock and were sometimes burnt at the stake because they had sworn on everything holy that they have found angels in words. Hermes was out of work, unable to move through kingdoms and moods as he once did. Psyche, too, was underemployed, because spirit had stolen the day and taken all the images that expressed soul since time began, depositing them at the feet of the one god, the Christ. Hercules, who for a few centuries helped the sages better understand the idea of Christ, was now found only in comic books alongside Apollo and his crowd, puffed up and out of shape.

Virgil, understanding the vastness of this existential quest, demurred but promised to pray for the right outcomes, God willing. Colette understood that the guide was worried about the old gods coming back, stinking up the place. How could the man who spent all that time with Dante, tracing circle after circle for the last medieval Christian epic, understand that the next essential journey would be about the soul, inside out? How could he know that we must all undertake that epic journey in miniature, inside ourselves, imagining as many demons as we could stomach?

Colette dispensed with guidebooks and soothsayers and imagined a mock audience of priests, monks, nuncios and gentlemen-in-waiting to try out her script, her tall tale from the heavens and her running narrative about Trent and beyond. Rebecca Aimes agreed to help with the décor; Luther Martin with the questions; and Murphy Braun with the jokes. There was an open invitation to Boccaccio, Ficino, Plotinus and others to attend. Her professors had promised to stop by. She proclaimed her unilateral right to speak in tongues. That announcement was received with a profound silence.

"Welcome one and all! It is with great pleasure I give back to you—heart heavily burdened—the wonders of the Council of Trent and other blessed gatherings of note, and those sturdy books of rules and chastisements which have guided the Church for centuries.

"I give you back your joyless and emotionless Christ and embrace the holy man who surrounded himself with women who watched over him, even until death.

"I give you back the shepherd Christ, the infant in swaddling clothes and the manger scene, but will keep with your indulgence the mangled, tortured and grotesque Christ, for I have picked up his blessed body parts in my dreams.

"I give you back the anti-feminine doctrines that come from Aristotle, Augustine and Aquinas and also their tortured and punishing biology of women who were considered passive and inferior participants in the birth process and mere receptacles for male sperm.

"I give you back the pronouncement by Ambrose, Bishop of Milan, that virginity was the blessed property of the Catholic Church.

241

"I give you back your council jokes, confessional banter and backyard gossip about whether it is more sinful to have sex with a beautiful or ugly woman.

"I give you back virginity and priestly celibacy, the twin gods parked on your altar of repression and exalted for centuries above earthly, imperfect marital love.

"I give you back your bachelor theology and the proposition that married love is essentially unchaste and leads to the feminization of the human heart.

"I give you back the images richly praised at the councils and then flattened by doctrine so I can see with the eyes of mystic Marguerite Porete who was burned at the stake for imagining a feminine godhead.

"I give you back your Trinity because it is a fiction, because it is masculine and incomplete, excluding the essential giver of life, the Mother and the Feminine, known to the ancients as the birth-giver of the gods.

"I give you back your Maria Cross, the Feminine impulse you have mixed with your wretched, doctrinal virginity and nailed to that cross of repression and denial and your dark, priestly imaginings that punish the bodies of our children."

Colette droned on: "I give you back, I give you back, and I give you back," stopping by instinct at the magic number three, listening for the sounds from those assembled in her mind. Was that the nuncio from Bologna wearing a cloak with images of the Papal States who nodded approvingly at first then said as calmly as a wave of the hand that she had placed herself outside the congregation of souls? Will the bombast follow, sir? Will you bind me in the chains your dutiful servant nearby carries? Will you drown me? Will your God finally show himself?

Was Boccaccio of the outer circle in conversation with Clement about lust among the pagan pantheon? Was Ficino working his Renaissance magic, a cover for his Platonic love? Was Plotinus covering the congregation with his cool, smooth language? Was Petrarch still climbing mountains in search of his soul? Was Jung lost in his dark, personal cathedral?

An old man she had not invited to the gathering caught her attention. Colette was almost sure she had seen this man on the news, in some oversized book or in her dreams engaged in some popish pantomime. He had a white beard and moved with the aid of a cane. She thought prophet, she thought guide, she thought this man's on my side. She mouthed the archetypal words, Wise Old Man, and waited for wisdom to pour forth. It was as if she were reading his mind:

"Dear Maiden, I have heard your litany of woes, your anxious giving back of gifts, your presumptions of soul. Remember what Petrarch said about the soul having endless depth and potential? You cannot fill the soul by proclamations and endless lists. The 'I will give you back' anthem sounds very much like 'Thou Shall Not.'"

"But, Dear Sir," she said, "the doctrine is soulless; it must be given back to the source. The doctrine must be imbued with soul. Christ must find His soul."

"Gentle lady, honor to all gods, to all things. Even in the pagan pantheon, humility still resides. The soul had its birth in religion. With some help from Hermes, we will find our way back."

"But Sir: what about the Council of Trent? What about the doctrine that has repressed the righteous for five hundred years? Sir, what about the burnings? What about the rapes implicit in the theology? Dear Sir: what about the women?"

"Women will assume their rightful place in the pantheon, in the ranks of the clergy and in the hearts of men."

"But, dear Sir," said Colette, "I have traveled through two thousand years of Church history and found more soul in my dreams and nightmares than I found in your doctrines and cathedrals."

The man turned away and left as quickly as he appeared, before she could reveal what remained in her heart.

"But sir," she said in a half-whisper to the shadows, "what about the baby, what about me?" Colette felt that she was falling again into that parsnip funnel, but this time with less fear and a good heart.

She was inside an amphitheater of her being, listening for signs and wonders, wary of tics and other devil voices that would lead her astray. She heard steel rushing along steel, back and forth, this way and that way. She sensed a curtain rising. Colette remembered an earlier scene, but this time she is fixed, almost nailed in place.

Her mother's voice hung in the air and offered the comfort of angels. Someone in white shined a flashlight in her eyes, and Colette wondered whether the light was a warning about a vision to come or perhaps another birth. We can't rule out a stroke, a voice said, and she remembered her father brushing her long hair. She now hears her mother. Please, not a stroke, please. I said Trent would kill her. It was probably not her workload, the man in white said. Perhaps a predisposition? Her mother screamed: Christ Almighty!

The familiar god came again and Colette blinked her eyes to let the other gods in. One side of her face felt like stone, and she assumed that a god had found an opening. The strong-born Iphigenia arrived, recognizing the place. Demeter brought grapes and harvest corn. Most high Athena entered, her mind filling the space with gravity. Then Aphrodite appeared, followed by her train of allures and endless compulsions.

243

Through the mist Colette sensed the gods were beginning a processional to another kingdom, Aphrodite leading the way. The pencil light moved this way and that way, adding urgency to the procession. She wanted to scream at the images invading her heart.

Colette felt that she was going underground again and somehow found her mother's hand and heard a voice that told her to hang on, baby. Everything will be all right. "I love you, Mum," she said through sea pebbles and saw in a distant mirror a St. Andrew's cross heading in her direction. As she tried to remember the kind of crucifixion St. Andrew endured, Colette felt a finger making the sign of the cross on her forehead with something gritty. There was the familiar mumbling that brought back the sounds of her youth and something being born in her. She was inside a small prayer waiting for a chorus to chant the feminine down.

She was falling into the parsnip funnel again, fleshy and bulbous, her heart full of joy, open to everything. The priest told her now, after all her suffering, God willing, she will indeed be born again. All she can see were Pepsi bottle caps scattered at the foot of an altar, well out of reach of the elect. She felt at home among the beggars and those without limbs. She could almost touch the god in her junk yard dream.

Was that the Sirens' call she heard in the distance like a faint church bell? Would she frolic with the three nymphs on some distant rock waving to Odysseus, ears full of wax and nailed to the mast, resisting the temptation on the last leg of his journey home? She would follow in Odysseus's wake, hoping this patient and soulful guide would lead her back to the source.

Colette longed for that blessed place where the gods were everywhere, in her tics, prayers, and heartfelt wanderings. And especially in her womb!

She heard one more summons, one last Angeles. Colette dreamed she was in the Port Authority Bus Station in New York City waiting to serve the poor, lame and lost. There was a processional. First to arrive through the front door was a pope dressed in rich blues and greens; then the cardinals, bishops, priests and nuncios. Their faces seemed to be painted cosmetic white, as if they had just left the final act of an Off-Off-Broadway play. They all passed in silence as if they were on their way to another Trent.

Under cover of darkness the outcasts arrived, dirty and stinking, as if they had just crawled out of the catacombs. Colette handed each a small offering, which contained pieces of placenta, as if it were meant to be a gift from God.

To each receiver of the gift, Colette said, "This is Our Body."

Colette thought the rapturous and thunderous "Amen" that filled her cathedral could only have come from the hearts of Boccaccio's famous women and all their daughters across the centuries who served as anthem, prayer and eternal chorus.

Colette could see the women walk out of the mist. They moved past statues of goddesses imagined and fashioned by men, past Jesus the Hermaphrodite, past the graves of the holy men who found a place for patriarchy and misogyny in the Godhead.

Colette could see Boccaccio's famous women, dressed to kill in a true Renaissance spirit of body and soul, re-enter the world as equals to men in all things. They walked passed the Trinity and into a true quaternity which was finally transformed and made whole by the full, pulsating presence of the feminine.

Colette could see a woman priest standing at the altar, hands outstretched and welcoming, waiting for the sacramental bread and wine and the words of consecration that would come from Colette's lips and from her heart.

She was giving birth.

Afterword - Into the Mist

Chanting the Feminine Down began as a dream, a poem, and a prayer. Colette's essential journey is psychological, a contemplation of her psychic space. It is also outward through time, history, mythology and religion as she searches for traces of the feminine in the Christian tradition.

While her private struggle takes place in her personal unconscious, her outward journey takes on an archetypal dimension, calling up the gods, the wounding and religious symbols from the collective unconscious. These two dimensions are frequently mashed up and at war with each other.

Her travel through two thousand years of church history, philosophy and hints of archetypal psychology found in the Italian Renaissance is not for the faint of heart. And it's not for the solitary traveler. Colette is joined by hundreds of seekers from Plotinus, to Boccaccio's *Famous Women* to Carl Jung. She joins these minds and these souls, men and women, gods of the night sky, the murdered and the damned, and those who reside outside God's mercy.

Colette's fellow travelers, who sometimes represent split off parts of herself, represent a study in and of itself. *Chanting* represents a kind of creation story that gives birth to a narrative that is always advancing, perfecting itself and drifting into the mist.

We can still imagine Colette, contemplating Boccaccio's noblewoman Marcia who is looking at her own reflection while painting her own image, imagining and mirroring other women endlessly over time.

Acknowledgements

A lifetime of poets, novelists, psychologists, religious leaders and ancient gods and goddesses were steadfast companions while I was writing this novel. To list them all would require another book. Going back in time, grappling with the gods and entering the fiction of mythology required excellent guides. I was fortunate to have Boccaccio, Plotinus and St. John Damascene at my elbow. The poet Rilke whispered constantly in my ear. William Blake kept the night light on. Dante's path was well-traveled and well-marked. I got a regular earful from a thousand years of church councils.

A wonderful array of popes, priests and a cast of characters from a more secular crowd showed up regularly in my dreams cheering me on, admonishing me and leading me astray. I listened to Psyche as if she were both a guest and a goddess. Carl Jung and James Hillman helped me navigate that delicate strip of land between religion and psychology. At times I felt as if the fiction was writing me.

Women mystics such as Hildegard of Bingen, Marguerite Porte, Anne Askew and others helped me imagine a feminine Godhead. Their voices, growing louder by the day, served as an emphatic chorus to the novel.

The novel is their gift and my prayer.

A more detailed list of Characters that appear in the novel and a more extensive Acknowledgement/Bibliography page can be found at www.chantingthefemininedown.com; a comprehensive Web site that explores the novel.

Made in the USA
Middletown, DE
27 July 2018